THE SPEAR OF CROM

THE SPEAR OF CROM

Tim Hodkinson

HEAD
ZEUS

An Aries Book

First published in the UK in 2013 by Acett Enterprises

This revised edition first published in the UK in 2022 by Head of Zeus Ltd,
part of Bloomsbury Publishing Plc

9 7 5 3 1 2 4 6 8

A catalogue record for this book is available from the British Library.

ISBN (PB): 9781801105392
ISBN (E): 9781801105378

Cover design: Ben Prior

Typeset by Siliconchips Services Ltd UK

Printed and bound in Great Britain by
CPI Group (UK) Ltd, Croydon CRO 4YY

Head of Zeus Ltd
First Floor East
5–8 Hardwick Street
London EC1R 4RG

WWW.HEADOFZEUS.COM

To Trudy, Emily, Clara and Alice

Mag Slecht

Here used to stand a lofty idol, that caused
many a fight,
Its name was the Crom Cruach; it caused every
tribe to live without peace.

He was their god, old wizened Crom, hidden
by many mists.
And for the folk who believed in him, the eternal
Kingdom of Heaven shall never be theirs.

For Him they ingloriously slew their hapless firstborn
babies, with much wailing and peril, and poured their
blood round Crom Cruach

From *The Metrical Dindsenchas*,
the old Irish lore of places

Glossary

Ala – Roman cavalry. The word means 'wing' in Latin. In the imperial era, the cavalry were elite units made up of auxiliaries (from the Latin word *auxilia*, 'help'), people from the Roman provinces who were free but did not hold Roman citizenship, something that was required to be a legionary. The Latin word *ala* (plural *alae*) gave us the modern term *allies*.

Brittunculi – *'Nasty little brits'*. It seems this derogatory term was used for the natives by Roman soldiers stationed in Britain. The term was recently discovered by archaeologists working on the Vindolanda tablets, a hoard of first- and second-century Roman military documents discovered near Hadrian's Wall in the North of England.

Cohort – A tactical unit of a Roman legion. About 480 men. A *maniple* was a smaller unit, about 120 men.

Cornu – (plural *cornua*). A long brass horn curled into the shape of the letter 'G'. Along with the other brass horn, the *buccina*, *cornua* were used by the Roman army for signalling and relaying orders during battle.

Decurion – An officer in the *ala*. Commander of a *turma*.

Dobunni – An ancient British tribe whose kingdom covered roughly what is now the English counties of North Somerset, Bristol and Gloucestershire and at times also parts of Oxfordshire, Wiltshire, Worcestershire and Warwickshire. Their capital acquired the Roman name of *Corinium Dobunnorum* (Cirencester). This is the name given to their capital in this book because it is Roman characters who refer to it. The hill fort (*oppidum*) that appears in this story is now called Bagendon. Its actual name is lost to history.

Duplicarius – A non-commissioned officer, second in command of a *turma*. The name means 'double pay', reflecting the higher salary of the duplicarius.

Erin/Hibernia – Ancient Ireland. The Roman name, Hibernia, supposedly reflects their opinion of the weather there (the Latin word *hibernus* can be translated as 'wintry'). The Romans also sometimes called Ireland Scotia, 'land of the Scoti' (Scots).

Fetial – A type of Roman priest. *Fetials* advised the senate on foreign affairs and international treaties and made formal proclamations of war. They also carried out the functions of ambassadors. The **College of Fetiales** was a legal body, the guild to which *fetial* priests belonged. They were devoted to Jupiter as the patron of good faith.

Finnabair – Finnabair appears in the ancient Irish epic, the *Táin Bó Cúailnge*. Her name could mean 'white phantom' and is the Gaelic equivalent of the Welsh name *Gwenhwyfar* (Guinevere).

Hasta – A long, heavy lance used by the Roman cavalry.

Legate – *Legatus*, commander of a Roman legion.

Optio – An officer in the Roman legion, roughly

equivalent to a modern-day lieutenant.

Pilum – The standard javelin carried by roman legionaries. The *pilum* (plural *pila*) was around 2 metres long overall, consisting of an iron shank about 60 cm long with a pyramidal head, its base connected to a wooden shaft.

Praefect – Commander of an *ala* regiment.

Silures – A war-like ancient British tribe whose kingdom occupied a large part of what is modern-day South Wales, as well as parts of Gloucestershire and Herefordshire in modern England. The Silures were a thorn in the side of the Romans, waging constant war against the invaders and even defeating the Second Legion in battle. It is a tribute to their indomitable character that the Roman historian Tacitus (Agricola's son-in-law and biographer) wrote of the Silures: *non atrocitate, non clementia mutabatur* – they were 'changed neither by cruelty nor by clemency'.

Torc – From Latin 'to twist'. The broad twisted rope of gold worn around the neck by Celts to denote noble rank. Torcs were also awarded by the Roman army for bravery.

Tribunus laticlavius – One of the six tribunes who commanded a Roman legion. Essentially second in command to the *legate*, the title *laticlavius* means 'broad-striped', reflecting the broad purple stripe that this tribune bore on his *paludamentum* – the scarlet cloak that was part of the uniform and denoted his rank as part of the senatorial class in Roman society.

Trinovantes – The Trinovantes were a tribe from Eastern Britain. Their territory was north of the Thames estuary in what is now Essex and Suffolk, including land now in Greater London. To the north of them were Boudicca's tribe, the Iceni, and the Trinovantes were partners in the rebellion led by her. The capital of the Trinovantes (and first target of Boudicca) was *Camulodunum* (modern Colchester), one proposed site of the legendary Camelot.

Turma – A unit of the *ala*. A troop of around thirty mounted warriors.

I

AD 59, Roman Province of Britannia

The cavalry trooper never saw it coming.

He had just removed his helmet to wipe the incessant rain from his face when the stone whistled out of the trees. It struck him squarely on the right cheekbone, shattering it with a crack like someone snapping a dry twig. The trooper gave a brief cry of shock and pain as he tumbled from his horse, both hands clutching his face. A bright red splash of blood sprayed the trooper riding on his left.

Fergus MacAmergin cursed. They were not yet half a mile away from camp and already they were under attack.

'Stone thrower, sir,' one of the other troopers shouted. 'Slingshot. It came from the trees.'

Fergus rode beside Viridovix, his fellow officer in the *Ala Augusta Gallorum* – the August Gaulish Cavalry. As usual, the big Gaul had been mocking the accent Fergus spoke Latin with when the slinger had struck.

Decurion Sedullus, the new commander of Fergus's

squad, swung his horse around and galloped in the direction of the fallen cavalryman.

A short distance to their right was a wood. A couple of British tribesmen stood at the edge of the trees. The bright warpaint that covered their almost naked bodies was starting to streak in the heavy rain. They whooped and jumped up and down, their glee at taking a Roman cavalry trooper down evident.

'Those bastard *Brittunculi* are lethal with slingshots,' Fergus said.

'Here we are, riding beside the Legio XIV, the most advanced army in the world,' Viridovix said through clenched teeth. He turned his head and spat to the side of his horse. 'We've the best equipment in the world and these savages cause casualties on us with shepherds' weapons!'

'Sometimes men have to fight with whatever they've got when someone bigger stomps all over their land,' Fergus said. 'If that's the contents of their farm store, then so be it.'

Viridovix shot a sideways glance at his friend.

'Don't get me wrong,' Fergus said. 'I'd still gut the bastards if I got my hands on them.'

He turned in the saddle.

'Keep in line,' Fergus barked to the troopers of his *turma*, Turma X, the thirty-man troop he led. 'Slingshots are a nuisance, not a threat. They're just a wasp stinging a bull.'

To his satisfaction, Fergus saw his men had kept their discipline. Not one had broken ranks.

The sound of approaching hooves in the soft ground made him turn around again. Sedullus the decurion was galloping back towards them.

'Turma Ten: wheel right,' he said.

Fergus's jaw dropped open. Then he dug in his spurs and goaded his Hispanic horse towards Sedullus.

'Sir, you're not planning to chase them are you?' he said. 'It's almost certainly a trap. They want us to chase them so they can lead us into an ambush.'

Sedullus's blue eyes blazed with fury. 'Are you questioning my orders, *Duplicarius*?' he said. 'Do you suggest we let this rabble wound our men with impunity and do nothing about it? In Gaul they say Hibernians are cowards. Now I see it might be true.'

Fergus glared at his commander. 'We are no cowards,' he said, his voice a low growl.

For a second Fergus and the younger Gaul locked eyes. Then Fergus swung his horse around to join his own troopers.

'Right, men: we're going to teach these savages a lesson,' Sedullus said, shouting so all the troopers heard him. 'Forward!'

The tenth troop of the Ala Gallorum crouched, their lances under their right arms, dug in their spurs and charged.

They rode in formation: Sedullus in the lead followed by Fergus, then the troopers formed into three rows of ten riders each behind them. Each trooper was clad in chain mail, a gleaming bronze helmet encased his head and most of his face was hidden behind the helmet's tightly strapped metal cheek guards. Unlike the legionaries of Legio XIV who marched behind them with their heavy, rectangular shields, each cavalryman bore an oval shield, light enough to hold on one arm while also holding his horse's reins. Two throwing javelins sat in a quiver slung across his back.

Couched under his right arm was a long, heavy lance: the *hasta*.

The Britons seemed undaunted by this intimidating sight. The two tribesmen stood their ground, taunting the approaching horsemen with jeers and obscene gestures. At the last minute they turned and fled into the woods.

'After them,' Sedullus said, his voice a high-pitched squeal, spit flying from his lips. 'Hunt them down!'

The tribesmen disappeared down a narrow track that led through closely packed ash and alder trees. Fergus followed Sedullus after them, trying to shake off the uneasy feeling that it was not the natives who were being hunted.

As the troopers arrived at the treeline they were forced to slow down to negotiate the branches and undergrowth. Thorns tore at their cloaks and pricked the horses' flanks as the cavalry forced its way through the thick vegetation. Spears caught in branches and their visibility was cut to the distance of the immediate surroundings. In moments their perfect formation became a confused mess.

'Keep going. Force your way through,' Sedullus shouted.

The cavalry troopers impelled their protesting mounts onward, struggling further into the densely packed undergrowth. The troopers were all over the place and Fergus found himself in front of the others. Then he broke through into a wide clearing.

Fergus reined his horse abruptly to a halt, looking around him. The clearing was quiet and seemed empty but every nerve in his body felt like it was stretched to the point of snapping. His ears strained for any sound but all he could hear was the panting of his horse and the pounding of his heart.

The rest of the troop burst into the clearing after him.

'What are you doing, Duplicarius?' Sedullus said as he arrived with him. 'Push on, man. They're getting away!'

Before Fergus could respond, a hail of spears and stones came from all sides at once.

Two troopers cried out and fell from their horses, transfixed through the chest by spear shafts.

'It's a trap,' Fergus shouted as he wheeled his horse. 'Go back!'

Tribesmen were pouring out of the trees from all sides. A trooper cried out in terror as he was dragged from his horse and disappeared beneath a crowd of frenzied Britons.

Fergus urged his horse forward towards the fallen man. His lance hit the naked back of a Briton who was crouching over the fallen trooper. The iron head powered right through the tribesman's body, the razor-sharp point erupting from his chest in a spray of bright crimson. choking him as he toppled forward, his weight twisting the shaft of the lance. With a crack the shaft of Fergus's hasta shattered into three pieces. He dropped the useless stump.

He kicked his heels and his horse's hooves trampled another Briton into the ground. Fergus ripped his *spatha* from the scabbard on his right hip.

'Get off him,' he shouted.

In his anger and excitement he momentarily forgot his Latin and yelled out in his native tongue. The British all looked up in shock, surprised at hearing a Roman cavalryman shouting in a Celtic language very like their own. Fergus brought the long cavalry sword swooping down. The heavy blade whooshed through the air and connected with the side of a tribesman's head. It skidded down onto his neck, opening up a horrible wound and releasing a gush of blood. The man tried to scream, but all that came out was a gurgle from his severed throat as he collapsed onto the forest floor.

His remaining companions, seeing half their number killed in as many seconds, decided to leave their victim and sprinted off as fast as they could back into the forest.

With dismay Fergus recognised the fallen Roman trooper was Valetiacus, an old mate from basic training. He was already dead. In the short time they had had their hands on him, the Britons had slit his throat and stabbed him under the armpits and anywhere else they could slide a blade beneath his body protection.

Fergus looked around. The forest clearing was in chaos. Two more of his troop were down and at least five Britons. The remaining troopers were milling frantically round and round, stabbing this way and that at the natives swarming around them. Sedullus's face was a mask of confusion.

Another trooper fell, skewered through the guts by a British spear. If they did not do something soon they would all be massacred.

Fergus grabbed the little bone whistle that hung on a leather thong around his neck. Hoping the sound would travel through the trees to the rest of the cavalry, he put it to his lips and blew three short, sharp blasts: the alarm signal. He then gave two short blasts and one longer one – the signal to regroup.

The beleaguered troopers responded and began forcing their way into the centre of the clearing.

'Circle ranks,' Fergus said, kicking his horse's flanks. He set off riding around the clearing in a left-hand direction.

The other horsemen fell in behind him and soon they formed a ring around the perimeter.

Several Britons cried in dismay as they found themselves trapped inside the circle. Moments later they were dead, killed by cavalry *hastas*. With the inner danger removed, the riders now rode at a controlled trot, their mounts nose to tail, each man's shield to the outside to protect him from the tribesmen around their circle. They were now unable to get in amongst the troopers to cause more havoc.

Fergus knew he had won the Tenth Turma a temporary respite, but they had to get out of the woods. While they remained in the clearing the cavalry formation could hold an attack at bay, but they could not keep riding in a circle all day. Once they tried to go back through the dense bushes and trees, they would have to break ranks and in the close confines of the undergrowth the tribesmen would once more be able to pick the troopers off one by one.

'What do we do now, sir?' Cetillus, one of the new recruits, said.

Fergus, realising the young trooper was addressing him, looked around uncomfortably.

Where was Sedullus? To his surprise and consternation he saw that the decurion was not taking part in the defensive circle but had ridden into the centre of it where he was protected by the circling horsemen.

'What shall we do now, sir?' Fergus repeated the question in a louder voice.

'Emm...' Sedullus's face creased with anxiety. Fergus knew how he felt. He had no idea himself how they were going to get out of this mess, but for a brief moment he enjoyed his young superior officer's predicament.

At that moment the drumming of approaching hooves signalled that help was coming. The rest of the cavalry was responding to his whistled alarm.

Turma XV came thundering through the trees, hacking and stabbing their way through the surprised Britons who were thrown into more confusion by their sudden arrival. Fergus grinned at the sight of the big Gaul, Viridovix, in the lead.

Sedullus, looking like a man who had just woken from a nightmare, shouted the order to withdraw. The Tenth Turma broke their circle and surged forward across the clearing to meet Turma XV. The tribesmen caught amongst the horses were quickly dispatched on the way.

'Viridovix! Good to see you.' Fergus touched his blade to his helmet by way of a salute.

The Gaul shook his head in mock admonishment.

'What are you lot up to, Fergus?' he said. 'My grandmother could have seen that was a trap.'

'Just following orders.' Fergus smiled, raised an eyebrow and cocked his head in the direction of his decurion. Viridovix grinned and rolled his eyes.

Their moment of shared contempt for Sedullus was interrupted by a sudden hail of ill-aimed slingshot from the Britons. By now the tribesmen had withdrawn to a safe distance where they could subject the Romans to further assault without risk of injury to themselves.

Attempting to control their agitated horses, the Roman troopers huddled behind their shields as deadly pebbles bounced and rattled off their helmets, shields and chain mail.

'Let's get out of here,' Viridovix said.

Needing no second bidding, the troopers began to withdraw from the clearing into the trees. Fergus slung his shield across his back by its long leather strap to protect him as he fled. Most of the troopers did likewise as they plunged through the thick undergrowth once more.

'Blood of Camulos!'

Fergus heard Viridovix cursing in the name of the Gaulish war god. He looked back to see that his fellow officer was well behind the rest of the troopers. He was clutching his right hand, which had been struck by a stone. The sudden pain of the blow had made him drop his spatha, which now lay on the forest floor amongst the undergrowth.

Fergus knew Viridovix would have to stop, dismount and pick up the sword or face punishment. Leaving a serviceable weapon on the battlefield was a disciplinary offence in the Roman army.

None of the other escaping cavalry had seen what had happened and Viridovix would be left behind alone. Fergus wheeled his horse around once again. He had to go back and help his friend. Viridovix was already dismounting as Fergus dug in his spurs to urge his horse back through the trees.

As if from nowhere, a huge Briton ran out of the undergrowth behind Viridovix who was stooping to pick up his sword. The tribesman was almost naked, his body smeared in blue warpaint and his long hair spiked up from his head in outlandish fashion, held in place by congealed limewash.

Fergus called out a warning. Viridovix looked up.

It was too late. The Briton swung his long Celtic sword and with a sickening crunch the blade caught the Gaul under the rim of his helmet at the back of his neck. Viridovix's head came off cleanly and his body pitched backwards, his recovered spatha still clutched tightly in his injured right hand. His severed head tumbled end over end across the forest floor while from his decapitated torso three huge jets of blood were pumped out by his dying heart before it stopped beating.

Fergus arrived as Viridovix's body collapsed to the forest floor. With a roar of frustration he hacked down with his spatha. It caught the still-running tribesman who had killed Viridovix across the skull, splitting his head almost in two.

More tribesmen flooded out of the woods in pursuit of the fleeing cavalry and Fergus realised with deep regret that he was going to have to abandon his friend's corpse or he would share his fate. With an angry curse he turned his horse and galloped after the rest of the troopers.

Within moments the remnants of Turmae X and XV had cleared the trees and made it back to the relative safety of the meadow to rejoin the legion.

2

General Gaius Suetonius Paulinus, the new governor of
the Roman Province of Britannia, was not happy.

All through dinner he had seethed with quiet rage and
hardly said a word. The other officers knew his fearsome
reputation and the conversation in the officers' dinner tent
during the meal had not strayed beyond the odd awkward
pleasantry.

Right in the centre of the army encampment, furthest
away from any danger, was the *praetorium*, the legion's
headquarters. Here the officers pitched their tents and now
the day's duties were over, after changing out of their leather
armour into formal togas, they gathered for dinner.

Reclining on couches, the XIV Legion's officers were
served by bustling slaves, while Paulinus's musicians
played soft music in the background. It was a scene similar
to that occurring at any upper-class dinner party in any
great villa in Rome itself, the general reflected, except that
this was under canvas in a muddy British field. These men
were Roman citizens, after all. Certain standards had to
be maintained. The only reminder of where they actually
were came from the incessant patter of rain on the tent roof.

The only concession made to the local climate was that some of the officers wore woollen socks under their sandals.

Paulinus eyed these with barely disguised contempt. To him it was typical of the state of Rome's legions in this dreadful province. Shortly after arriving in Britannia he had come to the conclusion that Rome's difficulties in subduing the natives was due to the weakness of the legions stationed here and he had seen little to contradict that impression since.

Rome had lost patience with her newest province. For nearly twenty years, four of her legions – more than was required for any other province – had been bogged down in this wretched island. Keeping any semblance of order here required more troops than any other part of the empire. The Britons refused to accept that they were conquered. Tribes-men picked off soldiers and colonists one at a time then melted away into the woods and mountains, while native kings pretended fealty to the emperor but refused to pay taxes and schemed with non-allied rebels.

Meanwhile, despite their numbers, the Roman army in Britain had become lazy and soft. The men patrolled safe territory, built roads and bridges instead of fighting and lay around in bathhouses and wine bars while their officers amused themselves and their wives in a constant round of dinner parties and socialising.

By Jupiter, thought Paulinus, his gaze on the wool-clad feet of a particularly overweight cavalry officer, things would be different now he was in charge. This time, Nero Caesar had picked a man to be governor whose reputation was already proven. The brutalised, decimated population of Mauretania – his last posting – could testify to that.

Paulinus now intended to bring to heel those Britons who stubbornly refused to realise they were part of the empire. His first step was the campaign they were now embarked on. He had marched the XIV Legion – better known as the *Gemina* – out of its safe, comfortable barracks in Viroconium and they were heading west.

The Kingdom of the *Silures* was to be the first to feel the new strong hand of Roman government. Rome had a score to settle with that wild, savage people who had not just humiliated Veranius, Paulinus's predecessor, and the XX Legion, but they had been in a constant state of rebellion since the Emperor Claudius invaded Britain two decades before.

The campaign would be a short, sharp and bloody shock designed by Paulinus to both knock the Britons into line and the XIV Legion back into shape.

Once the Silures were conquered, the Ordovices would be next, then the druids' nest of Mona. Beyond that a whole new island, *Hibernia*, as yet unconquered by Rome, lay before him. With conquest came honour and fame. The Roman public liked nothing more than a military hero who expanded the bounds of the empire and Paulinus intended to be such a hero.

Before he whipped the Britons into line, however, he would have to whip his own men into shape.

'Not a very auspicious start to the campaign, was it?' He finally broke the silence as the slaves cleared away the dishes from the *secundae mensae*, the last course of dinner. No one responded. All the officers avoided his gaze.

'Not even a mile from our camp and we are attacked,' he continued. Still no one spoke. 'And then some fool of a junior officer decides to charge straight into an ambush. Not good enough, is it?'

Titus Pomponius Proculianus, the *praefect* of the Gaulish cavalry, the officer whose socks had caused the general such offence, was finally goaded into speaking.

'Sir, with respect, Decurion Sedullus was only recently promoted,' he said. 'He's new to command and I can assure you he will prove to be a fine officer in time. Sedullus was keen to fight the enemy and I think we should not punish him for that. We all can make mistakes.'

'Mistakes get men killed, Pomponius!' Paulinus thundered. The Gaulish praefect noticeably flinched at the venom in the general's words.

'What casualties did we take?' Paulinus asked, though he knew full well the answer.

Pomponius looked slightly lost. He had no idea. A polite cough came from behind him and the Gaulish cavalry praefect turned to see the handsome, tanned features of the young tribune of the legion, Gnaeus Julius Agricola.

'If I may be so bold.' Agricola smiled provocatively at Pomponius. 'The XV Cavalry troop lost their decurion – killed – and duplicarius – also killed – as well as one man badly injured. The tenth troop lost nine troopers. All either confirmed dead or missing, presumed dead.'

Pomponius glared at Agricola with undisguised dislike but said nothing.

'Thank you, Agricola.' Paulinus's thin, almost bloodless lips curved slightly into what may have been a smile. 'Well. One troop of our cavalry almost decimated. A second with both officers dead. We cannot afford any more incidents like this. I will not tolerate indiscipline and I've a good mind to disband the tenth troop as an example to the rest. Unfortunately we are short of men as it is, so we need to regroup them. Decurion Sedullus is obviously not ready for command.'

'Sir, with respect,' Pomponius interjected, aghast. 'While Sedullus may have acted impetuously, it was only through eagerness to attack at the enemy. Also, once the troop was in danger, Sedullus tells me it was he who led them out of it again. They did kill many Britons after all. I think that should be taken into account.'

This time not bothering to disguise his contempt, Paulinus glared at the Gaul.

'You seem very fond of this young fool, Pomponius. Perhaps he is a relation of yours?'

Pomponius, his face flushing livid with anger, glowered at the general.

'I knew his father well,' he said. 'He comes from a good, noble Gaulish family. I am confident he will make a fine officer.'

Paulinus regarded the cavalry praefect for a few moments before replying, battling to control his scorn. In many ways, Pomponius represented in person a lot of the faults he saw in the modern Roman army. The Gaul was a Roman citizen, but only because his grandfather had been a king with enough common sense to submit to Rome when Julius Caesar conquered his tribe. Unlike himself, Pomponius did not come from generations of Roman forefathers. And yet here he now was, a man far too fat to be training every day with his men as he should, commanding an elite cavalry regiment of the Roman army. Paulinus, on the other hand, prided himself that his body was still lean and hard from continuous exercise, even though he was now in his early fifties and getting on in years.

With a conscious effort, he bit his tongue and swallowed his opinions. He still had to work with these people and they all had a job to do.

'Very well. This Sedullus will get a second chance, but from now on I hold you, Pomponius, completely responsible for his actions. Let's hope if he gets anyone else killed, then next time it's himself.'

Paulinus paused, considering the situation further.

'However,' he went on, 'an example must be set. You will regroup Turma Ten,' he ordered. 'Make it up to full strength with troopers from Turma XV and form whoever is left into a special operations group – a *numeres* punishment team – under the command of Turma Ten's duplicarius.'

'Sir, there's a problem with that,' Pomponius said. Although it was clear from his agitation that he feared his general's further wrath, his indignation at what he saw as interference in his jurisdiction gave him courage. 'The duplicarius of the tenth is not a Gaul. In fact he is not even from the empire or an ally: he's a Hibernian. I don't recommend we promote someone to a command position who may be, shall we say, unreliable. Remember Varus.'

Paulinus glanced away from the cavalry officer. As far as he was concerned the matter was decided.

'Pomponius, I don't care if he's from the moon. He's in the Roman army and he has taken the same vow of loyalty to the emperor as the rest of us.'

He was enough of a politician to know not to add that Hibernians, Gauls, Britons – whatever – were all the same to him: just barbarians. Celts.

'Besides,' he added, 'he's being put in charge of a punishment squad. This numeres will be given dangerous tasks that are too risky for other troopers. I intend this to serve as an example to the rest of the cavalry. They will see where indiscipline will lead them.'

Pomponius did not object further. The discussion was very obviously over.

'Now,' Paulinus addressed all the officers, 'I'm sure everyone has work to do. We have to be up early tomorrow. I'll not keep you any longer. Goodnight, gentlemen. Let's try and make tomorrow a better day, shall we?'

Realising they were being dismissed, the officers of the legion filed out of the headquarters tent, their sullen expressions betraying their disappointment – shock even – that the meal had not ended in the customary prolonged drinking session.

Watching them go, Paulinus picked up a stack of reports, sat down at his writing desk and sighed heavily. This was going to be a tough command. He looked up again to see that the tribune had remained behind.

'You see what we're up against here, Agricola?' Paulinus said, wearily running a hand through his short-cropped, iron-grey hair. 'Men like that will be the ruin of Rome. They're just barbarians in togas. They don't have our inner qualities. They wear Roman dress, but they don't have the *virtus* of men like us whose forefathers steered the course of Rome down through centuries. They are not patricians; they just don't have the breeding.'

Nodding in agreement, Agricola enquired, 'You're sure you want to place a non-alae – a Hibernian – in charge of the numeres? You must have a good reason?'

Paulinus smiled. From anyone else he would not have tolerated such a question. However, he liked Agricola, as much as he liked anyone.

'Well spotted, Agricola,' he said. 'In many ways you remind me of myself in my younger days. Of course I have a reason. Naturally I'm curious as to just how this Hibernian got into the emperor's army, but it's an unexpected piece of luck. As it happens, I just may have a very special task for a Hibernian cavalry officer.'

3

On the first day of basic training in the Roman army, Fergus MacAmergin's centurion had told the raw recruits: 'Even if you don't believe in the Roman gods, by Jupiter you will all worship them.'

It was soon clear to Fergus that the army was obsessed by religion. Not from any great sense of spiritual conviction, he realised, but because the observances required by the various imperial deities provided two things the army valued above all else: routine and discipline. Holy days were marked by parades, rituals were scrupulously observed and when any marching camp was established, the first thing constructed after the outer defences had been built were the altars to the gods. They were simple, quickly erected structures of wood, but they served two purposes: a focal point for the religious practices that needed to be performed, and a visible stake into whatever land was being entered. The statement they made was clear: 'Rome is here, and here is now Rome.'

As the drizzly, grey evening turned towards night, Fergus stood before the altar of Mars to say a prayer for Viridovix. His friend had worshipped the Gaulish god of war, Camulos, and Mars was the closest Roman equivalent. However, standing in front of the wooden altar decorated with imperial symbols, he felt slightly uncomfortable. Camulos had similar characteristics to Mars, but he was not really the same god. Viridovix may have worn a Roman uniform, but he was a Gaul.

Viridovix's death had been the shit end to a shit day. The Gaul had been Fergus's oldest friend in the army. They had joined up at the same time and gone through basic training together. Naturally gifted horsemen, both had been posted to the Ala Gallorum as troopers and both had been quickly promoted to the non-commissioned officer rank of duplicarius. Recently, to Fergus's chagrin, Viridovix had been promoted further to decurion of Turma XV. Not that Fergus had resented his friend's promotion, far from it; it was the fact that he had been passed over himself that rankled. He was duplicarius of the tenth troop, Turma X – one of the fifteen squadrons of troopers that made up the cavalry regiment – and had been for over a year. For most of that time the troop's commanding officer, the decurion, had been Casticus, a doughty Gaul whom everyone respected and with whom Fergus had got on well.

Three weeks ago, while leading a patrol out from the fort, Casticus had been killed by a British spear, which had sailed out of the forest and impaled him to a tree trunk. Fergus, being second in command and with years of experience in the army, had expected to receive Casticus's plumed helmet. Instead, Sedullus, a duplicarius from another troop who had joined the cavalry only six months ago, had been chosen to lead Turma X.

This had nothing to do with ability, experience or talent. Sedullus was the son of a Gaulish chieftain, while Fergus was from Hibernia, which was not even an allied nation of Rome. As their name proclaimed, the Ala Gallorum had an august, almost century-long history, and though it now supposedly welcomed recruits from all over the empire, there was still a strong Gaulish bias when it came to promotion.

All in all, thought Fergus, things were not working out the way he had planned. It was not just the lack of promotion that galled him. With a derisory grunt he recalled the words of the recruiting centurion from all those years before: *Join the Roman cavalry. It's a life of adventure.*

Beguiled by those stirring words, he had joined the Roman army hoping to see the world and get as far away from *Erin* – Hibernia as the Romans called it – as possible. He had dreamed of riding around the pyramids in Egypt; visiting the Pharos Lighthouse at Alexandria; traversing the Atlas Mountains.

Instead, he had ended up posted back to Britannia, somewhere he had never possessed the desire to see. Yet here he was, marching to Dinas Emrys on the way to Yr Wyddfa, where on a good day if he climbed to the top of that highest of mountains he could probably catch a glimpse of his homeland lurking on the other side of the sea to the west.

It had all been a mistake – a complete waste of time – and the thought of desertion was starting to simmer in his mind. He could slip away from camp during the night. Leave the army behind and move on to something else.

There were a few problems with that idea, however. Firstly, the penalty for desertion was death. Secondly, the minute he got away from camp he would be in enemy territory, and if the British got their hands on him they would see him as a Roman soldier and kill him. Either way, he'd end up dead. The Romans would beat him to a pulp while the British would give him to the druids, who would gut him alive in a ritual. He did not fancy either option much. Besides, even if he managed to escape both fates, he had nowhere else to go. Home, if he could still call it that, was no longer an option.

Bringing his thoughts back to Viridovix, Fergus completed the standard Roman prayers. He then decided to add another in the way of his own people, a way that Viridovix's god might more readily understand. Leaving the altars, Fergus climbed onto the defensive rampart that surrounded the camp. He was far from comfortable with any sort of prayer but he felt compelled to honour his friend's memory and faith in some way. From his pouch he took Viridovix's knife and held it in both hands. Closing his eyes, he held the cold iron of the blade to his lips.

'Gods my people swear by...' he murmured using the standard words. Even though he did not use their names he knew them well enough. One in particular hovered in his mind: *Crom Cruach* – Crom to bow down to. *Crom Dubh* – Crom the Black. It was a very long time since he had prayed to that greedy, vengeful god and he had vowed never to do so again, unless it was to spit a curse. As he stood on the rampart, the memory of a terrible *Samhain* night in Erin years before surfaced in his thoughts.

Fergus opened his eyes to dispel the memory. 'Accept this gift and look after Viridovix,' he said. 'Remember me to him and ask him to look after me from the other world. Viridovix, I hope the Great One of the Sun took your spirit an hour before Crom knew you were dead.'

With that, he hurled the knife high in the air. It tumbled

end over end in a wide arc, the bright blade flashing rhythmically as the setting sun's light caught it, until it finally fell with
a plop into the river that ran by the camp a short distance
from the rampart.

He was still watching the ripples subside and fade around
the spot where the knife had plunged into the water when
he heard his name being called.

It was Sedullus.

'Duplicarius, I've been looking all over for you,' Sedullus
said, striding up the rampart towards him. Not as tall as
Fergus, his dark hair was cut short, his handsome face oiled
and clean-shaven, apart from the wispy traces of hair on his
upper lip where he was attempting to grow a long, drooping
moustache, a tradition of the cavalry regiment harking back to
its Gaulish origins. Though born in Gaul of Gaulish parents,
Sedullus was from the aristocracy, now bred into the Roman
way of life with only the outward appearances of their people's
traditions. To Fergus, he was just another Roman playing at
being a Celt: a pampered rich boy who would not have lasted
a day amongst the *Cruithni*, Fergus's own people.

In stark contrast to Sedullus, Fergus's tribal origins were
more visible. Provided it was kept tidy, braided and out of
the way, long hair and moustaches were two of the very few
concessions to their own culture the Roman army allowed
recruits from the allied Gaulish nations, since, as they were
not legionaries, some leeway could be allowed. On either
side of his mouth, Fergus's moustache hung down below his
chin. He had been growing it since he was twelve years old.
Both his heavily muscled arms were covered from shoulder
to wrist in swirling tattoos and his braided hair hung down
his back.

Both men regarded each other with mutual contempt for a few seconds, before Sedullus finally spoke.

'You're to report to the praetorium. Don't ask me why, but Tribune Agricola wants to see you.'

Fergus raised his eyebrows. This was strange news indeed.

'Then I'd better not keep the tribune waiting,' he said, and made to set off down the rampart. Sedullus caught hold of his arm to stop him.

'Listen here, Duplicarius,' Sedullus said in a fierce whisper, 'if Agricola starts asking any questions about what happened this afternoon, just you remember that you disobeyed a direct order today. I haven't mentioned that to anyone, but just you remember that I always can. So keep whatever opinions you have about the ambush to yourself. Understand?'

Fergus nodded and pulled his arm free of Sedullus's grasp. He turned away and smiled to himself. The decurion was obviously scared that the truth would come out. Fergus had said nothing about his superior officer's ridiculous attempt at leadership that day. Then he remembered that the tribune, Agricola, was not just second in command of the legion but was also in charge of punishments. Had Sedullus somehow dropped him right in it?

It was with some apprehension that he walked towards headquarters at the centre of the camp.

4

Fergus had no need to ask directions to Agricola's tent. Every Roman army camp, no matter where it was, how permanent it was, or how many men it was designed to accommodate, was always constructed to exactly the same plan.

First, a huge rectangle shape was marked out and a ditch dug around its periphery. On the inside of the ditch the legionaries erected a rampart topped with a palisade of sharpened wooden stakes. Even at rest, the XIV Legion arrayed itself in battle formation. At the forward end of the camp, the part usually facing the enemy territory, was the *praetentura*: the area where the elite troops of the legion – the First *Cohort* and the other strongest cohorts – pitched their tents. The *retentura* was the rearward part of the camp where the veterans, the rest of the cohorts and the cavalry were quartered. At the exact centre of the camp was the praetorium: headquarters. Here the slaves pitched the tents of the commanding officers, and outside the biggest tent – that belonging to the general – they drove the standards of the cohorts and the legion's eagle, the holy battle flag of the unit, firmly into the ground.

This pattern was repeated wherever the army was,

anywhere in the world, such that this temporary overnight camp constructed by the XIV Legion conformed to exactly the same design as the permanent legionary fortress in Judea built to house Rome's soldiers for centuries to come. The only difference was that here in Britain, wooden palisades and leather tents replaced stone walls and brick-built barracks.

Not quite the only difference, Fergus mused ruefully as he trudged through the mud on that cold, rainy evening. A permanent fort had a bathhouse, where as an officer – even a non-commissioned one like him – he could have relaxed in the heat after the rigours of the day. If there was one thing he missed more than anything, it was the feeling of sinking into warm water.

Hearing horses' hooves thumping up behind him on the *via praetoria*, the road from the main gate to the praetorium, Fergus looked round and was surprised to see a party of Britons approaching. He counted eleven riders: eight were Celtic warriors in full battle dress. The other three, two women and a man, were more regally attired. Local nobility, judging by their gold neck jewellery and expensive woven cloaks. One of the women in particular caught Fergus's eye. She was stunning and even from a distance her snow-white skin and raven-black hair reminded him of a woman he had once known back home in Hibernia. She sat tall in the saddle, her rich, sumptuous dress and cloak flowing out behind her.

As she neared him, Fergus saw that although young, the woman was not in the first flush of youth. A few tell-tale crow's-feet lines crept from the sides of her eyes, but it was those eyes that were the most striking part of her. The colour of green ice in a mountain stream, they surveyed everything around her with a cold, scornful – almost mocking – gaze.

Glowering out from under a fringe of dark curly hair, the man riding beside her was younger than she. His clothes also spoke of wealth and status. From the surly, sour expression he regarded the camp around him, he looked far from happy at being there. Riding behind them, the second woman's clothes were of good quality, but less rich-looking. Fergus surmised that she was some form of attendant or lady-in-waiting to the black-haired beauty. He transferred his gaze to the warriors who rode with them. They each carried the finest equipment and all their shields bore the same swirling Celtic pattern.

Fergus stiffened at the sight of them. He knew they posed no danger or they would not have got through the main gate alive, but their appearance reminded him of old enemies. Like himself, they were tall and fair-skinned, their hair long, curly and blond. They had the look of Iberians, or worse, *Laigin*: warriors from Hibernia. Years before, he had faced many men like them in battle.

The group cantered past and went ahead of him to the headquarters tents of the praetorium, where they were stopped by the general's bodyguards. Fergus watched as the regal lady and her male companion dismounted and were ushered into the tent of the Tribune Agricola, leaving the warriors and female servant milling around outside. By the time Fergus arrived at the tent, the warriors and the general's bodyguards were eyeing each other with equal suspicion and bristling with mutual challenge.

'Duplicarius Fergus MacAmergin,' Fergus announced

himself to the commander of the bodyguards. 'I have been ordered to see the tribune.'

The commander narrowed his eyes and looked him up and down, but Fergus took no offence. He knew it was the man's job to be suspicious of everyone. After a few moments, apparently satisfied, the commander produced from the pouch on his belt a thinly cut sliver of wood that had been folded in half.

'You're to take this to the *aquilifer*,' he said. 'The tribune cannot see you now. He is meeting the Queen *Finnabair*.'

Fergus frowned. Finnabair was a Hibernian name. Perhaps the warriors with her were indeed Laigin men. He shot a narrow-eyed glance in their direction as he took the folded note, feeling the wood slightly rough against his fingers. In the northern provinces of the empire papyrus was scarce and orders, record keeping, letter writing and general note taking were all written in ink on these little slivers of birch, alder or oak, which were then folded in two for confidentiality. He wondered what message he now carried, but knew better than to look while the commander's gaze was on him.

Fergus headed off towards the tent of the aquilifer, the legion's standard bearer. Lucius Marius Faustus was a grizzled old warrior. He had been in the army for twenty years and risen through the ranks from legionary to *optio*, then transferred to *signifer* and finally had ended up as the highest-ranking duplicarius in the legion. The aquilifer carried the eagle, the legion's standard and symbol of its pride and honour. Almost equally important, he also looked after the men's finances. Even on campaign there was much work to do. Expenses had to be paid, wages calculated, fines imposed, and thus Fergus found Faustus in his tent sifting through the mound of documents that were gathered on his table.

A guttering oil lamp provided some light in the dismal British evening, and for warmth Faustus had wrapped himself in the wolfskin that was part of his uniform. The aquilifer ran his hand through his thinning, close-cropped grey hair and sighed at the amount of work piled up in front of him.

Fergus coughed to announce his presence.

Faustus looked up and saw standing before him the tall cavalry trooper. He raised an eyebrow by way of questioning Fergus's reason for being there.

'*Salve*,' Fergus raised his right hand and saluted. 'I've been told to give you this,' he said, passing the wooden note to the legionary standard bearer.

Faustus opened the note and read it. He rolled his eyes. 'More documentation,' he said. 'You know, people think the Roman army is the most efficient war machine in the world. It's not. It's the most efficient bureaucracy in the world. If we spent half as much time fighting as we do keeping our records up to date, the entire world would be under our command and we wouldn't be stuck in this gods-forsaken land at the arse end of the world. You've been misbehaving, I see.'

'What do you mean?' Fergus was confused.

'*Gradus deiectio*. You've been demoted,' Faustus replied flatly. 'You are moving from your present pay grade of duplicarius to that of *sesquiplicarius*.'

Fergus's mouth opened but he was rendered speechless. That meant his double standard pay was being reduced to basic pay and a half.

Before he could ask why, Faustus added, 'On the positive side, you've been granted a temporary command position – *praepositus* – you'll be in charge of a numeres special operations group made up of the remnants of the X Turma, Ala Gallorum.'

'A numeres? A punishment troop?' Fergus said. 'Why?'

'Please: a special operations team,' Faustus said. 'It says here that you are being punished for recklessly leading the troopers under your command into an ambush.'

'A suicide troop you mean. Numeres do all the dangerous work no one else wants,' the Hibernian said, gritting his teeth. 'I don't believe it! And anyway, I didn't lead those men into an ambush. Our decurion ordered us to charge. It was just bad luck that I was first into that clearing in the woods.'

'Well I have it here in the tribune's own writing,' Faustus said with a wan smile. 'You should count yourself lucky all you got was a pay cut. The tribune could have sentenced you to a beating.'

'But I haven't done anything,' Fergus said.

Faustus snorted. 'That's what they all say, son. That's what they all say.'

Fergus ripped his knife out of its sheath and stabbed it into the aquilifer's portable writing desk. 'You can take your damned army and shove it up your emperor's arse!'

'Put that weapon away, trooper, or you will find it shoved up your own arse!'

Faustus got to his feet, his own ire raised. He was a full head taller than the stocky Roman standard bearer, but nevertheless Faustus's dark eyes glittered with reproach and defiant challenge.

'Now you listen to me, son,' he said, stabbing a forefinger at Fergus. 'You curb that Gaulish temper and take your punishment like a man. I've fought all over this world in the name of Rome and that emperor you're so quick to disrespect, and I won't have it. Good friends of mine died in his service, and over the years the army has been good to me. Just you remember that before you go criticising the emperor or his damned army!'

'One of my best friends died today in the service of your emperor and I doubt Nero gives a shit. Do you?' Fergus said, meeting the smaller man's gaze.

Both men glared at each other for several seconds. Then Faustus smiled ruefully.

'No he probably doesn't.' He sighed. 'But what did you expect when you joined the army, trooper? Hugs and kisses?'

Despite his anger, Fergus could not help giving a bitter laugh and the tension between them subsided.

'I'm not a Gaul,' he said when his mirth had passed.

'What?' Faustus said.

'You told me to curb my Gaulish temper. I'm a Hibernian.'

Faustus raised his eyebrows in surprise. 'A Hibernian? They still sacrifice their children over there, don't they?'

A flicker of anger streaked across Fergus's face, followed by a spasm of guilt. Suddenly averting his eyes, he mumbled, 'Just the firstborn. It's a religious thing.'

'The Carthaginians were the same.' Faustus shook his head. 'Savages. We sorted that out when we finally conquered and civilised them.'

'We don't all do it,' Fergus said, adding flatly, 'only some tribes. Not all of us are slaves of the druids.'

'What's a Hibernian doing in the army of Rome?' the aquilifer said. 'You're not even from an allied nation. How did you get in?'

Fergus shrugged. 'I joined up in Gaul. I suppose to a Roman recruiting centurion we *Celtae* all look the same.'

'He's right. You do. But what I mean is *why*, not how?' Faustus said. 'Did you fancy a life of adventure or something? Join the cavalry to see the world, meet new people and then kill them. Was that it?'

Fergus smiled. 'Something like that.' Then he said, with conviction, 'No. More than just that. I want to be a citizen.'

Even to his own ears it sounded simplistic, almost childlike, so he was not surprised when Faustus sat down again, shaking his head in astonishment.

'Well, now. A citizen. Eh? You don't like the emperor but you want to be one of his subjects. Now there's a paradox. Things like that interest me.'

The aquilifer leaned back in his chair and regarded Fergus, curiosity sparking in his eyes.

'Do you have any idea how ironic that is?' he said at length. 'Do you know why we're here, trooper?'

Fergus was slightly confused. 'Of course I do. British tribes were sending aid to insurgents in Gaul, so the Roman army came to Britannia to stop it.'

'That was over twenty years ago, and we're still here,' Faustus said. 'Why is that?'

'Erm… because Rome has not finished the job yet? We're here to put down the insurgents and rebels who still fight Roman rule, aren't we?'

'Nothing to do with the British silver and tin mines, then?' Faustus said with a wicked smile. 'But seriously, you Celts never seem to wonder why we Romans insist on stomping all over your lands, imposing ourselves and our way of life on you.'

'You said it yourself: to bring civilisation,' Fergus said with a shrug. 'Aquilifer, in Hibernia I was born a noble and my home was a mud hut. There's more luxury and comfort in a Roman army barracks than the hovels my people call palaces. The baths, the games, the gymnasia, the theatre, roads, libraries, books, underfloor heating – I could go on. We have none of that, and that's what I want now, not superstitious terror, ignorance and primitive misery. Trust me; I have good reason to turn my back on that.'

Faustus chuckled. 'And yet there lies the irony, Hibernian. It's those very comforts and trappings of civilisation that makes us Romans feel insecure. We envy you. Barbarians still live the wild martial life. We worry that our soft, pampered existence somehow makes us less manly. Which is why fat, ageing senators in Rome – anxious about their own loss of virility – send us out to test Rome's mettle. It's the reason we constantly have to strive; to pit ourselves incessantly against those we see as free warrior tribes in order to prove our own manhood. Funny isn't it? You envy us our sophistication and we envy you your lack of it.'

Fergus screwed up his face. This sounded like nonsense to him, the sort of random, strange talk that Romans called 'philosophy'. Someday perhaps he would have time to sit down and study what it was all about, but for now there was only time for fighting. Still, the aquilifer seemed to be willing to discuss things and right now an influential officer like Faustus could possibly aid him in his plight.

'Aquilifer Faustus, I appeal to you,' Fergus said. 'This punishment is unjust. Can you help me contest it?'

Faustus pondered for a moment, then said, 'I have no idea whether this punishment is deserved or not, Sesquiplicarius.'

Fergus frowned at the first use of his new rank title.

'However,' Faustus went on, 'in my twenty years in the army I have to admit you wouldn't be the first soldier I've seen who had to take the blame for a useless officer's mistakes.'

Fergus nodded enthusiastically. 'Sedullus – our decurion – ordered us to chase a group of Britons into some woods. It was obviously an ambush—'

Faustus held up his hand to stop Fergus in mid-flow. 'Hibernian...' He paused, glanced down at the note before him to read the Celt's name. 'Fergus MacAmergin, the harsh truth you have to face is that once a tribune has made a decision there is no way he will go back on it, whether it be right or wrong. It would be seen as weakness. I would add that Tribune Agricola is very young and very new to the post, so this is more likely to be a direct order from the general himself, in which case there is even less chance of it being reversed.'

Fergus looked lost. 'Then what am I to do?'

'Well, for a start, you can't just run away,' the aquilifer said, looking him steadily in the eye. 'I know that's what you might be thinking and I wouldn't blame you. After all, this isn't your army. We're not fighting for your people. But you took an oath of allegiance, MacAmergin, and the Roman army takes a very dim view of deserters. A very dim view indeed. Believe me, you would welcome death by the time they'd finished with you.'

There were a few moments' silence as the implications of Faustus's words sank in. The only sound was the drumming of the rain on the goat leather of the aquilifer's tent as Fergus gazed forlornly into the guttering flame of the oil lamp, his mind in a turmoil of rage, disillusionment, resentment and the first kindling of a burning desire for revenge on Sedullus.

'You interest me, though,' Faustus finally said. 'You're not a Roman subject yet you want to achieve the things we believe in. You want to be a citizen, and why not? I will help you if I can, Hibernian.'

'How can you help me?' Fergus grunted. 'You might be the legion's aquilifer, but you're still just a non-commissioned officer. A duplicarius like me.'

'Like you *were*, you mean,' Faustus said. 'But I am *the* aquilifer. I have a privileged position that allows me to move in different circles to your average duplicarius. I have the ear of the senior officers. I also have twenty years' experience in this army and – if you choose to listen to me – I can maybe give you some good advice.'

'But you said yourself, there's no way the tribune will reverse this decision,' Fergus complained.

'No, he won't,' Faustus confirmed. 'But if you're ready to start listening to me, I can offer a few suggestions as to how you can make the best of things.'

Fergus shrugged, unable to imagine anything the aquilifer could say to improve his situation.

'You say you want to be a Roman. Well, the most important characteristic of any Roman is "virtus". Toughness. Morality. Good character. Accepting any situation stoically, no matter how adverse. View this as an opportunity, Hibernian,' Faustus said. 'You may have been demoted from duplicarius but you are now in command of your own troopers with no bumbling decurion over you. On top of that, as you said, numeres troops are given dangerous work that no one else wants to do. It's risky, yes, but with risks come opportunities. Look on this as a chance to win glory. Put it this way: there are two routes you can take to win Roman citizenship. You can complete twenty-five years' service in the army and be granted your diploma. You can then retire a citizen just in time to die. Or you can be granted it as a reward for a heroic act. Glory is your fastest route to your prize. Be brave, Hibernian, and one day you will wear a toga. That or be dead.'

Fergus felt his despair begin to disperse a little. He could also see why Faustus had been made aquilifer. He was the sort of man who inspired others; one who other men would follow into the very mouth of Hades.

He nodded his agreement.

'Good,' Faustus said. 'Now, if you don't mind, I have work to do, not least altering the pay records to reflect your change in status.'

Straightening up to attention, Fergus saluted again, before lifting the flap of the tent to leave.

'By the way, you're now officially a Gaul,' Faustus stated.

Fergus stopped and cast a questioning glance at the aquilifer.

'Hibernia is not an allied nation of Rome,' Faustus explained. 'Therefore no Hibernian should be in the Roman army. Officially, for the purpose of the army records, you are now a Gaul.'

Fergus rolled his eyes at the strange reasoning that

changed his people with a stroke of Faustus's pen. Shaking his head, he left the tent.

'And get your hair cut,' Faustus shouted after him. 'If you want to be a Roman you'd better damn well start looking like one!'

5

First thing next morning, the praefect of the regiment, Titus Pomponius Proculianus, accompanied by Sedullus, arrived at the collection of cavalry tents to begin the reorganisation of the troops. They had come accompanied by a centurion and three *contubernia* of legionaries – twenty-four soldiers in all – to enforce discipline lest there be any objections.

Sedullus created his new command, the XV Turma, by making it up to full strength with cronies and those members of the old Tenth who had kissed his backside the most. The ten remaining men were given to Fergus for the numeres troop. All of them had reacted to the news of their punishment with the same consternation as Fergus, but the threatening presence of legionaries had quelled all protests to mere angry words.

It was a hard thing for the troopers to accept. They were the elite of the army, the sons of Gaulish nobility. Some of them were of royal blood and to add insult to injury it was the common soldiery, whose pay was four-fifths of their own, who had come to enforce the punishment.

'Helmet,' Sedullus said in a demanding tone, his hand held out towards Fergus, a gloating smirk on his face.

Fergus felt the cold rage churning in his chest as he unbuckled his helmet with its horsehair crest running front to back, the symbol of his rank, and took it off. He handed it to Sedullus who in return gave him a standard imperial bronze helmet.

Fergus took a deep breath, fighting to quell the anger inside him. He longed to punch Sedullus in the face but knew that would only make everything worse. Sedullus would run crying to his Gaul commanders and he would be kicked out of the army. Or worse, executed.

He had spent all night mulling over his situation. He had given a lot of thought to what the aquilifer had said and was beginning to look on things in a more positive light. Perhaps Faustus was right and this was actually an opportunity for him. It might not have been what he had originally envisaged, but he had got his command after all. So what if it was a punishment squad instead of a cavalry turma. It was *his* punishment squad. Finally he had a chance to show he could lead and was determined he would make a success of whatever task he was given.

Fergus swallowed hard and put the plain bronze helmet on.

Nine of the numeres were Gauls. The tenth man, Masculus, was from Batavia – the low, flat country beside the sea that nestled between northern Gaul and Germania. Fergus liked Masculus for his black sense of humour and the fact that he too was an outsider.

'This is a fucking joke,' Liscus, one of the Gaul troopers said, deliberately pitching his voice loud enough to be heard by Fergus. 'They do this to us and as if it wasn't bad enough, they put the Hibernian in charge. If anyone is to blame it's officers like him. He's not even from an allied nation for fuck's sake.'

Fergus clenched his teeth again but decided on this occasion to let it go. They had as much right to be annoyed as he did. However, he realised that he now had his work cut out if he were to meld them into a team. They did not have to like him, but he needed to gain their respect.

The legionaries stripped them of their heavy lances, cloaks, regimental regalia and their horses' armour and sent it all off to the baggage train. In its place they were given quivers of light throwing spears. They each kept their spatha and helmet, but instead of heavy cavalry they were now a light troop. Obviously, whatever task awaited them required that they be as swift and agile as possible.

Pomponius ordered them to assemble outside the praetorium. The officers and the legionaries then left to prepare for departure from camp while Fergus and his new troop fetched their horses and walked them across to the praetorium and lined up.

'What are we waiting for now, sir?' Masculus said.

'Orders,' Fergus said.

Around them the camp that had taken so much effort to construct was being dismantled again. Tents were taken down and packed away, the rampart levelled by back-filling it into the ditch and anything that could not be carried away and could possibly be used by the enemy was burned.

'We build it all up then we take it back down again,' Masculus the Batavian said with a wry smile. 'We train, we fight, we form ourselves into effective teams and then we get reorganised. Sometimes you have to wonder what the point of it all is.'

'What are you moaning about, Masculus?' Fergus said to the flaxen-haired trooper. 'You don't do any of the building work. What do you care?'

The cavalry troopers were all *immunes*: exempt from the heavy construction duties that the legionaries were expected to do. Fergus and his new numeres troop sat, mounted on their Hispanian horses, watching as the foot soldiers slogged away.

'You can see why they call them *Marius's mules*,' Masculus said. The others laughed.

The legionaries loaded themselves down with armour, equipment satchels, entrenching tools, weapons, food and their big rectangular shields in preparation for leaving camp; the cavalry troopers could see how apt a name it was. Each legionary was expected to lug so much equipment that he had to carry a long, forked stick as well, designed to hang various impedimenta from so that as much as possible could be transported by each man.

'And there you can see the advantage of being a Roman citizen,' Masculus said. 'You get the honour of doing more work than us.'

'But you're still just another barbarian to them, Masculus,' Fergus said.

As the numeres waited at the centre of the camp, Queen Finnabair and her female companion emerged from one of the large tents. Behind him, Fergus heard Masculus give a low whistle of appreciation.

'Now that's what I call a lady,' the Batavian commented

softly. All eyes were drawn towards her and there were murmurs of appreciation from the troopers.

Fergus hid a smile; if there was one thing the Gauls all loved it was the sight of a good-looking woman.

'That, troopers, is a Hibernian queen,' he said, 'so none of you lot stand a chance with her.'

'Are all Hibernian women as beautiful as her, sir?' asked Dumorix, a young lad of nineteen.

'Of course,' said Fergus.

'If the mothers are so beautiful,' Liscus said, 'how come Hibernian men are so ugly?'

The troopers laughed. Fergus did not join them, wondering just how far Liscus would push things. The Gaul was taller than he, with broad shoulders and a long reach that would be hard to tackle if they came to blows, which was what was going have to happen if Liscus continued on his current course. He also wondered for the second time just what a Hibernian queen was doing in the Roman camp.

Agricola came out of his tent, his tribune's white leather armour gleaming and spotless despite the dismal, muddy surroundings.

'Right, lads. Here we go,' Fergus said. 'Straighten up, troopers. Sit high in your saddles and salute the *tribunus laticlavius*.'

After a barely noticeable hesitation, the numeres all raised their right hands in the Roman salute.

'Salve,' Agricola greeted them, returning the gesture with a small, slightly arrogant smile on his lips. The tribune stood and regarded the line of cavalrymen before him, his tanned skin glistening with oil, the muscled arms speaking of privilege and enough wealth to afford to spend time in the gymnasium. His eyes were so dark as to be almost black; his nose was unbroken and possessed of a long, straight profile. Short, stocky and powerful, Agricola was to Fergus every inch of what he liked to refer to as a typical, conceited little Roman.

Despite the fact that the mounted troopers towered over him the tribune met their eyes, his gaze steeled with confidence. He was an important cog in the most powerful military machine in the world and he knew it.

'Good morning, gentlemen,' he said. 'We have a very special task for you today.'

Out from the tent behind him came a worried-looking man in very strange clothes. He was gaunt almost to the point of starvation, with very close-cropped grey hair. He appeared to be in his late forties. His arms were scrawny and his bare legs, which had turned a mottled blue colour from the cold, were like those of a bird. From his leather skullcap and clean white robes, which he held carefully out of the British mud, the man was clearly a Roman priest of some description, though he was dressed differently to the priests Fergus saw officiating at the army rituals. In particular, he wore two extra pieces of headgear: a headband made from white wool and bound over it a wreath of what looked like dried twigs and leaves. In his hand he carried a spear, but it was no legionary javelin. It was some sort of ceremonial weapon, constructed more for style than violence, and the tip of it seemed to have been burned. Fresh blood, no doubt from some animal sacrifice, dribbled down its point.

'We Romans are not savages,' Agricola continued. 'We have ways of doing things: traditions, laws and rules. Though we now go to war it is not lightly or on a whim that we do so. There are certain formulae to follow, rules and ceremonies to perform. This man—' he rested a hand on the shoulder of the anxious-looking priest '—is a member of the College of Fetiales in Rome. They are the priests who act as guardians of public faith. When Rome goes to war, it is the *fetial* priests who declare war against the enemy. This priest here will carry the declaration of war right to the enemy's door. You men are to assist him in this sacred duty.'

Fergus frowned. 'We're warriors,' he said. 'We have no religious training, sir. How can we help him?'

Agricola laughed. 'I forgot, you're Gauls, aren't you? You're perhaps unfamiliar with the Roman way of declaring war – though your forefathers would have been all too aware of it.'

So far, Fergus's own involvement in the wars of Rome had always started when the fighting had already begun, when the only religion there was time for was a quick prayer that you would survive. He heard uneasy murmurings from some of the troopers behind him, signalling that some of them at least had more idea of what was coming than he did.

'You do not need any religious training,' Agricola said. 'When Rome has decided to make war, a priest representing the College of Fetiales rides with a burned spear dipped in blood into the lands of the enemy. When he meets the enemy, he will hurl the spear and declare the *clarigatio*, the official declaration of war. The legions can then march into the territory and the war has officially begun. It will be your job to get this priest into the land of the Silures, let him make the clarigatio and then get him safely back to us. The legion will be following behind. It may seem like a mere formality, but these things are important. It is what makes us civilised.'

The priest looked distinctly concerned now and turned his hollow, red-rimmed eyes towards Agricola.

'Tribune,' he said, casting a nervous glance at the drooping moustaches and long braided hair of the cavalry troopers before him. 'Will these men protect me? They look like barbarians themselves.'

There was reproach in the eyes of Agricola as he met the priest's gaze.

'Pater, these men are Roman soldiers. Rest assured they will carry out any mission they are assigned.'

'It's suicide,' Fergus heard a trooper behind him mutter in the Gaulish tongue. He was sure it was Liscus, and though he rankled at the man's insubordination, he had a strong feeling that the trooper was right.

6

Agricola watched as Fergus's new troop rode out to the west while all around the legionaries continued dismantling the camp.

At what was left of the main gate, several horsemen trotted in. Watching them from the doorway of his tent, the tribune could see these were not auxiliaries but mounted members of General Paulinus's own bodyguard, distinguishable by the dark green plumes on their helmets. They rode at a slow pace trailing a prisoner behind them. Both hands roped, he was being pulled along by one of the bodyguards and was forced to run at a trot to keep up with the horses or be dragged face down through the muck.

That he was a Celt was obvious, both to Agricola and to the toiling legionaries, who eyed him as he went by. He wore the plaid breeches of the natives. Despite the weather, he was naked from the waist up – most likely his captors had stripped him. His hair was long, braided and tied up in the shape of a horse's tail behind his head, and a long moustache drooped from his upper lip. His chest, back and arms were covered in the customary swirling blue and brown body paint, and round his neck gleamed a *torc*: the twisted rope of gold that signalled his noble status as the Celtic equivalent of the Roman equestrian class.

None of the legionaries raised an eyebrow. Another insurgent had been captured and was being brought in for questioning. After a quick glance in his direction they went back to their labours.

The bedraggled prisoner was hauled roughly up the temporary via praetoria to the command tent of General Paulinus. Although the camp was being taken down, the tents of the praetorium were customarily left intact until just before the legion was ready to march.

His curiosity aroused, Agricola decided to investigate further and followed them to Paulinus's tent. The body-guards were dismounting as he arrived.

'What have you got there?' he asked the officer.

'Prisoner,' the bodyguard said. 'The general wants to see him personally.'

Agricola entered through the tent flap and gave a slight cough to announce his presence. Inside the tent, the general was sitting at his writing table, reviewing a papyrus scroll and a sheaf of the thin wooden tablets that served as the medium for reports in Britannia. Paulinus raised his head with a questioning look at the tribune, one eyebrow raised.

'General, sir,' Agricola said. 'Some of your bodyguards are outside with a British prisoner. They say you asked to see him personally.' His tone of voice and the look on his face betrayed the fact that he thought this highly unlikely, but felt he should check anyway. To his surprise, Paulinus's face lit up in a rare smile.

'Ah, excellent! Send him in,' the general said.

Puzzled, Agricola went back out and quickly returned accompanied by the Briton and two burly bodyguards, who half-shoved, half-carried the prisoner in through the leather tent flap.

Paulinus stood when they entered. 'Thank you, men, you can go,' he said, gesturing for his bodyguards to leave.

Moving to obey, they paused as Agricola, his puzzlement turning to outright shock, blurted out, 'Sir, you can't be serious?!'

The general shot him a look that conveyed both disdain and disapproval.

'Really, Tribune. Show a bit of backbone before the men! I think we two Romans in our armour and with swords by our sides can handle one unarmed native without the aid of guards. Don't you?'

The bodyguards turned swiftly away, but not before Agricola had seen their stifled laughter. Blushing, he nodded, but his gaze slid over the mud-splattered Briton taking in the warpaint; the long, matted hair and the ring-pierced nose. His hand dropped to the hilt of the gladius that rested in its scabbard at his waist. To his consternation the prisoner returned his gaze with what could only be described as a contemptuous sneer.

Agricola was sure he heard guffaws from the bodyguards now outside the tent. His cheeks burned and he silently vowed that later he would make them sorry for mocking him.

Once they were gone, General Paulinus drew his dagger and approached the Celt. Agricola swallowed. He was far from squeamish but he disapproved of torture – not least because he considered it ineffectual. Unlike some, he gained no enjoyment from watching it either. While he had never seen Paulinus engage in the practice, he strongly suspected this was not a scruple the general shared.

To his further astonishment, Paulinus merely sliced through the ropes that bound the Briton's wrists.

Agricola started. He half drew his sword then stopped as he realised both men were now grinning at him.

'Tribune Agricola,' Paulinus said, 'there is no need to be frightened.'

His face creased with amusement as he laid one hand on the prisoner's shoulder.

'Let me introduce Titus Furious Falco, one of the most dedicated citizens and servants of the Senate and People of Rome that you will ever meet.'

Aware his jaw had dropped, Agricola struggled to regain his composure.

'Some wine, Titus?' Paulinus said, walking back to a jug that sat on the writing table.

'Jupiter, yes!' Falco said. 'I haven't tasted decent wine for months. The Brittunculi only have the cheap muck we sell them and it's rough enough to take the paint off a legionary's shield. Apart from that, all they have to drink is that dreadful concoction brewed from apples.'

Hearing Falco use the word 'Brittunculi' – *nasty little Brits* – the derogatory term by which Roman soldiers referred to British natives, confirmed to Agricola that despite appearances this man was no British tribesman.

Paulinus poured three goblets of crystal-clear white wine and passed one to Falco and one to Agricola.

'No doubt you are wondering what is going on, Agricola?' Paulinus said. 'I owe you an explanation.'

'I would not mind hearing that, sir,' Agricola said through tight lips.

'When the Roman army goes to war, Tribune, do you think it marches with its eyes closed?' the general said.

Agricola shook his head. 'Of course not. Roman merchants and tradesmen provide information for us,' he said. 'Also collaborators: natives sympathetic to Rome – or more likely with an axe to grind against their fellow countrymen. We know the local tribes, the harbours to land in, the routes to follow.'

Paulinus nodded. 'Indeed, but there are also dedicated men, Romans through and through, men like Falco here,' he said, tipping his goblet at the man in Celtic garb, 'who give up the comforts of civilised life to enter the world of the barbarians. They dress like them, interact with them, pretend to be one of them, but all the time they are gathering information for us. What they tell us is vital. Not only that, but sometimes they, er… shall we say engineer provocative actions by local tribes against the Roman Empire, which make it necessary for us to respond.'

'And Rome never goes to war without provocation,' Agricola said, drily.

'Of course not,' the general said. '*We* are civilised, after all. Titus here is one of those brave men. For most of the last three years he has been living as a native among the Britons, watching what they are up to and passing it back to us. Many times he has risked an unspeakable death to tell us information that has saved the lives of many men.'

Falco grunted. 'And got quite a few killed too,' he said with a wolfish grin.

'So, he's a spy,' Agricola said.

Some of the humour left Paulinus's smile. 'Yes, he is a spy. From your tone of voice I gather that you do not approve. If that is the case then I suggest it is time you grew up a little and put away your childish notions of combat, Tribune. Wars are not won by battle formations and cavalry charges alone. A truly successful general knows he must make use of every scrap of information, and obtain it by whatever means necessary, so that when the time comes for the legionaries to advance he has done everything in his power to gain an edge over the enemy. Titus is from one of the most illustrious patrician families, yet he has given up wealth, power, status and an easy life back home to live among the savages of this country.'

'I saw your bodyguards drag him roped and half-naked behind their horses,' Agricola said.

'Yes. I apologise for the play-acting, but it was necessary to keep Falco's identity secret,' Paulinus said. 'No one knows – not even the legionaries – that he works for us, and if word ever got out then I dread to think what the Britons would do to him.'

The general paused, then smiled.

'And when it comes to play-acting, the fact that Titus has been accepted as one of them for so long, shows he is not *just* a spy, Agricola,' he said, 'but surely one of the greatest actors who has ever lived, regardless of what our illustrious emperor thinks of himself.'

Falco and the general both laughed. Agricola did not join in. He was uncertain how he felt about spies. All his instincts told him the way to meet an enemy was head on in an open contest of strength, tactics and valour, not sneaking around behind enemy lines pretending to be one of them but all the time acting for the other side.

He was determined to forge a military career for himself, however. He was here with the general to learn about war, and if spies were a cog in Rome's military machine, then so be it. He would have to overcome his scruples if he wanted to become a hero of Rome. Which was exactly what he planned to do.

Most of the mirth left Falco's eyes as he turned to Agricola, subjecting him to the same contemptuous gaze as before.

'You look very young and fresh-faced to be a tribune,' he said. 'Ever killed a man? Ever been in a battle?'

Agricola blushed yet again. 'I've skirmished and been through full military training,' he said, puffing out his chest. 'I've taken part in manoeuvres and studied military tactics. I have read Xenophon, Caesar—'

The spy cut him off with a snort. 'Well your standard legionary tactics are useless here, boy,' he said. 'The Brittunculi hit you from the trees and run away. A native will talk to you one minute and slit your throat the next, just as soon as you turn your back. They don't do formations. Warfare here is not a symmetrical clash of armies. That's why the empire needs men like me.'

'Which is exactly what we need to talk about,' Paulinus intervened. 'So tell me, what is going on with our British subjects?'

Falco shot a suspicious glance at Agricola. 'Do you want him hearing any of this?'

His anger rising, Agricola glared at the spy.

'I am tribunus laticlavius of this legion and completely trustworthy. There is no dissembling in my character,' he said.

'That's what I am worried about, boy,' Falco said with a derisive sneer.

That was too much; Agricola was incensed. Already a tribune at his young age, he was also of senatorial rank, but this man, who could not have been ten years older than he, had no respect for him at all.

He opened his mouth to say so when Paulinus held up a hand. 'Don't worry about Agricola, Falco,' he said. 'I trust him and that's all you need to know.'

Somewhat mollified, Agricola felt a thrill of excitement, realising he had just crossed a form of personal rubicon in his career. He was seeing a new side to the general, one that he had never suspected before. In front of his men, Paulinus was always impassive, never letting his thoughts be known. Yet here with the spy, a man who spent all his time hiding his true self from those around him, the general was completely relaxed. It was as if he found in Falco a kindred spirit. It came to Agricola that in sharing in these moments with Paulinus and his spy, he had been accepted into the inner circle of the senior command of the legion. He had just taken an important step up the ladder of his career.

'It should be no secret to you that this whole island is a seething cauldron, General, ready to boil over into revolt at any moment,' Falco said with a sigh. 'The tribes champ at the bit of Roman rule. The ones who have not begun to adopt our customs are bitter at paying taxes and having to send their young men to fight in our army. The ones who have become Romanised now find themselves in debt to our money lenders. To make things worse, men like Seneca are starting to call in their debts.'

'Tell me something I don't know, Titus,' the general said. 'The damned money men are worried about their investments in this imperial venture. And they've good reason to be nervous. Do you know that the emperor actually considered abandoning Britannia? With all the trouble here and four legions still required to hold the place down, he seriously talked about withdrawing back to Gaul! Can you imagine the effect that would have?'

'Indeed I can,' Falco said, nodding. 'Every savage and barbarian from Iberia to the Rhine would see it for what it was. Weakness. They would all be up in arms demanding freedom. It would be the end of the Roman Empire.'

'And I'm damned if I'll be remembered by history as the man who opened up the first crack in the wall that let the barbarian hordes in,' Paulinus said. His eyes had become slightly glazed and had taken on a steel-like sheen. 'I'm damned if I'll be the last Roman Governor of Britannia.'

Agricola felt a further thrill, both of nervousness and excitement. To question the emperor's actions was treason. If someone overheard them it could mean a death sentence. This knowledge reinforced the gratifying feeling that he was his general's confidant and he began to relax.

'Thankfully the Brittunculi are so hopelessly divided they will never unite against us,' Paulinus went on. 'If they did, they could probably drive us into the sea. Now, tell me about this Hibernian queen. Agricola here has been entertaining her so he deserves to know more about what is going on. Tell me what you know of her. Is this offer of hers genuine?'

'Been "entertaining" her have you?' Falco's leer was unpleasant. 'Well what can I tell you about the fair Finnabair? She became queen of the *Dobunni* tribe to the south of here as part of an alliance with a tribe in southeast Hibernia, one the Dobunni trade with. Catti, the Dobunni king she married, died last year. The Britons are so degenerate that they allow themselves to be ruled by women, but Finnabair's position is far from assured. She's unpopular and a foreigner. Some of the tribe are openly asking if she should be replaced by one of their own. To try to bolster her position she has taken a consort, Comux – the old king's nephew. She has chosen badly though. Comux is an ambitious young brat who'll happily see her ousted so he can become king in his own right. She now looks to us as a way to hold on to power.'

The general snorted. 'When will they ever learn?' he said. 'She might hold on to power for the rest of her life, but we will expect her to name the emperor as her successor, just as the king of the Iceni had to last year. Prasutagus is not a well man and with him will die the last independent kingdom in the east of Britannia.'

Falco looked unconvinced. 'He may be loyal to us,' he said, 'but I've heard that his wife, Boudicca, does not share his affiliation. Finnabair, however, has very little choice. Nor, I suspect, does she care what happens to the Dobunni after her death, so long as she holds on to power until then. If she is to keep her position – and her life – she needs outside support. Us.'

'What about the spear?' the general said. He seemed slightly anxious.

'Ah yes, the mysterious spear,' Falco said. He turned to

Agricola and explained, 'The Dobunni are in possession of a sacred spear, which is rumoured to have mystical powers. The queen is offering it to us in return for our support.'

Agricola frowned and looked to his general.

'Magic weapons? What nonsense is this? Surely we have no interest in native superstitions?' he said.

Paulinus held up his hand. 'Perhaps we do, Agricola. There is often more to superstitions than meets the eye. They are not always nonsense,' he said. 'Take the place to the south of here that the Dobunni believe to be sacred to their water goddess, Sulis. I've been there and sure enough, hot water actually bubbles from the ground, though it comes from natural hot springs rather than divine origin. Can you imagine how much money is waiting to be made by the man who converts that place to medicinal baths like we have in Rome...?'

He fell silent, his eyes distant, until Falco gave a meaningful cough.

Paulinus laughed. 'Yes, well, as I was saying, this spear might have rather more useful properties,' he said. 'Quite what I cannot imagine, but it is clearly important to the Dobunni. The queen is being coy about the truth of it though. Falco, what have you found out? Has she got a sacred spear and if so what is it exactly?'

'It is said to be imbued with great power, which could well be genuine,' the spy said. 'It seems that even here at the far end of the civilised world the Christian superstition has spread its insidious influence.'

Agricola pricked up his ears. Even growing up in Frejus, in southern Gaul, he had heard of the followers of a Judean Jew called Christus, who had proclaimed himself a prophet and started his own religion. The man had been crucified in Judea for treason thirty years ago, before Agricola was born, but now the cult was spreading fast throughout the Western Empire and people were saying the emperor had lately become obsessed with it. The refusal of its followers, who called themselves Chrestians – or sometimes Christians – to accept his own divinity was a personal affront to Nero and he was determined to stamp the movement out. Even so, to learn that it had reached this island at the edge of the world seemed unbelievable to Agricola.

'It's not a religion, it's more like a disease,' Paulinus said. 'How in Hades' name did it get *here*?'

'The sect spreads from town to town, city to city, meeting underground or in secret,' Falco said. 'When we executed their founder, the rebel Jesus Christus, his followers scattered and went on the run. They took relics of Christus and sacred items of the cult with them. At that time, Britain was just about as far from Roman authority as you could get and some of these Christians must have come here. It's just their bad luck that fifteen years later the Roman army arrived. There are Christians among the Dobunni. They have some temples of their faith in the south near Aquae Sulis. The druids don't like them, but the cult is still too small to threaten their power, so for the time being they leave them alone.'

'That's as may be, but what of the spear?' Paulinus said.

'Among the religious relics the Dobunni Christians claim to have is the spear used by a Roman soldier to stab Christus when he was dying on the cross. They see it as divine and it is one of their most precious possessions.'

'If we can get our hands on that, Titus, the emperor will

be both grateful and generous with his rewards,' the general said, his eyes glittering. 'He hates the Christians with a venom I have not seen him direct at anyone else – except perhaps his royal mother! Gaining a relic of such power would allow Nero to crush the Christian sect once and for all.'

It dawned on Agricola what Paulinus was thinking. If the emperor destroyed the spear publicly, it would demonstrate that he was more powerful than the Christians' god, thus refuting their faith and stopping further converts to the cult. Or knowing the emperor, even make himself leader of it. Nero: the second Christus.

Lost in the thought, Agricola became aware that Paulinus was addressing him and snapped to attention.

'I want you to accompany this queen south, back to her lands, Tribune. You are to take that Fergus MacAmergin, with you – he could play a key role here, so keep him alive, at least until we learn what we need to. You are aware that he's a Hibernian?'

'Yes, General.' Agricola's chest tightened with a spasm of dread. He tried not to show it.

'Under no circumstances are you or he to reveal where he is from. As far as the world at large is concerned, he's a Gaul, understood?'

Speechless, Agricola nodded.

'He's to listen when Finnabair talks to her maidservants and bodyguards in their language,' Paulinus said. 'He will learn what he can about this spear and her real intentions, then rejoin us and we can make further plans.'

In the dim light of the tent, the general peered at Agricola's face.

'Is there something wrong, Tribune?' he said. 'You seem to have gone very pale.'

'Eh, no, General,' Agricola stammered. 'Erm... I am just concerned about the campaign against the Silures. There is a battle coming and you are ordering me away. I am worried I will miss the action.'

'Commendable, but battles come and battles go, Agricola,' Paulinus said. 'Don't worry, there will be fighting enough for you before all this is over. In the meantime this is more important, which is why I am sending you. Don't let me down. Now go, and the best of luck to you.' The general saluted.

Agricola raised his right hand to return the salute, nodded at Falco then turned and left the tent, painfully aware that unbeknownst to Paulinus, he had already sent the Hibernian cavalry officer, so vital to the general's plans, off on a mission that could very well end in his death.

7

As the sun rose behind its mask of relentless grey clouds, Fergus's new command rode westward away from the army. Ahead in the distance, mountains rose in jagged peaks towards the sky, while most of the undulating land around them was forest, occasionally slashed by deep valleys.

This terrain made the troopers nervous.

'I hate this country,' Masculus said, scanning the undergrowth with an uneasy eye. 'Too many trees. It's just like Germania.'

'You should feel at home then,' Liscus said.

'Piss off, Gaul,' Masculus retorted. 'Batavi are not Germans. We're better than them. We left Germania to join the empire. Unlike you lot we were not conquered. We willingly become citizens.'

Fergus rode in the middle of the group. He did not intervene in the conversation, although he thought Masculus's comments ironic. Fifty years before, the Batavis' cousins, the Chatti, had joined the Cherusci in a coalition of Germanic tribes that had wiped out three whole Roman legions in the Teutoburg Forest. It was Rome's greatest military disaster, and it had happened in country not unlike this.

Progress was not rapid. The engineers of the legions had not yet made it this far into Rome's newest province so there were no Roman roads. Instead they followed the native roads: cart tracks and at some points animal paths that twisted through forest and undergrowth, sometimes disappearing altogether. Every step of the way the men were tense, their free hands hovering near their sword hilts. At any minute they expected to see the trees or bushes erupt with British tribesmen. By the time the sun had risen high in the sky the troopers' nerves were stretched to breaking point. They were jumpy, every sound from the woods making heads twitch around and hands grab for weapons.

Eventually the trees thinned out and they came upon a small but fast-flowing river. Its brown waters meandered in several loops before disintegrating into a rock-strewn ford shallow enough to allow the troopers to walk their horses over.

Beside the ford was a standing stone. As tall as a mounted man, it was decorated with daubs of multicoloured paint. Caked on top of the paint, dark brown rivulets of dried blood streaked its surface. A veritable forest of wooden poles stood upright around the stone, one end buried in the earth. On the top end of every wooden stake was impaled a decapitated human head. Most were mere bony skulls, the flesh and eyes long picked clean by crows. A few strands of long, wispy hair still clung to some of them.

'This is the border,' Fergus said, pointing at the severed heads. 'When we cross that river we're in the land of the Silures.'

'How do you know?' the priest asked.

'This is how we mark boundaries,' Fergus said. 'We

execute our criminals and our enemies and plant their heads at the edges of our land as a message to outsiders.'

'We?' the priest almost squeaked.

'We Celtae, Pater. Celts.' Fergus smiled, momentarily enjoying the look of panic that crossed the Roman priest's face. His black humour was stopped abruptly, however, when he caught sight of one of the severed heads that sat skewered on a pole beside the standing stone. It was fresher than the rest and as yet had suffered only a few pecks from the beaks of scavenging birds. The eyes were gone though, leaving two deep holes, black with dried blood. It was still recognisable as the head of Viridovix.

Around it, spiked on other poles, were arranged the heads of the other Roman soldiers killed in the ambush the day before.

Fergus sighed and dismounted. He walked over to the Gaul's severed head and for a few moments regarded it.

'How long until I join you, old friend?' he said in a whisper as he grasped the hair and lifted the already stinking skull off the pole. It came away with a wet sucking sound. Turning around with it in his hands he saw the troopers and the priest all watching him with a mixture of fear and disgust.

'I'm not leaving it behind for the crows. He was a brave soldier and my friend,' Fergus said, his tone both defensive and bristling with challenge. 'What do you think I am? A savage?'

'He's insane,' he heard Liscus comment as he tied Viridovix's head to his saddle by its long hair. 'We're given a suicide mission and our leader is collecting body parts. At least we Gauls left headhunting behind years ago.'

'Have you got something to say, trooper?' Fergus said. He fixed Liscus with an unflinching stare. The Gaul at first met his gaze, but then his eyes flicked away.

'No,' Liscus said.

'No, what?'

'No. *Sir*.' Liscus spat the second word with an insolent smile playing on his lips.

Fergus knew that the time was coming fast when he would have to deal with Liscus. He could not let this continue if he were to retain any authority over the rest of the men.

'Well here we are at the border, Pater,' Fergus said to the priest as he swung himself back into his saddle. 'Perform your ritual and we can be on our way.'

The priest shook his head. 'We must go further,' he said. 'We must enter the territory of the enemy.'

'What?' Fergus said.

'The ritual is quite clear,' the priest said as he folded his arms and looked away. 'It has been followed since time immemorial and we cannot change it now. I repeat, it must be carried out inside the territory of the enemy. We have to cross the river.'

'By Mars Tiwaz!' Masculus rolled his eyes and swore by the combined names of the Roman and German gods of war. 'In this country, everywhere outside our forts is enemy territory. This is no time for pedantry, old man. Get on with it. The Brittunculi could attack us at any minute.'

The priest visibly flinched as if Masculus had spat on him.

'Don't say those names,' he said, his voice raised in anger. 'I am a priest of the Collegium of Fetials. Our ministry is in the legal and civic arena. We only invoke Jupiter, Juno and Quirinius. We must never invoke those other deities.'

'Are you telling me that the Roman priest responsible for declaring war isn't allowed to mention the name of the Roman god of war?' Fergus said. 'By Crom, that says a lot about you Romans.'

The priest narrowed his eyes.

'Who is this Crom you swear by – some barbarian god?' he said.

'Never you mind. He's not a war god. Content yourself with that,' Fergus said.

He frowned at the priest, who sat shivering on his horse in his ridiculous costume, his face a mask of determination. The man was cold, wet and frightened, but the light of religious conviction burned in his eyes. Some battles were worth fighting, but Fergus could tell that this would be a pointless one.

'Very well,' he said with a heavy sigh, 'let's cross the river and you can do your magic on the far side. Then we can all go home.'

For the first time that day, the priest actually looked happy. He was the only one.

'Fuck this,' Liscus muttered. 'We've gone far enough. Who knows what is waiting for us on the other side of that river. Let the mad priest go on his own. If the Hibernian wants to go too then let him. I'm not getting killed for some crazy Roman tradition.'

'Cross the ford. That's an order, Liscus,' Fergus said, his voice gravelly with implied threat.

'No,' Liscus said. His voice wavered, rising a couple of octaves. 'This is a numeres; a punishment squad. We don't *have* to do what you tell us. We're all the same in this unit and I say we're not crossing that river.'

He looked at the other troopers for support. The expression on his face betrayed his disappointment that no one openly agreed. On the other hand they didn't leap to Fergus's defence either. None of them wanted to cross the river, but it was clear they were waiting to see how this situation would resolve itself before choosing to support one side or the other.

The priest, seemingly oblivious to the brewing storm, goaded his horse forward and splashed over the ford. On the other side, seemingly unaware that none of the troopers had followed him, he dismounted and untied from his saddle-bow the bloodied spear he had brought from camp. With the spear held in both hands above his head, he knelt on the stony riverbank, bowed his head and began to recite prayers, the sound of his voice carrying over the water to where the troopers watched in fascination. The words were strange to their ears, slightly familiar but unintelligible. If it was Latin it was an extremely archaic form of it, Fergus thought.

Fergus judged that the time had come to do something about his insubordinate trooper, Liscus.

'There's a change of plan, men,' he said. 'You are not going to cross the river after all.'

Liscus smiled in triumph and a look of scorn crossed his face. Clearly he had not expected Fergus to capitulate so easily.

'Instead,' Fergus said, 'Liscus and I will cross alone while you guard our backs. We have things to discuss.'

The smile died on Liscus's face as he watched Fergus dismount once more, remove his helmet and lead his horse across the river. On the other side he looped the reins around a large boulder on the riverbank, then unbuckled his sword belt and took off the weapon, laying it and his helmet carefully beside his mount. A few feet away from him, the priest droned on, the cadence of his voice rising and falling as he uttered the ritualistic prayer. Ignoring him, Fergus stood, arms folded, and waited for Liscus to follow, confident that the Gaul would not want to lose face in front of his companions and would rise to the obvious challenge.

The other troopers all now looked at Liscus to see what he would do. Fergus knew the defiant Gaul had little choice now. He could turn away, but if he did, there was no way the men would accept him as their leader. With a shrug, Liscus dismounted and trudged through the water to the far bank to join Fergus. The watching troopers also dismounted, cheery grins breaking out on their faces at the entertaining prospect of a fight.

Fergus cracked his knuckles. The priest's orations got louder and seemed to be reaching some sort of climax. He had got back to his feet and was now shouting the strange words and gesticulating wildly at the mountains, the trees and the air with one hand while twirling the spear around with the other.

Liscus removed his helmet, warily watching Fergus as he did so.

'Have you got something to say to me?' he said, head to one side, an arrogant sneer on his lips.

Fergus's fist streaked straight towards Liscus's jaw. The Gaul had just enough time to turn his head away so that the blow struck him on the cheek instead of its intended target. It was still effective. Liscus's head snapped back.

Dazed, legs buckling, he stumbled backwards into the river, the insolent look replaced by one of shock and surprise.

Fists bunched, Fergus stepped forward looking for another target to strike. Liscus staggered further into the water, shielding his face with his hands in a vague attempt at a defensive stance.

Splashing after him, Fergus advanced, jabbing a right-hand punch at Liscus's head. The Gaul moved both hands up to block the blow. Immediately Fergus lashed out with his left. His fist smashed into Liscus's ribs, driving the wind from his lungs.

With a groan Liscus sank to his knees in the water, his face twisted with pain and his eyes closed. Stepping over him Fergus drove another merciless blow into the Gaul's upturned face. Liscus's nose shattered under it and his lower lip burst open. Howling he buried his face in his hands, blood, saliva and snot dribbling down between his fingers into the river.

'I'm in charge,' Fergus shouted in his face. Unflinching and intimidating, he stared down at the Gaul. 'Don't fucking forget it. You do what I say. Understand?'

Liscus, a pathetic, timid figure, nodded, not meeting his gaze.

'Good.' Fergus's shoulders relaxed and some of the fire died away in his eyes. He straightened up and turned back to the priest. 'Now, if you've finished—'

Fergus's breath whooshed out of his mouth, the blow taking him by surprise. Too late, he realised his elementary mistake in turning his back on Liscus. The Gaul had charged from a crouch and with his shoulder hit Fergus right in the middle of the back.

Propelled forwards onto the stones of the riverbank, Fergus cried out more in shock than pain. As he hit the ground, the impact forced an involuntary grunt from his lungs and he felt, rather than heard, a crunch in his mouth. Liscus leapt straight on top of him and straddled his spine, raining blows on the back of his exposed head. Fergus tasted blood and on one of his lower front teeth his tongue rasped along a jagged edge that had not been there before.

He spat out the chip that had broken off one of his molars. His chest heaved in a couple of involuntary gasps. Then rage took hold of him. For a moment his vision dimmed and the world appeared bathed in a deep red hue. He realised he was on the verge of losing all control.

Liscus stopped punching and grabbed his neck with both hands, squeezing hard to cut off his breathing. Already short of breath from the initial burst of fighting, Fergus knew he did not have much time before he passed out. Gritting his teeth he planted both hands flat on the gravel. Arm muscles bulging, he pushed himself into a press-up that lifted his chest off the ground with the Gaul still on his back. In the same movement, using all the power of his iron-strong thighs – a legacy of a lifetime spent on the back of a horse – he snapped his legs forward, tucked them under him and heaved upwards. In seconds he was back on his feet and Liscus, wide-eyed with amazement and dismay, now stood behind him.

Panting with effort, the Gaul changed his grip on Fergus's throat, sliding his left arm all the way around it to complete the stranglehold. He was certainly a persistent bastard, but hand-to-hand fighting was clearly not his strong point.

Fergus drove his head backwards, enjoying the satisfying crack as it collided with Liscus's face.

Howling with pain, Liscus loosened his grip on Fergus's throat and Fergus, gasping in a lungful of much-needed air, stamped back with his right foot, smashing his hobnailed sandal down onto Liscus's toes. Shrieking, the Gaul pulled his injured foot away, instinctively lifting it off the ground. With his opponent now off balance, Fergus completed the move by twisting down and to the right, driving his elbow into Liscus's ribs and thumping him near the spot where he had landed an earlier punch.

Liscus let go of Fergus's throat, pain doubling him over. Still on one leg he collapsed and fell face first onto the riverbank. Fergus spun round and placed a hefty kick into the other side of his ribcage. The Gaul made a grunting sound, half-groan, half-whine. He remained on the ground, his legs still in the water, his eyes tight shut, clearly waiting for the final blow to fall.

'You stupid bastard,' Fergus said, gulping in air to get his breathing back to normal. 'If you don't have the sense to know when to give up you should at least know how to fucking fight.'

As he spoke, he became aware of nervous laughter on the opposite bank. Insubordination was inexcusable in the army and doubtless the other troopers were wondering what would happen next.

At that moment, the priest let out a loud shout. Fergus turned to see him holding the spear in his right hand, ready to launch it, while with his left he pointed in the general direction of the trees a short distance away. He had also stopped chanting in the strange archaic tongue and now spoke loudly and clearly in modern Latin with the commanding tone of a practised orator.

'Hear this, people of the Silures: you have committed grievous offences against the Senate and People of Rome. You have been given ample time to provide restitution. That time has now expired, and as no satisfactory recompense has been received, the Senate and People of Rome now declare war against you!'

As he spoke the last words, he flung the spear. It was a feeble, ungainly attempt. He had only enough strength in his scrawny arm to launch the weapon about ten paces and it clattered into the long grass beyond the riverbank, not even making it as far as the trees that were his intended target. Despite this, the priest seemed extremely pleased with himself, for when he turned to confront Fergus and the troopers, his face was creased in a broad smile, the first any of them had seen from him all day.

'That's that,' he said, rubbing his hands together. 'War is declared. We have fulfilled the mission. Now, if you barbarians have quite finished fighting amongst yourselves, we can have a spot of lunch and then go home.'

As he was speaking, a figure burst from the trees behind the troopers on the opposite side of the river. As one, they stared wide-eyed at the newcomer.

She was a woman, there was no doubt about that, although she was very tall, at least as big as Masculus, but to Fergus, staring at her from across the narrow strip of water, she looked even taller. Her long, bright red hair stood straight up on her head, stuck in place with some concoction that made it radiate around her face in a way that reminded him of a burst of fire or a magnificent sunset. Her headdress consisted of a very thin bronze strip that circled her head above her eyebrows. Another strip ran from front to back across the centre of her skull. Her forehead seemed strangely long and, like her eyelids, was painted blue. She wore a multicoloured cloak that reached to the ground, its long hood hanging down her back. It shimmered somehow in the sunshine, first black then blue, but also brown and speckled, and Fergus realised that it was made from birds' feathers. The skin of her arms showed pure white through an intricate covering of blue paint, daubed in swirling, twisting patterns that seemed to reflect the sunlight, much like metal or enamel work.

They all stood open-mouthed, momentarily dumb-founded by the sheer beauty and power the woman exuded. At Fergus's feet, Liscus voiced what everyone else was thinking. Letting out a low whistle, a smile cracking his damaged face, he commented, 'Magnificent!'

Only the priest seemed unaffected.

'What in Jupiter's name?' he said, a look of aggrieved consternation wiping the rare smile from his features.

'I think your challenge has been answered,' Fergus said. An ominous feeling of dread growing in his chest, he started to move towards his horse.

The priest opened his mouth to speak, but before he did so the woman raised her right hand and pointed at the troopers. A terrifying, ear-piercing screech erupted from her lips and in that second, hordes of British warriors – bristling with spears and long, shining swords – burst out of the forest screaming their own bloody war cries.

The Silures' trap was sprung.

8

With a groan of dismay, Fergus realised he had screwed up in imperial style.

He could not believe his own stupidity. He had let Liscus's bickering get to him and been so focused on teaching the Gaul a lesson he had forgotten basic military practice. Not only had he neglected to post a lookout while the priest did his orations and performed his ritual, he had also allowed his troop to dismount. Now, as scores of British warriors came howling towards them, outnumbering them by at least four to one, they had lost the single advantage that being on horseback might have afforded them.

Silures swarmed towards them from the trees, screeching and whooping as they ran, venting the strange joy that gripped men anticipating battle, particularly when they saw their enemies at a disadvantage. Fergus could see these were no naked savages. These were trained warriors; men equipped with gleaming bronze helmets, mail coats and large square shields.

Too late, the startled troopers leapt for their mounts. The Britons, with so short a distance to cover, were already among them. As the lead warriors charged, they unleashed a deadly rain of spears. One gouged deep into a trooper's thigh, a second taking another in the chest, the point tearing through his leather tunic and bursting out of his back in a torrent of bright crimson blood. The trooper collapsed, clutching vainly at the shaft of the spear that protruded from his body as he died.

Another spear sank deep into the haunch of one of the horses. Screaming in terror and pain, the stricken animal reared up, panicking two of the other horses into bolting.

Yelling defiance, the remaining troopers drew their spathas and lined up, preparing to defend themselves as best they could.

On the other side of the river, Fergus could see that it was hopeless. He stood rooted to the spot, his instinct telling him to charge back over the water to join the fight; his head and eyes telling him that the battle was already lost.

A touch on his arm broke his trance. He looked round and saw to his surprise that it was Liscus.

'Come on,' the Gaul called, his voice thick from his split lip and broken nose. 'We still have a chance to save ourselves at least. Let's get out of here.'

Fergus knew he was right, yet still he hesitated, his heart urging him not to abandon his men. It did not matter that they did not like him; perhaps if he joined the fight he could make a difference. He looked back again and saw that two more troopers had fallen, their blood splattered around the rocks and stones of the riverbank. Masculus alone had managed to get on his horse and was surging forward into the enemy, slashing down death and injury with his spatha.

As Fergus teetered with indecision, a group of Silures warriors caught sight of the trio on the other side of the river and broke off from the main band to cross the water.

Fergus looked over his shoulder and saw that the priest was already mounted and was galloping away towards the trees.

Liscus, who had left his own mount back across the river, leapt onto Fergus's horse and rode up onto the bank. Then he stopped.

'Come on, you fool,' he shouted, wheeling around, one hand extended. 'Here. Jump on. I won't ask again.'

Fergus glanced at the Britons advancing towards him over the ford. There were seven of them. Not the best of odds.

He ran, pounding up the riverbank and into the long grass beyond it. Behind him the crunching on the stones told him that at least some of the Silures were already across, and from the intense look of anxiety on the watching Gaul's face he knew they were nearly upon him.

Just short of Liscus, Fergus spotted something in the grass. He dipped as he ran past, his right hand deftly plucking up the ritual spear the priest had thrown earlier. Little had they thought then that the war he had declared would start so soon.

'Look out!' Liscus called a warning.

Fergus had no time to turn and look. He threw himself forward in a headlong dive, twisting his body as he fell so that he was facing the way he had come, at the same time bringing the point of the spear up and round with him. It was an old boar-hunting movement, this time used against human quarry.

Directly behind him, a British warrior, his hair spiked up from his head, eyes wide with fury, was charging at full tilt, sword raised for a blow intended to cleave the back of

Fergus's skull. He had not anticipated that his target would leap and spin like a salmon before he could bring down the blade.

As Fergus hit the ground he grasped the spear shaft with both hands, the blade pointing upwards while he dug the butt into the earth behind him. A momentary look of surprise registered on the Briton's face as he charged forwards onto the point, breaking the metal rings of his mail shirt and skewering himself through his own guts. His momentum and the weight of his body carried him on halfway down the shaft until he stopped, suspended in the air above Fergus, his face mere inches away.

The warrior gasped and coughed out his last breath and Fergus felt the final hot exhalation on his own face. The sour odour – a mixture of ale, onions and bad breath – made his gorge rise.

As the light in the impaled tribesman's eyes died away to blankness Fergus scrambled out from under his corpse with only seconds to spare. The other warriors were nearly on him.

Liscus stuck out a hand and Fergus grasped it, using it as leverage to haul himself up behind the Gaul. Liscus dug in his spurs and the horse took off, quickly outstripping the pursuing British tribesmen. Expecting at any moment to feel a spear between his shoulder blades, Fergus sent up a prayer of gratitude that none of the British had horses, so there was no chance of them catching up. Even so, Liscus did not slow down. Neither he nor the priest had any intention of stopping until they were well away from danger. As they rode into the thick trees of the forest, Fergus wondered just when that would be. They had escaped the ambush at the river, but were now riding deeper and deeper into the lands of the Silures, a nation on whom they had just declared war.

He had thought the day before had been a bad one, but it paled into insignificance compared to today. It was not even midday and already he had lost his numeres troop to an ambush and was stuck with no heavy armour in enemy territory. They had only two horses for three of them, and his companions were a mad priest and a Gaul who a short time before had been trying to kill him.

It did not augur well. Could things really get any worse?

9

'Are you ready for war?' Aquilifer Faustus bawled. He screeched so hard that his face deepened to a dark purple and veins throbbed in blue ridges on his temples.

On his right General Gaius Suetonius Paulinus surveyed the troops of the XIV Legion – better known as the Gemina – arrayed before him in marching formation and full battle dress with a cold, disdainful gaze.

Faustus grasped the legion's standard, the eagle, in his two fists and raised it above his head for all the men to see. The silver emblem not only embodied the very spirit of the XIV Gemina, it literally resembled its formation. On either flank of the massed legionaries, the beak and the talons of the imperial bird of prey, the cavalry regiment – the Ala Augusta Gallorum – spread out like the wings – the ala.

With the camp dismantled, the XIV Legion – the iron fist of Rome – was ready to march. Even in the dull, grey British weather the scintillation of light that glittered on polished arms and armour dazzled the eyes.

As one, the five thousand legionaries raised their right hands, made the Roman salute and screamed back, '*We are ready,*' at the top of their lungs.

This fearsome roar echoed through the trees and off into

the distance as a new sound arose: the rhythmic thump of drums as the drummers began marking time for the legionaries to march to.

Led by their standard bearers, the Gemina Legion moved as one, ten thousand legs tramping in perfect military step like a vast, armour-plated leviathan.

As the foot soldiers began the march, the cavalry cohort spurred into a trot and divided into four sections to protect the legion's front, rear and flanks. Their commanding officer – the fat, balding Titus Pomponius Proculianus – galloped along their ranks.

'Straighten that line,' he barked. 'You look like a bunch of ill-disciplined barbarians, not Roman soldiers!'

After he had traversed the troopers from one end to the other, Pomponius wheeled his horse away from the vanguard and galloped back to the rear of the legion, falling into an easy trot beside Decurion Sedullus and the XV Turma.

'I hope the Brittunculi attack again, sir,' Sedullus said. 'I'm itching to make them pay for what they did to us yesterday.'

'Don't be a bloody fool, Sedullus,' Pomponius said. 'You made a right mess of things yesterday. It was only thanks to me that the general did not have you scrubbing the latrines. Let me tell you, son, I haven't got as far as I have and lived as long as I have by playing the hero. Be prudent with your bravery; that's my advice. Only apply it when it will be most effective and, more important, most noticeable.'

Anxious that none of the men had heard the praefect's words, Sedullus looked around, but Pomponius had been careful to check that no one was too close before he opened his mouth.

Catching sight of a horseman galloping along the ranks

towards them, the praefect sighed. The highly polished bronze cuirass moulded in the shape of a heavily muscled torso, and the red cloak billowing out behind – not just the plain red cloak of a tribune, but one with a broad purple stripe – identified the horseman as a tribune of senatorial rank.

'Look out,' Pomponius said in a hissed whisper, 'here comes that jumped-up little shit Agricola.'

'Dress that line, men,' Sedullus yelled at the troopers. 'Straighten up for the tribune.'

Agricola reined his horse as he drew level with them. The men saluted and the tribune returned the gesture.

'I was just saying to the praefect here, sir,' Sedullus said, 'that I can't wait to get into a fight with the barbarians.'

'Really?' Agricola raised an eyebrow. 'Well, this is your lucky day. I want you and your troop to accompany me on a special mission. This morning a squad led by the Hibernian, Fergus MacAmergin, were sent to escort a priest from the Fetial College to perform the ritual of declaring war on the Silures. We will ride ahead of the legion into enemy territory and make sure they have accomplished what they set out to do and return safely.'

'On our own?' Sedullus said.

'Sir, MacAmergin and his troop were a numeres,' Pomponius said. 'Surely it doesn't matter if a punishment squad gets back alive or not?'

The tribune frowned. 'They are still Roman soldiers, Praefect Pomponius. Surely you are not suggesting we abandon our brothers in arms to the whims of Fortuna?'

'No, not at all,' Pomponius said. The praefect, a consummate politician, quickly sensed Agricola's mood and adjusted his behaviour accordingly. 'I was just wondering if it was really an appropriate mission for elite troopers like the Turma XV.'

'I can think of no one more suited,' Agricola said with a smile. 'And who better to witness the performance of these elite troops than their commanding officer?'

'Me?' Pomponius said. He visibly paled.

'Why not?' the tribune said with a grin. 'Decurion Sedullus here is dying for a crack at the enemy. Surely you are too, Pomponius?'

'Of course, sir,' Pomponius said, though his throat had suddenly become very dry and his voice came out as a harsh croak.

'Good,' Agricola said. 'Let's go.' He wheeled his horse and set off at a gallop.

Sedullus looked at Pomponius who gave a resigned shrug.

'Don't worry. They're probably all dead by now anyway,' the praefect said. 'We'll discover their bodies and be back with the legion by midday.'

Sedullus nodded. He signalled for the troopers of the XV Turma to follow and set off after the tribune.

As they rode, the Praefect Pomponius glared at Agricola's back and thought about how, if the interfering tribune were to meet with an unfortunate accident on this adventure of his, they could all be back in relative safety with the legion long before midday.

10

'Sacrilege! Blasphemy!'
The Roman priest's red-rimmed eyes burned with accusation. His lips quivered with barely restrained rage. Saliva sprayed from his yellow teeth with every word.

Fergus stared back at the man in utter disbelief. They had ridden wildly through the woods, heedless of direction, just desperate to escape the pursuing tribesmen. After some distance, when it became apparent they were no longer being pursued, Fergus concluded they had too much of a head start and were unlikely to be caught. Not only were the Britons without horses, but most of them were probably also still engaged in fighting what remained of his troop.

Roman soldiers do not go down easily, he thought grimly. Regardless, he had not allowed them to slow down, pushing on for several more miles until the horses began to tire. Not wanting to kill the beast on which he and Liscus depended, at last he called a halt.

They had ridden into a small clearing where a spring bubbled out from a mossy wall of rocks. Nearby were two standing stones covered in brightly painted, swirling designs. Three smaller stones had been placed to form a triangle on the ground beside them. These were round and worn smooth, and looked as though they had come from a river.

'We'll stop here to rest the horses,' Fergus said.

It was then that the priest had turned on him and let his anger fly. He had ripped off the strange headgear to reveal a bald scalp surrounded by a half ring of sparse, grey hair and strutted forward like a scrawny, underfed cockerel.

The priest shook his fist.

'How dare you!' he screeched. 'How dare you defile the sacred spear by killing with it. It was meant for performing the clarigatio, not for use as a weapon. You have tainted it, you, you…' for a second his anger robbed him of speech then he narrowed his eyes and spat out the word '…*barbarian*!'

Controlling his temper with some difficulty, Fergus swung himself down from the spent horse. He briefly contemplated punching the man, but decided that the blow would probably snap the priest's scrawny neck.

'I think we have more important things to worry about right now, don't you?' he said instead from between gritted teeth.

'What is more important than the gods? Than tradition?' The priest continued to rave.

'Pay no mind to him,' Liscus said, dismounting. 'He's religious.'

'He's fucking mad,' Fergus said.

'Is there a difference?' The Gaul shrugged as he began rummaging through the saddlebags on Fergus's horse. 'It's time for lunch I think.'

'Don't think I've forgotten about our fight back there,' Fergus said.

Liscus stopped rummaging. He met Fergus's challenging gaze.

'Back home in southern Gaul my father is a prince,' Liscus said. 'I've served six years in the Roman army and then they turn round and reward me by putting me in a punishment troop. To crown it all, not content with shitting on me, they put a fucking barbarian from Hibernia in charge. What do you expect me to do? Just accept it? Anyway, you were being an idiot by insisting we fulfil this insane task.'

Despite himself, Fergus could not help smiling. The Gauls were always like this. They exploded with anger, yet when it passed it was like it had never happened.

'So what now?' Liscus said as he pulled some bread, ham and a hunk of cheese from the saddlebags.

'We rest the horses and then we complete the insane task,' Fergus said.

The Gaul rolled his eyes.

'And you said the priest was mad?' Liscus said. 'Are you serious? The army doesn't care if we live or die and you say we finish their stupid task? Well I say fuck you, General Paulinus, and fuck your damned army. We can disappear into these woods, ditch our equipment and pass ourselves off as natives.'

'Liscus, your grandfather gave up being a Celt and became a Roman citizen before you were even born. Whatever you want to think of yourself, you're a Roman soldier and it stands out a mile. We're well inside the Kingdom of the Silures here. You won't last until sundown, and if the locals do get their hands on you, they'll gut you like a fish or chop your face off and throw it in a lake. That's what they do here to honour their gods, by the way. Cut your face off. It stops your ghost coming back to haunt them.'

Liscus was silent for a moment. Then he said, 'What god would want that?'

'The hammer god,' Fergus said. 'We call him Tuireann in Hibernia. You Gauls call him—'

'Taranis,' Liscus said. He spoke in the cracked, hesitant voice of someone speaking a name he should not utter. 'My mother used to talk of the god of the wheel and hammer: the god of thunder.'

'That's him,' Fergus said.

'We could join the Brittunculi,' Liscus said. 'Offer our services as professional soldiers. They're going to need everything they can get when the legion gets here.'

'True – and that's putting it mildly,' Fergus said.

'So couldn't we persuade them to let us help instead of cutting our faces off?' Liscus took a bite of cheese.

'Even if we could, which I very much doubt, do you *really* want to be on the other side when the XIV Legion arrives?'

Liscus was silent for a few moments. 'No,' he said, looking down at his feet as the reality of their situation sank in. 'I saw the legio attack in Germania. It was like watching a line of men mowing a field. No one was left alive after they passed.'

'So no,' Fergus said. 'We complete the mission. We get the priest back to the legion and make sure we are on the right side when the killing starts.'

'You only want to get me back to the legion so I can be disciplined for insubordination,' Liscus said.

'No, Liscus,' Fergus said, shaking his head. 'I've lost most of my troop this morning and I'm damned if I'll lose any more. You're all that's left of it so you are going back to the legion and you are going to continue to be a Roman soldier, whether you want to or not. I think we've already sorted out who is in charge here? Or do you want another try?'

'Maybe,' the Gaul said, but there was no threat in his tone. He raised a hand to his bruised jaw and smiled. 'If the British had not attacked…'

The priest looked from one to the other and was not smiling. 'I'll be making a full report of your sacrilege to the general when I get back,' he said, waving away the bread and cheese Liscus offered him. 'No thank you. I have strict dietary rules I must follow. I do not know where this food has come from.'

'That's good,' Fergus said, as he began searching for more food in the saddlebags on the second horse. 'Two horses means only two lots of rations and there are three of us.'

Dividing what he found into two equal portions, he refilled the goatskins from the spring. Then he watered the horses and left them free to crop what little grass there was in the clearing. After that Fergus settled down with Liscus to eat. The priest cast a sour gaze on them both.

'Well all is not lost,' Fergus said through a mouthful of bread. 'At least I've still got Viridovix's head.' He pointed to the gruesome body part tied by its hair to his saddle.

Both the priest and the Gaul grimaced.

'What is it with you people and human heads?' the priest said. 'It's…' he searched for the word '…disturbing.'

'It's where the soul lives,' Fergus said. 'If you have someone's head you have them. Liscus here—' he clamped a hand on the Gaul's shoulder '—he and his people have forgotten all this. His granda knew it was true, but Liscus has forsaken his roots. The Gauls worship Roman gods now… I'm not saying that's a bad thing, mind. Some of our gods are real bastards. Crom is, for one. But you, Liscus, you look down on such things, and yet I'll bet when you were a child you scooped out turnips at Samhain, carved a face on them and put a candle inside just like we do in Hibernia.'

Liscus nodded. 'I did. Back home the Gauls still do.'

'You must know the turnips are substitutes for the real thing?' Fergus said. 'In Hibernia we still carry actual heads at Samhain. More than that: Samhain is the night when the year, the Earth and the Summer King both die. It is the night of sacrifice and Crom must be placated, so we kill our enemies – and sometimes our friends – to make new heads.'

'Well, like the priest said, you're a barbarian,' Liscus said. He grinned then looked all around the clearing, eyeing the painted stones and the bubbling spring. 'What is this place? It looks like it's tended by the Silures.'

'I'm not sure,' Fergus said. 'But it might be a sacred grove. The British worship their gods and goddesses outdoors in the forests, in clearings and groves, especially where there is water.'

Both Liscus and the priest looked around with an involuntary shiver.

'I've heard of these druid groves,' the priest said, 'but I thought they were supposed to be ghastly places, hung with the corpses of sacrificed animals and men, the trees dripping with blood. There's no sign of that here.'

'You read too much poetry,' Fergus said, though he too was slightly puzzled by the lack of any sign of religious practice, beyond the painted stones.

'Who do you think that woman was?' Liscus said, changing the subject.

'That, my friend, was a druid,' Fergus said.

'She was incredible,' Liscus said.

The priest shook his head. 'Queens? Female priests? Whatever next? I don't understand why you barbarians let yourselves be ruled by women,' he said.

Fergus shrugged. 'It's not a question of letting ourselves be ruled by women,' he said. 'It's just the way it is. Half the people in the world are women you know, though you wouldn't think so the way you Romans go on. You are just jealous, Priest. Or maybe you're afraid.'

'Jealous? Afraid?' The priest was incredulous. 'What could a woman do that I cannot?'

'Well…' Fergus said, choosing to ignore the crude gesture and accompanying snort that erupted from Liscus. 'What is your name, anyway?'

'Marcus Flavius Lucullis.'

'Well, Marcus Flavius, you might carry out a ritual to start a war, but that priestess can stop one,' Fergus said. 'The druids hold such sway with the tribes here that if one appears between two fighting armies they will stop and listen to what they have to say. If the druid pronounces that the fighting must stop, it will stop.'

Both Liscus and the priest stared at him, their incredulous expressions betraying the fact that they found this very hard to believe.

'They must truly respect them,' Liscus said.

'It's not respect,' Fergus said, a note of sharpness entering his voice. 'It's fear. A druid has the power to curse you. And they can ban you from attending worship, ritual and sacrifice. If you cannot attend the sacrifice you are cut off from the gods, and if you are cut off from the gods you're nothing. No one will have any dealings with you. It's like a death sentence.'

Taken aback by his vehemence and the note of bitterness in his response, Liscus and the priest fell silent. Fergus, his stomach pleasantly full, enjoyed the quiet for a moment, listening to the soporific sounds of bubbling water, and the horses tearing rhythmically at the grass.

Finally the priest spoke. 'These druids are powerful then. Can no one match their power in this country? Kings perhaps?'

'Kings could stand against them, yes. But they don't,' Fergus said. 'Kings are scared of their own people's disfavour and the people in turn are scared of the druids. Truly great warriors sometimes stand against them. In our land, in my grandfather's time, there was a hero called Cuchulainn. He wasn't scared to kill druids when he had to, but people say he was not quite human and he was the son of Lugh, the shining god, and thus himself a lesser god.' Fergus paused then added, 'There is something, though, that even the druids are scared of.'

'Really?' The priest leaned forward, his eyes sparking with interest. 'What?'

'I know of this,' Liscus said. 'Serpent stones, right? My grandmother told me of them. They're still respected in Gaul. Once a year, in the summer, serpents gather and become entangled in a heaving mass. They combine their spittle and it gathers in a ball, which hardens into a magical stone that can guard against curses, bad luck and evil magic.'

'And druids,' Fergus said. He reached inside his tunic and

withdrew a leather thong that was tied around his neck. Hanging from it was a small object that appeared to be half stone, half blue glass, the thong passing through a hole in the middle.

Liscus gave a little gasp. 'Is that one?'

Fergus nodded, holding it up for them to see. 'It cost me an arm and a leg. Almost literally,' he said. 'I wouldn't go anywhere without it.'

The priest let out an audible grunt. 'I've seen these trinkets before. They're not made by snakes. They are made by men. The Phoenicians have made them for centuries. They know the secrets of glass. The Egyptians too, revere them. Do you think they really work magic against druids?'

'I imagine it depends if you believe in their power or not,' Fergus said with a shrug. 'However, now I think of it, that woman we saw was probably more likely what we would call a *filed*, or a *vates*. They are a type of druid that performs sacrifices, divines the future and inspires men to war.'

'She inspires me all right.' Liscus gave a lascivious grin. 'But not to war.'

'Let me tell you what will happen to you, Liscus, if she gets her hands on you,' Fergus said.

'If having my face cut off was the price of a moment's passion with her I would consider it,' Liscus said, grinning.

'As a captured enemy, you will first be sacrificed to her gods,' Fergus said. 'She will stab you, slice your belly open and while you are still wriggling about she will use the patterns that your spilt guts make to tell the future. Only then, while you yet live, will she chop off your face and throw it into a sacred pool to stop your ghost coming back to haunt her.'

Liscus's grin faded a little. The priest shook his head again and tutted loudly.

'Barbarians,' he said.

'Bearing that in mind,' Fergus said, 'I think the horses have rested enough, so finish up eating and let's get back to the Gemina Legion before that vates or some of her friends find us.'

II

The further Agricola's small company rode, the more nervous Praefect Pomponius became. The more nervous he got, the more he talked and the more he talked, the angrier Agricola became.

The young tribune tutted, barely able to contain his scorn as he watched Pomponius constantly swivel his gaze from side to side and start at every slight noise that came from the surrounding forest.

He found it hard to believe such a fool had risen so far in the ranks. Clearly this was not on merit but thanks to good connections and his family name. Then he reasoned that Pomponius was far from unique in this. Many rich men's sons – himself included – were able to enjoy long careers in the army. That this was due largely to the professionalism and dedication of the centurions, decurions and legionaries who were able to carry on with the job regardless of what upper-class idiot led them, was a humbling thought.

They had ridden ahead of the XIV Legion, following the route that he had sent Fergus MacAmergin and the numeres down earlier, heading west into enemy territory. The further they travelled the more their pace slowed, the road degenerating into little more than an animal track through the ever-denser forest. Inevitably, before long it started to rain.

'This is a fool's errand,' Pomponius said. 'Even if they're still alive, we'll never find them in this forest.'

He glanced around apprehensively at the undergrowth and trees, as if expecting attack at any moment.

'Where are we anyway?' Sedullus asked. 'This damned country all looks the same to me.'

Agricola shook his head, unable to believe that an officer would even admit to such ignorance.

'We're riding into territory that lies between two British tribes, both hostile to Rome,' he said. 'To the north, the Ordovices. To the south, the Silures. The plan is to drive deep into the Silures' territory and root out their fighters, hopefully bring them to battle and finish them off, before we then sweep north and sort out the Ordovices. Did you not listen to the general's briefings?'

'They're all just Brittunculi to us, Tribune. We're simple cavalry officers, sir,' Pomponius said with a provocative smile.' We just kill the enemy and get the job done. We're not privy to all of the general's thoughts and plans. Unlike you, we do not share his tent.'

Agricola's cheeks burned. In many ways he was grateful to have such access to Suetonius and glad the general had taken him into his confidence. There was so much to learn about command and by living so much in the company of the commander, he was learning fast. But the fact that Suetonius wanted him to share his tent was a constant source of snide comments from the other officers. The fact that the tent was big enough to accommodate at least eight men and that he and Suetonius each had a separate bed in it, did nothing to abate the rumours.

To make it worse, the general seemed utterly oblivious to the idea that anyone could possibly infer that anything untoward was going on. The man was so austere that such thoughts simply never occurred to him. That did not stop others from having them though, and Agricola, knowing that to deny it would simply increase speculation, found the situation a constant source of embarrassment.

'Well they're not just Brittunculi, Pomponius,' he said, choosing to ignore the taunt. 'Underestimating your enemy is the one thing guaranteed to bring you defeat. Hubris, Pomponius, is as dangerous a threat to a commander as the enemy is.'

'Does the general say that, sir?' Pomponius said, his innocent tone belying the underlying jibe.

'Actually he does,' the tribune said. 'And it has got him far. He was the first Roman to cross the Atlas Mountains at the head of the army. Britannia, Pomponius, is actually a mesh of different kingdoms, from the Iceni and Parisi in the east to the Ordovices and the Dumnonii in the west. There are nineteen different tribes in this province, each with their own area, political system, allegiances and even religions. A lot of them hate us, some of them can tolerate us for their own ends, and a couple of them are even happy that we are here. Nearly all of them hate each other as well, and that's to our advantage. Thinking that they're all the same, Praefect, is something that will one day bite you in your overfed arse.'

The forest suddenly cleared and they rode out into a small meadow beside a shallow, meandering river.

'I believe this marks the border with the Silures' territory,' Agricola said. 'We should be on our guard from now on.'

'Can't we turn back now, sir?' Pomponius asked. 'We're right at the border and haven't found them. They're dead.'

Agricola turned to snarl a response at the cavalry praefect when a shout came from the trooper riding at the forward point of their formation. Turning back, Agricola saw that a bedraggled figure had emerged from the undergrowth near the river. The man had no horse, no helmet and no weapons, but wore the mail coat and dun-coloured breeches of a Roman auxiliary cavalry trooper. He appeared to be soaked to the skin as he stumbled towards them, waving his arms and shouting.

'Who is that?' Agricola said.

'I think it's Masculus,' one of the troopers said. 'He's a Batavian in the XV Turma.'

'One of the Hibernian's numeres,' Sedullus added.

'What's he shouting about?' Pomponius said, agitated. 'He'll bring the British down on us creating a racket like that!'

Agricola caught some of Masculus's words and his head whipped around to scan the surrounding trees and undergrowth. To his dismay he saw movement everywhere. Figures darting from tree to tree, running through the forest, coming both closer to the Roman soldiers and moving past them at the same time.

'It's a trap!' Agricola shouted. 'They're getting round behind us to cut us off!'

As he said these words, Silures tribesmen began pouring from the trees towards them. A flurry of spears and stones swarmed into the air. The missiles tore into the Roman troopers. Horses screamed, men shouted, the clanging of projectiles hitting armour and shields and the hiss of weapons being drawn created a sudden and unexpected maelstrom of noise in what had been a peaceful meadow.

Agricola looked behind his troop and saw that their retreat was already cut off. They were heavily outnumbered and would be extremely lucky if any of them got away alive.

12

Fergus, Liscus and the priest saw the ambush unfold with dismay.

They had almost reached the river crossing when they became aware of a strong force of British warriors moving through the trees up ahead of them. Hastily pulling their two exhausted mounts back into the undergrowth, the three of them waited to see what was happening. With growing dread they had seen the Roman troopers ride into the meadow on the opposite bank and straight into the waiting ambush.

When he saw Masculus clambering out of the river, Fergus allowed himself a brief smile of satisfaction. He should not be surprised that the canny Batavian had survived the earlier ambush. Like all Batavians the man was a superb swimmer. Fergus deduced that he must have escaped by hiding underwater among the reeds and rushes growing along the river's edge.

'What in the name of Mars are they doing riding into an ambush?' Liscus said in a hoarse whisper. 'And why are they on their own? Where's the rest of the legion? That's that idiot Sedullus leading them, isn't it?'

'To be fair to them,' Fergus said, 'we did exactly the same thing.'

'Pomponius is there too,' Liscus said.

Fergus looked at Liscus and grinned.

'I'm not sure I mind if Sedullus and Pomponius ride into an ambush,' he said.

'This is not something to joke about,' the priest said in a hissed whisper. 'The Tribune Agricola is with them too. We have to do something.'

'Like what?' Fergus shot an angry glance at the priest. 'There's only three of us and they are outnumbered by hundreds. We'd be throwing away our lives.'

Even as he spoke, the trap was sprung and the British began charging into the meadow. To Fergus's dismay the first casualty was Masculus. Speared through the chest and felled by a superbly aimed Silurian javelin before he had a chance to make it to the cavalry troop.

'At least he tried to warn them,' Liscus said in a murmur.

'They've come to help us. We must do something,' the priest said in an insistent voice.

Fergus rolled his eyes and looked up at the sky. *Do something brave and win glory*, the aquilifer had urged him. Rescuing a tribune would certainly be in that category, but what would be the use if they all died in the attempt?

'Crom,' he hissed through clenched teeth, more as a curse than a prayer as, like the boiling waters of an angry river, the Silures surged around the Roman cavalry troopers.

Despite being taken by surprise, more than half the troopers at the rear end of the column managed to close into a tight arrowhead formation and together were able to smash their way through the ranks of attacking tribesmen and get away, galloping back the way they had come and into the trees beyond the meadow. Watching them, Fergus noted with grim appreciation the troopers' rigid discipline, the result of years of training that overcame a man's natural instinct to drop his weapons and flee in the face of overwhelming odds.

Agricola, Pomponius and Sedullus – who had been near the front of the column – were not so lucky. They and the remaining troopers of the vanguard were cut off by hordes of Celtic tribesmen. The hail of stones and spears that preceded them took a heavy toll and four troopers were unhorsed before they even came to blows with the enemy. The Silures closed in around them, forcing the troopers to discard their lances almost immediately in favour of their spathas, a weapon made for close-quarters fighting. No sooner had a trooper struck down at one tribesman than another was leaping up to stab him in the back, or slash at his horse's flanks to bring him down. The anguished screams of wounded men and hamstrung horses filled the meadow.

'Run! Get out of there, damn you,' Fergus cried out in frustration. His shout was drowned by the cacophony of battle but Agricola must have realised this too. He was shouting for the remaining cavalry to disengage and regroup so as to force their way through the ranks of their enemies.

They managed with some difficulty to form two groups. Two troopers were with Agricola and Sedullus, the other five remaining troopers were with Pomponius, but there was still a horde of British tribesmen between them.

'They can still break out if they regroup,' Liscus said. 'Come on, lads!'

Agricola stabbed downwards with his sword, sending the blade smashing through the eye socket and deep into the skull of an attacker. As he did so the trooper to his left received a slashing blow from one of the British, the long, leaf-bladed sword opening his thigh to the bone. With the muscle split, the trooper could not grip the saddle and fell into the seething, howling, stabbing mass of warriors around his mount.

Another trooper took a spear thrust to the throat and toppled backwards from his horse, bright red blood spraying in an arc above him and splattering Sedullus across the chest and helmet.

At that moment Pomponius threw his sword down.

'Gods! What's that fat fool doing now?' Fergus said.

'He's thrown away a serviceable weapon,' Liscus said, unable to believe what he had seen.

The praefect raised his arms above his head, crying '*Pax! Ildio! Cedo!*'

'He's surrendering,' Fergus said.

'I don't think it's going to do him much good...' Liscus said as the trooper beside Pomponius was cut down from his horse.

At that moment harsh trumpet blasts cut through the clammer of the fighting. Two men had emerged from the trees onto the meadow, each one bearing a tall, upright *carnyx*, the Celtic boar-headed war trumpet. Between them stood the red-haired priestess who had initiated the earlier ambush on the numeres. The trumpet blasts must have been some sort of pre-arranged signal, because at their sound the British warriors reversed their spears, turning them into cudgels for battering rather than killing. They meant to take prisoners.

Seeing this, Pomponius jumped from his horse and fell to his knees, crying out his surrender for all who would listen.

Unsure what to do now that their commander had given up, the remaining troopers wavered, their training telling them they should follow their officer's lead, but their instincts urging them to abandon him and escape. Their hesitation allowed the tribesmen to get in amongst them and quickly they were overcome and brought to the ground.

The tribune, it seemed, had no such thoughts. He kept on fighting, wheeling his horse and slashing down with his sword at anyone who came near. One of the Silures hurled a spear into the animal's guts and the beast went down with an anguished scream, throwing Agricola off to the side. In the blink of an eye a swarm of warriors pounced on him.

As quickly as it had begun, the fighting was over. Seven troopers of the turma lay dead. Agricola, Pomponius, Sedullus and the four remaining troopers were captured. The tribesmen let out great whooping cries of victory, raising their hands to the heavens as they did so. More carnyx blasts rallied them to their pre-arranged battle plan and they began moving with renewed purpose, forcing their prisoners to kneel while their hands were bound behind their backs. Others stripped the dead troopers of weapons and armour then beheaded them, putting their heads into a large bag. When this was all completed the priestess shouted what were clearly some orders. The prisoners were hauled to their feet and the whole war band began to evacuate the meadow, lifting their own dead and wounded as they did so.

'What did she say?' Liscus said.

'I'm not sure,' Fergus said, frowning as he tried to make sense of the British language. It was related to his own native tongue but still different enough to make it a sound foreign to his ears. 'I think she said they would take them to meet their god.'

'That doesn't sound good,' the Gaul said.

'We should have done something!' the priest said, rage blazing in his red-rimmed eyes.

'If we had, we'd be dead too. Or prisoners with the rest of them,' Fergus said.

'They're coming our way,' Liscus pointed out. Fergus turned to see the British war band was hauling the prisoners in the direction of the river. Once they had forded it they would be in amongst the trees where he and his companions were hiding.

'Come on. We need to get away from here,' Fergus said.

'Running away again?' the priest said. 'This isn't very Roman.'

'Priest,' Fergus said, 'if you want to stay alive, shut your mouth.'

An idea had taken root in his head. Perhaps finally some luck had come his way. The British had not killed the tribune yet. In all probability the priestess had recognised the value of such a high-ranking prisoner.

If he rescued a tribune from the barbarians, what better chance could he get to win glory and restore his reputation?

13

As the tribesmen approached the river crossing, Fergus, Liscus and the priest pushed deeper into the undergrowth.

'We'll leave the horses here,' Fergus said and outlined his plan to attempt a rescue.

The priest nodded, but Liscus grimaced.

'You're going to get us all killed,' he said. 'We should get back and warn the legion. The general will dispatch a rescue party with enough men to complete the job.'

'There isn't time for that, Liscus,' Fergus said. 'The tribune will probably be dead by the time we get to the legion and a rescue party is organised. And how will they know where to look for them? I'm not asking you to do this. I'm ordering you. Just do as I tell you.'

They tied the horses to a tree amid a thicket of saplings where they were well hidden and could be retrieved later. Then they waited while the war band passed through the woods behind them. Once the Silures were out of sight, Fergus, Liscus and the priest crept along behind the British warriors, keeping at a safe distance. The Silures were on foot and moving cautiously but there were so many of them that tracking them was easy. The sounds of branches snapping, rustling undergrowth, and occasional shouted orders accompanied by excited whoops were clearly audible.

They travelled through the forest for a long time. For once it was not raining and the sun was visible through the treetops. Glancing up from time to time, Fergus watched its progress from directly overhead to lower in the sky and judged it to be well past noon. The Silures travelled quickly and he began to worry that the priest would not be able to keep up the pace. To his surprise, however, Marcus Flavius trudged doggedly onward with them, the only sign of effort being the sheen of sweat across his milk-pale face, even when the ground began to rise and they started climbing.

Eventually the sounds of movement ahead ceased and Fergus signalled that they should stop too. Moments later, an excited hubbub of chatter carried back to them from the Silures up ahead.

'What are they doing?' hissed the priest.

'I don't know,' Fergus said. 'Liscus, come here. Take that helmet off.'

The big Gaul walked over, unlacing his helmet as he did so, a slightly puzzled expression on his face. Fergus stooped and grabbed handfuls of black muck from a nearby puddle then reached up to rub it through Liscus's hair, pulling it up into spikes and points as he did so. The Gaul's puzzlement turned to consternation and he tried to pull away.

'Hold on,' Fergus said, grabbing him by the arm to stop him moving off. 'Get that mail coat and shirt off too. We need you to look more like one of the tribe.'

Liscus sighed, unlaced the armour and pulled it over his head, now realising just what Fergus had in mind. He pulled the mail shirt off over his head and then removed the leather jerkin he wore beneath it. Finally, Liscus stood bare-chested, his breeches tucked into the laces of his *caligae* boots, his longsword sheathed at his side. Fergus did a bit more work with the mud, drawing swirling patterns across the Gaul's face and torso in imitation of the warpaint designs that the British wore, then stepped back to admire his handiwork.

'There,' he said, smiling. 'Now you're much more native-looking – at least from a distance – and given that the Roman army stole the design for the spatha from the Celtic battle sword, your weapon won't look out of place. Now get up there and see what they are up to.'

'Why me?' Liscus said.

Fergus laid a hand on his shoulder.

'Because you're the most junior rank here, so you get all the shitty jobs,' he said. 'Now get on with it. We are going to rescue the tribune, so acquit yourself well and maybe you won't be court-martialled for striking a senior officer.'

'When they hear the senior officer was you,' Liscus said, 'they'll give me a medal.'

'Go,' Fergus said with a chuckle.

The Gaul slipped off through the trees ahead. Fergus and the priest crouched down beside a large holly bush. As they sat in silence, Fergus became aware of just how unnaturally quiet the forest was. There was no scuffling of animals; no birds were singing. The passage of so many armed men had scared everything away. The pungent smell of wild garlic, crushed beneath the feet of the warriors, rose from the forest floor to fill the late afternoon air. The sunlight filtered down casting shadows through the stunted, moss-covered trees, which were just bursting out into new green life with the arrival of spring.

After a short while the sound of stealthy movement in the undergrowth warned Fergus that someone was approaching. He tensed, poised to attack, the tip of his spear pointing in the direction of the sound.

Liscus emerged from the tangle of holly branches and both Fergus and the priest relaxed. 'Well?' Fergus said.

Liscus rolled his eyes. 'I don't know what they're up to,' he said. 'There's some sort of roadway or track that leads up to a gate. There are walls leading either side of the gate to cliffs that look like the sides of a ravine. It's strange because it looks like the British have fenced off the ravine to create some kind of enclosure. It's a ghastly, strange place. There are human heads on poles all along the walls and the trees along the path up to the gate are hung with all sorts of strips of cloth, pieces of clothing and little wood carvings from what I could see. It's weird. I don't like the look of it at all.'

'What about the tribune?' Fergus said.

'They have him and the other prisoners lined up in front of the gate,' Liscus said. 'That priestess is there too. She's screaming at them, but I couldn't understand what she was saying. It doesn't look good. I didn't want to get too close in case someone started talking to me.'

'You've done well,' Fergus said, taking his own helmet off and undoing his braided hair so that it fell loose around his shoulders. 'We'd better get back there.'

'I'd say there are nearly a hundred of them,' Liscus said. 'We don't stand much chance if a fight starts. What are you planning to do?'

'You think I have a plan?' Fergus said.

Leaving his helmet on the ground, he also took off the

cape of chain mail that reinforced the shoulders of his uniform, leaving the rest of the chain mail coat underneath on. He removed the spurs from his caligae and pulled his breeches out of the leather strapping that bound the boots around his lower legs.

'Do you think I'd pass as a local?' he asked.

'Probably better than I would,' Liscus said, observing the Hibernian's wildly long hair and the tattoos on his arms. 'But neither of us will get away with it if we get too close. Those patterns they have painted on their bodies have been done with real care and precision, not just streaks of muck. How come you get to keep your mail while I have to freeze my tits off with a bare chest?'

'That, my friend, is what is called the privilege of rank,' Fergus said. 'Besides, if we both wore our chain mail they'd spot straight away that we were dressed the same, and only one army in these parts wears a uniform: the Roman one. One person who definitely won't pass as a local is you.' He turned to the priest who flinched at his words.

'What are you going to do to me?' Marcus Flavius said.

'Nothing,' Fergus said. 'But you must wait here until we come back. Don't move a muscle and if anyone comes this way but us, hide in that holly bush.'

'You can't leave me here on my own!' The priest looked around with terrified eyes, as if the very trees posed a threat to him.

'You're right,' Fergus said, handing him Liscus's spear. 'You can have this to keep you company.'

'What if you don't come back?' Marcus Flavius said, gripping the shaft of the spear warily as if it could somehow damage him of its own accord.

'Well, you're a man of the gods,' Fergus said with a smile that was more threatening than pleasant as he lifted his own spear. 'I suggest you pray to them.'

Fergus and Liscus began to creep forward, moving cautiously from tree to tree until they got closer to the British warriors. Fergus saw for himself the items that had been suspended by twine from the branches of the surrounding trees: everything from pieces of clothing to bloodstained bandages and little wooden carvings of arms, legs, hands and other body parts. All of them twirling in the slight breeze.

'These are offerings to the gods,' he said quietly to Liscus. 'People with sickness or injuries make carvings of the affected part of their body and then hang it on the tree to ask for a cure. The clothing could be a sick child's, or just from someone who wants the gods' favour in some venture. They sacrifice something of their own to bring luck. This must be a holy place to these people.'

Ahead of them where the forest ended, a large cliff of black rock rose straight up from the ground to tower far above them. The cliff was divided in two by a wide fissure or canyon some fifty feet wide, which continued on through the higher ground to form a ravine. Fergus could see the large gate and sturdy turf walls, surmounted by a palisade fence of wooden stakes that had been built between the canyon walls to close off one end of it. What looked like a defensive walkway or battlement had been constructed on the back of the palisade and it was now crowded with excited warriors who were looking over the wall into whatever was on the other side, whooping, shouting and laughing. What was strange was that the defences seemed to be facing the wrong way. The canyon created a natural defensive position, but the rampart faced into it rather than outward from it.

The Tribune Agricola, Praefect Pomponius, Sedullus and two troopers stood guarded near the gate. Two of the captured troopers were now missing.

'What are they up to?' Fergus said, regarding the oddly placed rampart. 'If the rampart faced out, it would meet threats coming from the border. This way round, though, it's almost like instead of trying to keep someone out, they're…'

He was cut off as a huge bellow arose from the canyon. It came from some sort of living being, but certainly not from a human throat. The noise was accompanied by a thunder of hooves that almost drowned out the frantic screams coming from two anguished voices, which were definitely human. The warriors on the ramparts cheered.

Liscus finished Fergus's sentence for him. '…they're trying to keep something in?'

14

'We need to get closer,' Fergus said.

'Are you mad?' Liscus said, catching hold of his arm by the bicep. 'We won't pass as British at close range.'

'They're all distracted watching whatever's on the other side of that gate,' Fergus said. As if in answer, another bellow blared from the ravine followed by a loud snort. Fergus and Liscus could both feel the vibrations of heavy footfalls in the soft turf beneath their feet. Something very big smashed into the opposite side of the gate, making it bulge outward and rattle on its hinges. The stout oaks from which it was constructed held and the gate relaxed back to its original position. The warriors on the ramparts cheered again – a harsh, triumphant shout that was full of bloodlust. The last time Fergus had heard a cry like it was from the crowd at an arena in Gaul who were watching gladiators fight.

The body of one of the cavalry troopers rose above the height of the rampart as if tossed aloft by a giant hand. Limp as a half-stuffed scarecrow and covered in blood, the body tumbled through the air until it ran out of momentum and fell back down behind the wall again.

'Jupiter's blood! What monster is in there?' Liscus said.

'Come on. We don't have much time,' Fergus said. 'Act like you belong here – and remember: *qui audet adipiscitur*.'

'If glory comes at the price of death,' Liscus said with a derisive grunt, 'you can keep it.'

As nonchalantly as possible, trying to look as if they were simply late arrivals at this particular party, merely a couple of stragglers who had been left behind in the woods, they both strode from the trees and approached the group of warriors guarding the prisoners near the gate. Fergus began to size up whether they had any chance to grab the tribune. There were ten guards, as well as the priestess, but if he and Liscus could free the prisoners that could quickly change the odds.

They would still have to get away then. It would have to be done quietly too, or the warriors presently engrossed in watching the entertainment would be on them.

As he was wrestling with this problem two of the guards looked around. The chance of surprise gone, Fergus and Liscus kept walking past them to the set of steps that ran up the turf rampart. As they passed the prisoners, praying that they would not recognise them and give them away, Fergus heard the druid priestess haranguing the tribune. She seemed enraged, most probably by the arrogant, cool gaze with which Agricola met every word she said.

'What's she saying?' Liscus said out of the corner of his mouth as they climbed up onto the ramparts.

'She says that they are going to pay for trespassing into this kingdom,' Fergus said in a low voice. 'She says they're about to meet Esus.'

'Esus?' Liscus said. 'Doesn't that mean "The Lord"?'

Fergus nodded. 'She means their god. Whatever is

behind that gate seems to be an incarnation of the god they worship.'

They climbed the steps up onto the rampart and onto the battlements at the top of the wall. Now, among the other warriors, Fergus was acutely aware that their current position was suicidal. Luckily for them the attention of the British was focused on what was going on below on the other side of the wall. He and Liscus edged closer to the palisade and looked down into the enclosed canyon.

It was fortunate that Liscus's appalled gasp was drowned out by the renewed roar of bloodthirsty cheering from the tribesmen around them. Beyond the gate was indeed a wide canyon leading off between the cliffs. Its floor was covered by a carpet of long grass that had been trampled and flattened around the gate. The broken bodies of what was left of the two troopers were in several pieces near the gate. One seemed to have been reduced to little more than a scarlet smear across the back of the turf rampart with several long bones and pieces of armour amid it. One of his still-intact legs lay on the ground.

The smashed and bloodied remains of the other trooper were being prodded by the massive forehoof of a vast bull that snorted and shook its head as it examined the shattered body with agitated interest. The creature was truly gigantic: at its shoulders it was half as tall again as a man and its body was twice as long as it was tall. Its legs seemed almost too slender to support its enormous torso. Long, pointed horns curled forwards from either side of a huge head that sat on a massive, thick neck. A long dewlap hung down from its throat. The bull was ebony black all over except for one white stripe running down the ridge of its spine.

The creature snorted and swung its head this way and that in clear agitation.

'Gods...' Liscus breathed. 'An aurochs! I've never seen one so big... It's *enormous*.'

Eyes wide, Fergus stared at the huge bull. He knew wild forest oxen still existed in Gaul, though they were becoming rarer by the year. That the creatures had existed sometime in the past in Britannia and Hibernia was evidenced by their bones, which occasionally turned up in peat bogs and when the sea swept sand away from beaches, but no one could remember ever seeing a live one. No wonder these people thought it was the incarnation of their god.

Shouts from below made them turn round. A smaller, man-sized door in the gate had been opened and the guards were using their spears to prod the Roman prisoners towards the gap. The first trooper stopped in the threshold when he caught sight of what was on the other side. A warrior planted his foot in the small of the trooper's back and launched him through. From the top of the rampart, Fergus and Liscus saw him stumble forward on the other side of the gate and go sprawling face first onto the ground. The huge bull immediately noticed him and swung its head round to see what was happening.

The Silures warriors grabbed the second trooper and manhandled the struggling man through the door also. They then turned to grab the tribune. Agricola met them with his usual contemptuous gaze. He pushed out his chest and marched coolly through the doorway without them laying a hand on him. Sedullus was then poked through at spear point leaving the praefect. Pomponius wailed and fell to his knees, tears streaking down his plump cheeks. Fergus noted with disdain the dark stain on the man's breeches where he had wet himself. Despite their predicament, he allowed himself a smile. The contrast in these noble Romans' display of their virtus could not have been greater. Three men picked up the cavalry praefect and forced him through the door in the gate. Then it was slammed behind them.

The bull let out another massive bellow, dipped its head and charged towards this new group of men who had just invaded its realm. They scattered as best they could, each man running in a different direction. Pomponius fell over again, once more sprawling into the muck. It saved his life as the bull's horns passed over him and skewered into the trooper behind him. The beast tossed its head, throwing the gored cavalryman into the air, ribbons of blood gushing from torn arteries in his gut.

The bull planted its forelegs into the ground to stop its charge before it collided with the wall. Then it swung round to the left to charge after Sedullus and the tribune, who were running with all their might away from the gate towards the longer grass.

Fergus realised that the longer he waited, the chances of him rescuing the tribune alive were disappearing, and with them any chance of restoring his reputation.

'I'm going down there,' he said to Liscus.

'Are you mad?' the Gaul said.

'I wish you would stop asking me that,' Fergus said. 'I know what I'm doing. I've been fighting and riding bulls since I was a wee lad. You go and grab the druid woman.'

Liscus looked confused. 'Don't you need me to help you?' he said.

'You will be. Go and grab the druid. She's our only chance

of getting out of here,' Fergus said. 'They won't attack you if you have her as a hostage. Now hurry.'

With that, Fergus grabbed his spear and vaulted over the top of the palisade fence and was gone.

The sudden movement made the nearest British warriors turn around to see what was going on. Liscus realised that if he did not move fast any chance he had of success would be gone.

15

Fergus had not been joking about bulls.

In Hibernia, a tribe's wealth was measured by the number of cattle it possessed. Bulls were the personification of its power and potency. The bigger the bull the greater the measure of how much of the gods' favours were enjoyed by the king or queen of the tribe. Hibernia's tribes fought each other all the time and cattle raiding was a key tactic. There was no better way than stealing their cattle to bring a rival tribe's status down and raise that of your own. It was every young warrior's first introduction to war from the moment he came of age and a constant seasonal activity from then on. The point at which raiding ended and full-scale war began was sometimes hard to discern and in Fergus's experience, a simple incursion to steal a few cows had often exploded into an island-wide conflict.

Defeating the rival tribe's warriors was only part of the game, though. The cattle had to be stampeded and the quickest way to get the herd moving was to ride the bull. All the tribe's greatest warriors – and all the young men wanting to make a name for themselves – fought for the honour of being the first onto the beast. It was not always possible, of course, to carry off a tribe's cattle and sometimes the aim was simply to kill the bull, so warriors practised fighting the beasts as much as they practised riding them.

For all his experience, Fergus had however never faced a creature so large. He remembered when, as a boy, the king of the tribe, Cathach MacRoth, had possessed an enormous drinking horn that they said came from one of these great aurochs. It was a magnificent piece, its rim and point encased in golden bands and its entire length carved with intricate swirling patterns inlaid with silver. The horn was longer than a man's arm and no one but the king could drain it in one draught. Even it, though, was smaller than the two pointed horns now levelled at his chest.

The great bull snorted at the latest man who had just arrived into its realm and pawed the ground with a hoof. Fergus crouched down low, side on towards the bull, spear point extended towards it, ready to spring either right or left. His right hand was under the butt of the spear to give it maximum reach, his left was on the shaft to steady it. He screamed at the creature, a wild, high-pitched whooping that had not escaped his throat for years.

The bull charged.

As it approached, the massive bulk of the great beast's shoulders blotted out everything else. Fergus felt the turf beneath his feet vibrating with the bull's pounding hooves. He tried to stay as still as he could. He was searching for a target for the spear.

Moving too soon would be fatal. The bull would have time to change course as well. Moving too late would be just as deadly. There was also no point in trying to thrust his spear point through the massive, thick skull of the beast as the weapon would simply shatter on the bone without doing any damage. The muscles around the shoulders were too deep too to present a viable target.

There was a small bunch of muscles at the top of the neck that Fergus knew were critical to defeating the bull, but they could only be stabbed either from above or head on, which meant he had to hold his ground until the last possible moment.

The bull let out a mighty snort as it approached. Fergus felt the blast of its hot breath, and a shower of its snot splattered his face and hands.

He thrust forwards and upwards with the spear. The weapon's progress halted and Fergus felt the jarring impact of it hitting flesh. He had to let go as he leapt sideways to the left, flinging himself as far as he could from the deadly sweeping horns.

Fergus hit the ground, rolled and bounced quickly back onto his feet. The bull had missed him – the fact that he was still alive told him that. It barrelled past, the momentum of its huge bulk carrying it on. Fergus ran as hard as he could away from the bull, trying to get as much distance between him and it as possible before it turned to charge again.

He both heard and felt the thudding hoofbeats halt and knew the beast had stopped itself. Spinning around, he saw to his dismay that while the spear had gone into the flesh, it had not done the damage intended. He had wounded the creature but it was a useless gash to the shoulder muscle. Not even deep enough to remain embedded, the spear's weight pulled it back out of the bull's flesh and it fell to the ground. Now he had both lost his weapon and succeeded only in annoying the animal.

The huge beast swung around looking for the source of the annoying pain it had just experienced.

It saw Fergus and charged again.

Outside the gate, the group of warriors who had pushed the prisoners through to become sacrifices to the bull was breaking up, each man eager to get up onto the ramparts to watch the Romans' grisly end. Liscus knew he had a single moment in which to act before they became aware of him. Drawing his sword he leapt off the rampart walkway, landing just behind the closed gate and crouching to let his thighs absorb the impact.

He rose back up from the crouch. In the same movement he swung his blade left and right in two semicircles. He caught three of the unsuspecting guards with crippling blows across their exposed necks. As blood arced from his handiwork, he sprinted for the priestess. She had frozen, surprised by this sudden turn of events. Before she could react, Liscus was behind her, his left arm holding her in a bear hug against him and his sword blade held across her throat.

The warriors around him got over their initial shock fast. With shouts of rage they began to close in on this new threat. Liscus pulled the priestess backwards so that he was standing up against the gate and it protected his exposed back.

'Come any nearer and I'll kill her,' the Gaul screamed at the Silures. Even though they did not understand his Latin, his meaning was plain enough. To his relief they halted their advance. It seemed Fergus had been right about the regard the British had for their druids.

So far, so good, Liscus thought to himself. As to what he would do next he had no idea. The angry roars of the warriors on the ramparts told him that Fergus had done something to annoy them, but was he even still alive? Liscus could hear shouting and the thumping of hooves, but the lack of agonised screams gave him some hope that that was the case.

It also gave him an idea.

'Open the gate,' he shouted at the semicircle of warriors facing him. Their mystified expressions betrayed their lack of comprehension. Tightening his hold on the priestess, he raised his sword, quickly banged the great wooden bar that fastened the gate shut and shouted, 'Open!'

He returned the blade to his captive's neck and made a sawing motion to demonstrate what would happen if they did not do as he said. All the while Liscus struggled to hold on to the druidess with his other arm. She kicked and wriggled to get away, seemingly oblivious to the blade at her throat while spitting and cursing him – or so he assumed – as she did so. He realised that he would not be able to hold on to her for much longer, and when she got away his last hope of surviving this situation would go with her.

On the other side of the gate, Fergus made ready to dodge another charge. He crouched, weight distributed equally on both feet so he could jump in either direction, though there was not much room to his right as he was only a few feet from the inside of the wooden gate.

The ground trembled again at the bull's approach. Fergus flexed his right thigh, about to leap to the left, but the bull seemed to anticipate him this time and changed its path to intercept him. Fergus just had time to twist aside as he leapt into the air. Sideways on, instead of being impaled his body fitted between the points of the horns and crashed onto the bull's forehead. The impact drove the breath from his lungs.

The bull, unaware that it had not gored its target but aware of Fergus's weight, tossed its head up and back to throw him off. Its enormous strength propelled him through the air and he tumbled over the animal's back, falling heavily onto the ground somewhere near its back legs.

Dazed and winded, Fergus was dimly aware that he had to move fast or the bull would sweep round and finish him off. He raised his head and shoulders, but spinning stars and a strange darkness overcame his vision and he collapsed back to the ground.

Lying flat on his back, Fergus shook his head, trying to dispel the spinning multicoloured stars from his sight. Through them he could see that the bull had turned around and was pawing the grass, about to come at him again, this time its head lowered almost to the ground, the horns ready to impale him as he lay there, helpless in its path.

The beast was mere yards away and he did not have time to move out of the way. It had got him. He closed his eyes and prepared to die.

A sudden howling broke the air.

Fergus's eyes snapped open.

The Tribune Agricola leapt over him, the spear Fergus had lost earlier gripped in both hands. The Roman reached the bull before it started its run and, still roaring an unintelligible war cry, he drove the point of the spear deep into flesh around the animal's shoulders.

A spurt of blood erupted from the wound and the bull bellowed with pain. It turned away from both men, wrenching the spear from Agricola's grasp as it did so.

Fergus felt hands grabbing him under his armpits as Agricola and the one remaining cavalry trooper hauled him to his feet.

'Are you all right?' the tribune asked.

Before Fergus could reply the trooper beside him let out an anguished cry and collapsed to the ground. They looked around to see that a spear hurled from the ramparts above had transfixed the man through the chest. Blood bubbled out from the wound, mixed with a pink froth: the spear had gone through his lungs and he gurgled his last breath into the grass.

The Silures warriors on the ramparts had realised the situation had changed. They were hoisting their spears and readying to send the prisoners to the other world without the aid of the bull who personified their god. The bull itself was now gathering for another charge.

'Get behind the bull. Stay close to it,' Fergus said to Agricola. 'They'll be too worried about wounding the bull to throw their spears.'

The tribune shot a glance in his direction that initially suggested he thought Fergus was mad, then understanding dawned. They both scrambled forward towards the right flank of the bull, putting it between them and the ramparts. As they ran, Fergus felt rather than saw a spear thump into the ground a mere whisker-breadth behind his left heel. For an instant he considered turning back to grab the weapon but as he hesitated, he saw that the bull, maddened by pain, was about to charge.

Forsaking the spear, Fergus readied himself also. This time he knew exactly what he was going to do. It was dangerous, potentially suicidal, but his experience told him that it was the only way he stood a chance of bringing the creature down without a long weapon.

The bull came pounding forwards at him, Agricola's spear still stuck deep into its shoulder and waving up and down like an insane flagpole without any attached standard. Fergus positioned himself right in its path, legs wide and bent, thigh muscles corded and hands held out before him, open and ready to grasp.

As the bull reached him, Fergus leapt forwards and grabbed one horn in each hand, his right hand on the beast's left horn and his left on the right. At the same time he pushed up with his legs and thrust down from his shoulders, propelling himself upwards and over the top of the deadly points of the horns, somersaulting over the bull's head to land astride the massive animal's back.

The bull exploded with rage. It leapt, kicked, tossed its head wildly, rocked its back legs into the air and did everything it could to throw the strange burden off its back. Clamping his mouth shut to stop himself biting his tongue, Fergus hung on grimly, reaching behind him to grab one of the creature's ears in one hand and a great tuft of the hairy stripe that ran down the centre of its back in his other. The beast bucked, kicked and spun, and Fergus knew he would not be able to stay on for long, especially as he now had to let go with one hand to draw his sword.

At that moment a scraping, creaking could be heard as

the large gate swung open, revealing Liscus and the druid woman outside. The bull, suddenly confronted with seeing the door to what had been its prison for so long opened but still with a man on its back, was momentarily confused and stopped its wild thrashing. It was enough for Fergus to reach behind him, grab a couple of handfuls of the bull's hair and spin himself around on its back so he now faced forwards. The bull recovered its amazement and made straight for the open gate, bucking and kicking to try to throw Fergus off at the same time.

Liscus flattened himself against the open gate with the druid still hugged to his chest as the bull flew past and out of the enclosure. Fergus could do nothing but hang on for grim death. He grabbed the bull's right ear with one hand and a tuft of hair in the other, his legs clamped across the animal's back for added grip. He could smell the stench of its sweat. The bull spun around in a circle, its back legs kicking to knock four Silures warriors flying, smashing bones and causing terrible damage to them.

Letting go of the bull's ear, Fergus ripped his spatha from its sheath. He would have only one chance to strike before being thrown off. He raised the sword, point downward, grabbing the hilt in both hands. He drove it down into the bunch of muscles where the bull's neck met its shoulders.

The bull bellowed with pain and redoubled its efforts to throw Fergus off its back, but as the spatha severed some of the muscles that held its head up, its whole stance changed. Unable to withdraw the blade from the bull's flesh, Fergus let go of it. He grabbed the shaft of the spear that still protruded from its shoulder and jumped off the bull's back, letting his weight pull the weapon free as he fell to the ground. The bull felt the weight leave its back and turned, intent on finishing off this unusually persistent annoyance.

Fergus crouched once more, spear levelled towards the approaching bull. It was tiring now, weakened by blood loss and exertion, and its charge was little more than a lumbering trot. The damaged muscles in its neck would no longer support the weight of its massive horned head, so it came at him with its head and horns low down, still as deadly, but now exposing to attack the weak spot between its shoulders.

As the bull came close, Fergus ran forward to meet it. Placing his left foot on the top of its head between the horns he pushed himself up onto it once more. He drove the spear downwards into that vulnerable place, the point powering its way down through the beast's flesh and muscles, following the path through the bone cage straight into its heart.

A spurt of dark red heart blood bubbled up around the spear shaft. The bull gave a grunting cough. It staggered on for a few steps then collapsed with a huge snort onto the ground.

It was dead.

16

For a few seconds there was complete silence.

The Silures looked down from the ramparts, the expressions on their faces a mix of shock and utter consternation. Agricola and Sedullus came warily out through the open gate. They were followed by Pomponius, who had only just got up from where he had fallen on entering the enclosure.

The silence was finally shattered by a piercing scream from the druid woman. Liscus, his blade still held against her throat, hauled her kicking and screeching across to where Fergus stood. Fergus saw to his surprise that her face was streaked with tears.

'She's not happy,' he said.

'I imagine none of them are,' Liscus said, eyeing the ramparts above and the glowering, though not moving, warriors. 'That was their god you just killed.'

'We need to get out of here before they get over their shock,' Fergus said. 'Bring the woman.'

'Maybe you want to take her?' Liscus said, holding up one arm that bled from numerous cuts, scratches and bite marks.

The druid, feeling his grip relax, began yelling at the

warriors on the ramparts. He hastily clamped the arm back around her waist and pulled her roughly against him as the Silures began to jump down and stalk towards the small group of Roman soldiers.

'What will we do?' Sedullus said, his voice quavering slightly. 'There must be thirty of them.'

Liscus made his gesture to cut the druid's throat. A trickle of fresh blood dribbled down her neck from beneath the sharp edge of his blade, but this time it did not seem to halt the approach, albeit cautious, of the Silures.

'For Crom's sake shut her up,' Fergus said. 'She's telling them to kill us all, even if it means killing her in the process.'

The Gaul clamped a hand over the druid's mouth. Straight away she bit his fingers and he had to let go again. He moved to punch her but it would mean releasing one hand completely. Instead he cursed her and pulled the edge of his sword tighter against her throat.

'Any more weapons?' Agricola said as he wrenched Fergus's spatha from the neck of the dead bull.

Fergus shook his head, doing the same with the spear.

'We can't fight them anyway. There's too many,' Liscus said. 'If we run we'll get about as far as the trees before they catch us.'

'We must surrender,' Pomponius said. 'We don't stand a chance.'

'Shut up, Pomponius. They'll kill us anyway,' Agricola said. 'Well, so be it. At least I can die with a sword in my hand rather than being trampled to death by some sacred cow.'

Fergus suddenly felt a steady thrumming in the turf beneath his feet. The sound of horses' hoof beats came to their ears, along with a strange high-pitched yelling and shouting. Out from the trees to their left burst a herd of horses, whinnying, neighing and agitated.

The first bunch had no riders, but then a large black mare emerged from the trees and on it sat the gaunt skinny figure of the Roman priest they had left behind in the forest. He roared and screamed like a fury, slapping his horse's flanks and prodding the horses around him with Liscus's spear.

More horses poured out of the trees behind him, all of them saddled and bridled. They had blankets and little gold and silver ornaments hanging from their trappings, but not Roman army trappings. These were British horses.

With no time to ponder where the priest had found them, Fergus shouted, 'Grab one!' as the horses galloped between them and the approaching Britons.

No one needed telling twice. Mounting a running horse was one of the skills drilled into the cavalrymen from day one of basic training and regularly practised. In moments Agricola, Sedullus and Fergus were on a horse each. Pomponius was slightly slower because of his weight, but the instinct of self-preservation gave power to his legs and he was next to mount.

Fergus grabbed the reins of his horse and pulled back to halt its wild gallop. The creature reared up on its hind legs, trying to throw him off, but Fergus dug in his knees and gripped the reins, relentlessly pulling the bit in the horse's mouth to bring it under control. He wheeled it around to see what Liscus was doing.

The Gaul was still struggling with the druid, who had renewed her efforts to get away from his grasp. Fergus rode his horse over to them, bumping the creature's body up against the pair of them so the druid was sandwiched between the horse and Liscus. He reversed his spear and hit the woman a thump with the shaft across the top of her head. Her body sagged and Fergus reached down, grabbed a handful of her feathered cloak and hauled her up onto his horse. Liscus pushed from below and within a second the unconscious druid was draped across the front of Fergus's horse, between him and its neck.

Turning, Liscus grabbed a passing horse and swung himself onto its back. The whole action from first sight of the stampeding horses had taken only moments, but now the stunned Silures threw their caution to the wind and charged screaming towards them.

Driving the spooked herd of horses before them with whoops and cries, the Romans dug in their spurs and galloped into the trees, following the rough track that led away from the enclosure gate. Some of the pursuing Britons launched spears and slung stones after them, but they were soon out of range and before long were left completely behind. After a while the riderless horses began to slow and drop away and Fergus and his companions were on their own once more.

Slowing the punishing pace, Fergus pushed his winded mount forward to come up beside the Roman priest.

'By the gods! Where did you find them?' he said.

'I was afraid you would not come back,' Marcus Flavius said, his grin showing how pleased he was with himself. 'And even if you did we would still need some way to get away. I recalled the story of Hercules coming across the man with the broken wheel on his waggon.'

'What?' Fergus said.

'While on his travels,' the priest said, 'Hercules came upon a man who was praying. His waggon had a wheel stuck in mud and it could not move. "Thank the gods," the man said. "My waggon is stuck, I prayed for help and Jupiter has sent the mighty Hercules in my hour of need." "Have you tried pushing it?" Hercules asked. "No, first I prayed," was the reply.'

The priest fixed Fergus with a knowing look, as if this somehow explained everything.

Fergus raised an eyebrow, a frown of incomprehension still creasing his face.

'I still don't understand,' he said.

'Hercules did not help the man, but instead he said to him,' Marcus Flavius said, rolling his eyes at the barbarian's ignorance, '"By all means pray to the gods, but first put your shoulder to the wheel."'

'Are you saying that the gods help those who help themselves?' Fergus said.

'Well those who at least try,' the priest said. 'I realised that I had to do something. I was going to creep forward to see what you were up to, but then in the quiet I heard a horse neighing somewhere in the woods. I thought for a moment and realised that the British must have horses somewhere, so I went through the trees, following the noises until I found them. They had about fifty corralled in a clearing in the trees not far from that gate.'

'It makes sense,' Fergus said. 'Those warriors journeyed here somehow. They must have left their horses there and travelled on to the ambush point on foot so they would be quieter in the forest.'

'There were only three men guarding them,' Marcus

Flavius said, 'and not very well. They clearly were not expecting to be found. All I had to do was jump onto one horse and cause a commotion. A few pricks from this spear and they soon panicked. There was a stampede and the guards were swept aside in it.'

'Lucky for us,' Fergus said. 'We'd all be dead by now if you had not.'

Checking that the druidess was still unconscious, he settled back into the saddle as they rode on through the woods, away from the danger behind them and on towards the relative safety of the advancing legion. They had lost a lot of men, but he was bringing both the Roman priest and the tribune back with him to the XIV Legion. Perhaps for the first time in days luck was finally on his side and things were starting to look up.

He was wrong.

17

General Gaius Suetonius Paulinus looked at the bedraggled group of men who stood rigidly at attention before him. His gaze was withering, belligerent and the slight curl of his upper lip betrayed the anger that boiled within him.

It was late evening. The XIV Legion had pitched camp and the day's final labours of ditch digging, rampart building and tent pitching were nearly complete, leaving an hour or so for the legionaries to make their evening meal before sleep.

In the praetorium tent stood the Tribune Agricola, Praefect Pomponius, Sedullus and Fergus. They had been summoned to see the general to report on their activities. As officers, they would be held accountable, so Liscus was allowed to return to the quarters of the cavalry ala. The priest had gone to the altars at the centre of camp to give thanks to the gods for their return to the legion.

The general, sitting while they stood, had listened in stony silence to their account of what had happened, his gaze fixed on the floor before him, which Fergus noted had been strewn with comfortable fur rugs. After a long, intimidating silence, Suetonius had finally stood up and glared at them all with undisguised wrath.

'What in the name of all the gods do you men think you were playing at?' he said. He levelled a finger at Fergus. 'You were sent to perform the ritual of declaring war. You lost nearly all the men under your command. Admittedly it was a dangerous mission, but to lose everyone? You, Praefect, gallop off on some ridiculous rescue mission and lose even more men.'

'I was only following orders, sir,' Pomponius said, staring straight ahead.

Agricola shot a poisonous glance sideways at him. 'Sir, the praefect's behaviour was a disgrace—' he began.

'Shut up, Tribune!' the general roared. The ferocity of the anger in his voice startled all the men in the tent. 'You will speak when you are spoken to.'

Agricola snapped back to attention, a look of shock on his face. Fergus surmised it had been a very long time since someone had raised their voice to the young Roman nobleman.

'You are all a disgrace,' Suetonius said. 'Call yourself Roman soldiers? I've never seen such indiscipline, incompetence and insubordination! I should not need to remind you that the punishment for those misdemeanours is to be beaten to death by your fellow soldiers.'

For a few moments there was an icy silence as the four officers stood, waiting with bated breath to hear what their fate would be. Well aware of their discomfort, the general waited too, deliberately prolonging their moment of suspense. Finally he sighed and sank back into his chair.

'Luckily for you, news of your little adventure has already spread through the legion. They seem to see you as some sort of heroes, the gods alone know why. I doubt if I could find someone willing to beat you, and I don't want any more dissention in the ranks. If you were proper Roman citizens you'd have the decency to fall on your swords to annul your disgrace, but I doubt I can expect that. Since I arrived in this province, I've suspected that all the problems here are down to the softness and ill discipline of the legions stationed here. This proves it to me. You men are all dismissed.'

The officers breathed a collective sigh of relief.

'Don't think you're getting away with this though,' the general said. 'I need you men for another special mission. It won't be an easy one and it will certainly be dangerous. I had intended to send only the Hibernian but the rest of you have selected yourselves too by your own stupidity. On top of that, all your pay is reduced to nothing. Think yourselves fortunate. Now get out of my sight and I will send you further orders in the morning.'

Fergus, Pomponius and Sedullus saluted, turned and started to leave. Agricola remained.

'You are still here, Tribune?' the general asked.

'You mean me to go too?' Agricola's consternation and confusion were evident.

'Tribune, I am the general of a legion on campaign in hostile territory. I cannot be associated with failure and incompetence,' Suetonius said. 'I want you to move your belongings out of my tent and join the rest of the officers. Now go.'

He raised his head and looked Agricola in the eye once more.

The tribune saluted and turned to go. As he strode from the tent he was left with the impression that while the general's anger had been difficult enough to bear, what was even harder to endure was his final look of disappointment.

18

'Well fuck that,' Fergus said after they had left the praetorium. 'What an ungrateful bastard.'

Agricola grunted. Part of him agreed, but he would not be so disloyal to the general as to say it aloud.

'Such are the vagaries of Fortuna,' he said.

'Fortune my arse,' Fergus said. 'I thought by bringing you back alive I could get my old command back. How wrong could I be?'

Agricola did not reply. He was contemplating just where this left his own fortunes.

'What did he mean about a special mission?' Fergus said. 'I thought I'd already fulfilled that mission.'

'There's a Hibernian queen, married to a local prince,' Agricola said. 'She wants Roman protection and is offering some sort of magic spear as an enticement.'

'A magic spear?' Fergus said. 'Are you serious?'

'She told the general that it's sacred to the Christians,' the tribune said. 'So he wants it so he can gain the favour of the emperor.'

'Nero is a Christian?' Fergus said, raising his eyebrows.

'No,' Agricola said, shaking his head. 'Quite the opposite: he hates them. The emperor is obsessed with wiping them out. Having their sacred spear would give him power over them.'

'Only if you believe in its magic,' Fergus said.

Agricola just shrugged, unsure how to explain the power of symbolism to a barbarian cavalry auxiliary.

'It sounds like nonsense,' Fergus sneered. 'Or lies. Why would a Hibernian queen have a Christian magical weapon?'

'That's what the general wants to know,' Agricola said. 'He thought if you came along you might be able to glean some useful intelligence.'

'Another stupid mission then,' Fergus said.

'Don't look on it that way,' Agricola said. 'If we complete the mission and bring back that spear, we'll get back into the general's favour. This is just a temporary setback.'

'That's what the aquilifer told me before the last escapade,' Fergus said. 'I ended up deeper in shit. I should have deserted when I had the chance and left you to the bull.'

'Well, I'm a tribune, not the aquilifer,' Agricola said, realising his own chances of getting back into the general's favour now rested on this Hibernian helping him to get the spear. 'And I promise that if we come back with this spear your fortunes will be revived. You will get your old command back, regardless of what the praefect says.'

The last part was said deliberately louder so Pomponius could hear, but when he turned round to look, he saw that the praefect and Sedullus had already slunk away into the dark.

Fergus was silent for a moment, considering the tribune's words.

'Besides,' Agricola said with a smile, 'there's damn all you can do about it anyway. You may as well make the most of it. You're in the army. It's all part of the contract.'

Fergus laughed, though there was a bitter edge to his mirth.

Still smiling, Agricola locked eyes with Fergus.

'I never said thank you. I appreciate what you did. I am grateful.'

Fergus looked at the younger man with narrowed eyes. This was not normal behaviour for a Roman noble. He could see Agricola was very uncomfortable, his eyes constantly flicked this way and that, and Fergus was sure that if his skin had not been so sallow, the torchlight would have shown he was blushing.

'For saving my life, I mean,' the tribune said in a mumble, letting his hand drop. 'If my own fortunes were not fallen with yours, I would have rewarded you.'

'Don't talk bollocks,' Fergus said. 'You saved mine too when you distracted the bull. We owe each other nothing.'

Agricola looked almost relieved.

'All right,' Fergus said. 'If we are going to revive our fortunes we may as well start now.'

'What do you mean?'

'The druid woman. We have a prisoner so we may as well see what she knows.'

'Why would the woman know anything?'

'Spoken like a true Roman,' Fergus said, enjoying the novelty of the situation where he could speak to a senior officer as to an equal. 'The druids, whether they be men or women, work across all the tribes and kingdoms. They may come from one clan, but once they become a druid they are supposed to leave that allegiance behind and work only for the gods. She may know something. It won't do any harm to ask.'

'Why would she talk to us?' Agricola said.

'The druids are no friends of the Christians either,' Fergus said. 'They've arrived in this country and started to make converts already in Dumnonia and other kingdoms in the south.'

'Yes, I know.' Agricola's concern was evident in his voice. 'I can't believe that sect has even made its way here to Britannia.'

'They probably came with the legions.' Fergus's tone of voice betrayed the fact that he thought the tribune was being slightly naive. 'There are three things currently spreading across the empire like a plague: mosaics, underfloor heating and the Christian faith. Christianity is a new religion, the druids have no desire to share their power with a new god any more than the Emperor Nero does.'

Agricola nodded. 'It's worth a try,' he said.

They set off. Even though the camp had just been built that evening, there was no mystery as to where prisoners would be held. The two men headed east from the praetorium along the broad avenue that had been left between the ranks of legionary tents to form the *via principalis* – a roadway that bisected the camp widthways in the same way that the via praetoria divided it north to south. It was well past sunset. Numerous braziers and campfires blazed to keep away the darkness as legionaries, their day's toil over, finished up their meals of potage and bread and relaxed with either dice games or songs before they retired to their tents.

The *carcer*, where prisoners were held, was positioned

where the via principalis reached the outer defensive rampart of the camp, beside the main eastern gate, the *porta principalis sinistra*. In a more permanent legionary fort the carcer would have been built of stone, but in the marching camp it was a simple leather tent with guards posted at either end. No prisoners had been expected this early in the campaign so no palisade had been erected around it.

As Agricola and Fergus approached, the soldier at the front of the tent snapped to attention, spotting Agricola's uniform in the light from the braziers and torches that blazed around the porta principalis sinistra. The two guards were legionaries: short, squat citizens with broken noses, their bodies whipped hard by the vine canes of their centurions and constant drilling and marching. Every ounce of compassion and fellow feeling had likewise been thrashed out of them.

Agricola returned the guard's salute.

'We want to interrogate the prisoner,' he said.

The legionary's face split into an unpleasant smile.

'I can't wait to interrogate her myself, sir. She could do with a good talking-to.' His leer showed that talking was the last thing on his mind. 'She's a real beauty. Great tits. We took a look.'

Agricola frowned. He was becoming accustomed to the mistreatment of women that seemed to be an aspect of military life, but was as comfortable with it as he was with torture. In Roman society, the rape of a woman – if she was a citizen – was considered a crime punishable by death.

'That woman is a prisoner, soldier,' he said, 'and as such is a hostage of the Senate and People of Rome until you are told otherwise. I trust she has not been molested?'

The legionary's face dropped to a blank expression. 'No, sir.'

The guard's tone of insolence suggested he thought his senior officer was a prick. Agricola levelled a cold stare at the man until he dropped his gaze.

'Good,' Agricola said, as they brushed past the legionary and entered the tent. 'Now let's see what she has to say.'

19

The druid sat on the ground, her hands tied behind her head, around the central pole of the tent. Her cloak of bird feathers was wrapped around her, covering her body completely. She had somehow brushed her prodigious red hair down so that it now hung around her shoulders and partially hid her face. The bronze headdress she had worn before was gone, probably stolen by the guards, so they could now see the strange way in which her hair was shorn. It was cropped short high up on her forehead and at the back of her neck, leaving a crescent of long, bright red hair on the top of her scalp.

'Nice haircut,' Agricola said.

'That's the tonsure of a druid,' Fergus said. 'I saw Colphra, the Chief Druid of Mag Slecht once. He had his hair cut like that.'

The druid raised her head. 'What do you want?' she said.

'You speak Latin?' Agricola said, his eyebrows raised in surprise.

'Why wouldn't I?' the druid said with a sneer. 'I speak many tongues.'

Agricola stiffened and clasped his hands behind his back. His normal composure had been dented by the general's disapproval but the shock of that was beginning to wear off.

'Good,' he said. 'I won't need my interpreter after all.'

'Is that what you are?' the druid said to Fergus in the British language, her voice laden with disdain. 'An interpreter?'

'What is she saying?' Agricola demanded, then realised what the woman was doing.

'We will ask the questions,' he said.

'And what makes you think I will answer them?' the druid said.

'Let's just say it will be better for you if you do,' Agricola said, trying to sound as menacing as possible. 'We have much more unpleasant methods of questioning you if you don't co-operate.'

'I know all about Roman savagery,' the druid said. 'You think I care what you do to me? You can destroy my body but my soul will live on.'

'Really?' Agricola seemed interested. 'How so?'

Fergus coughed. 'We're not here to discuss religion, sir,' he said.

'Yes, of course,' the tribune said. 'Now what is your name?'

'What is yours?' the druid said.

'Stop pissing about,' Fergus said in the British language. 'You know what they'll do to you if you don't talk.'

'You are a *Gwyddel*? One the Romans call Hibernian?' the druid said. She began to speak in the Hibernian tongue. 'I should have known when I saw you ride the bull. I can speak *Goidelc* too.'

'What are you talking about now?' Agricola said, raising

his voice, a tone of unease creeping in now the two Celts were conversing and he had no idea what they were saying.

'Gwyddel, you have committed great sacrilege,' the druid said, switching back to British and rising from the floor to a standing position. She drew her left leg up so she balanced on her right foot and closed her left eye.

'What's she doing?' Agricola said. His voice held a tinge of panic.

'She's going to cast a spell,' Fergus said. 'Or tell my fortune. They make this position when they are going to do some magic. If her hands were free she would make a diamond of her thumbs and forefingers and look at me through it.'

'You killed *Donn Tawr*, the sacred bull. Now I curse you,' the druid said in a monotone voice. 'May the gods rain down punishments on you and all you hold dear. May you rot with disease. You are barred from attending sacrifice. You are—'

Fergus interrupted her, speaking a series of words that rattled from his mouth in a clatter of harsh syllables. It sounded neither British nor Hibernian. Nor was it Latin and from the puzzled look on her face Agricola saw that the druid did not understand what Fergus had said either.

'Well you may be clever, but you can't speak that language, can you?' Fergus smiled, switching back to Latin. 'Now, shall we all agree to converse in a tongue everyone understands?'

'What language was that?' Agricola asked.

'That was the ancient tongue of my people, the Cruithni,' Fergus said. 'It is not the Goidelc she talked of.'

He reached into the neck of his tunic and pulled out the

leather thong that held his serpent stone. With his other hand he undid the clasp of the necklace and held it up so the druid could see it.

'You and all your kind have no power over me. I bear a serpent stone,' he said.

The druid looked stunned and dropped her foot back to the floor. She hung her head, letting her hair fall down over her features. After a few seconds they realised tears were falling from her lowered face.

'By the gods, man,' Agricola said, amazed. 'What on earth is that amulet? Look what it has done to her. What great power does it have?'

Fergus shrugged. 'The power of superstition, which is possibly the most powerful magic there is,' he said. 'Perhaps I should question her now.'

Agricola nodded, impressed at how quickly Fergus had managed to get under the skin of the priestess. This sort of questioning was far more effective than the crude application of torture implements.

'My name is Fergus MacAmergin. I am from the tribe of the Cruithni in Ulaidh but I left there some years ago,' Fergus said. 'I once had a wife and a son and your kind took them away from me. So you know all about me, and should have no fear of telling me who you are.'

Agricola shot a sideways glance at the Hibernian. The woman looked up at him, the blue paint on her forehead now running and streaked, her long hair straggling and stuck to her face. She was young, but not in the first flush of youth. This did not surprise Fergus. It took twenty years of training to become a druid and a *filidh* took thirteen. A lot of the fire seemed to have disappeared from her glare and she now regarded him with something like resentment and even a touch of fear.

Fergus was perplexed by this change of attitude as he had not expected his serpent stone to be so effective.

'My name is Ceridwen,' she said at last in a low voice. 'I am a *gwawd*, a vates. You would call me a filidh in Hibernia. You should understand my position in society, which makes your treatment of me more appalling.'

Fergus nodded. He had been correct about her.

'We don't want to know anything about the Silures – don't worry about that,' he said. 'We don't expect you to betray your people.'

'How can that be? Your general, the great Suetonius, is here to wage war on the Silures,' Ceridwen said, some of the fire returning to her eyes. 'To crush us under his boot, kill our warriors, steal our treasure, enslave our people and burn our homes. Then, when there is nothing left but the silence of death, announce that he has brought peace: *Pax Romana*.' She spat on the ground.

'The general can ask his own questions,' Fergus said. 'We need to know more about the kingdom of the Dobunni. What do you know of Queen Finnabair?'

The scowl returned to the face of the woman.

'She's another *Gwyddeleg* like you. From Hibernia. Gods that she had stayed there!' She spat again, this time with a degree of real vehemence. 'She will do anything to try to cling on to power, but her time has passed. Her fortunes died with her husband, that lapdog of Rome. Now she whores herself to her late husband's armour bearer. She tries to bribe the old king's warriors to fight for her, but it's all for nothing. The gods are against her. Worse than that, the people are against her. She should go home to Hibernia before someone cuts her throat.'

'Have you heard about the religion of the Christians?' Fergus said.

'Of course,' the vates said, 'another of the infectious diseases that have crept into this land with the Romans. They're a strange cult. Blasphemers and tricksters. Religious fanatics who drink blood and eat human flesh.'

Fergus laughed, a short, bitter bark.

'What's so funny?' Ceridwen said.

'Religious fanatics?' he said. 'You don't see any irony in that? It was because of fanatics like you I left Hibernia. Is Finnabair a Christian?'

Ceridwen snorted with derision and sank back against the tent pole.

'I don't think so, but who knows with that woman?' she said. 'She'd do anything to cultivate support to keep her in power. One of the nobles of the Dobunni – a powerful chieftain called Peredur – definitely is, though. He forsook the gods of his own people and works for the Christians' god now. He is part of the queen's court. The gods will punish him for that, just like they will punish you for what you have done. You've forsaken them and joined these foreigners with their false gods. You killed the Donn Tawr, the bull sacred to Taranis.'

A sudden anger flared in the eyes of Fergus and he stepped towards the woman.

'By Crom! Don't speak to me of punishment,' he said. 'The gods have already punished me. I'm just getting my own back now.'

'You dare speak that name?' Ceridwen said, narrowing

her eyes. 'The name of the Black One? The Bloody Crooked One? What do you know of Crom?'

'Crom is the god of my people,' Fergus said.

'But life-giving Lugh, Son of Beli, put Crom to death,' the priestess said, 'and brought life back to the earth, and fertility to the fields.'

'The druids of Ulaidh preach that without the blood of our children, Lugh cannot win his victory,' Fergus said. 'The bastards still cut the throats of the firstborn. They give their innocent blood to their bloody, dark god.'

Agricola saw that Fergus was now angry. He stepped forward and laid a hand on Fergus's shoulder.

'As you said, Decurion, we are not here to discuss religion,' he said.

Fergus glared at him for a moment, then nodded and stepped aside.

'Have you heard if the queen possesses a magic spear, sacred to the Christians?' Agricola said.

'The queen says a lot of things, none of which are true,' Ceridwen said with a chuckle. Yes, I've heard that she claims to have a sacred weapon, but she is the sort of woman who claims to be all things to all people. She claims to have a magic spear, but to some she says it is a Christian relic, to others a gift of our gods. She is careful not to be specific so she can use it to try to trick the greatest number of people into supporting her. So yes, she has *a* spear. If it's the one you're looking for I can't say. She's pathetic. She cares for power more than what is right.'

'She sounds like the perfect politician,' Agricola said. 'If this spear exists, then we must get it.'

'I will speak no more to you,' the woman said, raising her

arms above her head to stretch them. 'I have said enough and I am tired.'

As the cloak fell away from her bare arms, Fergus caught sight for the first time of a swirling tattoo on her flesh just below the right elbow. It was of a three-armed wheel with spokes trailing as if it was spinning round in the direction of the sun. He leaned over to the druid to get a better look. The woman immediately dropped her hands behind her head again, but Fergus grabbed her right hand and held it while he examined the tattoo more closely.

'Well, well,' he said, looking into the woman's blue eyes for a long moment. 'It looks like neither of us are what we seem. This is a *Trinovantes* tribal symbol. You're not from the Silures at all, are you? What are you doing this far west inciting the Silures to rebellion?'

The woman simply glared back at him, her mouth resolutely closed. Both Agricola and Fergus realised that they would get nothing further out of her without resorting to more desperate methods.

'Let's go,' the tribune said. 'She's told us what we want to know anyway.'

Fergus nodded and they turned and left the tent.

'Is that the interrogation over?' the legionary guarding the entrance said, his face alight with eager anticipation.

'Ours is. Why?' Agricola said.

'We've got orders that once she has been questioned there is no further use for her,' the soldier said. 'She can be given to the legion for their enjoyment. There won't be much left of her after the first cohort has their go, so I'd like to get in early.'

The tribune frowned. He found it hard to believe that

the general would sanction that sort of behaviour, but he was also aware that Suetonius knew it was sometimes necessary to throw the soldiers the odd bone, particularly if he wanted them to do something difficult for him later. Harsh discipline only went so far.

'We are not the general's interrogators,' he said. 'They're still to come so you will just have to wait a while longer.'

'The general is making a big mistake,' Fergus said as they walked down the via principalis back towards the centre of the camp. 'If he has a druid raped it will incense all the local tribes, even those favourable to Rome. The whole country will rise in revolt.'

'Perhaps that is what he wants,' Agricola said with a sigh. 'There's no way to beat the Silures if they keep up their hit-and-run tactics. The only way the legion can defeat them is if we can draw them into open battle. Tell me something—'

The tribune stopped and turned to look Fergus directly in the eyes.

'Was that true about your wife and child?'

Fergus hesitated, then opened his mouth to reply but at that moment the darkness of the night was illuminated by sudden blazes of light that came from the direction of the *porta decumana*, the back gate of the camp.

Horns blasted and, through the dark, a man came running towards them. As he got near, the flames from a nearby brazier showed he was a legionary, but he was missing his helmet and blood poured from a deep cut on his forehead.

'Raise the alarm!' he shouted. 'The camp is under attack!'

20

'I'm going to get orders,' Agricola said and hurried off towards the command tents. Fergus tightened the straps of his cavalry helmet so the cheek guards covered most of his face, then jogged back down the via principalis towards the camp carcer once again.

Almost as soon as he had heard what the fate of the druid was to be, he had decided that he was not going to allow it to happen. The fact that an opportunity to prevent it had arisen so quickly convinced him even more that perhaps the capricious gods with their strange sense of humour were prompting him that it was the right course of action.

Fergus had no love of druids. He despised them and with good reason. The events of the day, however, coming on the back of the events of the day before, had left him feeling equally indisposed towards Rome and her fickle, ungrateful war machine. He was well aware that it was the weak and the powerless – women, children and slaves – who suffered most when the havoc of war was unleashed but he had never been comfortable with it. He found such behaviour cowardly and distasteful. Unmanly.

Unlike the Romans, in his culture women held common status with men and for all the antipathy Fergus now held for the folk he grew up among, he still held many of their principles. For his people, rape of a woman was a monstrosity. For that crime a man could expect to be bound, half strangled then drowned in a bog. The *Getae* – bands of landless, tribeless young warriors who roamed the countryside causing problems, stealing cattle and raping women – were the lowest of the low, a nuisance that wars were invented for to keep them busy. It seemed the Roman army, for all its supposed morals and virtus, could often behave just like them.

Ultimately, though, he'd had a gutful of his adopted army and was determined to at least give them a bloody nose, if only a small one, for the way they had treated him. His main issue was make sure he did not get caught. He had no intention of deserting – at least not yet – he would just let the druid go free. Freeing a prisoner was a crime liable to be punished by a fatal beating. Or worse, crucifixion. So he needed to make use of all his cunning.

He approached the carcer tent and the legionary on guard outside saw him coming.

'What's going on at the back gate?' the man said.

Fergus was careful to lurk in the half-darkness beyond the light cast by the braziers at the gate.

'The camp's under attack. You're to get down there straight away. Everyone has to repel the assault,' he said.

The legionary shook his head.

'Not carcer guards. We're never to leave our posts: standing orders,' he said.

'Tribune's orders,' Fergus said. 'They need everyone they can get.'

'Well the tribune would need to come down here himself

and tell me that,' the legionary said. 'Standing orders supersede everything. They don't need me. It's just a bunch of fucking savages having a go in the dark. The sentries will be able to handle it. It'll be over by the time we get there.'

'Well your mate has already gone,' Fergus said.

'What?!' The guard, amazed, turned round to see if that was indeed true.

Fergus lashed out with the butt of his spear. The shaft smashed across the side of the Roman's head, knocking his helmet off with a clang. Before the headgear had hit the ground Fergus whipped the spear shaft back in the opposite direction, cracking the soldier across the temples. His eyes crossed as consciousness left him and he collapsed onto the ground.

Fergus decided not to see what was actually going on with the other guard at the back of the tent. He drew his knife and pushed through the flap to find the druid still slumped at the base of the tent pole. She looked up when he entered, saw the knife in his hand, and a look of anger crossed her face.

'I might have guessed they'd send you to kill me,' she said.

'Come with me and keep your mouth shut if you want to live,' he said as he crossed to her and cut the ropes that tied her hands round the tent pole.

He grabbed her by the wrist and pulled her back out through the tent flap. The woman, dumbfounded, let herself be led until they were outside. To his relief the other guard appeared to have heard nothing. Fergus could see his shadow still in position at the back of the tent.

'What is going on?' the druid said.

'Keep your voice down or you'll get us both killed,' Fergus said in a hiss. 'I'm letting you go.'

'This is some sort of trick. Why?' she said.

'Look: I'm a Roman soldier, but there are some things I just won't stand for,' he said in a whisper. 'Your fate would not have been pleasant and sometimes it takes a barbarian to act in a civilised way. It's nothing personal either. I still despise druids and all they stand for. Now come with me to the rampart. Getting into a Roman fort is extremely difficult, but I think I know a way to sneak out of one.'

He unfastened the clasp that held his long cavalry cloak around his throat, then swept if off his shoulders.

'Take that bird thing off and put this on,' Fergus said.

'This is a sacred cloak of feathers, handed down through centuries,' the druid said, grasping it close around herself. 'I'd rather die than lose it.'

'You might do just that,' Fergus said, but he could see the hardened resolve glinting in the torchlight reflected in her eyes. 'Very well, put it on over it, and pull the hood up.'

The druid shot a vicious glance his way, but wrapped herself in his cloak. He grabbed her hand once more and started to pull her along again. This time she snatched her hand away.

'I should scream,' she said. 'They will come and punish you as well as me.'

Fergus turned to face her.

'And what would be the point of that?' he said. 'I should've known better than to try to rescue a religious fanatic. Let me tell you what they have planned, shall I? Once the general's torturers have finished with you, they will let the legionaries guarding you rape you, then when they are done you will be thrown to the first cohort, who will also rape you. If you're still alive after that, which I very much doubt, it will be the turn of the second cohort. Maybe you would prefer that? If not then shut your mouth and come with me.'

They hurried through the *intervallum*, the wide empty area between the protecting rampart and the legionaries' tents, left intentionally bare so enemy missiles, lobbed over the wall, would fall short of doing any damage. As a marching camp designed to house the legion for a single night, the defences were a lot less elaborate or extensive than those created for a longer stay. Beyond the intervallum was the rampart the legionaries had constructed all the way around the camp. On the inside it was just over the height of a man, with a step built into the back of it for defenders to stand on to repel attackers. At the foot of the rampart on the outside was a wedge-shaped ditch that nearly doubled the height of what an attacker needed to scale to get into the camp. The gate was a more sturdy wooden construction, being built from prefabricated pieces carted along in the legion's baggage train. Dotted along the rampart were blazing torches, and legionary sentries were posted every fifty paces.

They arrived at the rampart not far behind one of the sentries, whose attention was focused away from them towards the dark night outside the camp. Fergus led the druid about twenty paces along the back of the rampart to a point where the light between the torches was dimmest. He then jumped up onto the step, reached down and grabbed the druid around the waist. He swung her up so she sat on the top of the rampart.

'Off you go,' he said in a quiet voice. 'Be careful of the ditch on your way down. We like to leave a few surprises in there for unannounced guests.'

As she sat, perched on the top of the rampart, the druid turned to him, fixing him with her icy blue eyes.

'You expect me to be grateful for this?' she said. 'It was you who captured me. Now you don't have the strength to see me killed. You're pathetic.'

'The feeling is mutual, I can assure you,' Fergus said. 'The only thing I expect you to do is to get out of here. I don't care what happens to you from now on – though I want my cloak back.'

The woman tore it away from her and threw it at him. She paused again, still looking at him with an expression of confusion mixed with anger on her face.

'Well get going,' Fergus said.

'Your druids have led you astray,' Ceridwen said. 'Our message is life-affirming. But the worship of Crom Cruach is an abomination, a twisting of the holy story of the year. Crom is god of winter, darkness and death. Winter triumphs at Samhain, but Belinos sent his divine son Lugh to defeat Crom and bring life back to the world with spring. Your druids taught fear of Crom rather than love of Lugh—'

'Spare me the preaching. They taught us more than that,' Fergus said. 'My wife and child died because of them.'

'You are really of the Cruithni?' Ceridwen said, suddenly anxious, her brows knitted.

'Aye,' Fergus said.

Ceridwen sighed. 'There's a prophecy of our tribe that when a painted man comes from the north, great destruction will follow,' she said. 'A tide of blood will be loosed, fire will rain from the sky and great slaughter will come down. The Romans call your people the *Picti* – the painted ones – because of your tattoos...'

'I don't have time for this superstitious shit. Go!' Fergus said, glancing anxiously towards the nearest sentry on top of the rampart. If the man looked round now, all this effort would be for nothing.

'Wait, there is more to the prophecy—'

'I said go. Jump across the ditch if you don't want your ankles broken,' Fergus said as he leaned forwards and pushed the druid so she toppled over the rampart. Peering after her he saw her fall down the outside, hit the ground and tumble down it towards the ditch. Half expecting to hear a shout of alarm, he looked quickly left and right to see if any of the sentries had seen her go, but all were gazing off into the dark, staring fixedly ahead.

Below, Ceridwen regained her feet and did indeed jump over the defensive ditch. It was a good thing too, Fergus mused, as it was probably sown with caltrops, spikes and all manner of snares and traps to cause as much damage to attackers as was possible.

'Shit!' a sentry to his left called out. Fergus felt a stab of anxiety. Thinking Ceridwen had been seen, he ducked beneath the top of the rampart and looked apprehensively along it. The soldier, however, was still staring out into the darkness of the meadow beyond the ditch.

'Light! Get some light over there!' a voice down the rampart shouted and a blazing signal arrow ignited. The archer swung it aloft for a second as he drew his bow, then loosed into the night. The arrow, wrapped in pitch-soaked cloth, soared in an arc from the tower out into the darkness beyond the walls of the camp. As it travelled towards the trees a short distance away, its light glared across the bodies of many men, moving silently and swiftly through the darkness towards the ditch and rampart. Here and there fire from the arrow glittered on the unmistakable glint of metal.

'Crom,' Fergus said.

Hundreds of warriors were approaching the camp through the night. They could only have one purpose. The attack on the back gate was a feint and the real assault was about to be launched at the eastern rampart, where he now stood.

21

Praefect Titus Pomponius Proculianus whispered sweet nothings into the ear of his horse. He was in full battle dress: fighting helmet, armoured cuirass, chain mail, greaves and forearm guards, but was planning on not requiring its protection.

The Gaulish cavalry had been ordered to stand by while the camp was under attack. Their mounts were ready for battle – saddled, armed and bridled – but the troopers' main purpose was to keep their horses calm and avoid any potential stampede. In an enclosed space such as that within the ramparts of the camp, panicking horses could do more damage to the defenders than the enemy. Defence was to be left to the legionaries unless the camp looked as if it was likely to be overrun.

This suited Pomponius. Fighting was bad enough at the best of times, but the thought of fighting in the dark was positively frightening. Decurion Sedullus was not so content.

'We should be joining the battle,' he said.

Pomponius grunted. Sedullus represented the cream of Gaulish society: rich and thick. The young decurion was as exuberant as a four-week-old puppy with the brains and sense to match. He also worshipped Pomponius, which was why the praefect kept him around. A leader needed men who obeyed orders without question.

Behind them, to the rear of the camp, the crash of metal on metal, the screams of wounded men and roars of anger and pain filtered through the darkness from the battle that was taking place around the back gate. Braziers, bonfires and torches had been set afire along the ramparts to illuminate the night. Missiles, spears, stones and the occasional blazing arrow filtered into view from the dark outside and into the firelight to fall uselessly in the empty space of the intervallum.

'This is legionary work, Decurion,' Pomponius said. 'Let them repel the savages in the dark where no one can see their deeds. We will have plenty of chances to win glory in the daylight.'

'Do you think so?' Sedullus said. 'The general was really angry with us. I thought he was going to have us crucified. It will be a long time before he awards us any honours. I just hope this doesn't mean my career is ruined. What would my father say?'

Pomponius nodded. He had to agree with that. He knew Sedullus's father well. The big Gaulish nobleman was as stupid as his son but even in his old age was still built like a bull with a temper to match. Pomponius did not relish the idea of having to explain this to him either.

'It's all that damn fool of a tribune's fault,' he said. 'If he hadn't led us out on that stupid mission to rescue the Hibernian, none of this would have happened.'

'At least the general is as angry with him as he was with us,' Sedullus said.

'Yes, but for how long?' Pomponius said. 'That oily little shit will soon worm his way back into the general's affections. Then he will be telling tales and twisting things, making it look worse than it was. And then we really will be in the shit.'

By 'we' Pomponius meant 'I', but he wasn't going to say that out loud.

'I simply followed standard military procedures by surrendering in that ambush,' he said. 'If I hadn't, we'd all be dead.'

'You did the right thing, sir,' Sedullus said with conviction, though at the same time racking his brains to try to remember which procedure manual that particular process was in. As far as he could recall the word 'surrender' simply did not exist in the Roman army lexicon.

'Of course I did,' Pomponius said, his bottom lip jutting out in a pout. 'But that's not the way it will be portrayed by Master Agricola when I'm not around. Oh you can be sure that weasel will be playing it up.'

He adopted a whining, childlike tone that was supposed to sound like the tribune.

'"Pomponius surrendered," he'll say. "Pomponius threw his weapon away." And by the way, Sedullus, I didn't throw my weapon away. It slipped from my hand. The sweat of battle made me lose my grip.'

'I never thought it for one moment, sir,' Sedullus said, rearranging the whole incident in his own memory as he did so. 'It would be an injustice if you suffered because of his lies.'

'An injustice? Yes it would be,' Pomponius said, nodding enthusiastically. 'But it won't be just me who suffers,

Sedullus. You mark my words. You will too. I have no thoughts for myself, but to see a promising young officer like you have his career ruined because of the lies of that Roman and his snake-worshipping Hibernian lapdog? It makes my blood boil!'

'Me, sir?' Sedullus had not considered the possibility that he would share in the praefect's ignominy.

'Oh yes, Sedullus.' Pomponius, delighted to see in the flickering torchlight that the younger man's face had flushed with the first stirrings of real anger, was determined to stir him further. 'The tribune will want to cover all his mistakes and you went with him on his ridiculous mission. You can tell the truth about me and he won't want that. And he will get the Hibernian to back him up.'

'But MacAmergin is a cavalry officer of the Ala Gallorum, sir. One of our own,' Sedullus said. 'He wouldn't dishonour the corps, would he?'

Pomponius shook his head sadly. 'That's precisely it, Sedullus,' he said. 'He's *not* one of us. He is not a Gaul, he's a Hibernian. Worse, he's from some horrendous tribe of daemon-worshipping savages from the far north who still sacrifice their firstborn children. And he hates you, Sedullus. Maybe you don't realise that, but he's been jealous of you ever since you got that promotion. He thought he should have got it.'

Sedullus did not reply. He was not so great a fool that he did not realise it was family rank and influence that had secured his promotion ahead of the man who actually should have got it. In fact, only the day before he had ordered a trooper whipped for muttering that very thing behind his back.

'We can't allow this injustice to happen, sir,' he said.

'We cannot,' Pomponius said, pleased that he had managed to get the young officer round to his way of thinking so quickly. 'We must take action. We must rid ourselves of this liar of a tribune and his Hibernian wolfhound. Only then will our careers be safe and justice be done.'

For the first time both men met each other's gaze. Sedullus nodded. He was not shocked by this concept in any way. It was a ruthless world and in Roman army life, as in politics, the surest way to remove the threat of an enemy was to kill him.

'We need to work fast though. Who knows how long it will be before Agricola is back in the general's favour?' Pomponius said. 'The Hibernian should be easy. I'll leave him up to you. First chance you get in a raid, a battle or on patrol, stick your spatha in his back. If the opportunity doesn't arise in the next day or so, then we'll have to find some fatally dangerous work for him. The tribune, on the other hand, will be a different proposition. That will take planning and cunning, but I'm sure we'll find a way. We have to. And Justice herself is on our side. I want both those bastards dead at the first possible opportunity.'

22

As the soldiers in the watchtowers and eastern rampart began raising the alarm, lighting bonfires and preparing for the coming attack, Fergus jumped down from the step and sprinted as fast as he could along the via principalis towards the praetorium. Not for the first time that night he wondered what on earth he was doing. He had just facilitated the escape of an enemy prisoner, yet now here he was, sprinting with all his might to save the camp from being overrun.

He got to the praetorium just in time to see the small group of senior officers who comprised the leadership of the XIV Legion leaving to join the action at the back gate of the camp. They were surrounded by a squad of soldiers who would act as their bodyguards.

'Tribune!' Fergus shouted, spotting Agricola, now in full battle armour and helmet.

Several guards stepped forward to bar Fergus's approach, but Agricola waved them away.

'What is it? Make it fast. I've orders to oversee defence at the porta decumana,' the tribune said, walking over to meet Fergus.

'Sir, the attack on the back gate is a ruse,' Fergus said,

breathing heavily from his run halfway across the camp. 'There are hundreds of warriors launching an attack on the eastern ramparts.'

'Shit,' Agricola said. 'We've all been ordered to take the reserves to the back gate to fend off the attack there. It will take time to move the men round again.'

'Sir, I have an idea,' Fergus said. 'We should counter-attack. Ride the cavalry out of the porta principalis sinistra and hit them where and when they don't expect it.'

The tribune looked at him for a couple of seconds, both impressed at the strategic thinking from a junior officer and realising that it was exactly the right thing to do. He nodded.

'You're right. But I cannot go. I've orders to go to the back gate and if I show any more insubordination I'll be crucified. Perhaps literally,' he said. 'You must go. Tell Pomponius what's happening and order him to counter-attack. I'll send cohorts to back you up, but don't wait for them.'

Fergus shook his head. 'Sir, he'll not listen to me,' he said. 'We need a senior officer to give the order.'

Agricola rolled his eyes. There was not a moment to lose if the camp was to be saved, but he knew that the Hibernian was right again. Neither were there any senior officers available who would be able to go and deliver the orders. He thought briefly of having the *cornua* blow out the signal for a cavalry charge, but they needed to know where to charge to.

The tribune unclipped the fibula clasp at his right shoulder that held his large red cloak in place. All six of the legion's tribunes wore the *paludamentum* as part of their uniform and symbol of their rank. Only one, however – that of the tribunus laticlavius – bore a broad purple stripe. Agricola swept the cloak off his shoulders.

'Take this,' he said, handing it to Fergus. 'It will prove you're acting under my orders. Now go and tell that fool Pomponius to get his arse out the eastern gate and finish this attack off before we are overrun. If he still refuses even when you show him my cloak, then tell him he is no longer in command. Find someone who will take the horse out. Lead them out yourself if you have to.'

Fergus saluted, took the cloak and sprinted off once more, this time in the direction of the cavalry.

As he neared the stabling section of the camp, a familiar voice called out to him: 'Where are you going in such a hurry?'

Turning, he saw Liscus, armed and ready for battle but – like the rest of the cavalry – standing beside his mount trying to keep it calm. His eyes widened when he saw that Fergus wore the red cloak of a senatorial tribune.

'Got a promotion?' he said.

'Liscus.' Fergus stopped, realising that this was a stroke of luck. 'Ride to the porta principalis sinistra. Wait there until you see the ala coming then open the gates.'

'Orders are to stand by here and keep the horses quiet,' Liscus said. 'They came from the praefect himself.'

Fergus held up the hem of the cloak. 'This supersedes any orders. We're under attack from the east as well. Where can I get a horse?'

Liscus grabbed a mount from the nearest trooper.

'Orders of the tribune,' he said when the soldier looked as if he were about to object. 'Here you go.'

Liscus passed the reins to Fergus.

'Thanks. Now go,' Fergus said.

Liscus nodded and in one movement leapt onto his own horse. He shouted, 'Yah!' kicked his heels into the beast's flanks and took off at a gallop.

Two figures came hurrying over.

'What in Hades is that trooper up to?' Pomponius thundered. 'How dare he ride off!'

'New orders from the tribune,' Fergus said. 'We are to repel an attack on the east gate.'

'What nonsense is this?' the praefect said. There was a note of panic in his voice.

Fergus pointed to the cloak at his shoulder, taking pleasure in the expressions of consternation on the faces of Sedullus and Pomponius.

'You can question these orders but you will have to discuss it with the tribune himself later,' he said. 'Agricola also says if you do not obey these orders then you're relieved of command. Sir, if we don't ride out now, the camp will be overrun.'

Pomponius's mouth moved soundlessly for a few moments.

'Very well,' he finally said. 'Sedullus, go with him. Make sure this is not some sort of dangerous, damn fool, hare-brained scheme. I must stay behind to fulfil the original orders. Where is Aelius? Aelius!'

Aelius Augustinus – *decurio princeps* and second in command of the ala – trotted his horse over. The hard-faced warrior saluted.

'Aelius, the tribune orders that you are to lead the men out of camp,' Pomponius said. 'The Hibernian here can give you the details.'

Fergus saluted the decurio princeps. He respected the Gaul, knowing from experience the man's combat record and his ability as a soldier.

Fergus relayed the orders. Aelius Augustinus nodded grimly, understanding the situation straight away. Fergus swung himself into the saddle of his borrowed horse.

'Form up. Turmae in column formation.' The decurio princeps shouted orders to the other decuria nearby. 'We are under attack from the east. We ride to repel it.'

The other officers hurried to relay the orders to their own troopers. Cornua blared signals to broadcast the orders further down the line.

'Trooper,' Pomponius said to Fergus. 'I understand you lost the men under your command this morning. Join Sedullus's troop, Turma XV, for this mission.'

Fergus nodded. The flag of each troop was always carried by a mounted standard bearer so that everyone knew who was where and even in the half-dark of torchlight, Fergus was able to identify Turma XV. He dug in his spurs and took off to join that troop.

Sedullus was about to ride after him when Pomponius slapped his vine cane across the younger officer's chest.

'Did you see that red cloak, Sedullus?' the praefect said. 'What more proof do you need that those two are conspiring together?'

The thought had not actually occurred to Sedullus until Pomponius pointed it out. His face falling into a dour glower as he nodded.

'This is our chance to rid ourselves of one of our enemies,' Pomponius said. 'You're riding out into a battle. It'll be dark so it should be easy to stick your spear in the Hibernian's back. What better sign do you need that the gods are on our side? They've given us this opportunity to strike back at our enemies so soon. Do not waste it!'

Sedullus nodded again.

'Good luck,' Pomponius said.

Spurring away from him, Sedullus moved to take the lead of Turma XV.

'Move out,' Aelius Augustinus commanded and the Ala Gallorum rode into battle.

23

Liscus stood behind the porta principalis sinistra, listening as it rattled violently on its hinges. As he watched, it swayed and bucked from the battering it was taking from outside. Above and around him the sounds of fighting clattered as the legionaries on the ramparts around the gate desperately struggled to hold off the tide of warriors who hurled themselves on the camp defences.

The British seemed heedless of danger, fearless of death, and Liscus could tell from the desperation in the shouts from the Roman soldiers that the situation was getting critical. The braziers and beacons ablaze on the ramparts enabled the defenders to find targets for their javelins, but equally aided their enemies. The flickering orange light cast lurid shadows on the ground of men in the throes of combat, like so many grotesque dancers.

'Are you sure about this?' the optio commanding the gate said. He looked at Liscus with a mixture of doubt and concern on his face. Despite the chill of the night, sweat glistened on the parts of his face visible under his helmet.

'These are the orders of the tribune,' Liscus said. His face was impassive but inside he shared the optio's apprehension. The optio and six other legionaries stood behind the gate with him, all of them with their hands on the big wooden bar that passed through iron loops in both doors to hold the gate shut.

'As soon as we pull this away, they'll come pouring in. We won't be able to hold them back,' the optio said.

At that moment the sounds of cornua blaring reached their ears. It was an alarm from the rampart, the signal they had been dreading.

'The Brittunculi must be onto the rampart,' the optio said. 'The camp defences have been breached.'

The looks of concern on the legionaries' faces quickly turned to fear. Then, above the din of battle came the strident notes of another cornua blaring somewhere towards the centre of the camp, but rapidly approaching.

'Here come the cavalry,' Liscus said, a grin breaking on his face as he turned towards the praetorium in the centre of the camp. He saw horses and riders trotting around the corner from the via praetoria.

As they turned into the via principalis the lead rider, the decurio princeps, drew his spatha and held it aloft. Even at the gate they heard his loud commands. 'Draw spatha! Charge!'

The two cornua bearers riding two ranks behind him blasted out the signal to relay the order to the rest of the troopers. Almost as one, the Gaulish cavalry ripped swords from scabbards and dug in their spurs. The horses surged into a gallop and pounded their way towards the gate.

'Wait!' Liscus shouted to the optio. 'Wait.'

The horses thundered closer, closing the distance from the centre of the camp to the east gate in seconds.

'Now!' Liscus said, heaving the huge wooden bar at the same time.

The optio and legionaries joined him and together they slid the big bolt out of the bars behind the gate.

Liscus felt the gate surge open as the men outside threw their weight against it. With all resistance suddenly gone the gate swept open, carrying Liscus, the optio and legionaries with it. Silures warriors spilled into the camp through the gap, falling over each other as those behind pushed forward.

At that moment the Ala Gallorum smashed into them. A wave of horseflesh and iron surged outwards, sweeping the British back out of the fort with their charge. Five hundred men and steeds thundered past, riding three abreast, rushing out into the packed ranks of the attacking warriors. Their momentum was unstoppable and the cavalry cut a bloody swathe through the Silures whose ranks were too tightly packed for them to get out of the way.

The optio and the legionaries who had opened the gate watched the cavalry charge past, but Liscus ran to his horse, which he had left tethered in the intervallum. He mounted, drew his spatha and as the last trooper exited the fort, he galloped out after them. The optio and legionaries slammed the gate shut. They pulled the massive bar across before the warriors outside recovered enough from the onslaught to pour back into the opening.

Outside, the cavalry ploughed through the pressed ranks of warriors. Their sudden and unexpected counter-attack injected panic among the Britons and those nearest the gate tried to flee but were cut down immediately.

In the middle of Turma XV, Fergus forced his horse

forward through the throng of bodies. In such close-quarters fighting, spears and javelins were useless. The troopers, with their large, oval shields on their left arms, relied on their long-bladed swords, their spathas, to hack and slash down onto the enemy around them. It was bloody work. The horses' hooves crushed and smashed, breaking bones and splitting skulls, while the heavy blades of the spathas hewed off limbs and gouged into shoulders and heads, opening up horrific wounds that sprayed hot blood onto the riders.

In addition to the braziers on the ramparts, the Romans had built towers of wood soaked in oil out on the meadow beyond the camp. These were to be set ablaze for emergency lighting in an attack. The British had managed to dismantle a few of them before their assault had been detected, but most of them now blazed, ignited by burning arrows shot from the camp as soon as the alarm was raised. In their eerie, flickering light Fergus could see that the five hundred troopers of the Ala Gallorum were easily outnumbered by the horde of Celtic warriors outside the fort, but in the press of fighting his way through their ranks he had no time to worry about exactly how many there were.

The weight of the cavalry charge forced the troopers through, but the horses, despite their training, began to panic at being surrounded by such closely packed ranks of armed, screaming men. They became increasingly hard to handle. At the same time, the Silures were quickly recovering from the initial surprise of the assault and were beginning to fight back.

Several horses screamed as they were hamstrung, their bellies stabbed or slit open. The trooper riding to the right of Fergus shouted in pain as a spear, forced up behind his shield, broke the rings of his chain mail and skewered into his shoulder.

Fergus concentrated on the enemy before him. A warrior crouched, his spear aimed at his face. Fergus slashed his spatha in an upwards arc that took the spear point up in the air and away from its intended target. As his horse moved forward he swung the sword backwards again in a reverse of the first stroke, catching the warrior's back and opening up a bloody slice across his spine from left shoulder to waist, momentarily exposing the white bone of his ribs before dark red blood welled up and out of the wound.

The horse kept going and Fergus struck again, bringing his sword down on the next man in his path. This time the warrior countered with his shield and the spatha clattered harmlessly across it. Fergus spurred his horse and dropped his left shoulder to bring his own shield down and behind him, knowing that the warrior would counter-attack. Sure enough he felt the impact of the point of the man's sword hitting his shield, a blow that would have gone directly into his kidneys had he not blocked it.

Then they were through. The horses of the Ala Gallorum burst free of the ranks of the Silures and into open ground. They poured on across the meadow that lay between the camp and the edge of the nearby forest, riding to the limit of the light from the fires and the edge of the darkness of the trees beyond. Even in the meagre light they could see that the Silures' assault followed the usual barbarian tactic: everyone committed to one almighty onslaught designed to smash through the enemy and quickly overwhelm them in a tide of destruction. No reserves were left behind and by breaking through the Silures ranks the Ala Gallorum had now outflanked them.

Cornua blasted out new orders and the riders fanned out both left and right before they reached the trees, transforming their dense column into a long line that spread out across the meadow. The decurio princeps was shouting orders amid the din of the battle and the screaming of the wounded. The decurions and other optios repeated the orders and the cornua blared the signal that the Gaulish cavalry were to charge again.

Despite all the noise and confusion, Fergus suddenly realised that something was wrong. Instinctively he grasped his left shoulder when he recognised that the weight that had been there was gone. The heavy silvered clasp that had held the tribune's cloak was no longer there. His chain-mailed shoulders were otherwise bare. Somehow he had lost the tribune's cloak.

A sinking feeling hit his gut as he thought just how much money that piece of uniform must have cost. Officers' equipment was incredibly expensive, affordable only to the aristocrats who made up the upper echelons of the army and way beyond the means of a man in the ranks. The red cloak could well have cost more than a trooper like him would earn in a year. One of the Silures must have snagged it on the last charge and in the heat of battle he had not noticed. Fergus earnestly hoped that Agricola was the sort of officer who would appreciate that these things can happen in battle.

As the cavalry bridled their excited mounts into order for the upcoming charge, Fergus caught sight of someone waving a sword at him from ten horses down the line to his right. It was Liscus. A wave of relief swept over him as he saw that the Gaul was wearing the tribune's cloak.

'You dropped something,' Liscus shouted with a grin. 'That last Briton caught it off your back with his spear. Lucky I was coming along behind you and got it back.'

Fergus tipped his sword blade to his helmet in recognition.

'Thanks,' he said. 'Look after it. I don't fancy having to pay for a replacement.'

'Don't worry,' Liscus shouted back. 'I'll only charge you half its value to get it back.'

Fergus smiled but then the cornua signalled further commands. The troopers sheathed their swords on their right sides and lifted javelins from the quivers that sat on the front right of their saddles. It was time to attack again.

The Silures who were not engaged in fighting on the ramparts or inside the camp had become aware of the threat from behind them. As cornua sounded the charge and the Ala Gallorum surged forward across the meadow, the tribesmen turned to face them. This time they were ready and formed tightly packed ranks, a prickling hedge of spears to the fore. It was a standard anti-cavalry tactic. Horses, no matter how well trained, would never impale themselves on the deadly points and would either veer away or stop dead. Either way the momentum would falter. The first charge out of camp had succeeded because the horses had not seen what they were galloping into until the last minute. This time there was no mistaking what lay ahead of them.

The horses pounded towards the enemy, closing the

distance in moments. Every trooper knew the manoeuvre they were about to execute. It was practised relentlessly on the parade ground, but this was for real. The empty, level surface of the practice arena had been replaced by the uneven ground of a field with raised clumps of turf, hollows, and ditches. Waiting at the far end of it were not wooden practice targets but a living, screaming, defiant enemy who unlike the inert targets were hungry to fight back.

Despite this, the cavalry managed to keep a semblance of a straight line, filling the meadow from edge to edge, charging as one, javelins pointed towards the enemy. In the blazing firelight they could see the glittering, wickedly sharp points of the Silures' weapons and the warriors bunched so tightly together that every trooper knew there was no way their steeds would charge into them.

When they were slightly less than twenty horse-lengths away from them, the Silures let out a great roar as one. Half war cry, half bloodthirsty screech, it was designed to intimidate both riders and horses together.

The cavalry cornua blared almost at the same time. The troopers dug in their thighs and as one, wrenched the reins back with their left hands. The charge skidded to a halt so suddenly that had the troopers not been expecting it, it would have sent them tumbling head over heels over their saddle-bows.

Instead, together they launched their javelins. At such close range, the spears travelled almost horizontally. A wave of iron-tipped pain smashed into the enemy's front line. Warriors too tightly packed to be able to dodge the missiles were slaughtered where they stood. Spears broke through shields, skewered bodies and limbs and transfixed necks in an onslaught that saw most of the front rank dissolve, sinking to the ground in agony or death.

Without pausing to inspect the damage they had caused, the Ala Gallorum wheeled their steeds to the right, the entire line of cavalry turning as one to reverse their charge. Simultaneously, the troopers drew a second javelin from their quivers. The cornua blared again and they once more spurred their horses forward, this time charging away from the enemy. As they started, however, every man turned in the saddle to his right and loosed his spear, sending another volley of javelins back at the Silures. Even as the troopers turned back to face forwards once more, they could hear the crash of the weapons hitting their targets and the screeches of the men suffering beneath their deadly rain.

Without faltering, the cavalry galloped back to the edge of the field and turned again, the cornua sounding the signal to reform the line and take a very brief respite while they regrouped. The horses' breath rose in great clouds, steam rising from their heaving flanks. The cold night air was laden with the tangy reek of sweat from men and horses.

Fergus took the chance to wipe away the dribbles of his own sweat that despite the chill was running down from under his helmet to sting his eyes. In the firelight he could see the damage they had done. All along the front of the enemy line bodies lay piled on the ground, sometimes two and three deep. Javelin shafts, their points embedded downwards in the corpses, stood up like random higgledy-piggledy flagpoles that had lost their banners.

The Silures seemed undaunted, however. Men from the ranks behind stepped forwards and took the places of their fallen comrades. With another great roar they sounded their defiance at the Roman cavalry.

As the roar died away, across the field from inside the camp, the troopers heard the sound of Roman *buccinae* and cornua come blaring through the night. Silhouetted against the light from braziers inside the camp, the figures of many men in legionary armour began to appear on the ramparts. They arrived so suddenly and in such numbers that the attackers on the ramparts were overcome in moments. Bodies of Silures warriors dropped out of the camp and down the rampart as the legionaries swept them back to retake the defences. Soon the only figures on the ramparts were ones in Roman armour.

Agricola had made good on his promise and reinforcements had arrived. Despite still outnumbering the cavalry, the Silures now found themselves surrounded by Roman soldiers and their foothold in the camp lost. Someone in their leadership clearly recognised this, for the harsh sound of the great boar-headed Celtic trumpets began to bellow over the noise of battle.

The signal was evidently a retreat. The ranks of Silures began to dissolve, warriors running in all directions, fleeing for the trees. It was not a rout, they just scattered.

The gate of the camp opened and legionaries jogged out, marching at the double in both directions to form an offensive line at what was now the rear of the enemy.

At the other end of the meadow the cavalry waited as the Silures came running across the field towards them. Fergus looked left and right along the line of troopers. Cavalry being charged by infantry was not a situation covered by the manual and he could see from their expressions that most of them were wondering what to do.

They held firm. The Silures' intentions were simply to get past them and into the trees rather than any sort of deliberate tactic.

Decurio princeps, Aelius Augustinus, was screaming orders, the veins standing out on his neck. Fergus could not hear most of what he said over the din but caught the final words: '…let's take a few more of these bastards down!'

The signallers took up the orders and relayed them to the rest of the cavalry by the cornua. Each man knew what to do. A third javelin was drawn from the quiver and they made ready.

The Silures were not so much charging as simply rushing forwards. Their attack thwarted, they were now simply trying to get away. They closed the gap across the field, forty horse-lengths, then thirty, then twenty.

Again the cornua blasted and the Ala Gallorum unleashed their javelins. Once more the weapons took their toll on the Silures as the front ranks fell, transfixed by the deadly spears. The troopers drew their spathas and the charge was sounded. The Ala Gallorum once more surged forwards across the meadow to meet the warriors coming towards them.

Unlike the stolid Roman legionaries trained to stand in silence in the face of an enemy, the Gaulish cavalry screamed their own war cry, every bit as raucous and loud as the oncoming British. As they charged, they bellowed out the name of the Gaulish horse goddess: Epona.

Fergus was no different, yelling at the top of his lungs as he charged his horse forwards, sword held aloft and ready to strike, though he screamed the name of Macha – the goddess's name in his homeland.

The two sides clashed in a confused mess. Fergus brought his sword down on the first man he met, feeling the blade skitter off the enemy's helmet and cut deep into his shoulder. As the man fell beneath the hooves of his horse he tugged it free then looked for another target.

The Silures were no longer in the mood for battle. Some countered blows, protected themselves, and a few inflicted casualties on the cavalrymen, but most simply ducked out of the way of the riders' weapons and hooves and kept running. Unlike the close-packed ranks the cavalry had earlier struggled to force their mounts through, their problem now was to stop their horses from surging ahead through the chaotic mass of men running in the opposite direction before they had a chance to inflict damage on the fleeing enemy.

Then they were through and out the other side, riding on towards the lines of legionaries that had formed up outside the camp walls. By the time the troopers had turned their horses around once again to face the enemy, the Silures had gone, disappeared into the darkness and the trees, leaving behind only the dying and the dead.

24

A sickly dawn broke over the field beside the camp where the previous night's battle had raged. Wan sunlight filtered down through grey clouds, the dew raising a mist that wrapped and curled around the trees. Smoke from the smouldering remains of the beacon fires drifted across the field of slaughter like the wraiths of the dead leaving their corpses to float on the wind. Already crows were gathering in the trees and wheeling around in the air above, waiting for their chance to get stuck into the feast of dead flesh laid out before them.

A cohort of legionaries stood in defensive formation close to the treeline in case of further attack. The rest were busy either clearing up after the battle or dismantling the camp. No one had had any sleep and the red eyes and gaunt faces of the soldiers showed their weariness. To make things worse they now faced the draining prospect of a day's march deeper into enemy territory and possibly more fighting.

The troopers of the Ala Gallorum had been ordered to retrieve any of their javelins that were still serviceable and catch any horses who, having lost their riders in the battle, still wandered aimlessly across the battlefield. They picked their way through the dead, stopping here and there to place a foot on the chest of a corpse and heave an embedded weapon out of it. Unlike the legionary *pilum*, the cavalry javelin was not designed to bend on impact so as to weigh down an enemy's shield. Most of the javelins had broken shafts but the hard iron heads were intact and could be used again.

As Fergus picked his way through the field, a splash of colour caught his eye. Blood, now dried to black, was everywhere, so the patch of scarlet that lay near a pile of bodies in the centre of the field was arresting. A sinking feeling lurched through his gut as he jogged his weary legs over to take a better look.

'Shit,' Fergus said with a sigh.

Liscus was dead. He lay face down where he had fallen from his horse. Two dead Silures warriors were beneath him. Fergus rolled him over and saw his face was frozen in a snarl of rage, his now sightless eyes still glaring at whatever his last target had been. His sword was still gripped in his fist but his helmet was gone. The tribune's red cloak, its clasp broken when Fergus had lost it, was still tied around Liscus's throat. The spear that had killed him had been driven with such force through his cloak, armour and his back that its blade protruded from his chest. A congealed, sticky black puddle of blood lay beneath him.

Fergus knelt down and closed the Gaul's eyes. He fumbled in the purse he had on his belt and removed a sestertius coin.

'There you go, friend,' he said, placing the coin underneath

Liscus's dry, cold tongue. Then he carefully pushed the Gaul's mouth closed. 'Payment for looking after the cloak. Use that for the ferryman.'

Fergus sighed again. Liscus had been insubordinate but a good soldier. He could have worked well with him. The Gaul would have made a great optio for his turma – if he ever got it back. He undid the knot that tied the cloak around Liscus's neck, but realised he could not take it off while the spear still transfixed the body.

He placed his left foot on the shaft where it entered Liscus's back, grabbed the end of it and wrenched backwards like a man rowing on an oar. With a sharp crack the wood of the shaft broke and Fergus almost toppled over backwards. He tossed the broken shaft over his shoulder then pulled the point of the spear clear of the Gaul's chest. Apart from an initial sticking, it came out easily once the dried blood that held it in place was broken.

Picking up the tribune's cloak he rose back to his feet, still looking down at his dead friend. Catching sight of movement from the corner of his eye he looked around to see a couple of legionaries nearby. They were leading a mule that dragged a small cart onto which they were loading bodies of Roman soldiers for burial.

'Over here,' Fergus said, pointing to the body of Liscus.

As the legionaries lifted Liscus onto the cart, Fergus turned and began walking back towards the camp. Realising he still held the head of the spear that had killed Liscus, he hefted it to toss away onto the heap of corpses.

He stopped.

Fergus looked down at the head of the spear in his right

hand, for the first time realising that it was not the right shape. It was not the wide, leaf-bladed weapon that a Silures or other Celtic warrior would have used. It was the narrow, iron-sheathed head of a Roman heavy lance.

Liscus had been killed by a Roman weapon.

25

General Suetonius Paulinus glared at the cart laden with the bodies of Roman soldiers that trundled its way into the camp through the porta principalis sinistra. Around him the campsite was being dismantled. Tents were taken down and packed away while the impedimenta of the camp were loaded onto mules and waggons. Even the gate was being disassembled into several sections for transportation to the next campsite.

The general tutted and shook his head. Around him stood all the senior command of the XIV Legion: tribunes, senior centurions, the praefect castrorum, the praefect alae and the *legate*. Suetonius's lips were a tight, bloodless line. His jaw muscles continually flexed as he repeatedly clenched and unclenched his teeth. His breathing rushed in and out through his pinched nose as he struggled to contain his rage.

'How did they do it?' Suetonius said.

'They crept up in the dark,' Quintus Flavelis, the legate, said. 'Quietly killed the men on picket duty and by the time the sentries on the rampart spotted them they were nearly at the walls. Thank Fortuna we spotted them when we did.'

'Nearly at the walls?' the general said in a growl. 'They

got over them! They broke into our camp and freed that infernal druidess of theirs.'

The anger bubbling beneath the surface was clear from Suetonius's thick tone of voice and it cowed the other officers into silence.

'We were lucky last night,' he said quietly. 'Very lucky.'

None of the officers had the courage to respond. They all knew how right he was.

'Gentlemen, I've had enough,' the general said, turning his baleful gaze on the commanders. 'We're here to once and for all put down the rebellion of the Silures. Instead, two days into the campaign it is we who are taking the casualties. This bunch of stone-throwing savages are hitting us at will, at the time and the place of their choosing, not ours. It should not be this way!'

'Sir, this is the way of warfare in Britannia,' the legate said. Quintus Flavelis was a tall, grizzled veteran in his forties with iron grey hair. 'The enemy knows he's no match for the legions in open battle, so he hits us and runs away, back to the woods, the hills – wherever he can hide. The Silures have been in revolt for nearly twenty years. You can't expect to put them down in a couple of days.'

'They're humiliating us, Quintus!' Suetonius said. 'They're mocking Rome! What sort of message does it send out to every bare-arsed barbarian in the empire if we cannot pacify this one backward island with four legions?'

An awkward silence descended, the officers suddenly finding their footwear very interesting.

'Sir, Quintus is right,' Pomponius spoke up. 'This isn't Mauritania or Gaul. The British have no honour. They know we will defeat them in a fair fight so they resort to these cowardly bandit tactics. A legion fights best on open, flat ground against an enemy who stands and fights, or better, comes on to us. All this...' The cavalry praefect waved a hand in the general direction of the trees and the hills. 'This suits them, not us. They can hit us when they want and melt away into the trees again.'

The general rounded on Pomponius with a glare that could have withered the grass. The cavalry praefect's Adam's apple heaved as he tried to swallow, his throat suddenly arid.

'Pomponius,' the general said in a very low, very even tone that dripped threat with every syllable, 'I hope for your sake you are not suggesting that we simply give up? I am sick of hearing why we can't beat these bastards. What I want to hear is how we can and I expect you men to come up with the answers.'

There was another embarrassed silence. As it became almost unbearable, Agricola gave a cough.

The general raised an eyebrow.

'Tribunus laticlavius, perhaps you have an opinion to voice?'

'Well, sir,' Agricola said, 'it strikes me that we should be making more use of the auxiliaries. Let the alae harry the Silures until we can draw them into open battle where the legion will finish them off.'

Pomponius rolled his eyes and gave an indignant: 'Pshaw!'

'You disagree, Pomponius?' Suetonius said.

'Of course. The Ala Gallorum are elite cavalry, not bandit hunters,' Pomponius said with bluster. 'We win battles; we don't scurry about the woods looking for rebels. I respect the tribune's rank, but at the same time, sir, we must also bear in mind his youth and lack of experience. Matters of tactics should be left in the hands of those with a few more years of service under their belts.'

A half-amused smile flickered across the general's face. He folded his arms and turned back towards Agricola.

'There you go, Tribune,' he said. 'The praefect alae respectfully says you don't know what you are talking about. What is your response to that?'

Agricola felt the challenge, not just from Pomponius, but from the general himself. Suetonius was testing him to see if he had the guts to hold his own among the senior officers.

'My response, sir, is simply to point out the make-up of the auxiliary troops,' Agricola said. 'Most of them are Celtae themselves. Nearly all of the cavalry are Gauls. Some of the auxiliaries are even British, for Mars' sake. They understand how these people fight. Let them do what the Silures are doing to us. Hit them hard and run away again. Keep at it until we draw them out into open battle, but by then it will be in a time and a place of our choosing, when we will have them at our mercy.'

Suetonius nodded, turning down the corners of his mouth to indicate he may have been impressed, or perhaps he was being sarcastic.

'You make a good point, Tribune,' he said. 'And you have come to the same conclusion I had come to myself. We need to draw the bastards out. Provoke them and harass them until they can't take any more and we draw them out to fight in the open. Then we have them.'

All the senior officers, with the exception of Pomponius,

suddenly nodded as if this was what they had been thinking of too.

'I would go further though,' Suetonius said, holding up a forefinger. 'I don't have time to wait around until we finally annoy them enough with conventional tactics that they attempt a battle. We need to be more... provoking. Pomponius, while the camp is broken up you and your men will act as rearguard, then we will set you to work on punitive actions. Villages, farms, crops, settlements – anything you come across no matter how small, I want it destroyed. Burn everything to the ground. Put to the sword their women and children, old people and especially any men of military age. Slaughter them all. We will bring terror to the Silures until they can endure no more and come out to fight.'

The senior officers nodded again. The ruthless logic of the general's plan was obvious. Agricola swallowed.

'Perhaps the tribune will accompany us in these special duties?' Pomponius said. 'I'm sure we could do with the benefit of his extensive experience.'

Suetonius ignored the sarcasm and shook his head. 'I have the special duty I mentioned last night lined up for the tribune and it begins this morning,' he said. 'Agricola, I need you to ride east to Dobunnia on the mission we discussed earlier.'

Agricola bristled. 'Sir: The fight is with the legion,' the young tribune said. 'I don't want to be sent back behind the lines while the rest of the men battle the insurgents.'

Suetonius smiled. 'This is a long war, Tribune,' he said. 'Don't fret if you miss a few of the battles. We will win in the end. I admire your courage, but you still need to appreciate the value of long-term strategy. If you come back with that spear we will win the emperor's favour, which will be much more valuable in the long run. Do not fear. The Silures are just one rebel tribe on this dreadful island. There will be plenty more for you to fight over the next few years.'

Agricola sighed and nodded his acceptance. 'What about the Hibernian – MacAmergin?' he said.

'Ah yes. Pomponius, I need to borrow that Hibernian trooper of yours,' the general said. 'He is to accompany Agricola on this mission.'

The face of the cavalry praefect fell into such a studied expression of grieving that Agricola was unsure that it was not practised.

'Unfortunately, I'm sorry to say that the Hibernian was killed during last night's action.' Pomponius sighed.

The general tutted. 'Gods blast it,' he said. 'He was going to play a key role in my little scheme with that Hibernian queen.'

'He was a damn fine warrior too,' Agricola said. 'It was MacAmergin who alerted us to the attack on the east gate last night.'

'Indeed. He will be a sore loss to the ala,' Pomponius said, shaking his head, sadly.

'Wait a minute,' Agricola said, catching sight of something over the shoulder of the cavalry praefect. At that moment a bedraggled figure in battered cavalry armour, splashed with dried blood, his face smeared with grime, wandered through the opening in the rampart that had been the gate before it was dismantled. He carried a tribune's red cloak rolled up under one arm and a broken spear in the other hand.

The tribune pointed.

'Unless I'm seeing a ghost,' he said. 'Isn't that him?'

Pomponius spun around, a look of complete astonishment on his face.

'No need to look so shocked, Pomponius,' the general said, a faint smile of amusement flickering across his lips. 'You're not the first commander to receive incorrect casualty reports. Anyway, this is excellent. It means we can proceed as originally planned.'

'Trooper. Over here,' Agricola said, raising his voice. Fergus looked around and paused, seeing the top ranks of the legion gathered together. The tribune gestured to him and he approached with some apprehension, raising his hand in a perfunctory salute. All the senior officers noted how lacking in conviction the gesture was. They also noted with distaste the Hibernian's long hair, which had come loose during the battle and now hung down around his shoulders.

'I'm glad you still have my cloak.' Agricola smiled. 'It cost me a fortune, I can tell you.'

'It cost trooper Liscus his life,' Fergus replied, looking hard at Pomponius.

'Another damn fine trooper lost.' The praefect shook his head. Then his face creased into a greasy smile. 'But here's some good news. I was told you were dead, MacAmergin. I'm glad to see that isn't true.'

'Were you now? By who?' Fergus said, eyes narrowed.

Fergus felt his breathing shallow as cold rage pooled in his gut. His arm itched to slam the point of the broken spear into Pomponius's throat, but self-preservation prevailed. If he killed the praefect in cold blood no one would be able to save him, not even the tribune. The senior officers would all fall on him and if he wasn't summarily executed he would surely be crucified later. If there was one crime beyond forgiveness it was assaulting a senior officer. The other thing that stayed his hand was the fact that he knew it was not Pomponius who had shoved the spear through Liscus's back, although he was prepared to bet a considerable sum that the bastard had ordered it. But it was not the praefect who had actually done the deed, and if Fergus killed him now, he would never find out who had.

'It doesn't matter about that now, trooper,' the general interrupted. 'I need you to accompany the Tribune Agricola on a special mission.'

Suetonius went on to describe what the task was to be and Fergus pretended that he had not heard about it the night before from Agricola.

'Are we going on our own?' Fergus said to Agricola when the general had finished.

Before the tribune could answer, Suetonius interrupted. 'The Dobunni are friendly to Rome so once you reach the border of their kingdom you will be fine alone,' he said. 'On top of that an auxiliary cohort of the XX Legion is stationed in their capital. But I will send along a turma of cavalry to escort you to the edge of the kingdom of the Silures. The queen has promised that an escort of her warriors will meet you there to make sure you get to *Corinium Dobunnorum*, their capital. It won't just be the two of you though. This is a diplomatic mission so I will be sending along a religious representative who is skilled in these matters.'

Fergus looked at Agricola and rolled his eyes.

'Not that priest?' he said.

Agricola nodded. 'Yes, I'm afraid so.'

'Well, no need to stand around here gossiping,' Suetonius said. 'You men need to get going.'

As Agricola and Fergus turned to go, the general spoke again.

'Just one more thing, Tribune,' he said.

Agricola turned back to face him once more.

'Sir?'

The general met his questioning expression with a cold glare.

'Don't think this means you are back in my favour,' he said. 'What you did yesterday was gross insubordination. However, perhaps if you are successful in this mission then things will change. If, on the other hand, you don't get that spear, don't bother coming back.'

26

As the legion left the camp, the Ala Gallorum split into four divisions. One rode vanguard to the marching legion, one on either flank and a final one to guard the rear. The Praefect Pomponius had reserved the rearguard section for his own command.

Bonfires blazed as the camp rubbish and everything that could not be carried away but might be of use to an enemy was burned. The rampart had been collapsed to fill in the ditch. Patches of freshly dug earth marked where the Roman dead from the battle had been buried. The British dead lay heaped in a stinking pile to rot. A black cloud of crows had already settled to feast on the bodies.

Pomponius judged that it was time to go. Abandoned legionary camps tended to attract unwelcome attention, and bearing in mind last night's attack, he would prefer to stick close to the rest of the legion. He nodded to the signaller who sounded on his cornu the command to move off. The troopers began to file forwards in the wake of the already departed legion.

Pomponius noticed a rider approaching back along the line. It was one of the scouts sent ahead to prevent surprise attack on the column. The praefect frowned, hoping that this did not mean trouble already.

The scout approached and saluted.

'Yes? What is it?' Pomponius said, returning the salute.

'Sir, there is a Briton wants to see you,' the scout said. 'He rode up to us when we were patrolling, said he needed to speak to the general urgently. We told him the general had already departed with the legion and he insisted on seeing the most senior officer in charge instead.'

'We don't jump at the beck and call of Brittunculi, trooper,' Pomponius said. 'What does he want?'

'He will only talk to you, sir,' the scout said. 'I think this is no ordinary barbarian.'

'Why do you say that?'

'He speaks perfect Latin, sir,' the scout said. 'No wait, not perfect. Not like he has learnt it. He speaks it like a native. A *Roman.*'

'What does this Briton look like?' Pomponius said, narrowing his eyes.

'Like any other of the Brittunculi,' the scout said with a shrug. 'Long hair, going grey. Long moustache. Average build, but a bit smaller than most of them. Wiry though. Sharp face too: prominent nose and little eyes like a rat.'

Pomponius matched the description to the man who had been seen meeting the general a few days before.

'Where is he?' he said.

'He's waiting in the woods,' the trooper said. 'He's a bit cagey. Seems reluctant to be seen by anyone.'

The praefect considered the situation for a few moments.

'He is definitely alone?' he asked.

The trooper nodded.

'Right. Let's go and see what he wants.'

They galloped off, overtaking the cavalry turmae that were proceeding at a more orderly pace along a track through the woods away from the abandoned camp. A little way ahead they came upon the rest of the patrol who waited on the track.

'This way, sir. We must dismount,' the scout said. They got off their horses and he led Pomponius off the track and up an even narrower path that led deeper into the trees.

'You're absolutely sure about this man?' Pomponius said, glancing nervously around at the trees, hedges and undergrowth, all of which could be hiding a horde of Silures just waiting to leap out and cut his throat.

'He's guarded,' the trooper said. 'We took away his weapon as well.'

They entered a little clearing in which stood four very bored-looking troopers, their swords drawn, surrounding a man who looked like any other Celt.

'Salve,' the warrior said in Latin. 'You are the commander?'

Pomponius nodded. 'Who are you and what do you want?'

'I wish to speak to you alone,' the man said, his gaze flicking towards the troopers around him. 'I am a friend of General Suetonius.'

Pomponius considered the situation for a few moments. The man had no weapon, but who knew what these people could do with their bare hands. On the other hand he was alone, and almost certainly a Roman agent. Pomponius was fairly sure he was the one who had recently visited the general. It was his duty as a Roman officer to talk to the man, but he also suspected that some advantage could come his way from this meeting.

'Leave us,' Pomponius said to the troopers. 'Wait for me back at the track.'

The lead scout looked as though he was about to object, but Pomponius silenced him with a glare. They left.

'I'm not a Briton,' the man who looked like one said once the troopers had gone. 'I'm a Roman. My name is Titus Furious Falco and I am a soldier in the army of the empire.'

'You don't look like a soldier,' Pomponius said.

'You think I like looking like a barbarian?' Falco said, anger flaring in his eyes. 'You think I like having long, lice-ridden hair, wearing these ridiculous clothes? Well I don't. I do it for the good of Rome. I am Rome's eyes and ears among the Brittunculi.'

'I have no doubt your duty is a hard one,' Pomponius said, holding out a calming hand. 'But I'm an old-fashioned, regular soldier who likes to confront his enemy wearing my uniform, face to face, not scurrying around behind enemy lines. I like to make it very clear which side I'm on.'

For several moments both men locked gazes that radiated mutual dislike. Finally, Pomponius broke the silence.

'You have a message for me?'

'Not for you,' Falco said with a sneer, 'for the general.'

'I will ensure he gets it.'

'You'd better. You've no idea what I am risking by contacting you like this,' Falco said. 'I've compromised my cover. Your men now know who I am. If word ever gets back to the British, I'm a dead man.'

'Calm down,' Pomponius said. 'There's no reason why

that would happen. Now get on with it. I'm sure you have a human sacrifice or something to get back to.'

Falco narrowed his eyes but did not respond to the provocation. He had made up his mind that the praefect was an idiot on whom he would not waste any more time than he had to.

'I have an urgent message that the general must hear,' he said. 'He was planning to send men to the Queen of the Dobunni to seal a treaty with her and receive a certain spear from her as a sign of good faith.'

Pomponius nodded. 'I know. The Tribune Agricola has already left for Dobunnia.'

'They're walking into a trap,' Falco said. 'I've been travelling among the Dobunni and I've found out that there's a conspiracy against the queen. On top of that, the spear is not what she says it is. You must send men to get Agricola back immediately.'

'What do you mean?' Pomponius said.

'The Dobunni are split between the people in the north, who are pro-Roman, and the southerners who hate us,' Falco said. 'It's a tribal thing that goes back years, centuries probably. You know what these savages are like. The last king, Catti, who the Hibernian woman was married to, tried to unite them by making a southern prince – his cousin, Comux – his second in command. *Tywysog* is their name for it. Anyway, it worked for a time and when Catti died last year Queen Finnabair thought she could consolidate matters by making Comux her consort. What she doesn't know is that Comux was just biding his time. The south was too weak militarily to challenge the north, but now Catti has died without an heir and Finnabair is far from popular, he thinks his time has come. As the most prominent challenger for the Dobunni throne, he believes he can now overcome the south's military weakness by uniting the people in an uprising behind him. He hates us and the Christians and he blames the queen for allowing both into their kingdom. He intends to sweep all from his lands in one blow.'

Pomponius's eyes widened. 'Sounds like trouble.'

'Trouble? That's not the half of it,' Falco said. 'I've found out that there is a conspiracy right across the Brittunculi. The Iceni over in the east are trying to ferment a rebellion against Rome. If it succeeds and all the tribes rise up together, the whole Province of Britannia will be lost. Even four legions won't be able to hold down the whole country. Comux intends to make his move now. He knows the tribune is coming on a diplomatic mission and sees this as a perfect chance to get rid of the queen and strike a blow against Rome. Agricola and anyone with him are riding to their deaths. I've got to let the general know.'

'Don't worry, I will deal with it,' Pomponius said, turning away from the spy.

'I'm not prepared to accept that,' Falco said. 'In my line of work I've learnt to trust no one but myself. I order you to send word to the general, send riders after the Tribune Agricola and get me to Suetonius.'

Pomponius stopped and sighed. His right hand came to rest on the hilt of his spatha. 'How unfortunate,' he said.

'What are you talking about?' Falco said, indignant. 'I hold the rank of tribune in the army. I outrank you. Do what I say or you'll pay for it. Agricola's life depends on it.'

With surprising speed for a man his size, Pomponius ripped his sword from its sheath. In the same movement, he spun round and lunged at Falco. The point of the blade went straight into the agent's mouth, smashing his front teeth backwards and driving up through his soft palate into his skull. Falco's eyes bulged as the sword passed through his brain and broke through the back of his skull. The force of the blow shoved him backwards against a tree as the point of the sword stabbed into the trunk.

Falco tried to shout but all that came out was a strange choking sound. His eyes locked with those of Pomponius and the Gaul could see the consternation and rage in them. It was something that caused him satisfaction. Then a torrent of blood poured down the sword from inside Falco's head, his eyes rolled up and he was dead.

Pomponius tugged the blade back out of both the tree and Falco's skull. The agent's corpse collapsed onto its knees, then pitched forward onto his face, another rush of blood running from his mouth like scarlet vomit onto the forest floor.

Pomponius looked down at the body for a few moments then sheathed his sword. He made his way out of the clearing and back to the track. The scouts who waited for him there looked at the praefect with questioning eyes.

'You are wondering what happened to our friend?' Pomponius said. 'That man, trooper, was a secret agent of Rome. A hero. But his success – and ours – depends on secrecy. Forget you ever saw him. Understood?'

'Understood, sir.'

'Now get me a messenger rider,' the praefect said, the plan for what he must now do already formulating in his mind. 'And get me Decurion Sedullus.'

27

The sun was sinking from a gloriously crimson sky as evening arrived. Insects flitted randomly above the undergrowth and the bark of a fox echoed through the trees that surrounded the little meadow. The black, fast-moving specks that were bats darted to and fro among the trees and around the eaves of a small, square building that sat squarely in the middle of the open ground.

Marcus the priest, Agricola and the troopers from the cavalry turma who had accompanied them on their ride, sat on the ground beside a cooking fire that spat and cracked with the damp wood that had been used to light it. Its smoke drifted up and around them, blowing this way and that in the light breeze, making eyes smart and throats cough. Three leather tents stood nearby and the horses were corralled beside them, happy to be munching the fresh green grass. The saliva-inducing aroma of freshly baked bread filled the air, along with the smell of the garlic and bacon that hissed in the heavy-bottomed frying pan over the fire.

They had ridden east, away from the legion camp and towards the kingdom of the Dobunni, travelling all day until they reached the border between it and the territory of the Silures. As evening approached they had dismounted and set up camp beside the little shrine in the meadow that marked the boundary between the territories of the two tribes.

After the battle of the night before, then the long day of exertion in the saddle, the rest was very welcome and even though they passed around wineskins, it was highly unlikely that a night of carousing around the campfire lay ahead. Exhausted, red-rimmed eyes stared from pale faces at the fire, each man longing for his sleeping mat as soon as he had eaten, and fervently hoping he would not draw the short straw of first guard watch.

The small temple in the middle of the meadow was an octagonal structure made of wood, about forty paces across with a wooden portico around the entrance. The building was surrounded by a small, horseshoe-shaped ditch that ended on either side of the doorway. The faint sound of chanting could be heard from inside and a vague mist of herbal-scented smoke wafted out into the dusk. Now and again faces could be seen peering out of the doorway, keeping a nervous eye on the foreign soldiers camped nearby.

Fergus emerged from the trees on the other side of the meadow, his arms laden with firewood. He ambled across to join the rest of the squad.

'I thought you might be saying your prayers,' Agricola said, nodding towards the temple as Fergus dropped the wood and sat down beside the fire.

Fergus grunted and spat into the fire. His mouth curled into a sardonic sneer.

'No,' he said.

'It seems a strange place to build a temple,' the tribune said. 'Surely this is no-man's land between two kingdoms.'

'It's what the tribes do in Britannia,' Fergus said. 'Its purpose is officially to mark the border without either tribe building a fort or wall. Can you imagine what would happen if each side had warriors stationed here glaring at each other across the field all the time? There would be constant war. So instead of forts they build a temple to mark the border and both kings pay for druids to sit in it and pray all day. It stops them killing each other all the time. Alternatively they put a line of stakes with heads on them.'

'Just having druids here stops kingdoms going to war?' Agricola said.

'Usually, but not all the time,' Fergus said. 'Their spells and threats only work so far. When the tribes really want to go to war nothing will stop them. And then the druids usually lead the way at the head of the army of whichever king pays them more.'

'You don't like them, do you?' Agricola said, handing Fergus a wineskin.

'The British?' Fergus said. 'I've nothing against them. They're just like my own people in many ways. Some of them are the same clans. We speak virtually the same language.'

'No, I mean the druids,' Agricola said.

Fergus cast a contemptuous glance back towards the temple where a pale face still hovered in the gloom just beyond the doorway, warily maintaining its watch.

'No. I don't,' he said and took a long swig of the sour wine. When he finished he belched and let out an appreciative sigh before handing the wineskin back to the tribune. Agricola took it, but his sips were considerably more measured and Fergus smirked at the grimace even that little amount provoked on the young Roman's face. An aristocrat like the tribune, used to the taste of much more refined wines, was bound to find the harsh vinegar the common soldiery drank a tad caustic.

Still, he was impressed by the way the younger man embraced the hardships of military life. Unusually for an officer of such rank, Agricola eschewed the luxuries some others insisted on and mucked in with the rank-and-file soldiers. On an expedition such as this, most of his peers would have brought along at least one body slave as well as their own personal tent. Not Agricola. He had come alone and would sleep with the rest of them in the eight-man *contubernium* tent.

'But how can that be?' Agricola said. 'Druids are the priests of your people. They intercede between you and your gods. I may think old Marcus here is a pompous, judgemental windbag, but I still respect his position as a representative of the College of Fetial priests.'

He patted the old man on the shoulder. Clearly not amused, the priest returned a sour look in his direction but remained silent.

'Without them how do you commune with your gods?' Agricola said.

'What if your god is an evil bastard and all his servants murderous scum? Would you want to commune with him?' Fergus said.

There was an audible gasp from the others around the campfire and many of the troopers hastily spat or made the horned hand gesture to ward off bad luck.

The priest harrumphed. 'Typical barbarian,' he muttered. 'No respect for anything. Not even the gods.'

'Come now,' Agricola said, a half-smile frozen on his face. 'Everyone's gods are capricious. We're just toys to them. You can't take their fickle games personally. They play their games and we play ours. Better to keep them on your side.'

Fergus looked at him for a long moment without making a sound. The tribune proffered the wineskin again and he took it. Aware that all eyes were now directed at him, Fergus took another swig from the wineskin.

'The god of my people – my god,' he said, finally, 'is Crom. Sometimes he is called "Crom Cruach"; also "Crom Dubh", which means Black Crom. Crom the bent, bloody one. He's not just capricious. He is a tyrant. He demands blood as his drink and oh, is he the thirsty one.'

'All gods demand blood. Blood is the price of favour,' the priest said. 'It's part of the agreement with them. I have never heard of this *Crom*, but most of your barbarian gods are simply aspects of our Roman gods under different names. They're the true gods and they all require blood of some kind. In reality this is just an allegory, a symbol of the fact that we must all sacrifice something of our own lives in favour of the way the gods want us to live. You barbarians just don't understand the true nature of sacrifice.'

Fergus shot a suddenly fiery glance in the priest's direction.

'Oh, I understand the nature of sacrifice all right,' he said. 'An *allegory* you say? Everything I held dear was sacrificed to Crom Cruach. *Everything*. Crom is one of the oldest gods in Erin – that's what the people who live there call the island that you call Hibernia. The faith of Crom is the worship of the standing stones and he's been worshipped in Erin since my people and the Sons of Mil arrived there nearly two thousand years ago, probably longer. Long before anyone had even dreamed of Rome and your so-called "true gods".'

Fergus turned his glare away from the priest to the flames of the fire.

'Most Hibernians have forsaken Him for the sun god, Lugh, but his faith clings on in the north,' he continued. 'And in the wild places where the mountains rise at the edge of the vast ocean that marks the end of the world. In the north is a place called Mag Slecht, a rats' nest of druids and their like. There you will find a ring of twelve standing stones – all representing lesser gods – and in the middle is one big one that stands slightly crooked. That is the idol of Crom. The druids and the ancient kings covered it completely in gold. On two days of the year the sun strikes the stone directly. The first time is after the Beltane festival, when the spring comes and life is returning to the fields. On that morning the rays of the rising sun hit the stone and it shines so bright you can see it miles away. And that is a good sign, for Crom brings the harvest. He lets the cows bear milk and allows the fields to bring forth corn. The shining shows he is keeping his promise and the harvest will return.'

'He is a good god, then,' the priest said. 'Without him you all would starve.'

'Good?' Fergus shook his head. 'He's crafty. *Sleekit*. He knows that starvation is the one sure thing that will make any man, no matter how brave, bow the knee and obey his will. He controls the harvest so he controls the people. No one wants to anger him in case next year the crops fail. The sort of man your philosophers would call a "cynic" might even say that it's his druids who understand this truth, and use it to have power over the people.'

'He just wants what's due to him,' the priest said. 'All gods are the same. We owe them our duty.'

'At the end of the year,' Fergus said, 'is the festival of Samhain. Then the harvest has been gathered in, winter is coming and the Great Feast of the Dead is held. The sun strikes that stone again, but this time at sunset. The red light of the setting sun makes the stone glow crimson, and the druids say this shows that Crom is thirsty for blood. When the sun rises the next morning the stone is black, covered with the clotted blood of the sacrifices made over it during the night. This is the price Crom demands for letting the May queen go and returning the harvest in the New Year. Crom demands all our firstborn. Not just animals, but everything, including our children. The druids go through the land at summer's end and collect the firstborn animals and babies born since last Samhain and take them to Mag Slecht for butchery.'

Fergus's words hung heavy in the evening air and for a few moments no one spoke.

'The Carthaginians did the same thing,' Agricola eventually said, breaking the uneasy silence. 'They sacrificed their children in times of need. We put an end to that practice when Scipio destroyed them.'

'Thank Jupiter,' the priest said. 'Human sacrifice is repulsive to the laws of both the gods and Rome.'

'We've done it ourselves in the past, after our defeat by Carthage at the Battle of Cannae,' Agricola said. 'Two Greeks and two Gauls were buried alive as a sacrifice to Dis to ward off further disaster.'

'Dis. Chronos. Saturn. Crom,' Fergus said. 'I'm told that they are all names for the same god. In Britannia they call him "Gwynn".'

'Cannae was nearly three hundred years ago and at a time of direst national emergency,' the priest said. 'We would never resort to that today. We are more civilised.'

'You Romans make gladiators fight to the death for your pleasure and you call it *games*,' Fergus said with a derisive grunt. 'How much more civilised is that?'

'You defend the sacrifice of children?' Agricola said. He looked slightly shocked.

'No I do not,' Fergus said. 'But I've seen enough now of Roman "civilisation" to know you have no right to hold yourselves superior.'

'And yet you joined our army?'

'Don't get me wrong, I prefer Roman hypocrisy to Hibernian superstition,' Fergus said.

'You sacrificed your own child to this Crom?' Agricola said, frowning at the thought.

Fergus was quiet for a moment.

'Not willingly,' he said eventually. 'I had been married less than a year when our first child, a boy, Connor, was born. My wife was a beautiful girl. Nes was her name. She had hair as black as coal. A true Hibernian beauty. When Samhain came we tried to hide our child. The king was scared of the druids and sent his warriors to find Connor. Colphra and MacRoth, the head druids, demanded not just Connor but his mother too. I tried to save them but couldn't fight all of the king's warriors. They killed them both, mother and baby, and poured their blood over Crom's stone. I let it happen. I was beaten and thrown out of Erin, exiled.'

Fergus bowed his head, his voice trailing away as he finished the story.

The soldiers around the fire shifted positions uncomfortably. Agricola cleared his throat.

'What else could you have done?' he said, his voice sounding thick.

'I could have tried to fight them,' Fergus said. 'I could have killed some of them.'

'And what would have been the point?' Agricola said. 'You know what the outcome would have been.'

'Yes. I would've been killed,' Fergus said. 'And it would've made no difference to what happened, I know that. But it doesn't make it any easier. I often wonder if I'd be better off dead. It still keeps me awake at night. Some men don't believe in the gods. To them I say, look what my god did to me. I concede to Crom His greater power, but I vowed from that day on to fight him; to do my utmost to thwart his plans, to deny him his wishes. And the same goes for his lackeys, the druids.'

There were several moments of silence that was both awkward and horrified. Finally, Marcus Flavius broke the quiet.

'Did it work?' he said.

Everyone turned questioning eyes on him.

'Did the sacrifice work?' the priest said. 'Did the god Crom return the harvest once your child was sacrificed?'

Fergus heaved a heavy sigh. He straightened his back and rolled his neck, the stretching vertebrae cracking and clicking as it rotated. He stood up and then looked down at the priest.

His right fist lashed out. It connected with Marcus's jaw, just to the right of his chin. The priest's head snapped back, his eyes rolled up into his head and he toppled over backwards, unconscious.

Fergus turned and walked away, spitting as he went in the general direction of the little temple. At his glowering look, the pale face hovering in the doorway disappeared back into the darkness of the interior.

Agricola watched him go, taking another wincing draught of the sour wine as he did so.

'I think that was a no,' he said.

28

Fergus was woken for his turn at watch in the dead of night by a cold, tired trooper whose pale face loomed above him in the dark of the tent.

'Anything I should be worried about?' Fergus said.

The trooper gave a weary shake of the head. 'Nothing. It's as quiet as the grave. I relieved Lantomarus and he said that a rider passed by round about midnight. There's been nothing since.'

'A rider?' Fergus said, pulling on his chain mail shirt.

'Nothing to be concerned about. Lantomarus said it was one of ours,' the trooper said, dropping his weary body onto the bedroll Fergus had just vacated. 'Rode straight past and headed on towards the Dobunni kingdom. Some sort of messenger he reckoned.'

'How did he know it was one of ours in the dark?' Fergus said.

'How would I know?' the trooper said. 'Probably made too much noise on his way past. The Brittunculi move quietly.'

'Will you two shut up?' an angry voice said from the other end of the tent. 'Some of us are trying to sleep.'

Fergus had made his way out of the tent to begin his

watch. He went to the tethered horses to retrieve his mount, his fingers fumbling with the straps as he tightened the girth. All was quiet in the surrounding forest, but the news continued to bother him. If the rider had followed their path he could only have come from the XIV Legion and why would the general send a messenger to the Dobunni when they were already on their way there? It did not make sense.

The purpose of watch duty was to patrol the area to detect any possible attack before it was on the rest of the troop, so Fergus decided to make his way in the direction that the mysterious rider would have taken.

Mounting his horse, he trotted across the wide meadow, passing the silent, dark temple and heading for the gap in the trees on the other side where the track continued into the woods. The rider would by now have a long head start so he had no chance of catching him, but at least he could investigate, just in case something unpleasant was coming back their way from that direction.

The night was clear. Stars and a waxing moon cast a strong silver light over the countryside; it was enough to see by and even cast shadows. Fergus decided to take a gamble and go further away from the campsite than he probably should have. The track continued through a wooded area for some time then opened up into a plain that stretched as far as the eye could see. It was dotted with low, hump-backed hills and he was on the edge of one of them affording him a view of the moonlit landscape. A wide, open field lay beneath him; in the distance, some miles away, more trees covered the ground.

Fergus judged that this was a good place from which

to watch. He swung himself out of the saddle and settled down to see if anything happened.

A rather boring, cold time passed during which nothing more interesting than the odd cry of a fox disturbed the quiet. Far off in the woods the howls of wolves echoed through the dark, reminding Fergus that he needed to keep a watch all around, not just on the land below. Eventually the sky began to brighten and the sun pushed itself above the horizon. In the cold light of dawn, Fergus rubbed his sore eyes and decided he had waited long enough. It was probably well past the time he should be back at the campsite. He was exhausted and perhaps there would be time to grab some sleep before they went on their way again.

He had just climbed into the saddle when movement caught his eye. He squinted down the hill to the meadow below. On the far side of it, horsemen emerged from the woods. They were too far away to make out any details, but Fergus could see shields and spears glinting in the pale light of the sun. Clearly they were warriors and as they came nearer, he counted eleven of them. They rode out into the meadow then stopped, coalescing into a brief huddle for a moment.

Three riders split off from the group and headed off to the west. The other eight warriors began riding again, crossing the plain in the direction of the hill on which Fergus waited.

Fergus drew back in case they spotted him, pondering what was going on. The obvious answer when you saw a bunch of warriors divide was some sort of ambush, but in this case there were not enough in the breakaway group to make an effective flank attack. The tribune had mentioned that they were to be met by an escort of the Dobunni and he guessed that this was probably it. What the other three were up to was a mystery, but not one he judged to be worth worrying about now. Turning his horse he galloped back towards the camp.

As he returned across the meadow past the temple to the campsite, he was met by Agricola who galloped out to meet him. Fergus reined his horse to a stop.

'What in the name of Hades do you think you're playing at?' Agricola said. 'You should have been back here long ago! After that speech of yours last night we all thought you'd deserted. You strike a fetial priest and then, when you are supposed to be on guard, you disappear into the woods. I could have you beaten for this.'

Fergus was surprised at how angry the Roman was. Beneath his tan his face was pale, his brown eyes glared and he jutted his chin out in the same way he had when faced with the charging bull a couple of days before.

'I had good reason to go into the woods, sir,' Fergus said, then related what had happened during the night and what he had seen at dawn.

'All right,' Agricola said, some of his anger abating. 'I agree there's something odd about that messenger. If he was from the general he would've been ordered to relay the message to us on the way.'

'What about the band of warriors?' Fergus said. 'They're heading our way.'

'That is most probably our escort to Corinium Dobunnorum,' Agricola said. 'The Queen of the Dobunni is sending her most trusted warriors, some of her own bodyguard, to make sure we make it to her palace without incident. That's why you're here, remember? They will be the Hibernians who travel everywhere with her. When they arrive keep quiet, don't let them know you are one of them. That way they'll feel free to talk in their own language and you can hopefully learn a bit about the queen's true intentions.'

'Understood,' Fergus said. 'Though I'm not "one of them", as you put it. My guess is that they're from the Laigin tribe.'

'But you speak the same language?'

'Near enough.'

'Right. We need to break camp and get ready to ride.'

Agricola grasped the reins of his horse and turned its head but as Fergus made to follow, the tribune leaned over and grabbed him by the forearm.

'I'm warning you, MacAmergin,' he said, locking eyes with Fergus. 'No more of this insubordination. During the attack on the legion's camp the night before last that captive druidess got free. It's assumed that some of her countrymen freed her when they broke into the camp, but one of the carcer guards swears that an auxiliary cavalry trooper was involved.'

'What's that got to do with me?' Fergus said. He met Agricola's gaze coolly.

'By coincidence you were in that area of the camp, otherwise you would not have spotted the surprise attack from the east,' Agricola said. 'If I find out you had something to do with her escape, I'll make sure you face full military justice. Understood? You may be important to this particular mission, but you aren't irreplaceable.'

Fergus did not reply, but held the gaze of the tribune for a few moments longer.

'You need to decide whose side you are on, trooper,' Agricola said finally, spurring his horse forward with a lot more force than was required.

29

A thick pall of smoke drifted through the trees from the burning village. Voracious flames crackled and spat as they destroyed the wattle-and-daub roundhouses, their thatched roofs succumbing to the fires quickly and releasing roiling black clouds that were driven by the wind into the nearby forest then up into the sky.

Here and there on the ground lay corpses. Men, women and children cut down by Roman cavalry spathas as they ran in panic. They had been left to die where they fell. A cart laden with their dead pigs, the village's livestock, stood a safe distance from the blazing buildings, its mules waiting patiently between the shafts.

Decimus Julius Masivo spat in disgust and contemplated that if nothing else came out of their day's work, the pigs would at least ensure the troopers would eat well tonight. Not that they had been forced to work hard for their supper. The detachment of Roman cavalry had swooped on the British village from the track that ran through the woods, taking everyone by surprise. They made one pass through the houses, cutting down anyone within range. The villagers who escaped the Roman swords fled in panic to their fort for protection.

The so-called fort was a pathetic circle ditch with a rampart behind it, surmounted by a wooden palisade fence. It was barely forty paces across, designed as a simple defensive position that the villagers could run to in the event of an attack. It was sufficient only to cope with the hit-and-run tribal raids they were used to. British warriors wanted to get in and out as fast as possible, so when attacked the villagers had only to wait behind their fort's defences until the enemy tribe took what they came for – livestock and anything of value that was easily carried – and rode away again.

This time it was different. The average British raiding party did not have Decimus Julius Masivo and his war machines.

They had trundled into the village in the wake of the cavalry: four mule-drawn carts accompanied by Masivo and his crew of specially trained legionaries. While the troopers went about setting the houses ablaze, the carts were manoeuvred into positions around the fort, just beyond the range of the javelins and slingshot stones launched by the defenders from behind the ramparts. Then, efficiently, methodically, the Romans began their killing work.

Masivo hated these punitive operations. He was a soldier whose job was to confront the enemies of Rome in open battle, man to man. This was just terrorism: slaughtering innocents to punish the tribe for daring to rebel. There was not even anyone left behind to put up a decent fight. The young men were away fighting with the Silures' war band, so only old men and boys were left with the women and babies of the village. It was all such a waste, not least because the Brittunculi would have fetched a decent price on the slave markets. Now they were all dead.

Masivo was not just any soldier, however. He was a *supernumerarius* in the legion, meaning he was an officer with special functions. In his case an *architectus* – a highly trained engineer and a specialist in artillery – a skilled job in which he took great pride. He and his men had recently received special instruction in a brand-new innovation: a smaller and lighter form of the standard army ballistae.

He had spent years working with that huge iron and wood torsion weapon. Resembling a giant crossbow, the great beast was usually set up in emplacements where batteries of them, operated by crews of men, could rain huge, iron-tipped missiles down on an enemy over great distances. It was a devastating weapon but not very dynamic. If the enemy moved out of their way, the ballistae could not hit them anymore. A veteran of several such situations, Masivo had been particularly impressed to discover that advances in technology had allowed the construction of a version built from materials that made it light and small enough to be loaded onto a specially constructed cart. The new version was now highly manoeuvrable.

With a spring mechanism and skeins made entirely of metal, these new ballistae were almost as powerful as the full-size device but only required a team of three soldiers to operate each one with a fourth to keep the mules in check. It was still in the experimental stage, but given the nature of warfare in Britain, the army hierarchy had thought it would be of particular use there and so had issued a few to the XIV Legion on a trial basis.

Once the village was ablaze, the troopers settled down

to pass the time rolling dice while Masivo's teams began firing the ballistae into the fort. Iron bolts smashed through the palisade and the gate, each one cutting straight through both the wooden defences and the flesh and bone of anyone on the other side unlucky enough to be in its path. At such short range, some of the projectiles passed right through the fort and burst out of the fence on the far side. The air was filled with a constant rattle and snap of the weapon being loosed, the crack of splitting wood, screams from inside the fort as the bolt tore through bodies, then the ratcheting of the weapon being cranked back into the firing position. As one of the troopers remarked, it was like shooting fish in a pond. The Britons could not even hit back. All they could do was cower behind their inadequate defences and wait for the end.

Eventually, realising that their situation was hopeless, a tall elder of the village with a mane of silver hair, raised himself above the parapet and appealed for mercy. Masivo's orders had been clear: 'No prisoners'.

The stunningly accurate ballista was trained on the man then loosed. The cavalry troopers gave a derisory cheer as the bolt struck the old man mid-chest and his shoulders and head disappeared in a pink mist. With the message clearly delivered that there would be no surrender accepted, the ballista teams resumed their work.

Masivo guessed that about thirty people had fled into the fort. From the cries of the wounded he calculated over half of them had been hit by ballista bolts. Soon it would be safe enough for the troopers to rush in and finish the whole sordid business. He surveyed his men with a grim sense of pride, satisfied that even in this unpleasant, murderous work they continued to operate in a calm, well-disciplined and professional manner.

Turning at the sound of horses approaching, Masivo saw a new turma of cavalry in full battle armour riding up the track towards him into the remnants of the devastated village. The grime, soot, blood and gore that smeared their clothes and horses showed they too had been engaged on a punishment mission to another of the nearby Silures villages.

He squinted through the smoke and recognised the lead horseman as Decurion Sedullus, a jumped-up rich boy of a Gaul whom he did not like at all. In all honesty, Masivo was not that fond of many of the auxiliaries, even the officers. He may have had a dirt-poor upbringing, but at least he came from generations of men who had fought for Rome, every last one of them citizens. These Gauls were a mere generation away from living in mud huts, much like the savages they were fighting here in Britannia, yet they strutted about as if their forefathers had all been senators.

Sedullus rode up and pulled off his helmet.

'Salve,' he said, raising a salute. 'We need a couple of your machines.'

Masivo raised an eyebrow. 'Oh do you? Well you're out of luck. Can you not see they are all busy right now?'

'Not these ones. There are four spare in the legion's baggage train that are not in use,' Sedullus said. 'These are the orders of the praefect. He wants them deployed in support of another punitive action west of here. It's a special mission.'

'I'm sorry, Decurion, but I cannot spare any crews to man them,' Masivo said. 'We have our own orders to fulfil.'

'We have some legionaries trained in the standard ballista. They will be able to handle the work,' Sedullus said. His tone of voice suggested he was reciting words that he had learnt by rote, which was highly likely, thought Masivo. Sedullus's commanding officer, realising how thick the man was, had probably rehearsed him in exactly what he was to say.

'These are not standard ballistae, Decurion—' Masivo began.

'These are the orders of the praefect!' Sedullus cut him off, impatience and anger flaring in his eyes. We have a job to do and all I need from you is the watchword to authorise me to take those weapons from the baggage train. Now, are you going to detain me further or do I have to let the praefect know that you are refusing to obey his commands?'

Masivo tutted, then straightened up, pushing out his chest.

'No need for that,' he said. 'I just need you to tell me Pomponius's watchword first so that I know this order comes from him. Standard procedure, as you know.'

'Spartacus,' Sedullus said, with an unpleasant smile reflecting a petty sense of triumph at getting his own way.

Masivo recognised that day's watchword as the correct one.

'Very well,' he said. 'Our watchword is *Marius*. And where are you taking my ballistae?'

'As I said, it's a special mission,' Sedullus said. 'I can't tell you the details.'

With that he replaced his helmet, turned his horse and galloped away, followed by his turma.

Masivo watched them go, wondering just what the man

was up to. The watchword had been correct, which meant the order was a legitimate one. Knowing Gaulish cavalrymen they were probably engaged in some death-or-glory exploit, but without proper training in the new weapons Sedullus could well end up shooting himself instead of the enemy.

As he turned back to his own bloody work, Masivo privately hoped that he would.

30

The promised escort from the Dobunni met Agricola's company shortly after they started on their journey. Eight of Queen Finnabair's Hibernian bodyguards rode out of the woods and agreed watchwords were exchanged. After the uneasy introductions were completed the cavalry turma who had accompanied Agricola's band on the journey so far turned back to rejoin the XIV Legion.

The company that continued on to Corinium Dobunnorum consisted of the Tribune Agricola, the priest, Fergus and the Hibernian bodyguards.

Fergus did as he was told. He took his place in the company beside Agricola and was careful that the few words he said were in Latin. As they rode he listened to the conversation of the bodyguards. They were taciturn enough but now and again they passed some comments between them.

All eight of them wore thick black bearskins around their torsos over the finest of chain mail. Their bronze helmets, round on the skull with a long neck guard in the Gaulish fashion, shone in the early summer sunshine. On one arm each man bore a shield with a four-legged, swirling spiral design painted on it, and in the other hand he held a heavy, leaf-bladed spear.

It took most of the day to get to their destination. As they rode, the landscape of the kingdom of the Silures – with its forests, rugged hills and deep valleys – gradually gave way to the undulating hills and wide planes of Dobunnia. A broad river, named after the goddess Sabrina, meandered its way through a wide, open valley.

Fergus could see that the Kingdom of the Dobunni was rich and fertile. Vast plains of arable land stretched as far as the eye could see. Fergus could understand why the Dobunni would not want the Roman army stomping all over them and why they would do any sort of deal, accept any conditions, to avoid that and preserve their position and way of life. At least some of them, anyway: the privileged ones with the most to lose, Fergus reflected, observing the teams of slaves who toiled at ploughing and sowing the fields, overseen by their Dobunni taskmasters. Like the tribes of his homeland, the Britons were as enthusiastic at the practice of slavery as the Romans. For the poor bastards who worked in the fields, it probably did not matter if the man standing over them was a native taskmaster or a Roman one.

They saw their final destination from miles away. It rose up from the flat plain: a massive, flat-topped hill that dominated the landscape. As they got closer they could make out the defensive sculpting of the hilltop. Ditches and ramparts ringed the summit. Palisade fences surmounted the ramparts and at one end of the hilltop was a massive gateway, the trackway leading into it cut deep into the slope of the hillside.

'Caesar would have called that an *oppidum* in Gaul,' Agricola said for the benefit of Marcus the priest. 'It's a hill fort, but also the administrative centre of their kingdom. It's the main settlement and their capital.'

At the base of the hill was a building site. Overseen by specialist builders, several large buildings were being constructed by an army of slaves. The biggest, both in terms of floor size and height, looked to be near completion. It was still masked in scaffolding, but its brick-built walls were finished to a height of two storeys and the red, clay-tiled roof was already in place. Workmen on the wooden scaffolding were applying a white facing of lime to the exterior walls over the brickwork. The columns around the entranceway marked out the design as Roman. The next largest building was square and without a roof, its walls only half built. The third building was still in its early stages, but the amount of excavation that had been done for its foundation revealed an extensive underfloor heating system and deep pits that could only be bathing pools.

'If I'm not mistaken that's a Roman villa, a temple and a bathhouse they're building,' Marcus the priest said, pointing at the building work as they rode past. 'Is there a governor here?'

'No. Just an auxiliary cohort of the II Legion: Tungrians,' Agricola said. 'Their commander would not have the wealth to build that sort of palace.'

They rode past the construction site and up onto the sloping road that led to the impressive gates of the hill fort. The road climbed around the contour of the hillside, flanked on one side by a rampart topped with a palisade that allowed defenders to rain down missiles on anyone hostile approaching the entrance. As it neared the top of the hill the road became a deep cleft cut into the hillside with ramparts on both sides, finally ending in a massive pair of wooden gates. These sat between two defensive towers, which were connected by a walkway that ran across the top lintel of the gates, thus providing another position from which anyone approaching the gates could be attacked.

That morning, the formidable defences were open and a crowd was gathered around the entrance, clearly to welcome the Roman party. Men and woman of the Dobunni nobility waited, all of them dressed in fine clothes, the men in woollen breeches and multicoloured, knee-length tunics belted at the waist. The women wore long dresses, similarly multicoloured and woven in the square, criss-crossed manner that reminded Fergus of the fashions of his homeland. Both men and women wore long, woollen cloaks that were swept back and fastened at their left shoulders by large, impressive, gold and silver brooches that shone in the sunlight. A collection of musicians had gathered there as well. Two men bearing carnyx – the great boar-headed Celtic war trumpets – blasted out notes that echoed across the hillside. Drums were beaten and a couple of men playing harps vainly tried to be heard above the discordant cacophony.

In the middle of it all stood the queen. Her long black hair was curled and tumbled around her shoulders. Unlike her compatriots she wore a *stola*: a short-sleeved, long white tunic that reached to the ground. The bottom hem of the stola was decorated by a wide, colourful border of a dark crimson, almost purple, key-style pattern. Over the stola she wore a *palla*: a wide cloak that wrapped around her body and was draped over one shoulder. It was the female equivalent of the Roman man's toga.

At the sight of this, Fergus heard the priest audibly catch his breath.

'By Jupiter!' he exclaimed, his tone of voice expressing both shock and disapproval.

'Easy, Pater,' Agricola said in a low voice, 'the queen is perfectly entitled to wear those clothes. The royalty of client Roman states are given citizenship so can wear the clothing of a citizen.'

Fergus hid a smile as the priest tutted, sighing at what he clearly saw as the disgraceful sight of a barbarian in Roman dress.

'Salve,' the queen greeted them in good Latin. 'Welcome to my home and the Kingdom of the Dobunni.'

Beside the queen stood the young man with long, curly dark hair who had been with her in the legion encampment a few days before. Though dressed in finery, his hair and moustache neatly combed, he looked no less surly than he had then and he met the newcomers with an arrogant, almost confrontational stare.

'I am Queen Finnabair,' the queen said. 'And this is my prince, Comux.'

She made a gracious gesture to the young man.

Fergus regarded Comux and surmised immediately that he represented trouble. Letting his eyes wander beyond the queen and her prince, he looked around to check the situation they were in. Behind the welcoming committee, the flat top of the hill inside the ring of ramparts was covered in buildings. A huge roundhouse with a conical thatched roof stood at one end of the enclosure. Many other similar but smaller buildings, typical British dwellings, were dotted around, along with fences and pens for animals, mostly pigs and goats.

Everywhere he could see Dobunni tribespeople, both men and women, going about their daily business. Some tending the animals, others making bread or washing clothes. Women were spinning, men practising with weapons, while around their feet numerous children played. The oppidum was huge. Hundreds, if not thousands of people could live in the enclosed space on the hilltop, which was comparable in size to a modest Roman town.

At the far end of it were the unmistakable regular, whitewashed walls of a Roman army fortification. Above it fluttered the banner of the Second Cohort of Tungrians. A fort within a fort, the soldiers had obviously been stationed right among the tribal capital in order to keep a close eye on them. While their quarters were in one corner of the larger interior of the hill fort, there was a clear separation between it and any neighbouring native building.

A large parade and drill square had been marked out before the front gate of the Roman fort. This flattened area served several purposes. Primarily it was intended for practising military manoeuvres and marching, but by doing this in full view of the locals it also served as a continual reminder of the discipline and professional capabilities of the Roman soldiers in their midst, which would help keep them in their place. Lastly, from a purely practical point of view it provided a wide, clear space between the walls of the Roman fort and the tribes' many buildings and enclosures, making it difficult for anyone to sneak up on the Romans from the front, while at the rear, the rampart of the small fort butted against the inside of the massive southern rampart of the hill fort itself.

'I see you have spotted our lodgers,' the queen said with a smile. 'The Dobunni are friends of Rome, and we like to keep our friends close by.'

'Keep your friends close and your enemies closer still,' Agricola muttered, then in a louder voice: 'Thank you for your gracious welcome, my lady. We are glad to be here.'

'You are most welcome,' the queen said. 'What do you think of my new villa?'

'That's yours?' Agricola said. He was clearly impressed. 'When it's finished it will be a splendid mansion and the height of fashion. It would not look out of place in Rome herself.'

'Unfortunately, however, it is not yet finished,' the queen said, her eyes demurely downcast, 'so I regret that the welcome banquet we have planned for you must be in the old chieftain's house.' She wafted a dismissive hand in the direction of the large roundhouse. 'I can only apologise that a man of your rank, a tribune of the Roman senatorial class, must endure such primitive surroundings.'

'I'm sure it is more than sufficient,' Agricola said.

'Of course it is,' Prince Comux said with a frown. 'It was good enough for my uncle and generations of Dobunni royalty before him. I'm sure it is good enough for you.'

His tone was provocative and both men locked eyes in what was an unmistakable moment of mutual challenge.

'Comux, my dear, show some respect for our guests,' the queen said, flashing a flirtatious glance at Agricola from under her eyelashes. 'Now come along, Senator, you must be tired after your journey. Come and relax with us before the feast.'

'I will, Your Highness,' Agricola said, 'but first I must report to the commander of the Tungrian *cohortes*. The general expects me to report my arrival.'

The queen's smile took on a fixed aspect. The light of it dissolved from her eyes.

'Don't worry about that,' she said. 'We can send messengers to him.'

'I'm sorry, Your Majesty, but it is military procedure,' Agricola said. 'I must report in person.'

A flash of irritation passed across the queen's face, but Fergus could see she was at pains to hide it, masking it with a faux smile. Comux, on the other hand, did not bother to hide his expression of genuine disdain.

'I hope I've not caused offence,' Agricola said. 'But I have standing orders I must obey. I trust you understand? It shouldn't take too long.'

The queen nodded and her obsequious smile broadened, but Fergus noted that it did not reach her eyes.

'Of course I understand,' she said. 'If there is one thing that has made the Roman Empire great it is discipline. Go and make your report, but hurry back to us.'

Agricola saluted and bowed his head to show his gratitude. Looking round at Fergus and the priest, he indicated they were to follow then spurred his horse in the direction of the little Roman fort. Marcus Flavius rode after him. Fergus brought up the rear, glad to be getting away, if only momentarily, to the relative safety of a Roman army installation.

Something about the situation at the hill fort was making Fergus feel very uneasy, though he could not put his finger on what. Glancing over his shoulder he spotted the queen's smile drop from her face the moment Agricola's back was turned as she shot a look at her lapdog prince that set his teeth on edge.

Diplomatic protocol be damned. General Paulinus should have allowed them to bring an escort of their own.

31

Gaius Suetonius Paulinus was in a much happier mood. The legion had settled down for the night in a new marching camp. This time he had personally supervised the standing of the pickets outside the camp, inspected the sentries guarding the ramparts and organised the pattern and the roster that the patrols would follow through the night as they ranged through the woods and meadows outside the perimeter of the camp.

He was determined there would be no repeat of the shambles of the previous evening. No Brittunculi would get within a mile of the camp without being spotted. Not just spotted. He had given strict orders that any native encountered was to be killed on the spot. No questions asked. As an extra measure the senior officer who had been in charge of camp security the night before had been brought to the praetorium at the centre of the camp. Before the assembled legion he had been stripped of his arms and toga and flogged as an example to the others of what would happen to anyone who failed in his duty.

Suetonius was reasonably confident that this had had the desired effect. The senior officers were downright shocked that one of their number had been so brutally treated and punished like a common soldier. The general was happy that they would now be much more conscientious in their duty, and that each one of them would exert downward pressure on the rank below him to do the same, who would in turn transfer that imperative, right down to the lowliest foot soldier. Thus each one of them would do his job with the utmost diligence because they all knew what would happen if they did not.

Sitting in his folding chair outside his tent, the general regarded the blood-splattered post that stood about twenty paces away, to which the shamed officer had earlier been tied. Discipline was the key to victory, of that Suetonius was convinced. And complete victory was the only outcome he would allow. Completing the conquest of Britannia was a vital step in a bigger game he had to play, a contest that stretched well beyond the shores of this provincial backwater, namely his rivalry with Gnaeus Domitius Corbulo.

Suetonius took a sip of wine and thought about the pompous, self-promoting General Corbulo. He was currently the darling of Rome, her most vaunted hero. Paulinus believed he deserved that position more than Corbulo. What was the bastard up to now? Hopefully he had got himself killed on some glory-hunting mission. No, not killed. That would be too easy. Better by far if he met with some horrendous disaster. A consummate defeat at the hands of the Parthians would be good. Something that resulted in his return in disgrace to Rome, to live out whatever remained of his existence in misery and ignominy.

There had been a time when Romans spoke of no one but him: Gaius Suetonius Paulinus. He had been the first Roman to cross the Atlas Mountains. He had subdued the tribes on the other side of them and extended the boundaries of the empire into lands previously unknown. For a time he had been the hero of Rome. Then Corbulo, damn him, had gone adventuring into Germania, quelling rebellions by the Cherusci and Chauci, and the fickle Romans had switched their adulation to him. When Suetonius was appointed Governor of Britannia, the empire's newest and most dangerous posting, he had expected that all the attention would return to him. And so it should have, except that Corbulo, then posted in the East, had started a war against Parthia. The man was fighting and winning not just battles, but the adulation of the masses back in Rome.

Suetonius bit his lower lip. Thanks to Corbulo, his own achievements were yesterday's news. He had every intention, however, of being the man of tomorrow. He had a plan and if it worked no one would talk of Corbulo anymore. When he had accepted the post in Britannia many had been surprised, puzzled even. They had whispered behind hands that this would be the end of his career if not the death of him. Britannia was the worst posting in the empire. There had been four Roman governors here so far, and half of them had died in office. Since the Emperor Claudius had invaded the damned island twenty years ago, the chances of achieving further glory were slim. Although Britannia's rich mines were important to Rome's economy, the work here was not in conquering new territories, unknown lands and exotic, wild peoples, as Corbulo was doing, but putting down insurgent natives who were old news to the people back home.

Step one of Suetonius's plan was doing just that. He would stamp out the remaining rebellious tribes in the west. First the Silures and when they were put down it would be safe to strike north to conquer their insubordinate neighbours, the Ordovices. Once that was complete the whole of Britannia would be finally pacified under the legions; while to the north, the Roman client kingdom of the Brigantes could provide a buffer against the lunatic savages who dwelt in the bogs and mountains of the northern wastes.

Some glory would come of this. He would have achieved what no other Roman governor had done and pacified Britannia, but Suetonius had no intention of stopping there. At the north-east corner of the kingdom was a large, fertile island that the Britons called 'Mona'. Spies had identified this island as not only the bread basket for the whole area, but a rats' nest of druids. It was some sort of headquarters or college for them and Suetonius knew that Nero would be more than happy if he wiped them out. That was not the only aim in capturing Mona though. A century before, Caesar himself had recognised the strategic importance of that island, not just for Britannia, but as a jumping-off point from which armies could be launched at the one last country remaining beyond the realms of the empire: Hibernia.

Conquer Hibernia and the name of Gaius Suetonius Paulinus would be back on everyone's lips and his place in history would be secure. Once he held Mona he would have the point to attack from. By his side he would have a wronged Hibernian queen, Finnabair, and she would provide the justification. Some story would be constructed of how she was being denied her birthright in her homeland, and this would legitimise sending a Roman army over to right the wrong. His fame would be restored and no one would speak any more of that damn fool Corbulo.

The general took another sip of wine and contemplated his strategy as he sat in the glow of the setting sun, occasionally raising a hand to slap away the midges attracted by the scent of oil on his face. He narrowed his eyes at the sight of the overweight figure of Titus Pomponius Proculianus, the praefect of the Gaulish cavalry, who was ambling towards him. The thought crossed his mind that if he was going to achieve his aims he still had a fair amount of work to do in toughening up his troops.

Pomponius saluted. 'I am here to deliver my report, sir,' he said.

Suetonius returned the salute and nodded for him to proceed. The praefect outlined the day's work his cavalry units had performed, a litany of atrocities from burned villages to destroyed crops, looted farms and slaughtered innocents.

The general listened with satisfaction. Unpleasant as it was, every settlement destroyed, every child murdered and woman raped was another blatant provocation for the Silures warriors. Sooner or later the pain and affront would become too great. They would not be able to hold back and they would attack. Even if their leaders were cold-blooded enough to curb their instincts, the demand for revenge from their warriors would be too great to refuse. The Silures' war band would come out of their hiding places in the woods or mountains or wherever they were and there would be an open battle.

Then he would have them. The Brittunculi might be able to cause damage by hitting and running away, but no one could defeat a Roman legion in open battle.

'Any casualties on our side?' Suetonius said.

'None, sir,' Pomponius said, adding with a broad grin: 'Some of the lads are a bit shagged out though.'

Suetonius's scowl revealed his distaste at the vulgarity, but before he could respond Pomponius's face became serious.

'I'm sorry to say that we lost some equipment, however,' he said. 'Four of the new experimental ballistae fell into enemy hands.'

Suetonius sat bolt upright in his chair. '*What?*'

'A turma was taking them to provide artillery support for attacking a village stronghold,' Pomponius said. 'They ran into an ambush on the way. Severely outnumbered, they had to retreat in a hurry. Unfortunately they were forced to leave the ballistae behind. By the time they returned with reinforcements, the weapons had disappeared. The mission was completed and the village wiped out, but there was no sign of the ballistae.'

'I want them back, Pomponius,' the general said, getting up from his chair. 'The last thing we need is British tribesmen armed with Roman long-range weaponry. Tomorrow your men are to carry on with their punitive actions, but you are to make it your personal objective to find those weapons and bring them back. See to it. Now go. Goodnight.'

Pomponius nodded again and saluted, then turned and left the general. As he walked away a smile crossed his lips. He was more than happy to be given this mission. He knew exactly where the ballistae had gone. More than that, this task would give him the opportunity he needed to clear up a few loose ends too.

32

'The queen's love of all things Roman is mostly due to the desperation of her situation, rather than any respect for our culture,' Quintus Flavius Valens, the commander of the Tungrian auxiliaries, said.

He took another heavy gulp of wine, resting both elbows on the rough wooden table as he regarded his visitors. He had the haggard, dark-eyed expression of a man whose nerves had been under too much strain for far too long.

They were sitting in the small whitewashed room that served as the officers' mess for the small Roman fort within the walls of the larger Dobunni hill fort at Corinium Dobunnorum. When they had been admitted through the gates, Fergus had been dismayed by the meagre number of soldiers who manned the fortification. Taking a quick tally of the men on the gate, the ramparts and around the parade square, he totted up about fifty soldiers. Allowing for some being away on patrol, the complete strength of the garrison could not be much more than about eighty men, or one century.

'I thought there was supposed to be a cohort here,' Fergus said from the corner of his mouth to Agricola. 'There's not even enough men to make up a *maniple*.'

He saw the concern on the face of the tribune also. Eighty soldiers would not be much use if the horde of surrounding British tribesmen decided to turn on them.

'I was under the impression that there were a few more soldiers here,' Agricola said with an uneasy smile.

'I only wish there were, Agricola,' Valens said with a bitter laugh. 'I have to spread my men across four forts. I'm expected to hold down a kingdom with little more than a cohort: five hundred men. And auxiliaries to boot – barbarians like the bastards outside the walls – not even actual Roman legionaries. It's a joke.'

He shot a sideways glance at Fergus. Realising he had probably been rather indiscreet, he took a swig of what was already his second cup of wine.

'Why don't you report your concerns to your commander?' Agricola said, his own wine cup still untouched on the table before him. 'You're aligned to the II Legion aren't you?'

'Of course I have done that,' Valens said. 'The II are down in Isca Dumnoniorum in the Kingdom of the Dumnonii. I raise the issue in every single report I send to the legate there, but he cannot spare any men. We've received intelligence that the Dumnonii are about to revolt so the legion must stay down there. The Dobunni are considered friendly and allies of Rome so my forces will not be augmented.'

'You disagree with that assessment?' Agricola said.

'Not entirely,' Valens said as he refilled his cup. 'I understand that with General Suetonius launching the campaign against the Silures with the XIV Legion, every man is needed in holding down the rest of the country and that troops must be deployed where there is most need. On the face of it the Dobunni are on our side, but it's a very precarious alliance and it depends very much on individual people, the queen in particular. If one factor changes the balance of power, they'll turn on us and there won't be much I can do with a century sitting right in the middle of their capital. You can guess who'll be the first ones they'll hit.'

'You think the Dobunni would overthrow their queen?' Agricola said.

'Since her husband, the old king, died last year the queen has been desperate to hold on to power,' Valens said. 'She's a foreigner here. She's not popular and she is cultivating alliances with anyone who can help keep her on the throne. On top of that she's put the kingdom up to its ears in debt to a Roman money lender – Lucius Seneca of all people – to build that palace at the foot of the hill. Not a popular move, I can tell you. The Brittunculi don't like paying taxes to pay for symbols of their own subjugation. Can you blame them? But she's gambling that by showing how loyal she is to Rome and how keen she is to embrace our culture, we'll recognise her as a valuable ally, protect her and invest soldiers to keep her in power.'

Agricola scratched his chin, uncomfortably aware of the day's stubble that had grown on their journey.

'That could be a big mistake,' he said. 'Rome will only support a ruler who will bring advantage. If she can't hold down the kingdom by herself then Rome won't prop her up. If we have to commit troops to keep her in power then we may as well invade and make the place a province instead of a client kingdom.'

'That's only part of her worries,' Valens said. 'The Dobunni are divided amongst themselves. Until about a century ago when a royal marriage united them, they were actually two different tribes who had been at war with each other since time immemorial. Now the old differences between north and south are starting to show again. The queen thinks that by taking Comux – a southerner – as her consort she can reunite the kingdom, but I think she's made another mistake. He's an arrogant, insolent little prick who hates Rome. She thinks by marrying him she can control him and with him the anti-Roman faction in her kingdom. I think she is letting a wolf into her house. Then there are religious problems—'

'Ah,' Agricola said, raising a finger. 'That's partly why we are here. General Suetonius believes the queen can give us a spear sacred to the Christian sect in return for us supporting her.'

'I don't know about a spear,' Valens said, frowning. 'But there are definitely Christians in the kingdom. How they've got here Jupiter alone knows. They've one of their temples built down in the Vale of Avalon and the queen definitely courts a couple of their leaders. She thinks we don't know, but informers tell us what's going on.'

'Is the queen one of these Christians, do you think?' Agricola said.

Valens shook his head with a derisive grunt. 'Her? A Christian? I doubt it,' he said. 'There would be too much self-sacrifice involved. No it's the same old story. She sees that they have a foothold in the kingdom and a growing power base, so she is courting them. Perhaps so she can steal this spear from them. There is very little you can teach this woman about the art of politics. She's a born survivor, but I think Fate is against her now. She does the same with the druids and the weird cult of the black god.'

'Who are they?' Fergus said.

'There's a strange cult in the south of this kingdom. They say it predates the druids,' Valens said, frowning at Fergus's oddly accented Latin. 'They worship some sort of black-faced god. It's a primitive superstition. Human sacrifice and all that sort of thing. You know what these people are like. Anyway, it's a strong cult led by a druid whose name translates as "The Wicked". A lot of southern Dobunni follow this faith and naturally the queen courts their favour too.'

'What do they call this black god? Is it Crom?' Fergus said, fixing the fort commander with a piercing glare.

'I don't know,' Valens said, returning his look with one equally confrontational. 'Wait. I remember now: I think it's Gwynn or something like that. What do I care? It's all just native superstition.'

'Let's not get sidetracked,' Agricola said, laying a hand on Fergus's forearm. 'What's your assessment of the situation, Valens? What about this banquet tonight? Is it safe for us to attend?'

Valens paused for a moment to think. 'Like I said, the Dobunni are officially friends of Rome,' he said, taking another swig of wine. 'On the face of it, you should have nothing to worry about. I'm not so sure though. I'd be very careful if I were you, though perhaps my nerves are just overwrought. I'm one Roman surrounded by hundreds of barbarians. You don't know what it's like, Agricola – the sheer stress of sitting here behind these walls right in the middle of potential enemies, just waiting for them to turn on you at any minute.'

A look of disdain crossed Agricola's face. 'Pull yourself together, Valens,' he said. 'Remember that's just what you are: a Roman surrounded by barbarians. What sort of example are you giving? Show some backbone, man. Where is your virtus?'

The commander's face fell. He visibly paled and blinked as if someone had thrown cold water in his face.

'Of course,' he said, blushing. 'You're right. You must attend the feast tonight. It would be a gross insult to the queen if you didn't. In fact, it could well show her weakness and provoke a rebellion.'

'I'm looking forward to meeting this queen in a more relaxed setting,' Agricola said.

'All the same,' Valens said, 'for your own safety, I'd recommend you return here after the feast and sleep inside this fort tonight.'

33

'Gwynn ap Nudd is what the British call Crom,' Fergus said as he, Agricola and Marcus Flavius left the Roman quarters early that evening on their way to the feast.

While not having a full bathhouse, the little fort did still have a washroom and Agricola had taken full advantage of it. He had washed and shaved, combed his black hair and now wore his finest dress uniform. Marcus had changed into clean white robes of office and this time bore on his head a priest's red, padded skullcap instead of the laurel wreath he had worn the last time Fergus had seen him on official duty. Having nothing to change into, Fergus had done his best to wipe the mud from his tunic, armour and helmet. He had tidied his hair and combed his moustache. Posing as Agricola's personal bodyguard he was the only one wearing proper body protection, for although the tribune wore military dress uniform, its gleaming bronze cuirass was meant for decoration and was useless as armour.

'Drop it, MacAmergin,' the tribune said. 'We've a mission to fulfil here so forget about going off on your own private religious war.'

'I just think it's a bad omen, sir,' Fergus said as they skirted thatched houses and animal pens, passing local tribesmen and women who shot curious glances at the strangely dressed Romans in their midst. 'There are a lot of things about this I don't like.'

'Not you as well,' Agricola said, rolling his eyes. 'Don't let the ramblings of Valens get to you, trooper. That man is a nervous wreck. Too long away from civilised company has led him to take refuge in a wine cup and that is addling his judgement. We've nothing to fear here as long as we remain in control of ourselves. The general would not have sent me to my death on some fool's errand.'

Though Agricola spoke loudly, to Fergus's ears the last part lacked any conviction.

'Maybe we can ride our luck and get out before the situation turns to shit,' Fergus said. 'But there's something odd going on. I still wonder what that messenger was up to last night, then this morning I saw a group of riders break away from the queen's bodyguards before they came to meet us. Odd that they never rejoined us all day, don't you think? Where were they going? And then there's her bodyguard, those Laigin men who escorted us to—'

'What about them?' Agricola stopped walking and, pulling Fergus to a standstill, looked him in the eye. Marcus glanced back at them and hesitated, but Agricola waved him on. 'Keep walking, Pater. We'll catch you up.'

'I've been listening to them all day,' Fergus said. 'They didn't say much, but what they did say was interesting. They were laughing about something that was to happen at this feast tonight. From what I could gather some sort of surprise is planned for the enemies of the queen. I tried to ride in among them to learn more but they clammed up when I did. I don't know any more than that, which is why I didn't mention it to you earlier.'

For a moment Agricola did not reply as he digested the information, turning over the various possibilities in his mind. Finally he started walking again.

'Come on. Let's get on with it,' he said, but the aggressive tone of authority had gone from his voice. 'As I told you, we don't have much choice now anyway. If I don't return to Suetonius with that spear I may as well be killed by the Dobunni.'

Fergus followed him, sniffing the air as he went. The delectable aroma of roasting pig wafted over the settlement, instantly provoking a rush of saliva into his mouth.

'Well, at least we'll die with a decent meal in our bellies,' he said. 'Surely they wouldn't be so inhospitable as to murder us before we get our dinner?'

The early summer evening was warm and for once dry, so the feast was being cooked outside the chieftain's roundhouse. This would make the experience infinitely more pleasant, Fergus reflected. The windowless dwelling would be smoky enough from the many torches stuck around the interior, without the added smoke of roasting meat.

There was certainly plenty of meat roasting. Four hog boars hunted from the forests slowly revolved over beds of glowing embers, the spits rotated by red-faced, sweating kitchen slaves. Fat sizzled and dripped down into the fire as they turned, sending up occasional gouts of flame that licked the meat. In the centre of them was one huge boar, almost twice as big as the others and Fergus wondered at what prowess it must have taken to bring such a beast down.

Two huge cauldrons sat on another firepit, clouds of steam rising from the seething contents as great chunks of beef were boiled inside them. Smaller pots of bean stew bubbled away alongside the meat, and over a final firepit were spits lined with the roasting carcasses of all manner of wild birds, trapped with nets from the woods, and some other larger, four-legged beasts that reminded Fergus sharply of his childhood.

'What are those?' Agricola said, pointing at them.

'Badgers,' Fergus said, enjoying the look of consternation on the tribune's face. 'They're really tasty. And you Romans eat mice so I don't think you have any grounds to get high and mighty.'

They were already aware that they would not be the only guests at the feast that night. Tungrian sentries posted on the Roman fort walls had reported the arrival of other parties during the afternoon. The first was a small group of rather simply clad men. The second, a larger band, included warriors and a big man who wore the robes and bronze crown of a druid. Various other British noblemen and women, the aristocracy of the Dobunni kingdom, had continued to arrive on horseback and in chariots as the afternoon wore on.

Agricola and Fergus caught up with the priest and the three men continued walking towards the big roundhouse. There was no sign of the queen's other visitors outside, although the horse corral behind the chieftain's house brimmed with their horses, and several impressive, two-wheeled fighting chariots were lined up in a row alongside the cooking pits.

Queen Finnabair stood at the entrance to the house. She

was still dressed in the Roman finery she had worn earlier, a broad smile of welcome on her lips, but as before, it did not make it as far as her eyes.

'My honoured guests,' she said. 'I'm glad you have returned. I was starting to wonder what you were up to. You've been away so long.'

'I thought I should make myself presentable,' Agricola said giving a small bow.

'Oh come now,' the queen said, eyeing him up and down, her flirtatious gaze lingering on his muscled arms and his glittering cuirass. 'That wouldn't take a handsome young man like you too long.'

Fergus was amused to see the earnest young Roman's face flush a deep crimson. There was no question that Finnabair was a woman of exceptional beauty. It was a long time since he had been with a woman and her mere presence invoked a groin-tightening intoxication, but he could see exactly what she was up to. He hoped Agricola was not so wet behind the ears as to fall for it.

'Come inside and meet our other guests,' the queen said, ushering them in with a dramatic sweep of her arm.

They walked in through the crescent-shaped doorway. Fergus had grown up around houses like this and knew what to expect, but as they entered into the vast round room, which took up most of the interior of the building, he could see that Agricola was taken aback by how light it was inside. A huge fire blazed in the centre and torches burned in brackets attached to the ring of wooden pillars that circled the room to hold up the roof. As well as braziers there were oil lamps, their combined effect providing enough illumination such that there was no need to blink and readjust their vision when they entered from the evening sunlight outside.

While at the doorway the roof was a mere hand's stretch over their heads, in the middle of the building it soared to a height far above, and here, well away from the diners below, the rising smoke coalesced and seeped out through the thatch. The walls of the room were panelled with polished wood and hung with brightly coloured banners. Many doorways in the circular wall led off to other rooms situated in the space between the central large room and the outer walls.

Slaves appeared with horn cups brimming with wine, which Agricola and Fergus accepted but the priest waved away. Agricola took a sip and Fergus barely suppressed a smirk as the Roman's eyes widened, watered and a cough burst from his lips.

'They like to drink it neat here,' Fergus said. 'Not watered down the way you Romans prefer.'

He saw the queen shoot a sharp glance in his direction and realised she must have overheard him. For a moment he had forgotten he was supposed to be posing as a Roman and inwardly cursed his carelessness.

Comux stepped forward, flanked by a couple of hefty-looking warriors. They were both a head and shoulders taller than the young prince consort. Their long hair and moustaches were combed and they wore tunics that left their heavily muscled arms bare. Unlike the queen, Comux had chosen not to wear the Roman toga. As her consort and therefore an adopted Roman citizen he was entitled to. Instead he wore a fine, white linen tunic and dark woollen breeches. His torc, a massive rope of twisted gold as thick as a man's thumb, encircled his throat.

Agricola saluted him but the prince simply returned an insolent, challenging stare and held out his hand as if waiting for something.

The queen stepped forward, her customary poise clearly dented, a flush of embarrassment darkening her white cheeks.

'I am sorry, Tribune,' she said, shooting a fiery look at her partner. 'Comux is now my consort, but he still retains his former position as my late husband's armour bearer.'

They both now looked expectantly at Agricola whose mystified expression revealed he had no idea what was going on.

Fergus had been expecting this, though.

'This is a royal house,' he said. 'No one can enter with weapons. We must give up our swords. It's the custom here.'

The queen nodded. 'Your bodyguard is correct. Please surrender your weapons to Comux. He will make sure they're well looked after in the armoury until after the feast.'

'I don't think so...' Agricola said. Instinctively his hand dropped to the ivory hilt of the sword that sat high on his right-hand side.

'I know it's far from ideal, but it's expected,' Fergus said.

'I'm so sorry, Tribune, but I'm afraid this is true,' the queen said, clearly uncomfortable with the whole situation. 'Everyone else has done the same thing. No one here has a weapon, as you can see.'

She gestured around the room and a quick glance confirmed that none of the other guests carried a sword or spear.

'Yes, but they're not the only Romans in the room,' Agricola muttered to Fergus under his breath.

It was clear even to the tribune, however, that they would either have to comply or risk creating a diplomatic incident, and then there would be no chance of getting the magic spear for the general. With a sigh, he unbuckled his sword belt and handed it to Comux, who took it with a smirk then passed it to one of the warriors beside him.

Agricola gestured to Fergus, who rolled his eyes then also handed over his spatha and the knife from his belt. The warrior took all the weapons and with a quick bow to the queen, left the room. A look of relief washed over her face and her fixed, white-toothed grin returned.

'There. Thank you. Now come with me and I will introduce you to everyone,' she said, once more taking Agricola by the arm. Ignoring Fergus and the priest, she steered him towards the centre of the room.

Aware of Comux's belligerent gaze boring into his back, Fergus followed close behind, feeling suddenly very naked and vulnerable without his weapons and surrounded by a roomful of potential enemies.

34

The queen led them into the centre of the room, which had been laid out for a banquet. Fergus was surprised to see that they would not be sitting on cushions on the floor. Instead, couches were laid out for diners to recline on in the Roman fashion, each one with a little table beside it. The other guests were already seated, though most declined to lie down and were sitting upright, perched on the ends of the couches. A harper sat near the central fire, the iron strings of his instrument twanging out a lively tune.

'Let me introduce our other honoured guests this evening,' the queen said, addressing the company in a loud voice. 'This handsome young man is Gnaeus Julius Agricola, tribunus laticlavius of the XIV Legion of the Roman army. With him are his bodyguard and one of the legion's priests.'

She waved a dismissive hand in the direction of Fergus.

Cool eyes regarded them from all around the room, not least those of Prince Comux, who slouched on a carved wooden throne, clearly having eschewed the Roman furniture for something native and British.

Taking hold of Agricola's hand, the queen led him towards the couches until they came to a middle-aged man who was standing awkwardly beside the large fire. Fergus, following close behind, judged him to be in his forties, though still fit and active-looking. His black hair was streaked with silver but cropped quite short for a Briton. He was very simply dressed, his body wrapped in a woollen *cucullus* – a loose, hooded cloak that reached down to his knees. As Agricola approached he began to raise his arm then seemed to hesitate, changing the movement into running his hand self-consciously through his hair.

'This is Caerwyn,' the queen said. 'He is a high priest of the Christians in this land and servant of the Lord Peredur, one of the most powerful nobles in my kingdom.'

The man gave a short, nervous nod, his eyes flicking from the queen to Agricola, who responded with a curt nod of his own.

Seeing the tribune's look of consternation, Fergus hid a smile. The queen had noted it too. She took Agricola's elbow and steered him away towards the next set of couches.

'You disapprove?' she said in a low voice.

'The Christian religion is banned by the emperor,' Agricola said. 'I'm disappointed that you seem to tolerate their strange cult.'

'Sometimes we must cultivate all sorts of people to keep a kingdom together,' the queen said, then added with a wink: 'Perhaps when you hear what the Christians in my realm possess, you will not be so judgemental.'

'Do you mean the spear?' Agricola said.

'Well that made your eyes light up!' the queen said. Then she held a finger to her lips as they arrived at the next couch.

Even though the man on the couch was seated, Fergus could tell he was unusually tall. He too was middle-aged, yet seemed fit, unbowed and strong. His long, dark, wide-sleeved robe was belted at the waist and hooded, though the hood was down. Over it he wore a sleeveless jerkin of untanned animal hide which – judging by the long, black hair still clinging to it – Fergus thought was probably made from bull or cow skin. Hung from his belt was a large leather bag that had feathers poking out of the top of it. His bronze headdress shone like gold in the firelight and comprised a wide metal band that circled his head above the forehead, and another strip, smaller and thinner, that ran over the top of his skull. Beneath it his head was shaved both at the back and the front, leaving a crescent-shaped band of hair from ear to ear over his crown. It was the unmistakable haircut of a druid.

The man stood up and his true stature became clear. He was a good head taller than Fergus and towered over the diminutive Roman, Agricola.

'This is Anfad,' the queen said. 'He is a powerful priest-chieftain from the south of our kingdom and a druid.'

Fergus felt as if a cold hand seized his heart. The ancient memory of that terrible Samhain night when his wife and child had been killed, surfaced in his mind.

Agricola saluted, but the giant druid merely grinned, his expression somehow conveying both delight and pure malice at the same time.

'Never mind him, he cannot speak Latin,' the queen said hastily, a sudden look of concern crossing her face. 'Come; let me introduce you to everyone else.'

With that, she led them on around the room, introducing various warriors, chieftains and nobles of the Dobunni tribe, translating their native titles into the Latin equivalents, such as *comes* or *dux*, to give the Romans some sort of context for where they stood in the pecking order of the kingdom. Between druids, lords and ladies, warriors and their consorts, there were altogether about thirty people – the elite of Dobunni society – gathered in the royal house for the feast.

Finally, when they had completed a circuit of the room and were once more near the door, the queen stopped and turned to Fergus.

'I'm interested in your accent, which sounds unusual for a Roman soldier,' she said. 'I believe you're from my own country, Hibernia?'

Wondering if he should claim to be a Gaul, Fergus glanced at Agricola for guidance, but the tribune merely shrugged, his expression saying there was no sense in denying it now.

'I am,' Fergus said in Latin.

'What part?'

'I am of the Cruithni in the north, but left there many years ago.'

'How interesting,' the queen said, her tone suggesting the complete opposite. 'Then perhaps we will catch up on old Erin later. For the moment, however, this is your place for the feast.'

She gave him a cool, insincere smile and gestured to the pile of cushions close to the door. There was clearly to be no Roman dining couch for Fergus.

Still ignoring the priest, who lurked awkwardly behind them, the queen once more linked her arm through Agricola's.

'Tribune, if you would accompany me to our places we can get the celebration underway.'

'MacAmergin is my bodyguard, Your Highness,' Agricola said. 'He is supposed to stay at my side.'

'Oh nonsense, Gnaeus!' the queen said with a smile that reminded Fergus of a wolf looking at a doe. 'You speak as though you don't trust us. You're amongst friends here. There's no need for us to dine in the company of the common soldiery. You're safe in my hands.'

The tribune's cheeks, already flushed from the strong wine, turned a deeper shade of pink at her suggestive, husky tone. To Fergus's dismay, Agricola sighed and gave an apologetic shrug in his direction.

Watching the queen lead him away, Fergus was reminded of a sacrificial bull being led to the slaughter. The priest, trotting along behind them like a surly child, seemed oblivious to any threat. At least, Fergus reflected as he settled himself down on the hard, straw-filled cushions, his stomach growling, he would get a decent meal out of it. And if things started to go wrong he was near the door; a good position for a quick getaway.

Agricola and Marcus Flavius, on the other hand, being right in the middle of the room, would be in real trouble.

35

Conversation bubbled up around the room. Slaves carrying trays laden with cups of wine, tankards of beer and small packages of meat-filled pastry that served as appetisers, circulated among the dinner guests.

Deciding that he may as well enjoy himself, Fergus beckoned one of the slaves over. The young girl hurried over and Fergus helped himself to a cup of wine from her tray. As he began to glug it down like water the slave turned to leave but Fergus held up a hand to stop her. With a loud sigh of appreciation he replaced the now empty cup on the tray and took two more, one for each hand. He winked at the slave and nodded to signal that she could now leave.

Fergus sat down cross-legged on the cushions and slurped his second cup with slightly more restraint. As he glanced idly around the room he saw the Christian priest wandering towards him. The man stopped and looked down at him.

'Apparently my seat is over here with you,' he said, speaking in the Latin tongue. 'I am Caerwyn.'

Fergus smiled up at the squat, uncomfortable-looking priest.

'You're as welcome as I am at this feast, then, Caerwyn,' he said, speaking in the British language. 'Queen Finnabair clearly thinks as much about the Christians as she does about Roman cavalrymen.'

Caerwyn turned down the corners of his mouth as he eased himself down on the cushions.

'I don't really know why I was invited at all to be honest,' he said. 'Everyone in this kingdom, apart from the Lord Peredur, hates us.'

Fergus grunted and took another slug of wine.

'The queen wants something from you. That's why we're all here.' Switching back to Latin, he said, 'But a legionary like you should be used to getting the shitty end of the stick, eh? What's your real name, *Caerwyn*?'

The Christian looked at him for a long moment then shook his head. 'Longinus,' he said with a sigh. 'How did you know?'

Fergus laughed and finished off his second cup of wine. The heady, undiluted drink was already giving him a warm, fuzzy feeling inside.

'It's obvious, man. Your haircut for a start, and the way you hold yourself upright, so straight you'd think someone had shoved a plank down your back. But apart from that, the fact that you nearly saluted the tribune when he was introduced to you was a dead giveaway. Old habits die hard, especially when they've been hammered into you over the years by a centurion's vine cane. What are you up to, Longinus? Are you really a Christian?'

'Yes,' the reply came without hesitation and with a conviction that took Fergus back a little. 'And I'm not *up to anything*, as you put it. I really am bishop of the Dobunni.'

'That's a brave religious choice for a Roman legionary,'

Fergus said, raising his eyebrows. 'In Nero's army one might even say suicidal.'

'I'm not in his army now. I'm a veteran,' Longinus said. 'I've done my twenty-five years in the army. I did what I was told to do and believed what I was told to believe. Now I'm retired. I've been granted my plot of land near Camulodunum and I'm free to do what I please and believe what I want. I've found the one true God and I'll dedicate the rest of my life to spreading his word in Britannia.'

'The way the emperor feels about your religion,' Fergus said, 'that's not likely to be a very long time. But at the end of the day it's your choice, I suppose. Your funeral anyway. I don't get it myself.'

'I used to obey the will of the emperor,' Longinus said. 'Now I follow my own conscience. I submit to the will of God.'

'My god forsook me,' Fergus said. 'Now I just kill who I'm told to kill and life is much simpler that way. That's how I get to sleep at night anyway.'

He set down his empty wine cup and moved on to his third. Longinus eyed him for a moment.

'That's the way I used to think until I learnt about Jesus,' he said. 'Now my life has real meaning and I have absolutely no fear of dying.'

'That's probably a good thing,' Fergus said. 'If the governor finds out what you're up to he'll crucify you. So did you bring this magic spear with you? The one they are all after?'

The look of complete bewilderment on the face of Longinus told Fergus that the Christian ex-legionary was

THE SPEAR OF CROM

genuinely mystified and had no idea what he was talking about. Either that or he was an excellent dissembler.

'Magic spear?' Longinus met Fergus's gaze and frowned. There was no trace of guile in his eyes. 'I don't know what you mean.'

'The governor, Suetonius Paulinus, is under the impression that the queen can offer Rome a spear that's sacred to the Christians,' Fergus said. 'It's supposed to have been used to stab your Christus when he was crucified and became imbued with magical powers. The queen has led the governor to believe that she can supply it to us in return for Rome keeping her on the throne. It is why the Tribune Agricola and I are here. We've come to get it. When we saw you here we naturally assumed you possessed this magic spear.'

Longinus did not reply for a moment as he thought over what Fergus had said.

'I have heard of such a spear, it's true,' he said at length. 'However, if I had it, I would never, *never* give up such a holy relic to the queen. Certainly not if I thought it might end up in the hands of Suetonius Paulinus, and through him the Emperor Nero.'

There was an uneasiness in his voice that Fergus was unsure what to make of.

'So why, precisely, are you here tonight?' he said.

'As I told you, I do not know. That is to say, the queen invited me here, but she made no mention of a feast, nor of Tribune Agricola being here. She told me that she wanted to talk of an alliance and that if the Christians agree to support her, she will recognise Christianity as an official religion of her kingdom. You see, despite your emperor, the Christians are now big enough to be taken seriously as a political force in this land. Naturally, I am keen to extend this influence.'

'What about him?' Fergus pointed at the massive druid, Anfad, who sat on a couch, a cup of wine grasped in one huge fist, glaring around him at the other guests. His whole being seemed to exude raw menace as foul as the stink of stale sweat and uncured bull hide that also surrounded him. 'Do you think he is interested in an alliance with Christians? I imagine the queen has told him a similar tale to get him here. He's been given a much better seat too. I think you can tell whose support the queen values more.'

'That man is evil. I can think of no other word to describe him,' Longinus said with a sigh. 'He's very powerful, virtually a king himself. He leads a terrible cult in the south of the kingdom. They perform human sacrifices and worship the Devil himself: Satan. Thankfully, the question of being in an alliance with him is not going to be an issue. If the queen thinks she can count on his support she is wasting her time.'

'Really? What makes you say that?'

'He's a southerner. The southern Dobunni want to separate from the kingdom and Anfad wants to lead them away. On top of that, his opposition to everything foreign – from the Christian religion to the queen herself – is well known. She would need to tempt him with something very special in order for Anfad to offer her his allegiance.'

At that moment the queen's bodyguards entered the room, four of them carrying between them a large vat of sloshing, viscous liquid. Protruding from the liquid was a long metal pole that a fifth bodyguard held steady, keeping it from falling out of the cauldron. The sixth bodyguard followed them carrying a large pair of long-sleeved gloves made of thick, padded leather covered with metal chain mail. The cauldron itself was either made or coated with shining, polished bronze and it was completely covered in engraved and embossed pictures of gods, monsters and heroes. On the front panel an entire army trooped along beneath the massive face of a long-haired deity, who held two human beings aloft, one in each gigantic hand. The bodyguards set the cauldron down in front of the queen in the middle of the room. As it came to rest some of the contents sloshed over its lip and it was obvious that the deep red liquid that ran down the face of the cauldron was blood.

The queen stepped into the middle of the room and held up her hands to quiet the chatter that bubbled around her. Once quiet had descended, she began to speak.

'Friends, allies and our esteemed Roman guests, you have all come here tonight to witness and take part in the forging of a grand alliance that will secure peace and prosperity for our kingdom from today until the foreseeable future.'

There was a mixed reaction from around the room. Some people cheered, others murmured angry dissent. The queen motioned her hands for calm again.

'Some of you, I know, are uneasy with this plan,' she went on, speaking in a loud, commanding tone, 'but to you I have brought a great sign that the power above us – the deity – favours it. I have told many of you of the sacred spear that I have been given as a symbol that the heavenly powers favour me as your queen and now I will show it to you, to dispel any doubts you may still have. I have told you all that I possess the sacred spear. Some of you do not believe me, I know, so now the time has come to prove it.'

With that she looked deliberately at Agricola, Anfad

and her consort, Comux, locking eyes with each of them in turn. Then she strode to the blood-filled cauldron. Her bodyguard handed her the thick metal gauntlets and the queen pulled them on. Their large size looked outlandish on her slender white arms and the protective sleeves came right up to her elbows.

Grasping the long metal shaft in both hands, the queen pulled the spear out of the cauldron. She inverted the weapon, grasped it in both gauntleted hands and struck the butt of the shaft off the ground, releasing a shower of dark blood off the head that splattered crimson over her white stola. Seemingly heedless to the mess, she repeated the movement, shaking more of the blood from the metallic head to reveal more of its silver, patterned surface. Gasps erupted around the room as the queen raised the spear a third time then thumped the butt emphatically down to the ground. This time, instead of a shower of blood, bright sparks of yellow fire cascaded to the ground from the head of the spear.

What happened next astounded everyone. A bright flame awoke in the metal top of the spear. Moments later it was ablaze like a burning torch. Yelps of surprise, unease and even fear came from the guests gathered around the room and increased in volume as the light intensified and expanded. The strange fire popped and spat as it burned around the top of the spear. The queen, who was holding it up above her, had to turn her head and face away as sparks dropped down, bouncing off the metal gauntlets that protected her arms.

With a sweeping motion the queen suddenly plunged the blazing top of the spear back into the cauldron of blood.

The thick liquid hissed and bubbled as the burning metal sank into it and the weird fire was once more extinguished, leaving a strange blue haze in the air.

Amid the astonished silence that descended on the royal house, the queen released the shaft of the spear. She removed the gauntlets and handed them back to her bodyguard.

'Now,' she said, smiling at the guests who gawped at her in wide-eyed awe. 'Let no one question the magic that lives in this spear. Let's eat!'

An excited chatter erupted around the room as the queen made her way to her dining couch beside Agricola.

'Witchcraft! This is the work of Satan!' Longinus said in a breathy voice. He reached into the neck of his tunic and pulled out a small metal cross that was suspended around his neck by a leather thong.

Fergus became aware that his mouth was hanging open and he quickly closed it.

'I don't know who Satan is,' he said, 'but I don't believe that is his work. It's more like the artwork of Lugh.'

'You know what this weapon is?' Longinus stared at him in astonishment.

'There's a mythical weapon famous in Hibernia called the Spear of Lugh. It's also known as the *Lúin of Celtchar*,' Fergus said. 'It was a burning spear created by the god Lugh and wielded by the legendary hero of my tribe, Celtchar. It's one of the Great Treasures of Erin but it's just a legend and it's most definitely not a Christian spear.'

'You don't need to tell me that,' Longinus said. 'Our holy spear is a relic of the crucifixion of our Lord Jesus. We – the Romans that is – killed him: executed him for crimes against the empire. While he was hanging crucified and dying, a legionary took his spear and stabbed him, putting him out of his misery.'

Fergus's head was spinning, but he detected something in the tone of Longinus's voice and the strangely haunted look on the man's face told him there was more to this story than the priest was telling.

'A legionary stabbed this Jesus, you say?' Fergus said. 'Was it *you*?'

Longinus looked away. 'What I mean is that the holy spear of the Christians is not some extravagant conjuring trick like we have just witnessed,' he said, avoiding the question. 'A common legionary stabbed the Lord Jesus, so the spear he used was simply an ordinary legionary's javelin.'

'Well we agree on one thing,' Fergus said. 'I don't know how she did it, but when you say conjuring trick I think you're close to the truth.'

Fergus was about to talk further but noticed that the queen's bodyguards had lifted the cauldron and spear once again and were carrying it towards the door.

'I'm going outside for a piss,' he muttered before standing up and following them, determined to get a closer look at this magical weapon.

36

Growing up in Erin, Fergus knew well the legends about the mystical spear of Lugh. For generations, whether sung by bards before the king while warriors feasted, or told around the campfire on a winter's night, tales of the heroes, gods like Lugh and monsters of old were staples and had been a part of his childhood. One element was the magic weapon that once had belonged to the many-talented, bright, shining one with the long, strong arm: Lugh, the god of light. While Fergus's tribe had worshipped Crom, the dark god of winter, who captures the maiden representing the life of the fields and plunges the world into darkness, most of the other tribes in Erin had revered Crom's nemesis, Lugh, the god of summer, whose power triumphs over darkness and wins the maiden back, bringing the harvest.

It was not that the tribes believed different things, Fergus reflected, it was just a question of emphasis, which god they chose to pay more reverence to. In the years since he had left his homeland, Fergus – having denied allegiance to Crom – had often thought about Lugh. In his travels as a soldier of Rome he discovered that Lugh was honoured throughout the Celtic lands, not just in Hibernia. The Gauls called him Lugus and the tribes of Britannia called him Lleu. It was said in Erin that he had once lived among the people there and possessed many magical items, including a sword that compelled enemies to tell the truth when the blade was held to their throats, and a horse that could carry him over both land and sea. Of all Lugh's treasures, though, none was as fearsome as the *Areadbhar* – the Slaughterer – the burning spear that guaranteed victory in battle to whoever bore it.

If someone talked about a magic spear, Fergus reasoned, it would be the Spear of Lugh that he would think of. The queen would know those legends too, and her references would be the same.

This did not bode well for his and Agricola's mission. Fergus still had not worked out how she made the spear burn, but he did believe she was faking it, and the offer of the Christian spear to the general was a fraud. The queen must be desperate to hold on to power. She heard there was a spear sacred to the Christians the Romans wanted to get their hands on, so she had manufactured a magic spear claiming that was it. She was clearly unaware of the Christian legend Longinus had told him and instead created what she thought of when someone said the words *magic spear*.

Leaving the royal house, Fergus walked out into the evening air, pausing at the door to see which way the queen's bodyguards had gone. As he looked around he realised that he was not the only one to have left the building. A little way away, standing beside the parked chariots, was Comux. He was talking to a woman. Not so much talking to as arguing with, judging by his animated stance and the way he was gesticulating and stabbing his fingers at her. Despite this, they were keeping their voices down and Fergus could not hear what they were arguing about. The woman was obviously giving as good as she got, prodding Comux's chest with an accusing finger as she spoke. She wore a long, embroidered green tunic with a hood, which was pulled up over her head, making it impossible for Fergus to see her face. Fergus frowned, for although the evening was starting to cool down it was by no means cold enough to warrant a hood. Clearly she did not wish to be recognised.

While intrigued by what was going on between them, Fergus had more important business. Looking around, he glimpsed the queen's bodyguards disappearing into an adjacent building. Fergus melted into the shadows cast by the big roundhouse and headed after them, hoping that Comux and his lady friend were too engrossed in their argument to notice him.

The building, which butted onto the side of the royal house, had the unmistakable square outline of a British temple. Its walls were ridged and irregular and, as he neared it, Fergus saw that they were made from entire tree trunks set upright, side by side. He had seen similar buildings, both in Britannia and Gaul. From time immemorial the sacred oak groves of the druids had been clearings in the forest with tree branches woven together overhead to provide a covering. The temples the Britons had begun to build under the influence of the Romanised Gauls were made to mimic these ancient, natural groves.

As he was approaching the door, the bodyguards

re-emerged. They no longer carried the cauldron with its strange spear, but remained at the doorway, clearly now on guard duty. At the sight of Fergus's Roman uniform they stiffened, their hands dropping immediately to their sword hilts.

'Hello there,' Fergus hailed the bodyguards in his best Latin, trying to imitate how Agricola spoke and eliminate any traces of his Hibernian accent. 'The Tribune Agricola has asked me to examine the sacred spear.'

There was no relaxation from the bodyguards. One of them, a tall, broad-shouldered man, probably in his thirties, who appeared to be the leader of the group, frowned and raised his shoulders in a shrug as if to say he did not understand.

'The queen tells me you understand Latin,' Fergus said. She had not, but he reasoned that it was highly unlikely at least one of them did not know the language. He was also gambling that the queen had not had time to tell her bodyguards he was a Hibernian just as they were. If she had, he was in deep trouble.

The lead bodyguard smirked like a boy caught stealing apples from an orchard. 'I'm afraid she has also told us that no one is to see the spear without her being present,' he said in Latin. 'So it's out of the question.'

'The tribune needs to ensure the spear is the real thing before the treaty can be sealed,' Fergus tried again.

'Well he can get the queen to bring him here himself then,' the bodyguard said. With a half-smile that held no hint of humour but a lot of threat he regarded Fergus from hostile blue eyes.

Fergus smiled and shrugged as though conceding the point.

'So it's really the spear of Jesus then?'

The bodyguard hesitated for a moment then looked sideways at one of his colleagues, a confused and questioning look on his face.

'Ulli, what was the story we are supposed to tell the Romans?' he asked, speaking in the Hibernian tongue.

Relieved that he had fooled them into thinking him Roman, Fergus continued his charade by looking blankly from one to the other, a slight frown of puzzlement on his brow.

Ulli nodded and replied, also in Hibernian: 'Your memory's going, Ferchu, first sign of old age. She said we were to tell the Romans it's the spear that stabbed Jesus. But if any of the Dobunni ask, we can say it's Lugh's Slaughterer.'

Ferchu nodded and returned his attention to Fergus, switching back to Latin.

'It is indeed, Roman,' he said. 'If you were in the royal house a few moments ago you'll have seen enough proof of its power.'

There was silence as all six bodyguards stared at Fergus through half-closed, suspicious and implicitly belligerent eyes. Realising he would get nowhere with them, he nodded farewell, turned away and retraced his steps. As he walked he could feel the gazes of the bodyguards boring into his back. Knowing they would continue to watch him until they were sure he had gone, he carried on walking until he was almost back at the door of the roundhouse and once more out of their line of sight. He could hear laughter from within and the hum of inebriated people enjoying the feast. For a brief moment he was tempted to rejoin them, the smells of roasting meat almost too much to endure. Instead of going back in, however, he kept close in to the wall and skirted the circumference of the royal house until he was three-quarters of the way round. There, as expected, he found himself coming up on the back of the small temple housing the spear.

He edged closer, hoping that all the queen's bodyguards were stationed at the only door, which like most Celtic houses was at the front. He could now see an enclosure behind the building where horses were corralled. To Fergus's delight there was no one around. The guards must indeed all be at the front.

He vaulted over the shoulder-high wooden fence, planning to climb up onto the temple's roof and make a hole in the thatch big enough to clamber through. Quickly he crossed the paddock, but at his approach the horses, which had been pressed into a tightly packed bunch near the far side, scattered, kicking up clods of mud as they sped past him.

Fergus froze. Another person, it seemed, had had the same idea as him and was scrambling up onto the sloping roof at the back. Even in the half-light of the advancing evening he recognised the distinctive green hooded tunic and knew it was the woman he had seen arguing with Comux.

She glanced furtively around but missed him as he was standing directly behind her. She then crouched down and with a long-bladed knife began digging into the thatch. In no time she had a hole big enough to fit into and with another glance to be sure she was unobserved, planted her hands on either side and dropped through into the building.

As she disappeared from view, Fergus wondered what to do next. Something strange was going on. The meaning of it all was beyond him but one thing was for sure: the spear was somehow the key. Whoever this mysterious woman was, she was after it just as he was.

He made up his mind to follow her and crept across the paddock, taking care to avoid spooking the horses again. Using the fence as a ladder to climb onto the roof, he scrambled up to the hole the woman had made and peered inside. The interior of the building was too dark to make anything out. There was nothing for it but to go in. He swung his legs into the gap and, clutching onto the thatch on either side, let himself drop.

For a moment he hung suspended, waiting until his eyes adjusted to the gloom. Beneath him he saw a room with a bare earth floor and what looked like three large wooden altars made from tree stumps. The tree trunks from which the temple walls had been constructed were still covered in bark and gave the impression of being surrounded by tightly packed living trees in a real forest. There were three statues, representations of the gods, each one taller than the height of a man and carved from a single block of wood. In the middle of the three altars was a hole in the ground, a square pit with a wooden edging, and before it stood the big, blood-filled cauldron from which protruded the shaft of the magic spear. The woman in the green embroidered tunic stood in front of it. She had taken down her hood to reveal a shock of red hair.

Fergus let go and dropped to the floor. The sound made the woman turn round and for a few seconds she and Fergus locked gazes, both frozen in mutual shock. He recognised her at once, and she him.

It was the druidess – Ceridwen.

37

'Well now, what have we here?'

The sound of a third voice, speaking in Latin with a strong Hibernian accent, made both Fergus and Ceridwen turn towards the only door. In the entrance stood Ferchu, the queen's bodyguard, his long, leaf-bladed sword grasped in his right fist.

Fergus reached for his own sword then, as his fingers clutched at nothing, remembered that he had surrendered his weapon on the way into the feast. As Ferchu moved into the room, followed by the other five bodyguards, Fergus glanced up at the hole in the roof above. It was too high to jump back up unaided, which meant he was now trapped; cornered by six armed, hostile and violent men in a room with only one exit.

The queen's bodyguards fanned out in a semicircle, blocking the way out.

'This looks like a couple of people are trying to steal the spear,' Ulli said, grinning round at his companions.

Ceridwen stepped forward. 'I am a druid,' she said, her confident tone indicating that she expected this fact to have an effect on the warriors. 'I am engaged in highly important work. Do not get in my way or you will regret it.'

Looking both puzzled and annoyed, Ferchu screwed up his face and pointed at Ceridwen's druidic tonsure.

'We can see you're a druid,' he said. 'Don't you worry. We know exactly who you are and what you're up to. You're the partner in crime of the queen's fancy man, Comux. And druid or not, your little games have just come to an end.'

'How dare you talk to me like that,' Ceridwen said, spitting out the words through clenched teeth. 'It's the reign of that bitch you serve that's coming to an end.'

Ferchu smirked at her.

Fergus could see Ceridwen was taken aback by Ferchu's seeming lack of fear, as indeed was he. Tall, her red hair radiating like a burst of fire around her head, her startling eyes flashing with anger beneath her blue painted eyebrows, the filidh was enough to frighten any man, especially a Hibernian familiar with the effects of a druid's curse.

'Oh you think so?' Ferchu said. 'Maybe you don't realise that she has watched your every move? She knows what you have been plotting with Comux. Putting the spear in here was just the bait so we could catch you, and it's worked a treat. Only it looks like we've caught ourselves a Roman trout along with the salmon we were after.'

He nodded at Fergus.

'Very well,' Ceridwen said. 'You have asked for this.'

Drawing up her left leg and balancing on her right foot, she took up her cursing stance. Then, closing her left eye, she placed her thumbs and forefingers together. The druid raised her left elbow and dipped her right so her hands turned horizontally and Fergus saw that the space between her hands resembled the outline of an eye. Through this third 'eye' Ceridwen squinted at the bodyguards with her still-open right eye.

'I curse you,' she began in ringing tones. 'May the gods rain down punishments on you—'

A couple of the bodyguards began to back away from the filidh towards the door.

'Don't worry, lads,' Ferchu said to them. 'Lucky we've brought our own druid along, eh? He can counter her magic. We've nothing to fear from her curses.'

At that moment a massive figure entered the room behind the bodyguards, stooping to get through the door. It was Anfad. He straightened up, then took a look around the room, his wide grin revealing a mouthful of large teeth like a row of standing stones.

A smile broke out on Ceridwen's face also and, lowering her arms, she put her foot back to the floor.

'You've made yet another mistake. Anfad and I know each other well.'

'It's you who've made the mistake,' Ferchu said.

Anfad, still grinning, stepped forward and swept his long arms around in a dramatic gesture. In a deep, booming voice he uttered some arcane pronouncements in an obscure tongue then held his two massive hands over the heads of the bodyguards.

'These men are now under the protection of my spell,' Anfad said in the British language. 'No druid spell can harm them. To add to my power I give you this.'

He reached into a pouch on the belt at his waist and

retrieved an object. He held it up for all to see then handed it to the bodyguard.

'This will nullify her magic.'

Fergus saw he passed a large snakestone to Ferchu. He also noted Ceridwen's reaction and although he was not surprised, he still felt a surge of disappointment when he saw her shoulders sag.

'They're only stones for fuck's sake!' he said in Latin. 'They only have power over you because you believe they do.'

'Without my beliefs I am nothing,' Ceridwen said. 'Anfad, what are you doing? You are a southerner, part of Comux's faction. You're supposed to be on our side. Why are you siding with these Roman lapdogs?'

'We all have our own goals and games to play,' Anfad said. 'I let you and that fool Comux believe I was on your side. What you didn't know is that I studied the path of druidism in Hibernia. My master in the faith was the great arch-druid Colphra. Queen Finnabair is the daughter of Colphra's sister. When the queen made me an offer to counter Comux's, how could I not join sides with the niece of my venerable mentor?'

Fergus's mind raced. Arch-druid Colphra was the butcher who oversaw the slaughter of the firstborn children every year at Samhain. It was on his command his wife Nes and son Connor had been put to death. And the queen was a blood relative of the bastard.

The tall druid whistled through his teeth and three more British warriors entered the room. Anfad pointed to the cauldron and they came forward and lifted it, one of the warriors carefully holding the spear shaft to ensure the head remained submerged in the glutinous dark blood. Working together, they manoeuvred the heavy metal vessel outside.

Anfad nodded to Ceridwen.

'I believe we shall meet again later,' he said with a grin that conveyed a huge threat much more convincingly than a glare. 'And I shall offer *you* as a gift for the Divine Lord, Gwynn ap Nudd.' Then he turned and left, ducking to get through the doorway.

Ferchu and the other bodyguards chuckled at the look of consternation on Ceridwen's face.

'You'll not be laughing for long,' she said.

'Oh, you mean because of your plot with Comux to overthrow the queen and put him on the throne?' Ferchu grinned. 'Like I said, the queen knows all about it.'

'My work is part of a much wider strategy,' Ceridwen said, a note of desperation entering her voice. 'Comux may not be able to see beyond the borders of Dobunnia, but this isn't just about putting him on the throne. It's about throwing the Romans out of Britain! Surely you want that too?'

'Now why would we want that?' Ferchu said with a sardonic laugh. 'The Romans keep the queen on the throne here and the queen pays us – and pays us well – to keep her safe on it. What do any of us care if all the kingdoms of Britain are under Roman control? It's not our country after all. Once we've made our fortune here we can return to Erin and live out the rest of our lives in luxury.'

'You fools,' Ceridwen said. 'Rome is a ravenous wolf whose hunger for conquest and blood cannot be sated.

Once they've crushed Britain completely Hibernia will be next. Have you no feeling for your cousins here?'

Like thunderclouds sweeping over the sun, Ferchu's expression changed, anger flaring in his eyes. He dropped the serpent stone and strode forward, his left hand clamping Ceridwen's face in a vice-like grip, one meaty thumb pressing into her right cheek, his fingers squashing the left. He squeezed further and she let out a short gasp of pain from her compressed lips. Maintaining his grip, with his other hand he levelled his sword directly at the druid's right eye, the razor-sharp point a mere finger's breadth away from it.

'You're the fool,' he said and spat into her face. 'You're not our cousins. You talk of the Romans, but if you weren't so busy fighting them you'd be fighting us. You think we don't know that? You'd already started before Claudius brought the legions here and gave you something else to think about. Before then Dumnonii from southern Britain had invaded and settled in the lands of the Laigin in Erin, and the Pretani and Setantii from the north had done the same in Ulaidh. If the Romans hadn't arrived we'd have been overrun by you Britons, but you've been too busy fighting them to think about invading us. And all the while you keep them busy they won't start thinking of conquering us either. And that's the way we'd like to keep things.'

Fergus, finding he agreed with much of what Ferchu was saying, forgot himself for a moment and with a grimace of sympathy nodded. Too late he tried to cover it by scratching his head, but Ferchu had spotted it.

'What are you nodding about, Roman? Do you speak the British language?'

Fergus shrugged. 'A little,' he said, accentuating his fake Roman accent and making a gesture with his finger and thumb as if he were holding something small.

For a moment Ferchu's eyes narrowed with suspicion and he stared at Fergus as if reassessing his appearance.

'What sort of a Roman soldier are you?' he said, releasing Ceridwen and turning to point his sword at Fergus. 'What sort of Roman has long hair? A moustache? And what are those tattoos on your arms?'

His voice dripped threat as he stepped closer. He spoke in the British language and Fergus looked back at him blankly. The bodyguard scowled and repeated the questions in Latin.

'I'm an auxiliary cavalry trooper,' Fergus said. 'Not regular army. Allied nation of Rome. From Gaul.'

'A Gaul?' Ferchu spat on the floor. 'If there is anyone I find more pathetic than the people of Britain it's the Gauls. It's only a hundred years since Caesar conquered you and already you've forgotten your own culture and try to be more Roman than the Romans.'

Contempt creasing his features, he turned away, seemingly satisfied with the explanation.

'Right lads – Cet, Col and Mebul – you three come with me,' Ferchu said, switching back to his native tongue. 'We'll take the lovely prisoner here to the armoury house where she can be safely held until the queen is ready to make her move. This druid is going to die, but Anfad wants it to be done at a sacred time. Maybe we will have a little fun with her until that time arrives, eh?'

He leered at Ceridwen and reached out to grope her breasts, laughing as she flinched away.

'Ulli and Lerga, you two stay here with the Gaul.'

With lewd grins on their faces, the men nodded, three of them stepping forward and grabbing Ceridwen roughly by the arms. She struggled against their grip, but there were too many of them and they were too strong.

'Take your hands off me,' she shouted. 'I curse you all!'

'You have no power over us,' Ferchu, grinning, reminded her.

'What about him?' Ulli cocked his head in the direction of Fergus.

'Kill him when we have taken the druid away. The idiot has no idea what is going on so won't be expecting it,' Ferchu replied. 'You should find it easy enough to slit his throat.'

Maintaining a puzzled frown, Fergus did his best to appear nonchalant, but his mind was racing. He had only a few moments to work out a plan to escape or else he was a dead man. He was unarmed and would be outnumbered two to one, the men who intended to kill him standing between him and the only exit to the room. There were not exactly many options open to him.

The other four bodyguards dragged Ceridwen out of the room. As the door closed behind them, Lerga and Ulli turned towards him. His time was up.

Fergus made up his mind. If there was a clever way to get out of the situation, it was beyond him. He was just going to have to fight them. At least he had surprise on his side.

Fergus shrugged and smiled inanely, as if he accepted that he was to remain a guarded prisoner. Then he surged forwards, running straight into a very startled Ulli and wrapping his arms around the bodyguard in a massive bear hug. Fergus brought his knee up with a vicious jab into the man's groin. Ulli screamed.

With a shout of surprise, Lerga grabbed his sword in both hands, swept it back then scythed it down in a vicious cut designed to slice across Fergus's spine. Fergus had already moved, thrusting his right hip into Ulli's gut and lifting him bodily around in a semicircle.

Instead of cutting Fergus, Lerga's blade bit into Ulli. The sword sliced deep into the base of his neck right to the bone, separating the nape from the shoulder and opening his throat to unleash a torrent of hot blood.

Fergus pushed the dying man away from him and Ulli, reaching with both hands for his dreadful wound, dropped his sword and staggered backwards, colliding with Lerga. Fergus dived for the weapon, seized it and danced away, creating space between himself and the remaining bodyguard. With a frown of annoyance, Lerga shoved the dying Ulli away from him. Ulli staggered forwards a few steps then dropped to his knees, choking and gurgling, the iron reek of his hot blood mingling with the smell of urine and stench of shit as his bowels evacuated. A moment later he pitched forwards face first onto the ground.

'You should be careful what you say,' Fergus said in Hibernian. 'You never know who's listening.'

Lerga narrowed his eyes. 'You're no Gaul. You are from Erin like us,' he said. 'Well it makes no difference. You still have to die.'

With a roar the bodyguard stepped forward and swung his sword at Fergus in a massive blow. Fergus blocked it with Ulli's weapon. The blow jarred his shoulder as the blades met. Lerga raised his leg and kicked forward, hitting Fergus on the left hip. He extended his leg, shoving Fergus backwards and knocking him off balance.

Staggering from the blow, Fergus sprawled sideways onto the floor, cursing himself that he had not anticipated the bodyguard's move.

Lerga was on top of him in an instant, sword raised for the kill. Out of the corner of his eye, Fergus caught sight of something lying on the ground beside his head. It was the serpent stone. Ferchu must have dropped it when he was wrestling Ceridwen to the door.

Fergus grabbed it with his free hand and lashed upwards. The force of his throw was enough to smash the bodyguard's front teeth. Lerga let out a yelp of surprise and jerked his head back, his sword stroke momentarily forgotten. Fergus sat up, driving his own sword upwards as he did so, its point smashing the rings of Lerga's chain mail shirt and slicing deep into the man's belly. Fergus grabbed the hilt in both hands and thrust further until both arms were fully extended above him. The blade drove into the bodyguard's chest and heart. His lifeblood flooded down the sword, coating Fergus's arms and splattering his face. Lerga grunted, coughed up blood and toppled backwards off the blade. Fergus leapt to his feet, but could see that the bodyguard was dead before he hit the ground.

Panting, Fergus used both men's cloaks to wipe his sword and arms clean, grimacing at the stink that now pervaded the temple. He picked up the serpent stone and regarded it for a moment.

'So what do you know?' he said to himself. 'They are useful after all.'

He put it away in the leather pouch attached to his sword belt and moved to the door. He needed to get back and warn the tribune. He still was not sure what the queen was up to, but the fact that her bodyguards had been prepared to kill him gave him the nasty feeling that her life-threatening plans did not just involve Comux and Ceridwen.

38

Agricola was having a tremendous time. The heady effects of the strong, undiluted wine flowing freely into his goblet forced him to relax and he was unaware that a slightly silly smile had become stuck to his face. The earlier anxiety over the situation in which he found himself dissolved in the wine and he found himself warming to both his fellow feasters and the surroundings that had at first seemed so barbaric to him.

He now saw the round daub-and-wattle royal house, the food and the tribesmen and nobles around him as wonderfully charming. They were a delightful contrast to the stark solemnity of Roman social life. They added a splash of real local colour that the Romans had lost touch with in their ascent to civilisation.

While the guests feasted, a group of musicians played on pipes and *crwth*, the Celtic version of the lyre. In the curious local style of half-singing and half-chanting, the bards recited songs and poetry and although Agricola had no idea what they were about, the sound was sometimes haunting, sometimes stirring and provided an extremely pleasant backdrop to the dinner.

The food was generous if a little bland, but the queen

seemed to have managed to obtain two small jars of Roman sauces – one of *garum* and one of *liquamen* – which he dribbled over the variety of roasted and boiled meats brought to him on wooden platters by slaves. He found the conversation of the British guests around him an incomprehensible babble, but the queen spoke excellent Latin and kept him constantly entertained. Her sparkling wit and depth of knowledge surprised him and the way she kept casting flirtatious glances at him from the sides of her eyes gave him the distinct impression that she was interested in him for more than just diplomatic reasons.

While just past the first flush of youth, the queen was nevertheless still stunningly beautiful and he was flattered by her interest. After months of military camp life with the legion, the thought that this very attractive, powerful woman might later be entertaining him in her bed made him feel smug and gave him a warm feeling in his loins.

For once, thought Agricola, life as a Roman tribune was actually enjoyable. Up until now it had all been a lot of hard work and the rigours of military life on campaign. He deserved a little rest and relaxation. This was one of the rare occasions when his rank and position actually brought him some benefits and he might as well make the most of it.

That decided, Agricola became determined to enjoy it to the full. The one dent in his enjoyment was the priest Marcus, who sat on his right and seemed wrapped in a permanent cloud of stony, silent disapproval at everything going on around him. The priest drank the merest amount of wine and refused nearly all the food that was placed before him. Abandoning attempts to draw him into the conversation, Agricola decided to ignore the man and not let him spoil his fun. If he wanted to be miserable then that was his lookout.

'I'm impressed by the musicians,' Agricola said to the queen. 'I had understood from the writings of Cicero that the people of Britannia have no musical knowledge.'

The queen laughed. 'What would a Roman philosopher know of music?' she said. 'Or any Roman, come to that? With your rigorous forms and your stylised singing you've formalised the life out of it. The Gauls, the Britons and best of all, the Hibernians, are the greatest musicians in the world.'

'Our emperor sees himself as one of the greatest musicians in the world and he is neither Gaul nor Hibernian,' Agricola said, remonstrating silently with himself for the slight slur in his words. He needed to watch what he was drinking.

'I did not mean to question the august Nero's talent,' the queen said. She blushed and looked down.

'Don't worry, I'm not offended,' Agricola said in a mumble. 'The man's a clown. An embarrassment to Rome.'

As soon as the words were out of his mouth he knew he should not have said them. The sharp look the queen shot at him told him she thought the same. The wine was getting to him more than he had realised. Regardless of what his private thoughts were about the emperor, he should never let himself express them in front of the natives. It was a chink in the aura of command, a small display of sympathy with the conquered and, with it, weakness.

'The spear was amazing,' he said, attempting to change the subject. 'So how is it done?'

'What do you mean?' the queen asked. 'It is a sacred

object of the Christians. It has great magical power. You saw that with your own eyes.'

'I've seen many such "miracles" before, Your Highness,' Agricola said with a knowing smile. 'Egyptian soothsayers and wizards are particularly good at it. They perform all sorts of tricks and all of them claim it is the work of a god.'

A fleeting look of annoyance replaced the queen's teasing smile. 'It's Christian magic,' she said. 'I do not share their faith. So I don't know how it works.'

'Oh come now,' Agricola said with a frown. 'You and I both don't believe the Christians' hocus-pocus. Surely we can discuss this like reasonable adults? The blood the spear is immersed in – pigs' is it? I've heard of strange metals discovered deep in the bowels of the earth that when exposed to the air suddenly ignite into flames. They're a hazard to miners in Dacia and the only way to get them up to the surface is to keep them submerged in water. Is this spear made from that sort of metal?'

The queen suddenly stood up, a perceptible look of relief on her face that Agricola could not fail to notice.

'Ah!' she said, with a clap of her hands. 'At last, the main course is here.'

She stepped forward to the centre of the room.

A group of slaves had just entered carrying a roasted boar. It was so huge it took four of them, two at the front and two behind, to carry the spit on which the massive carcass had been cooked. The delicious aroma of flame-roasted pork filled the room as the slaves carried their burden towards the queen. They set it down on a vast wooden carving table, which appeared to have been made for the purpose, from the entire cross-section of a mature oak tree and positioned beside the central fire.

A strange hush descended on the diners as a slave handed the queen an enormous carving knife, so big it was almost a shortsword. The slave also gave her a long-handled, two-pronged device resembling a pitchfork. Holding this in her left hand, she skewered it into the boar's haunch, crunching through the crisp, blackened skin and releasing twin rivers of clear, succulent juices. Clutching the knife in her other hand, the blade glittering in the torchlight, she sliced into the hindquarters, unleashing clouds of fragrant steam. Working the knife around the haunch, the queen dug in deeper, separating bones and joints.

Knife poised and dripping with grease and juices, she stood back a little and gestured to one of the slaves, a young boy, who came forward, his head bowed. He grasped the boar's left hock and wrenched the whole hindquarter away, set it down on the carving block then helped the queen as she went to work again, carving deep into the body, working the point of the long-bladed knife along the beast's spine. Finally she stepped back and the slave, his hands now wrapped in a cloth to protect them from the heat, lifted out a long, thin portion of meat and laid it down on the block beside the previously removed hind leg.

Agricola was puzzled at how quiet the room had become. The guests watched the queen carve these pieces of meat with a strange intensity and there was a definite sense of expectation in the air. This was clearly some sort of barbarian ceremony or tradition that he did not understand.

The queen beckoned to him to come forward, then gestured to the long cut of meat. He was both flattered and pleased. She was offering him the tenderloin fillet, the best cut on the animal. Clearly he was being honoured as an important guest.

With a smile he got to his feet and stepped forward to accept the queen's offer. As he did so gasps and cries of surprise and astonishment burst from the others in the room. Puzzled, hand outstretched, his fingers about to lift the cut of pork, Agricola glanced around and caught sight of movement out of the corner of his eye.

He turned to see the Hibernian trooper, Fergus MacAmergin, running into the room, pushing past a row of seated diners and heading straight for him. To Agricola's further consternation, the man seemed to be splattered with blood.

'Don't touch that meat!' Fergus shouted.

39

Had he stopped to think about it, Fergus would probably not have run straight into the middle of the royal house and the centre of a gathering of the elite warriors of Dobunnia, who outnumbered the Romans by about fifty to three. After the fight with the bodyguards, however, his blood was up and his first instinct was to warn the tribune. He ran to the centre of the room where Agricola stood, his hand hovering above the hunk of roast pork.

'That's the *curadmír*,' he said. 'If you take it there'll be a fight!'

Agricola frowned, wondering what Fergus was shouting about. He looked around and suddenly realised that all eyes in the room were staring at him. The other guests' faces displayed a mixture of astonishment, apprehension and downright anger. Several men were on their feet, among them Comux, who stood glaring at him, shoulders back, his top lip curled in a snarl and his eyes wide with undisguised rage.

'That piece of meat is called the curadmír,' Fergus said again. 'They call it *the champion's portion*. In this country it is the right of only the bravest warrior in the tribe to take it.'

'Then I am honoured that it has been offered to me,' Agricola said.

'You don't understand,' Fergus said. 'This is tradition. It belongs to a warrior here who everyone acknowledges is the bravest and hardest. You can't just take it. If you want it you have to fight whoever normally takes it.'

'The curadmír belongs to me!' Comux shouted. 'I'm the champion of this tribe and I will slaughter any man who disputes that.'

'Don't lift it, sir,' Fergus said, speaking directly to Agricola. 'This is all about the hardest man in the room; the one who has the biggest balls. You're being set up. Don't get tricked into it.'

Agricola, the wine coursing through his veins, tilted his head back and looked down his aquiline nose at Comux.

'Why not?' he said. 'I'm not afraid of this Brittunculi upstart. If he wants to fight me for a bit of pork then let him try.'

An inarticulate roar erupted from Comux and he started forward, charging straight towards Agricola. A couple of warriors jumped up and grabbed him by the arms to stop him in his tracks.

'Not in here,' the black-bearded warrior hanging on to Comux's right arm growled in his ear, but loud enough for everyone around the fire to hear. 'You can settle this properly outside, with weapons. Show the Roman dog who's the real champion here.'

'She contrived all this,' Fergus said, pointing at the queen. 'That spear has nothing to do with the Christians. It's a trick. It's all part of some scheme she's cooking up. I don't know what, but she's up to something.'

'How dare you speak of me like that!' the queen shrieked, her stately composure gone and her face livid with anger. 'How dare a mere bodyguard accuse me, Queen of the Dobunni.'

'You knew exactly what you were doing when you offered that meat to the tribune in front of everyone,' Fergus said. 'You knew the tribe's champion would have to challenge him for it or lose face.'

Comux suddenly stopped struggling against the restraint of his fellow warriors, a look of dawning realisation on his face.

'The Roman's right,' he said, turning an accusing glare on the queen. 'The champion's portion is always mine. What are you playing at offering it to another man, and a Roman at that?'

The queen's expression changed from one of anger to pure scorn. 'I know all about your plot to overthrow me, Comux. I know about the pathetic plans you have made with that ridiculous druid woman and your treacherous alliances with the other betrayers from my kingdom,' she said. She emphasised each word with a jab of the carving knife in his direction, her lips curled in a sneer that was both triumphant and contemptuous. 'Well it has all come to nothing. I'm one step ahead of you. How could you think you would ever outwit me, you pathetic little man? You were always just a means to an end for me; someone to give me legitimacy as queen after Catti died. I needed someone not too smart and easy to control so you were perfect. But now it seems you've outlived your usefulness.'

All around the room the other guests were on their feet. Unsettled murmurs and angry voices started to rumble. Warriors were facing off against each other as the room began dividing into two factions. Accusatory fingers were pointed, some shoved others as curses and threats were pronounced.

'You were hoping I would kill him in a fight?' Agricola said, the slight tone of astonishment in his voice betraying his amazement that a woman had manipulated him so easily.

The queen laughed. It was a short, bitter bark. 'My preferred outcome was that you would kill each other,' she said. 'At the very least that would save me the trouble of killing whoever won a fight between you.'

'You dare to threaten a tribune of Rome?' Agricola said.

'Your death is part of the agreement,' the queen said, a nasty, scornful grin spreading across her face.

'Agreement? What do you mean agreement?' Agricola said, and his jaw dropped open. He turned to look at Fergus, but the Hibernian was watching the queen, his eyes narrowed. 'Agreement with who?'

'I suspected Comux was about to make his move, but until yesterday I had no proof,' Finnabair said. 'It was one of your own comrades who alerted me to how far advanced his plans were.'

Agricola gaped at her. He shook his head to try to clear some of the wine fumes.

'What do you mean, one of my own comrades?' he said.

'I mean a Roman, you fool,' the queen said. 'A message arrived from Praefect Titus Pomponius last night, telling me about Comux's plot. It seems your praefect was anxious for me to know exactly when and how my consort means to overthrow me.'

She returned her attention to Comux.

'I have moved quickly and put my counter-plans against you in place.'

'You cannot win,' Comux said. 'You have no support. Who can you count on? Most of the nobles in the kingdom support me. My forces are gathered in the forest outside the hill fort. They will attack and your reign will be over. You may as well give up now.'

As if to confirm his words, a band of warriors and nobles gathered around him. Their wives were pushed to the inside of the group as they formed a protective ring around Comux, all facing outward, prepared to face any assault.

The rest of the nobles in the room gathered around the queen. There were fewer of them, though not by enough for Comux to have a definite advantage. For a moment the two factions glared at each other, nobody making a move. As everyone had surrendered their weapons on the way in to the hall for the moment there was little either side could do.

'Get out of here,' the queen spat at Comux. 'And take these traitors with you. Run to the woods and don't come back. If you do I'll be ready for you. My own warriors are prepared.'

'I'm going,' Comux said with a smile. 'But I'll return soon and when I do I'll take back the throne of this kingdom in the name of the people to whom it rightfully belongs, the Dobunni, not a foreign bitch like you. And then we will drive the Roman dogs from our land.'

Surrounded by his ring of warriors and their wives, Comux pushed past the remaining guests in the room and strode out of the door.

Fergus considered what had just been revealed. He had

suspected Pomponius wanted him dead and that it was he who was behind the botched attempt that had led to Liscus being killed. To kill a trooper was one thing, but to try to kill a tribune took things to a new level. The praefect was gambling with very high stakes.

Regardless, it was also time for him to go.

Fergus turned to run only to find himself confronted by the queen's remaining four bodyguards, who had come up behind him while his attention had been on Agricola.

'Seize them,' the queen said.

The bodyguards, along with some of the nobles, ran forward and fell on Agricola and Fergus. Fergus swung a fist at the first man who came onto him, connecting with his chin and sending him reeling sideways. Arms grabbed him from behind around the shoulders, but he thrust his head backwards and felt his skull connect with something soft that crunched. A man cried out in pain just beside his right ear and the arms released him.

Fergus stumbled forward, then four men went for him at once. Their sheer weight drove him to the floor. They rained blows and kicks down on him, smashing into his face, head and body and he could feel the weight of someone on his back, sitting on him and forcing his head to the ground. Realising there was nothing he could do for the moment he stopped struggling so as to abate the assault on him before he was knocked senseless.

The blows stopped. As he caught his breath he twisted around and saw that Agricola too had been captured. The tribune was on his knees, a man on either side of him forcing his arms behind his back. A third stood with his foot planted between the tribune's shoulder blades.

Fergus looked around for Marcus and saw that he too had been taken prisoner, and with him the Christian, Longinus.

'What do you think you're doing?' Agricola shouted at the queen. 'Comux is right. He has left with more than half the nobles here. You cannot hope to survive without Roman support. General Suetonius will have you crucified for treating me in this way.'

'Oh I have Roman support, don't worry,' the queen said. 'Your friend Pomponius has sent me some weapons that will help me defend against the attacks of Comux's rabble. He has also pledged to ride to my aid with cavalry and legionaries. Indeed, he approaches as we speak. He asks but a small price in return – a debt that I shall take great pleasure in discharging.'

Finnabair plunged the carving knife into the boar with such force that the point of the blade went right through the carcass and twanged into the wooden block. She lifted a chunk of the curadmír, the succulent portion of meat earlier offered to Agricola. Popping it into her mouth she chewed with relish, a rivulet of grease escaping to run down her chin.

Swallowing, the queen smiled at Agricola.

'He asks me to dispose of you and your companions while you are in my power,' she said. 'My druid, Anfad, will do this for me. Before morning he will sacrifice you to the black god.'

40

The bodyguards and Dobunni warriors dragged Fergus and the others outside.

The interior of the hill fort was a scene of chaos. Men and women were running about in every direction, shouting and yelling orders and warnings. Huddles of children watched the agitated adults with wide, frightened eyes.

The evening gloom was gathering, but it was still light enough for Fergus to see the anarchy around them. The conflict had begun in earnest as several bloodied corpses lay on the ground. It looked like Comux and his supporters had made straight for the armoury to retrieve their weapons, and that the queen had anticipated this. Once the feast had begun she must have ordered the building secured and ensured her warriors were ready for the fight.

Consequently, while they were outnumbered by Comux's band, the queen's warriors were armed and armoured and able to resist the assault. After losing several of his men it seemed that Comux had realised it was futile to continue. He had a sizeable faction around him, but he did not have enough men to take the fort.

Fergus, struggling in vain against his captors, saw the group of rebelling Dobunni were now charging for the horse corral. Swinging open the gates, men and women leapt onto horses. Riding bareback, clinging on to manes, they goaded the startled animals towards the gate of the fort. Some of the wealthier nobles – those who owned some of the chariots lined up beside the royal house – managed in all the confusion to yoke up horses. In moments, with a rumble of iron-rimmed wheels, they clattered after the riders storming out of the fort and set off down the road.

No one stood in their way. The defences of the fort were built to keep people out, not in. As they left, the queen's warriors rained slingshot stones and throwing darts on the escaping nobles, intending to inflict as many casualties as possible.

The huge gates were slammed shut behind them. The men hauling Fergus and the others stopped to bind their wrists together. Around them warriors began frenetic preparations to defend the fort. The armoury building was thrown open. Swords, spears and armour were distributed. Barrels of slingstones and throwing darts were hauled up onto the ramparts.

'There's nowhere near enough men to defend this place,' Agricola said. Fergus could see what he meant. The circumference of the hill fort was massive and, with relatively few warriors at the queen's disposal, only a part of the ramparts could be defended at one time, leaving the remainder open to attack.

The warriors holding them resumed their journey. Agricola, Fergus and Marcus were dragged, prodded and kicked along.

'Where are you taking us?' Agricola shouted, but their

captors did not respond. They kept dragging them on, away from both the main gate and the royal house.

'To the Roman fort...' Fergus said.

It looked like all of Quintus Valens' nightmares were about to come true. If the queen was prepared to kill Agricola, a Roman tribune, then she could not leave the garrison untouched. Sooner or later Valens would start asking where Agricola was.

The queen's Dobunni warriors had already surrounded the inner fortlet. He could see Roman soldiers, the Tungrian auxiliaries, on the torchlit ramparts, nervously eyeing the gathering natives.

The prisoners were brought to the edge of the ring of warriors and once more forced to their knees. Fergus heard the thumping of hooves and looking up saw the queen mounted on a white horse. She galloped to the front, pulling the animal to an abrupt halt so that it reared up then settled down again, prancing a couple of times while she got it under control. Fergus could not help thinking how magnificent she looked, her black hair rippling down her back in the late evening breeze.

'Bring the weapons into position!' the queen said.

From behind the four kneeling captives carts rumbled into view.

'Jupiter!' Agricola swore. 'They've got artillery.'

Squinting up at the carts, Fergus saw that mounted on the back of each one was what looked very like a ballista, except it was much smaller than the massive wooden crossbows that he had seen accompanying the legions. Normally they were twice the height of a man.

'What are they? They look like toys,' he commented,

aware that Finnabair had ridden back to where he knelt and was looking down at him. A surge of hope entered Fergus with the thought that perhaps Pomponius had supplied the queen with fake weapons.

'Oh they're real enough,' she said. 'Where is our Christian friend?'

Two burly warriors dragged Longinus forward and dumped him at the feet of her mount, making the beast skitter backwards. The Christian sprawled forwards onto his hands and knees and raised his head to look up at the queen.

'Ah, Caerwyn, or should I call you Longinus? I'm afraid I have brought you here under false pretences,' she said with an unpleasant smile. 'You thought you were here to complete an agreement with me that I would recognise your religion in return for your support. That was my intention, but circumstances have changed. Anfad, as you know, is the arch-druid of Gwynn ap Nudd. He has many more followers than you and the unfortunate truth – for you – is that neither he nor the Roman general, Suetonius Paulinus, will support me if I count Christians among my supporters. I am sorry, but events have overtaken you.'

The gloating look of triumph on her face betrayed that the queen was very far from sorry. Agricola was looking at the queen with an expression that betrayed his Roman astonishment that a mere woman should possess such scheming abilities.

'But I have another use for you,' the queen said. 'You may have tried to hide it, but I'm aware of the years you spent serving in the Roman legions. My spies in the Roman veteran colony also tell me that you have a particular skill, which is most fortuitous to my current plans.'

Longinus hung his head. 'I am no longer a soldier. I cannot help you,' he said in a mumble.

'What a pity,' the queen said. 'Unfortunately that means Flavia, Aulus and Petrus will pay for your lack of co-operation.'

The Christian stiffened. He looked up at her, his face creased with a frown of dismay.

'I have warriors ready to move,' Finnabair said. 'At my command your wife and children will be slaughtered, as will that pathetic crowd of followers you call your "herd".'

'My flock?' Longinus said. 'They are all innocent. They have no part in this. You have no reason to harm them.'

'I will if you don't comply with my wishes,' the queen said, gesturing towards the carts. 'I need you to show us how to aim and fire these weapons.'

'So Pomponius gave you the weapons but did not tell you how to use them?' Agricola said with a snort. The queen ignored him, but a warrior standing behind him cuffed him hard about the head.

'What is the target?' Longinus said.

'I'm afraid your former comrades are now a problem I must deal with,' the queen said, pointing at the small legionary fort. 'These weapons should help my warriors take that ridiculous fortification without incurring too many casualties of our own in the process.'

'But why?' Agricola said. 'You expect Roman support, yet you are going to kill Roman soldiers?'

'You signed their death warrant!' the queen said. 'If you hadn't insisted on visiting them this afternoon they would have been fine. But now they know you're here. They have to go. I will tell your general that Comux killed them.'

Longinus was hauled forwards and yanked to his feet beside the ballistae. One of the queen's bodyguards held a sword to his throat, but Longinus pushed the blade away with a resigned sigh.

'I will help you,' he said. 'Just leave my people alone.'

'How can you turn on your former comrades?' Agricola said with contempt. 'Though what else would anyone expect from a Christian?'

'It's them or my family and my flock,' Longinus said. 'Those soldiers knew what they were signing up for when they joined the army.'

He moved to examine one of the weapons.

'These ballistae are new,' he said. 'I've not seen anything like them before. The ones I was trained on when I was in the army were about four times the size of these.'

'Praefect Pomponius has assured me that the principles are the same,' the queen said. 'Enough talk. We have little time. Let us rid ourselves of these unwelcome guests before my prince gets his rabble together and attacks. Advance the carts.'

At her command, her warriors wheeled the ballistae carts to just outside javelin range of the Roman fort. There were four of the artillery weapons, Agricola noted, and it seemed Pomponius had supplied a wealth of ammunition to go with them. Barrels of the short, pyramid-headed, iron-clad bolts stood ready at the back of the carts and more were packed onto a fifth cart that waited nearby.

The Tungrians watching from the ramparts of the fortlet could see what was happening. A couple of them launched their javelins, but they were out of range and fell well short of doing any damage.

Longinus mounted one of the carts, accompanied by Ferchu and several other warriors, who watched and listened as the stocky ex-legionary outlined the basic principles of the weapon.

'These weapons are large, torsion-powered crossbows mounted on swivelling stands,' he said. 'The front of the metal bow part is covered by a large metal plate to protect the firing crew from spears, stones and other projectiles while they go about their business. The long main body has a sliding block inside the bowstring.'

Listening, Agricola noted the change that came over the man. His tone of voice lapsed unconsciously into the practised, lecturing tone of an artificer, almost as though he were on a practice ground instructing a group of new recruits on siege warfare.

Finnabair's warriors crowded round to watch as, with the ease of a much-drilled movement, Longinus placed one foot forward beside a long-handled lever attached to a cog on the back of the base of the ballista, and began cranking it backwards like a man rowing on an oar. With a rattling this began to ratchet back the bowstring into the firing position.

'Now, watch the sliding loading block,' Longinus said. 'See how it comes back with the bowstring until it is fully drawn and ready to aim?'

There was an audible click as the metal claw engaged to hold the bowstring drawn until unleashed. Longinus slid a bolt into place in front of the sliding block then stepped behind the ballista to aim it.

Longinus examined the weapon with the eye of an expert. He was so absorbed in the mechanics of the weapon that he seemed to have forgotten what was happening around him. Despite himself he could not help but be impressed by how light and manoeuvrable the ballista was, turning easily on the well-greased ball joint topping the supporting post. To his surprise he was able to move the heavy wood and iron construction by himself and was genuinely intrigued to find out if the weapon would match the power and range of the much larger versions that he had formerly been used to. Yet he sensed the almost palpable power waiting to be unleashed from the taut, drawn rope bowstring and the bent, iron-bound bow, which had been enhanced by a set of torsion springs made from ropes of animal sinew twisted around the arms of the bow.

'The bolt that this weapon launches is not like an arrow,' Longinus said. 'Arrows have a trajectory and fly in an arc with the wind. A ballista bolt always falls at exactly the same rate—'

'Shut up and just show us,' Ferchu said.

'Very well,' Longinus said. 'But don't blame me if you lose a hand or a couple of fingers.'

Sighting the weapon through a round hole in the forward protecting shield, Longinus aimed it directly at the gates of the fort, about one hundred and twenty paces away. With a steady hand he pulled the small lever that loosed the weapon. There was a crack as the bowstring shot forward, propelling the sliding block forwards. The torsion springs thrummed and the bolt shot towards its target, so fast it was a mere blur in the air.

There was a bang and a chunk of the gate about the size of a man's head disappeared, the broken-off piece of wood simply vanishing from sight as the bolt slammed through.

For a moment there was stunned silence, then a cheer

rose from the Dobunni warriors as they realised the power of the weapons now in their hands. Simultaneously, a cry of dismay arose inside the fort. The fort's defences had been built to keep the native tribes out but the Britons were not supposed to have weapons like the ballista.

Longinus gaped in astonishment at the power of so small a ballista.

'God forgive me,' he murmured.

'The gate,' the queen said, pointing in the direction of the fort with a look of delight on her face. 'Shoot at the gate.'

She made a hand gesture and a group of men carrying carnyx ran forward blowing on their instruments. The noise was ear-shattering. Made of bronze, the carnyx were fashioned in the shape of a boar's head. The bell of the war trumpet funnelled and amplified the sound but in addition, loosely connected wooden 'tongues' were fitted into the mouths of the 'boars', which added a rattling clatter to the noise, designed to terrify the enemy.

The warriors manning the other three ballistae eagerly leapt to try their own hand with the new weapons. In quick succession the bows cracked as they were loosed. One bolt sailed high over the little Roman fortification, the second hit the ground before reaching its target, kicking up a lump of turf into the air, but the third punched straight through the wood of the gate, opening up another hole.

Longinus, years of legionary training and military professionalism overcoming all else, moved between the two ballistae that had missed their target, coaching their crews on what they were doing wrong. No one stopped him. Ferchu was too intent on reloading the ballista for another shot to pay any heed.

All four ballistae loosed again and this time all hit the gates. The gate on the right-hand side twisted backwards then collapsed inward, tearing itself off its hinges. More cheers erupted from the gathered Dobunni warriors.

The warriors on the ballistae worked in an intense frenzy, one cranking the weapon, another loading and a third firing. In no time they were working like seasoned legionaries. Ballista bolts smashed the remaining gate to firewood, the walls were peppered with holes and the crenelated battlement tops began to crumble. Sprays of bright crimson blood, cries of pain, screams of anguish and urgent shouting from inside the fortification conveyed the message that the Tungrians were taking casualties. Fergus tried to calculate how many, but it was impossible as they remained crouched behind the inadequate cover of the walls.

The assault continued, a relentless hail of iron-tipped missiles that, having destroyed the crenelations, began to smack through the walls themselves.

A rumble of wheels accompanied by a strange humming and whirring noise, audible even above the din of the ballistae and cries of the wounded, made everyone turn to see what it was.

Anfad had arrived. The huge druid stood on the platform of a chariot, but from what Fergus could see in the half-light, it was not a normal British war chariot. The two horses drawing it were fitted with protective iron-inlaid breastplates that sprouted spears and spikes. Their flanks were similarly covered. The chariot was much wider than normal and its central axle extended way out beyond the wheels. Above the extensions was a long wooden platform that reached out like a wing on each side of the chariot. At the end of the wings were metal cogs that drove wheels on either side of the axle. These revolved horizontally to the ground in time to the rotation of the chariot wheels.

Three long, heavy, oversized scythe blades were attached to the hubs on top of the horizontal wheels on both sides, and these also rotated, just above the height of a man's knee, swooping through the air with a deep, whooping noise. The huge blades, their edges honed to wicked sharpness, were highly polished and gleamed even in the gathering dark of evening.

'Jupiter noblest and strongest!' Agricola said. 'What on earth is that?'

'It's a sickle chariot,' Fergus said, raising his voice to be heard above the din. 'It's vicious but particularly effective against foot soldiers.'

An appalled expression clouded Agricola's face as he realised both the potential number of casualties and the horrific nature of the damage such a weapon could inflict on infantry.

'I've heard of these chariots. The Persians used them,' he said. 'But I thought the blades were supposed to be in the centre of the wheels.'

'That wouldn't make any sense,' Fergus said. 'Those blades will cut a man off at the knee first, then as he falls one of the other two blades will make sure he is dead.'

Quintus Flavius Valens, instantly recognisable by the crimson plume on his helmet, suddenly appeared on the battlements of the Roman fort. To his right and left Tungrian auxiliaries also showed themselves, their oval shields held up above their heads in a seldom seen gesture that only meant one thing.

'He's surrendering,' Agricola said, both disbelief and disappointment cracking his voice.

Fergus was not that surprised. Valens had clearly been at the end of his tether, his nerves already shot to pieces. The idea of him holding out for long against this onslaught was absurd.

Glancing around to see what the queen's response would be, Fergus saw Ferchu was lining up his ballista in the firing position. One eye closed, he couched his shoulder behind the end of the weapon and took careful aim.

With a bang the ballista loosed, and the bolt streaked through the air. A crimson cloud exploded around Valens. The bolt went through him at the base of his neck and his head came off, the bronze, crested helmet with his head still in it tumbling backward, chin first, to disappear into the interior of the fort. His decapitated body, a fountain of blood spouting from his destroyed neck, toppled slowly forward onto the rampart.

Clearly astounded at the power and accuracy of the weapon now in his control Ferchu let out a yelp of delight.

'He was trying to surrender!' Agricola cried.

'I didn't accept his terms,' Ferchu said, grinning. 'Keep at it, lads.'

The relentless attack continued. With the gates gone, bolts sailed into the interior of the fort unhindered and smashed through the clay walls of the barrack room inside. Chunks fell away from the wall and pieces dissolved into dust. Red roof tiles exploded as bolts went through them.

'They're being slaughtered like cattle,' Agricola said grimly.

As he spoke, there was movement inside the fort. The

Tungrians formed up in battle order. They advanced at a jog out of the open gateway, shields held before them, *pila* at the ready, the javelins couched under their right arms.

'They're coming out,' Fergus said.

'I don't blame them,' Agricola said. 'What would you rather do? Sit inside the fort and be massacred or take your chance and try to break out?'

'They don't stand a chance,' Fergus said.

'That's how a Roman soldier should behave,' Agricola said. His voice cracked with pride.

The Tungrians' shields were useless against the ballistae. A volley of four ballista bolts took six of them down as they left the cover of the walls. The missiles sheared straight through their shields as if they were not there. The bolts that hit the first two men travelled with such velocity that they also impaled the men running directly behind them.

As if smacked by a giant hand the auxiliaries pounding forwards at a run were swatted backwards by the impacts and sent flying off their feet to land in shattered, bloodstained heaps. Another bolt pounded into a Tungrian's chest and his torso fell apart, his arms, legs and head tumbling to the ground in different directions. The sixth bolt sheared the head of an auxiliary clean from his shoulders. His decapitated body, its severed neck pumping blood high into the air, carried on running for several steps before it fell forwards.

A second salvo took another five Tungrians down. With so many dead so quickly, the auxiliaries' discipline disintegrated. They broke ranks. Their orderly advance fell apart and all of them started running across the parade ground, desperate to close the gap with the surrounding warriors to give themselves even half a chance of fighting their way out. The ballistae were able to reload and shoot so rapidly that another ten Tungrians had been cut down before they even made it halfway.

There was a blast from the Dobunni carnyx. With a loud, rattling hum Anfad's sickle chariot began rolling forwards. The scythe blades whooped like beating swan wings as they rotated faster and faster. At a second blast from the carnyx, the ballistae stopped shooting as the chariot came within their range. A crowd of Dobunni warriors charged behind it to meet the Tungrians.

The auxiliaries saw the chariot coming and began to break sideways in both directions in an attempt to get away from the reach of the deadly vehicle. The move should have opened a gap through which the chariot would harmlessly pass while the soldiers escaped to the right and left, but Anfad's charioteer had other ideas.

Hauling on the reins, he turned the horses, first to the right, then back to the left in an incredibly skilled manoeuvre that swung the chariot through ninety degrees and should have seen it tip over. Somehow the charioteer kept it on its wheels so that the right-hand side of the chariot was now in killing distance of the front rank of Tungrians.

It swept alongside them, reaping a terrible harvest. Screams of shock and agony filled the air. A haze of crimson rose beside the chariot as the heavy spinning blades scythed through the knees, thighs and lower bodies of the running men, severing limbs and chopping men into bloody chunks of meat. At the end of its pass the chariot turned left again, back towards the ballistae. As soon as it withdrew, the ballistae unleashed another volley into what was left of the auxiliaries. By the time the Dobunni warriors reached the few Tungrians who were still on their feet, it was pretty much all over. All they had to do was kill the injured and maimed as they lay writhing on the ground.

As a hush descended on the parade ground that had become a scene of massacre, Agricola and Fergus gazed in horrified silence at the bloodied lumps that only moments ago had been living men.

With the quiet came the sound of commotion happening elsewhere in the fort. A warrior on a horse galloped up to the queen.

'Majesty, Comux is approaching the main gate with an army,' the warrior said. 'They were waiting in the forest near your villa. They will be here soon.'

A wild glint appeared in the queen's eyes. 'Let's get these new weapons to the gate so we can prepare a little surprise for my ex-consort,' she said. 'I think they have already proved their worth admirably here this evening. Longinus, I still have work for you. You'll come with us to help with these machines. Anfad,' she shouted to the druid as she swept her hand towards Fergus and Agricola, 'the other prisoners are now yours to do with as you will. Just make sure they end up dead.'

'I will, don't worry about that,' Anfad said, climbing down from the back of the death machine and stretching his long limbs as he looked up at the sky. 'But the time is not yet right. Have them locked up with the other prisoner until later. I will deal with them when the moon is in the correct position.'

As they were hauled to their feet and led away, Fergus contemplated their options.

There were not many. He was aware of some of the ways in which the druids sacrificed people, so who knew what unpleasant death Anfad intended for them. If they escaped Anfad somehow and Comux won the upcoming battle, then he would certainly kill them too. If Pomponius arrived with the legionaries then he would want to cover his tracks and would ensure they didn't live to tell any tales. All in all, unless they could work out a way to escape, their options consisted of nothing more than different ways to die.

41

Fergus, Agricola and Marcus were marched at spear point to the temple beside the royal house, then shoved roughly through the door. Fergus felt a sudden surge of hope, knowing he had got into the building earlier and now he had Agricola with him he could probably get out of it too.

The door banged shut, followed by the sound of a heavy bar being drawn across it, and they looked around at their surroundings. A couple of blazing torches, set into brackets high up on the wall, provided some light and from it they saw a cloaked figure sitting on the bare, packed mud floor. It was Ceridwen the druidess who, last time he had seen her, was being dragged away by Cet, Col and Mebul.

'This is going to be interesting,' Fergus said, observing the desultory expression on Ceridwen's bruised face and the glares of mutual animosity that passed between her and the Roman priest.

'What is this place?' Agricola asked, looking around warily at their surroundings. 'What's that hole in the ground for?'

His gaze slid to the wooden altars, which resembled huge chopping blocks.

'I don't like the look of that,' he said, pointing at the dark brown stains that decorated them. Whether it was human or animal blood it was impossible to tell.

'This is a temple to their dark gods,' the priest commented miserably. 'We are to be slaughtered, victims of a barbaric religion.'

'How dare a Roman accuse anyone of barbarism?' Ceridwen said. 'You who destroy whole cultures—'

Agricola held up his hands. '*Please*, this is no time for religious arguments,' he said. 'It appears we're all now in the same boat, a fact that I would venture to suggest none of us is particularly pleased about. However, if we are to escape from this, can I suggest that we temporarily set aside our differences and work together?'

For a long moment they all looked back at him in stony silence.

Finally Ceridwen shrugged. 'What other choice do we have?' she said.

Fergus eyed her warily, surprised and suspicious at how readily she accepted the situation.

'Good,' Agricola said. 'So let us—'

Whatever the tribune had been about to say was lost as a great noise came from outside. It was the sound of many men's raised voices. War cries and screams of pain and terror mingled into one massive, incoherent roar.

'Comux is attacking,' Fergus said.

'Perhaps I won't be forced to help you after all,' Ceridwen said, her eyes lighting up. 'Comux will be victorious and I will be freed. You'll all die anyway.'

'You didn't seem to be getting on very well with Comux

last time I saw you together,' Fergus said. 'From what I could see you were arguing.'

'Comux is a fool,' the druid said with a tut.

'I thought you and he had some sort of arrangement?' Fergus said. 'Earlier you said you were both part of some "higher plan".'

Ceridwen rolled her eyes and let out a short, exasperated cry. Fergus got the distinct impression that she was less self-assured, even lost. Although she fell silent he was sure she had more to say but was holding it back. The proud, feisty woman he had seen before had changed. Something had gone from her and it seemed to him that an air of defeat and despondency hung around her. He wondered what the queen's bodyguards had done to her.

'I was a fool,' she said in Hibernian, almost as if to herself. 'I said too much, things that I shouldn't have. Not that it matters now. There is no way out of here. The gods seem to have stepped in to make sure the greater plan continues.'

'No way out?' Fergus said. 'You forget you and I broke in here earlier. We can break out the same way.'

She raised her eyes to look at him but he saw nothing in them but hopelessness.

'What is she saying?' Agricola said. 'What are you two talking about?'

Switching back to Latin, Fergus quickly outlined what had happened earlier that evening. He pointed to the disturbed area of thatch in the roof where he and Ceridwen had gained access.

'What are we waiting for?' Agricola said, peering up at the roof. 'Get up on my shoulders.'

Fergus shook his head. 'You get on mine,' he said. 'I'm a head and shoulders taller than you.'

Fergus crouched down. The tribune climbed onto his back and knelt on his shoulders. With a flex of his powerful thighs, Fergus stood upright again, pushing Agricola up towards the roof. He still was not high enough and had to scramble up from his knees, precariously placing his feet on either side of Fergus's neck so he could poke his head through the hole in the thatch.

'Jupiter!' he said almost immediately.

'Hold still, damn you!' Fergus said, but Agricola was ducking back down. He came back too quickly and both men unbalanced, Fergus falling onto his backside while Agricola sprawled away from him, slamming into the ground and rolling forwards, just managing to stop himself before he toppled into the square pit in front of the three altars.

Marcus, who had been peering up at the thatch, leapt backwards. Above them came the sound of heavy thumps as missiles hit the roof hard in several places near the hole where only moments before Agricola's head had been.

'That was close,' Agricola said, rubbing his ribs where they had smashed into the hard-packed earth.

'I'll say it was!' Fergus pointed at the hole in the ground. 'You nearly fell down that.'

'What is it?' Agricola said, observing the square, wood-lined shaft that disappeared down into darkness.

'It's a sacrificial pit,' Fergus said. 'It goes way down into the earth, who knows how deep. The offerings to the gods are thrown down it. There's usually a big spike at the bottom to ensure anything that goes down it alive doesn't stay that way too long. In the slight chance that they do, the shaft is smooth-sided so they can't climb back out. The gods will not be denied what is their right.'

Fergus took a small coin from the purse on his belt. He flicked it up into the air, letting it fall into the pit where it disappeared into the darkness. For several seconds there was silence until the faint sound of a splash reached their ears from far below. It was clear the pit was both very deep and filled with water at the bottom.

'I should have made a wish,' Fergus said with a bleak grin.

Agricola looked down at the sheer, smooth walls of the pit and Fergus noted the little involuntary shiver that ran through the tribune as he realised the horror of the death he had just narrowly avoided.

'When I looked through the hole in the roof I saw there are guards standing in a horse corral at the back of the temple,' Agricola said. 'They're waiting for anyone poking their head out. Soon as they saw me they were ready with throwing spears, those short darts of theirs and slingshots too. I was lucky not to get my head knocked off.'

A sullen silence descended as the realisation set in that there was no way out of this temple after all. It had become their prison and there was little they could do but sit and wait for death.

'What's she doing here anyway?' Agricola finally said, nodding towards Ceridwen.

'She was up to something with Comux,' Fergus said. 'I saw them plotting earlier. The giant druid with the sickle chariot is in on it too. It seems everyone double-crossed everyone else and the queen was one step ahead of them all.'

'She was one step ahead of all of *us*,' Agricola said. 'By Jupiter, she would go far in Rome. She'd give the emperor's mother a run for her money when it comes to politics.'

Ceridwen grunted. She had not moved from the position they had first seen her in, sitting on the floor with her back to one of the wooden altars.

'Finnabair is a stupid, self-seeking bitch,' she said. 'She has ruined everything.'

'What were you two up to anyway?' Fergus asked. 'You said something about some sort of grand plan to kick the Romans out?'

Ceridwen looked away then heaved a sigh.

'We're all going to die anyway,' she said. 'I may as well tell you. You were right: I am of the Trinovantes. Our tribe and our neighbours in the east, the Iceni, are planning a rebellion against Rome. We know that two tribes are not powerful enough on their own, not with four Roman legions in Britain. For the last year I have been travelling round Britain through all the tribes and kingdoms, working out who will join our fight and who will not, and helping to co-ordinate the strategy.'

'The Iceni are loyal to Rome,' Agricola said. 'Their king is a client and has made the emperor his successor.'

'His queen, Boudicca, has not,' Ceridwen said. 'The Silures' revolt was the first step, but the time is not yet right for the rest of the rebellion to begin. Comux could not see beyond the borders of the Dobunni kingdom so has launched this war too early for his own selfish reasons. He risks wrecking the whole plan, which will only work if all of us – all the separate tribes – work together and rise at the same time.'

'Which is why it'll never work,' Fergus said. 'The Britons hate the Romans, but they hate each other more.'

'And for the same reason the Romans will conquer Hibernia,' Ceridwen said.

'So when is the "right time" for this rebellion?' Agricola said.

Ceridwen just shook her head and Fergus surmised she had decided that she had already said too much.

Outside the roaring reached a deafening crescendo, now mingled with screeches and wails of pain and the clash and bang of weapons colliding. The noise was so great it killed the conversation in the temple.

Agricola began examining the walls and door to see if there were any possible means of escape. Fergus went over and sat down on the ground beside Ceridwen.

'Perhaps I should tell him it was you who let me escape from the legionary camp?' Ceridwen said in a whisper, nodding her head in Agricola's direction. 'What would your tribune make of you then?'

'He already has a fair idea that it was me,' Fergus said. 'Look: you were talking about working together. The only chance we have of getting out of here is if we all work together. You don't like Romans and I don't like druids, so neither of us are happy with this situation, but we can settle our differences once we've got out of this.'

'It's pointless. We're going to die,' Ceridwen said.

'You seem very sure about that,' Fergus said.

'I'm certain,' Ceridwen said, looking him in the eyes. 'I told you before about the prophecy that was pronounced on the day I became a druid?'

Fergus, who found her gaze strangely captivating, nodded.

'Well it said that a painted man would come from the north,' she continued. 'With him he will bring violence and death, fire will rain from the sky and it will be the end of my path. You are of the Cruithni, the people the Romans call Picti "painted people".'

She pointed at the tattoos that decorated Fergus's arms.

'You are my doom,' she said.

'Prophecies, superstitions?' Fergus said. 'It's all nonsense.'

'It is my faith,' Ceridwen said bitterly, glaring at him with accusation in her eyes. 'And it once was yours. Anyway, I can do nothing against these men. The queen has given her bodyguards snakestones. I am powerless against them.'

Fergus shook his head and stood up. He took a couple of steps away then turned suddenly.

'Catch,' he said, throwing something at her.

Instinctively Ceridwen caught it. She opened her hand to see what it was. With a yelp she dropped the object as if it was red hot. Fergus's snakestone amulet rolled across the floor.

'See?' he said, returning, picking up the stone and pressing it back into the astonished druid's palm. 'It's just a stone. It's only your belief that gives it power over you.'

Ceridwen looked down at the stone as though scarcely able to believe she was able to hold it.

'Without my powers I am nothing,' she said in a breathless voice. 'My powers come from my faith.'

'Right now we don't need your magic, druid. We just need your sword arm,' Fergus said.

Ceridwen nodded, realisation and a new look of resolution dawning on her face.

'Great,' Fergus said. 'Now all we need is a plan for how to get out of here.'

42

Longinus felt exhausted. He was tired from the physical effort of directing the ballistae onslaught but his heart was also weary at the destruction and waste of human life he was overseeing.

After the slaughter at the Roman fortlet, the ballistae had been hurried to the main gate of the oppidum and positioned in the gateway, which was open so they had clear aim at the approaching enemy. The ramparts around the gate were lined with warriors armed with throwing spears, darts, slingshots and plain old rocks to hurl down onto whoever got close enough to the gates, while others stood ready to slam the gates shut when the prince's forces got close enough.

Comux's warriors had gathered in a wood near the villa at the base of the hill, waiting for the order to attack. When he came running out of the hill fort they had emerged from the trees and mustered into fighting order, whipping themselves into battle frenzy as the sun sank. As darkness came, the first thing they did was to set ablaze the magnificent Roman villa. It was a gesture of anger and resistance but they failed to realise the serious consequences it brought down on them. The firelight allowed Longinus to direct the ballistae's aim much better than the gathering gloom would otherwise have allowed.

The gathering host of warriors at the base of the hill was a formidable sight. There were hundreds of men stood ready for war. They outnumbered those preparing to defend the hill fort by about three to one. Their nobles rode up and down the ranks in their battle chariots, haranguing the forces and urging them on to brave deeds. The last rays of the setting sun glinted red-gold on great battle shields, leaf-bladed spears, longswords and the gold and silver torcs round the necks of the fighting men. They whipped themselves into a war fury, screaming battle cries at the darkening sky. Some wore chain mail armour but many were stripped to the waist, their drooping moustaches combed smooth and their long hair brushed back and limewashed so that it stood up from their heads in the outlandish fashion of the tribes.

Seeing the closely packed ranks of the gathered warriors at the bottom of the hill, the professional soldier in Longinus took over once more. He made a shrewd assessment and ordered the ballistae crews to replace the narrow, bolt-firing sliding blocks to ones with a wider, semicircular base. These fitted round stones and several barrels of stone balls, ranging in size from just bigger than a fist to slightly smaller than the size of a man's head, were carried to the ballistae by warriors supporting the crews.

Longinus directed them to load the stones into the weapons then instructed Ferchu and the other men to gather round one of the ballistae while he demonstrated firing the different kind of ammunition.

With a huge shout Comux's force began surging up the hill to attack.

'We will be firing downhill,' Longinus said, his voice calm and unflustered, despite the approaching menace, 'so we must take account of that by aiming over the heads of the enemy. Remember what I said about the shot falling at a uniform rate.'

He pulled the lever and loosed the ballistae. The stone flew down the hill and like a huge, invisible finger being laid down on a field of long grass, it ploughed a bloody path through the throng of warriors. A gasp arose from the hill fort defenders. The stones powered through man after man, pulverising flesh and bone, smashing heads and tearing off limbs. A whole rank of warriors, at least ten deep, was mowed down, leaving a flattened path of mangled body parts and shattered bodies. Incredibly, even when it had passed right through all the warriors from the front ranks to the back, it kept going. When it finally struck the earth it still had enough momentum to bounce high into the air.

With an excited whoop Ferchu pushed Longinus aside to take control of the ballista. The other warriors ran to man the other three weapons. Longinus stepped down from the cart, his heart heavy once more. Even though he had seen it many times while in the army, the sudden, shocking sight of the devastation caused by the ballista hit him like a bucket of ice-cold water.

Sickened by his own actions he bowed his head and offered up a prayer to the Lord to forgive him for what he had done, and guide him in the best path to take next. As more stones were loaded into the ballista, he reflected that at the very least there might still be a chance the queen would look favourably on the belief in Christ when this was all over. Whatever she had said earlier about Anfad, she would still be short of support and would require help from whoever she could get. This was probably all part of God's higher plan.

Knowing he was playing a part in that, Longinus felt slightly more content. Comux, he knew, would not hesitate to wipe out the Christians as a foreign, Roman cult. Given the stark choice between helping to fight Comux's army of pagans or the queen killing his family, he had done the right thing. That was what his god would understand, or so he fervently hoped.

Almost simultaneously, the four ballistae loosed a volley of stones into the lines of men charging up the hill. More holes were torn open in their ranks. One stone smashed the head of one of the pair of horses pulling a war chariot that pounded slightly ahead of the throng. As a shower of blood, brains and bone fragments splattered its companion, the beast went down, dragging the chariot traces with it, twisting the central shaft and pulling the other horse over as well. The charioteer, reins bound around his forearms, was hauled from the vehicle's platform and fell into the chaos of thrashing horseflesh. The chariot flipped over, spilling the aristocratic warrior on its platform onto the ground then smashing down on top of him. The rolling vehicle swept more charging warriors to death and injury, shattering into splinters on the way.

By now the surging warriors were almost halfway up the hill. They quickly filled the gaps in their ranks and continued charging towards the gate. Within seconds the ballistae were reloaded and another volley ploughed four new bloody troughs through the lines of warriors.

Fuelled by battle madness the charge continued, but now the attackers were in range of the defenders on the ramparts. A deadly hail of darts, spears, slingshots and rocks scythed into the front ranks, quickly followed by another withering salvo from the ballistae that reaped another bloody harvest.

As the entire front ranks were obliterated and three more nobles in their chariots were destroyed before even reaching the still-open gates of the hill fort, the indiscriminate slaughter wreaked by the ballistae finally had its effect. The attack faltered. Dismay and shock at the sheer scale and speed of their losses hit the charging warriors in a wave of despair and terror. At first they simply halted, then quickly turned on their heels and began running back down the hill even faster than they had come up it.

Three noblemen in their chariots tried to stop the rout by halting their war vehicles on the slope and shouting encouragement and threats, but another vicious volley from the ballistae smashed them to bloody pieces in moments.

Victorious cheers rose from the defenders as Comux's forces retreated. They suffered several more withering volleys from the ballistae as they fled. Leaving their dead and dying behind them, they withdrew into the darkness at the foot of the hill beyond the glow of the blazing fires from the burning villa.

Longinus sat on the ground with his back against the ballista, his forehead resting on his cradled fingers. As the clamour of battle died away to be replaced by the screams and groans of the dying and injured outside the ramparts, he felt a large hand come to rest on his shoulder.

He raised his head and found himself looking into the leering face of Anfad the arch-druid.

'Your work is done. It is time to join your friends,' Anfad said with an unpleasant grin. 'It's time to die.'

43

Longinus was unceremoniously shoved through the door of the temple. Fergus was talking to Agricola, trying to work out what options they had. It had not been a fruitful conversation. They all had noticed the substantial decrease in the noise of battle from outside. Eager to learn what was happening they rushed over to question him.

As the door slammed shut behind him, Longinus picked himself up off the floor. Recognising Fergus, he responded to their questioning and related the story of Comux's failed assault.

'His forces are now at the foot of the hill,' he said. 'They know if they advance the ballistae will slaughter them. At the same time they know they still have more men than are defending the hill fort for the queen, so they have laid siege. It's a stand-off.'

'What are they going to do with us?' the priest said.

'Anfad said we are all to be sacrificed to the devil,' Longinus said. 'Sometime before dawn.'

'So the queen betrayed you too,' Fergus said.

'I only hope she leaves my family and flock alone,' Longinus said, sadly. 'At least I will die a martyr's death. The Lord Jesus looks favourably on that.'

'A Christian?' Marcus the priest said, a horrified look on his face. 'Must I die surrounded by druids, barbarians and now Christians?'

'We feel exactly the same way about you, Roman,' Ceridwen said.

'Well whatever we think about each another, if we don't work out a plan we'll all die here together,' Fergus said. 'We need a way to escape.'

'We could rush them when they come in,' Agricola said.

'We have no weapons, we wouldn't stand a chance,' Fergus said.

'Do you want to just sit here and wait for death?' Agricola said, his eyes glittering with challenge.

His suggestion was met with silence and a row of surly faces. Agricola was right though; the only thing left was to try to fight their way out. It was hopeless but preferable to being thrown down the dark, deep sacrificial pit.

The night wore on. The guttering torches began to burn low. With the adrenaline rush of confrontation gone and nothing to do but wait, Fergus actually found himself nodding off. Deciding that there was no real reason not to, he lay down beside one of the altars and drifted off to sleep.

He was rudely awakened by Agricola shaking him by the shoulder.

'They are coming,' the Roman said.

Fergus rolled to his feet, rubbing his eyes. He could hear raised voices approaching outside and there was a rattling of the bar being withdrawn from the door.

Agricola and Fergus tensed. The door swung open, but no one came in. Instead, warriors were arranged in a semicircle around the door outside. They all had spears ready and some held torches.

The massive druid Anfad ducked down and entered the room, a drawn sword in his hand.

'It is nearly morning,' he said, indicating with the point of his sword that Fergus and Agricola should back off. They shuffled backwards, realising their moment of attack had passed.

Eight warriors followed Anfad into the temple and then the queen's four remaining bodyguards, struggling under the weight of the huge, blood-filled cauldron in which rested the magical spear. Two women druids in black robes brought up the rear and suddenly the room seemed full of people.

Agricola and Fergus were pushed back at spear point while the bodyguards set the cauldron down before the dark pit in front of the wooden altars. The warriors grabbed each of the prisoners and bound their hands behind their backs, forcing them to sit in a row on the ground so that they were facing Anfad and the cauldron.

'What manner of rope is this?' Agricola said as he struggled against his bonds, feeling hairs from it rubbing against his wrists.

'It's fox fur,' Ceridwen said. 'We use it to bind those to be sacrificed to the gods. It cannot be broken.'

Anfad gestured to the warriors to withdraw.

'The queen told us to guard you at all times,' Ferchu said, 'and there are five of them.'

'Thank Her Majesty, but I am no weakling who needs nursemaids. I can deal with four bound men and one woman,' the druid said. 'This sacred act is only to be witnessed by the devotees of Gwynn ap Nudd. Now go.'

Fergus could see the bodyguard's uncertainty. Judging by his expression, the superstitious part of Ferchu wanted to be away from anything to do with Crom, the horrific black god the Britons called Gwynn ap Nudd.

After another moment's hesitation, Ferchu nodded. Clicking his fingers at the other warriors to follow, he strode out of the temple without a backward glance.

When they had left, Anfad walked to the cauldron and grasped the shaft of the magic spear. He rotated it slowly, keeping the head of the spear submerged, stirring the black, viscous blood. He gazed fixedly into the dark liquid and gave a low chuckle.

'That spear is sacred to Lugh, the god who every year slays Gwynn and forces him back into the darkness of winter,' Ceridwen said. 'If you wield it you will simply be reminding everyone of the eternal defeat of your god.'

Anfad shook his head.

'It is indeed the spear of Lugh, cursed be his name,' he said. 'Therefore it will make a fitting tool to make a sacrifice to Gwynn. You five will be offerings to him. You will have the honour of the threefold death. After you are dead I will take the spear south and it will serve Gwynn as a symbol of his power over Lugh. In my hands it will be a reminder to all that it is darkness that triumphs over light, not the other way around. The spear of Lugh will become the spear of Gwynn.'

'So that's really why you sent the queen's warriors away,' Fergus said. 'She won't be happy when she finds you plan to steal the bargaining tool she used to buy Pomponius's military aid. The spear the general wants as well.'

'She would not have it at all if it were not for me,' Anfad said, his extremely long, smooth beard split by his wide, unpleasant grin. 'It was I who brought it from my mentor Colphra in Hibernia. It was only on loan to her to further our ends. She should know better than to offer what is not in her gift to give. My chariot is yoked and ready. I will leave when the sacrifice is complete. The queen will never know what happened.'

'Crom's blood! Can no one be trusted?' Fergus said. He spat on the ground. 'What a vipers' nest this country is.'

'You speak the name of Crom, Roman,' Anfad said, narrowing his eyes. 'In Hibernia that is the name for my god, Gwynn. What do you know of Crom?'

'I know he's a worthless bastard of a god,' Fergus said, leering provocatively.

Anfad gazed at Fergus for a long moment.

'Well you will soon be able to tell him that face to face,' the druid said in a growl. 'The threefold death awaits you.'

'What sort of scum are you?' Ceridwen said. 'You betray Comux and me, and now the queen as well. Have you no honour or integrity at all? Does nothing matter to you but your own ends?'

'Nothing matters but the will of Gwynn,' Anfad replied, his blue eyes glittering in the torchlight. 'Comux is a fool who cannot lead the Dobunni. This way they will destroy each other and leave only one power strong enough to rule this land.'

'You,' Ceridwen said, the light in her eyes dimming as

she comprehended the druid's strategy. Sitting beside her, Fergus felt her shoulders sag against him.

'I was a fool to think we could unite the tribes of Britain against the Romans,' she said in a murmur, looking sideways at Fergus. 'You were right: the divisions between our people are too deep, our ancient hatreds too great. What hope did our plan have when the tribes themselves cannot unite?'

'What's going on?' Agricola demanded in Latin. 'What are they saying and what is this threefold death thing?'

'You don't want to know,' Fergus said. 'It won't be pleasant I can assure you.'

'Offer him wealth in exchange for the spear and letting us go,' Agricola said. 'Say he can rule the kingdom in Rome's name if he wants. It doesn't matter to Caesar what petty king governs the tribes so long as he keeps the peace and pays the taxes.'

'You don't understand,' Fergus said. 'The man is a religious fanatic. He isn't going to be impressed by that sort of offer.'

'We should at least try,' Agricola said.

Fergus sighed and with a meaningful glance at Agricola, shook his head.

The huge druid chuckled.

'You think me so ignorant that I do not understand Latin, Roman?' he said in his deep baritone voice. 'I am a druid. I was tutored from an early age in many tongues both living and long dead, including yours. Why would I want to rule in Rome's name? A king of slaves is merely the most important slave. I have no wish to be that. Enough talk. It's time for the ritual to begin.'

The women in black began a terrible howling that was

a weird mixture somewhere between a chant, a song and a scream. Anfad stood among them intoning strange, archaic pronouncements in a tongue that sounded familiar to the ear and yet was unintelligible.

As the noise grew to a terrible crescendo, Fergus cocked his head to one side towards Ceridwen.

'Try and untie me,' he said out of the corner of his mouth. At the same time he turned his shoulders slightly so that his bound hands were closer to hers.

At first Ceridwen did not seem to notice. Then, when Anfad, his eyes closed, seemed totally absorbed in the ritual, she shifted slightly so as to bring her own tied hands in closer proximity to Fergus's. He felt her fingers begin working furtively on the knots. They were well tied, however. With restricted movement and behind her back, the task seemed next to impossible.

One of the women priests handed a long coil of thick rope to Anfad, who held it up to the prisoners so they could all see that it was tied at one end into the unmistakable shape of a noose. He swung this back and forth a few times then threw it high into the air towards the stout wooden crossbeam that supported the roof. He let the rope play out as the noose travelled up and over the middle of the beam and snaked down the other side where it swung to and fro, its purpose clear and ominous.

The centre of the room had become a gallows.

44

'Let us see what power the gods of Rome have,' Anfad intoned in the British language as he pointed at Marcus Flavius.

Neither the priest nor Agricola could understand the words said, but the meaning was clear from the gloating leer on the druid's face as he stood beside the ominous sacrificial pit with the noose swaying above it.

Marcus let out a little gasp. The two black-clad women each lifted a long, leaf-bladed stabbing spear and approached the seated priest. Marcus, hands tied behind his back, stood up of his own accord. He straightened his back and stuck out his chin. The priest attempted a glare of defiance, but with his bare, scrawny legs hanging from the bottom of his robes and his scraggy, emaciated neck poking out from the top, he looked more pathetic than challenging.

'You have no right to threaten me,' Marcus said. 'I am a Roman citizen and a member of the College of Fetial priests. I represent the Roman state and the gods of Rome. You have no right to touch me or make me take part in your filthy barbarian rituals.'

Fergus remained silent, glad that the priest had no idea what awaited him. The women in black prodded Marcus forward with their spears. With a contemptuous sneer he approached and stared up at Anfad, who towered over him like an immense black cloud. The druid pushed the noose over the priest's head and pulled it so that the rope constricted around the skin of his neck in a rough embrace.

Marcus's attempted look of defiance dissolved to one of terror. 'You simply cannot do this!' he cried, his voice rising to a high squeal. 'I am a sacred priest of Jupiter, noblest and strongest...'

'Enough Roman prattle,' Anfad shouted, his eyes flashing with anger. He wrenched the other end of the rope and looked up. Following his gaze, Fergus saw for the first time that Anfad's gallows were not makeshift: the stout beam that ran across the roof was grooved on top to allow a rope to slide easily over it, and a metal cleat was fixed to one of the altars. Far from being an improvised contraption, these refinements were provided for the very purpose of hanging.

The noose tightened and the priest was hauled up off the ground and forwards so he was suspended directly over the dark, sacrificial pit. His eyes bulged manically, his mouth opened and his tongue was forced out. The rope cut into his neck with a terrible crunching of gristle as it crushed his windpipe and Adam's apple. With immense strength, the druid hauled on the rope yet again and the priest rose higher into the air, his feet kicking and flailing. Anfad then wound the rope twice round the cleat on the altar to stop his victim returning to the ground.

Marcus's face darkened to puce. His lips worked but no sound escaped his constricted throat. His back arched and twisted as he tried frantically to find some purchase for his feet and his thrashing made his body spin on the end of the rope. Blood vessels behind his eyes exploded and the whites filled with deep crimson.

For several moments Anfad looked up at the struggling priest, a strange look of detached interest on his face as if he were studying a mildly interesting bird.

A stream of urine splashed down the priest's legs as his bladder loosened. He thrashed and kicked violently. Fergus watched with grim fascination, wishing the Roman priest would just give up and die and put an end to his own suffering. At the same time he was also aware that the grim spectacle created a diversion while Ceridwen once more worked at his bonds.

Anfad suddenly broke from his reverie and walked to the cauldron of blood. He pulled on the long, chain mail gauntlets that hung from a hook on its side then grasped the shaft of the mystical spear in both hands, raising the head of it up out of the dark, congealing blood and into the air. Anfad now shook the spear to release a shower of blood droplets then thumped the end of the shaft on the ground a couple of times. A shower of sparks cascaded from the rough tip. The same intense, blue fire erupted, seemingly from the metal itself, and spread to cover the whole of the spearhead. In an instant it was ablaze.

Anfad grinned a crazy smile, his teeth illuminated by the light, white against the deep black of his beard. Turning away from the cauldron he went back to where the struggling priest hung suspended in the air. The druid thrust the spear up and into the dying man's heaving chest. Marcus's body went rigid, his bowels releasing a torrent of faeces that cascaded from beneath his robe. There was a loud hissing as the burning metal went through the skin and flesh. The strong smell of roasting meat filled the air mixed with the stink of shit. Despite the constriction of the rope, a strangled grunting sound exploded from the priest's throat.

'Jupiter!' Agricola exclaimed, horror written all over his face.

'It's not over yet,' Fergus said, glaring, unable to tear his eyes away from the spectacle. 'There's more to come.'

Anfad pulled the spear out. It was still on fire. He shifted his grip on the spear towards the base of the shaft. This allowed him to reach up above the priest's head and saw the gallows rope with the point of the spear. He worked it back and forth across the taut rope several times, then the fibres parted. Marcus's body dropped like a stone straight down into the sacrificial pit. He disappeared into the darkness and for several seconds there was silence, then came the sound of a deep splash from far below.

Anfad plunged the burning spear back into the cauldron, extinguishing its fire with a hissing, thick bubbling of blood. The air was thick with blue smoke. The druid leaned over the pit and made a few hand gestures as he bowed his head, his lips moving in a silent prayer of dedication. Silently, his black-robed acolytes did the same.

'Jupiter, noblest and strongest,' Agricola said, breaking the shocked silence. 'He killed him three times over.'

'That's why it is called the threefold death,' Ceridwen said. 'It honours three chief gods in one sacrifice.'

'That's barbaric!' Agricola said.

Anfad finished his prayer and moved to the wooden altar beside the pit. He unwound the rope from the cleat and tugged at it until the burnt end slithered back to the floor. The druid grasped it, formed a loop with it and began to tie another noose.

'So,' he said, grinning at the remaining prisoners. 'Who's next?'

45

Fergus realised that Ceridwen had become mesmerised by the horrific scene unfolding before them and had stopped working on the knots at his wrists. He coughed deliberately and nudged her with his shoulder. His cough was loud enough that Longinus looked around as well. The ex-legionary exchanged a knowing look with Fergus as he realised what was going on.

Fergus felt Ceridwen flinch and recommence fumbling with his bonds, but her movements were clumsy and slow. His own fingers were growing numb as the fox fur cut off the blood supply to his hands and he guessed that it was the same for Ceridwen. The situation was hopeless. Fergus felt a surge of bitterness at the thought that Crom and his minions would defeat him. The feeling was so strong he could taste it.

'I think now we have proved the Roman gods have no power against Gwynn, we shall see what Lugh's representative can do,' Anfad said, pulling the noose and pointing at Ceridwen, his lip curling into a mocking sneer.

Fergus felt Ceridwen tense and once more her fingers stopped working on the fox fur binding his hands. The women in black moved forward, spear points levelled towards Ceridwen. She struggled to her feet, spitting in their direction as she did so.

'I'm not afraid to die,' she said.

Longinus jumped to his feet. 'You spawn of Satan!' he shouted. 'Jesus Christ – the only true God – is more powerful than any of your demons or conjuring!'

'What are you doing?' Ceridwen said, a bewildered expression on her face.

Turning his back on Anfad, the Christian priest smiled briefly at Ceridwen and then down at Fergus, giving him a quick wink.

'Forsake those demons you call gods,' he said in a loud voice. 'Accept the Lord Jesus, the one true God, and let him free you of the bonds of sin.'

Fergus realised that Longinus was trying to sacrifice himself to give Ceridwen more time to untie him.

'What is this?' Anfad said. 'What are you saying?'

Longinus swung back to face the druid.

'If you kill her, this woman is destined for the burning fires of Hell, unless she embraces the one true God,' he said. 'Like all you pagans, Jesus will punish you for following false gods. He will save me. Your god is just a demon who deceives; a minion of Satan the Enemy of God. He has no power over Christ.'

'Oh really?' Anfad said. 'Let's put that to the test, shall we? You'll go next instead of her.'

He nodded at the women in black, who pushed Ceridwen away then turned their spears on the priest.

Longinus stiffened and visibly paled, but his defiance remained.

'Christ will protect me,' he said.

'Then come and let us put your faith to the test,' Anfad said, holding up the noose and beckoning Longinus forward with a mocking gesture of invitation.

Anfad's women helpers circled behind Longinus and prodded him forward towards the druid.

Ceridwen sat down again, shifting herself right up against Fergus and half turned away from him, giving her better access to his hands and the bonds that tied them.

'What's the fool doing?' she breathed. 'I don't even know him.'

'He's bought us some time, so don't waste it,' Fergus hissed back.

Anfad roughly shoved the noose over the ex-legionary's head. Unlike Marcus, Longinus did not try to proclaim anything else. He stood up straight with his shoulders back, as if at attention on the parade square, but his eyes were closed and his lips moving silently as he said a final prayer.

Anfad shook his head then walked around to the other end of the rope. Grabbing the rope in both hands he braced his legs, bent his knees and tugged downward with a mighty pull. Longinus was hauled up off the ground and the grotesque spectacle began again.

'Where is your god now?' Anfad shouted as Longinus's face darkened to a deep purple colour and his legs kicked and flailed. 'Where is his power, eh? Nowhere to be seen! Gwynn ap Nudd, the bent and bloody one, triumphs again!'

For a time the grinning druid watched with apparent interest as the ex-legionary's struggles grew weaker, then he walked towards the cauldron to begin the second grisly stage of the execution.

Fergus looked on with growing rage. Longinus's stoicism and self-sacrifice moved him. What made it worse was that he was yet another victim of the bloody religion of Crom. The British may call him Gwynn ap Nudd, but he was the same greedy, bloodthirsty bastard whatever his name. Fergus's lip curled as he vowed to himself that if it was the last thing he did, Crom would have no more blood that day.

Briefly he considered praying to Crom's nemesis, the god Lugh, but then reasoned that would be hypocritical. He had not prayed to Lugh before and would not turn to him now, like a coward who cries for help from gods only when he knows all is lost.

Fergus was starting to think that Longinus had sacrificed himself in vain, when he felt his bonds loosen. Ceridwen had managed to undo at least one of the knots. Keeping his gaze fixed on the dying Roman, Fergus felt a tingling pain as blood began to return to his hands.

Anfad had removed the sacred spear from the cauldron and shaken off the pigs' blood. Now, as it ignited once more into its blaze he moved, and dripping a trail of sparks, positioned himself ready to thrust the white-hot blade into the belly of Longinus. The spear's baleful light illuminated the druid's face from below and as before, a broad grin split his beard to reveal his standing-stone teeth.

Perhaps feeling the heat of the burning blade, Longinus opened his eyes and stopped struggling. His face was almost black and his tongue protruded from his mouth, while his eyes were dark with blood. Despite this, he somehow had the presence of mind to lock eyes with Anfad.

A look of surprise followed quickly by annoyance chased

across the druid's face and he shoved the spear up and into Longinus's abdomen. The spear slid into the man's body with a puff of trailing smoke.

At the same time Longinus suddenly pulled his knees up and wrapped his legs around Anfad's head. It was a truly Herculean effort from a dying man. The ex-legionary squeezed the druid's skull with his thighs, using every shred of strength he had left even as Anfad thrust the spear further into his body.

Fergus knew he would not get another chance like this. His wrists were not yet fully released, but he could not wait for Ceridwen to finish.

With both feet planted firmly on the ground he flexed his iron-strong thigh muscles and powered himself onto his feet. He charged forward, shoulders dipped. In six steps, while Anfad's women were still frozen with surprise and the druid himself was struggling to free himself from the grip of Longinus's legs, he reached his target.

Fergus was a big man, but Anfad was much bigger and Fergus knew he had little chance of knocking the druid over if he struck him squarely in the back, so he dived the final steps and with all his weight, shoulder-charged the back of Anfad's knees. With a muffled cry, Anfad's legs buckled and he went down. His falling weight wrenched him from the grip of Longinus's thighs and pulled the sacred spear from the priest's body. Impelled by the impact of Fergus's shoulder, the druid pitched forwards and dropped the spear. Still burning, it fell to the floor.

Fergus thumped painfully into the ground. Anfad, however, went knees first into the sacrificial pit. His momentum carried him forwards, his torso colliding with the opposite wall of the pit shaft as he fell. He flung out his arms to stop himself falling further, his big fingers digging into the earth floor for purchase. With immense strength he held himself suspended at the top of the shaft, scrabbling with his legs in an attempt to pull himself up and out of the pit.

Fergus scrambled into a sitting position. He pushed with his legs, thrusting himself backwards across the floor. His hands, though able to move more freely, were still tied behind his back, and his fingers scrabbled along the ground searching for the shaft of the spear, which he knew lay behind him somewhere.

The two women in black, who had been momentarily frozen in shock, recovered and ran forward, spears at the ready, one to help Anfad, the other to attack Fergus. He felt the heat of the burning spear behind him and his fingers closed around its metal shaft. He struggled to his feet but as he did so realised he was too late: the woman was nearly on him and his restricted movement made it impossible to defend himself.

Agricola launched himself forward, colliding with the woman just as she was about to stab Fergus. She was knocked sprawling to the ground, her spear flying from her grasp. Seeing this, the second woman left Anfad and rushed to her companion's aid. Almost at the same moment, Ceridwen rushed the second priestess. Though of lighter build she still managed to knock her sideways from her intended path.

Fergus staggered towards the pit, the burning spear grasped behind him. Anfad was reaching across the floor, clutching for further purchase to pull himself back out of the shaft. The light from the blazing spear alerted him to Fergus's approach and he looked up.

'Get away from me, Hibernian,' Anfad said. He broke into maniacal laughter. 'By Crom, as you call Him, you may kill me, but my two companions, Du and Griffudd, will continue to lead our religion. Our gods will prevail.'

A vision sprang into Fergus's mind of his baby son Connor, his throat cut and his lifeblood streaming down from the wound as Anfad, one tiny ankle grasped in his huge paw, held his pathetic corpse above the standing stone of Crom.

'Fuck you,' Fergus said. He turned sideways and bent over, thrusting the burning spear point into Anfad's face. The druid let out a high-pitched shriek as his beard ignited and the spear burned and sliced its way through his right cheek. Desperate to escape the burning pain Anfad let go. The big druid slithered back into the shaft. Then he was falling and disappeared into the blackness of the sacrificial pit. His cries echoed up the shaft for a few moments, getting further and further away. A sudden wet crunch and an agonised scream told Fergus that the druid had landed on the spike at the bottom of the pit.

A horrible sucking sound accompanied Anfad's agonised groans as he slid down the spike that impaled him. The druid's cries turned to a short gargle then were drowned by a distant splash as he slipped down under the black, cold water that filled the bottom of the shaft.

Fergus smelt burning and realised the fire from the spear was singing his arms. He gritted his teeth, determined not to drop the only weapon he had, and looked up to see if there was anything he could do for Longinus. He was already dead, however. The ex-legionary's corpse hung swaying from the noose, the wound in his chest bleeding and smoking slightly. His face was bloated and discoloured but somehow seemed to bear an expression of contented repose, despite the horrific nature of his death.

Fergus turned to the others and saw that Ceridwen was circling warily around the black-garbed woman she had shoulder-charged. The priestess, now back on her feet, stood watching Ceridwen like a wildcat, looking for a chance to strike, her spear point following the druidess as she circled.

Agricola was standing by the other priestess, patiently waiting as she picked herself groggily up from the floor. He delivered a swift but hefty kick to the woman's face while she was still on her hands and knees. Her head snapped back, her eyes rolled up and she fell back to the ground, unconscious.

'Get the last one,' Fergus said, cocking his head towards the remaining priestess as she jabbed the spear at Ceridwen. Ceridwen arched her back and the deadly point just shaved past her.

Agricola nodded. He and Fergus advanced towards the priestess. Although her back was to the pit and she was outnumbered three to one, she did not look too worried. After all, her opponents still had their hands bound behind their backs, while she had a long-reaching weapon to defend herself with so could pick them off one at a time.

'If we rush her she can only kill one of us,' Fergus said.

'Speak in Latin,' Ceridwen said quickly. 'She'll not know what we say.'

'You know Latin?' Agricola said, not taking his gaze off the priestess.

'I am a druid and a vates,' Ceridwen said. 'I am an educated woman, unlike this priestess of Gwynn. She and her kind are just ignorant witches.'

As if to confirm her words, the priestess frowned and stabbed at Fergus with the spear. He danced backwards out of the way and the deadly point missed him. As he did so he noticed that his hands were no longer hot. Glancing over his shoulder he saw to his dismay that the strange fire had died away from the tip, leaving only the clean metal of the blade.

'The cursed thing has stopped working,' he said. 'Whatever made it burn must have run out.'

'This is hardly the time to debate the matter,' Ceridwen said. 'If we don't make a move soon, Ferchu and his friends will be back. We should all rush the witch at once. Like he said, she'll only be able to get one of us.'

Her words ended on a gasp as she dodged another thrust.

'I don't much fancy being the one she gets,' Fergus said, contemplating just how close the priestess's spear had been to piercing his gut.

'Coward!' Ceridwen said. 'You're the only one with a weapon.'

'That's why I know she'll go for me,' Fergus said.

'Enough talking,' Agricola said, the authoritative tone returning to his voice. 'This is the only course open to us, so let's get it over with before her friends arrive. That's an order, trooper. On my command: one, two, three, charge!'

All three rushed forwards together. At Agricola's shout the priestess swung towards him and drove the spear directly at his belly. The tribune's eyes widened. He tried to change course and leap sideways away from the spear point. At the same moment Ceridwen smashed her forehead into the priestess's left cheek. There was an audible crack and the woman cried out in pain. As Agricola fell away to the left, her spear blade bypassed his guts, but tore through his uniform and gouged deep into the flesh of the front of his right thigh. Fergus barged into the priestess, the weight of his charge knocked her flying backwards. She missed the pit as she went, but ended up flat on her back on the other side of it.

Fergus and Ceridwen leapt over the pit and rained down a devastating torrent of kicks and stamps on the priestess as she was trying to rise. She slumped back to earth, whether unconscious or dead Fergus could not tell and did not care.

Agricola cried out in pain as he lay on his side, the spear still hanging out of his leg.

'Get that other spear and cut me free,' Fergus said, nodding towards the weapon that lay by the priestess he had first kicked unconscious. He was relieved to note she was still not stirring.

Ceridwen nodded and crouched to retrieve it, holding it awkwardly behind her, point towards Fergus. He dropped the magic spear and turned his back. He began sawing his bonds along the sharpened edge of the spear blade. In a few moments the fox fur parted and his hands were free.

He took the spear from her and repeated the process, working at her bonds until she too was free. Ceridwen flexed her fingers and grimaced as the feeling returned.

'You could have killed me instead of freeing me,' Fergus said.

'I'm saving that pleasure for a more convenient time,' she said with a smile. 'However, this means we're now even, Gwyddel. I am no longer in your debt.'

Crossing the room she began to examine Agricola's wound. It was deep, but only cut into the muscle; no veins or arteries had been pierced. She got up again and pulled the black cloak off the nearest unconscious priestess. Returning to Agricola, with little mercy the druidess pulled the spear tip out of his leg. As he cried out, she ripped the hem off the cloak and wrapped it around his thigh, pulling it tight to staunch the blood welling from the wound.

'Can you walk?' Fergus asked.

Agricola nodded but his grimace and grey pallor suggested it would be far from easy.

'We can help him if he needs it,' Ceridwen said.

'Well will you look at that,' Fergus said. He had picked up the magic spear again and was examining the butt of it. He pressed the end and there was an audible click from the opposite end where the blade was. 'There's a button on the bottom of it. When they strike it off the ground it sets something off in the head.'

He rotated the weapon to look at the pyramid-shaped blade. Noticing a clasp on one side he pulled it back and one section of the blade came away. Inside was a piece of flint attached to some sort of hammer mechanism, with a wire leading down the shaft. Burned remnants of moss and wadding tumbled out to the floor, as well as the strong smell of oil.

'The button somehow pulls the wire that makes the flint strike in the head,' Fergus said. 'It ignites kindling hidden in the head that was soaked in oil.'

'So it was all just trickery after all,' Agricola said, grimacing in pain. 'Though I suppose we shouldn't be surprised. For someone who made that death machine of a chariot, a simple mechanism like that would be child's play.'

'I'm almost disappointed,' Fergus said. 'But right now we need to get out of here before someone comes back and finds us.'

'What about him?' Ceridwen nodded in the direction of the swinging body of Longinus.

'He's long dead,' Fergus said. 'There's nothing we can do for him now.'

'He knew I was trying to untie you and he made Anfad pick him instead of me,' the druidess said. 'He must have known it meant certain death. Why do you think he did it?'

'Who knows,' Fergus said with a shrug. 'The Christians have strange notions about self-sacrifice.'

'He was a Roman legionary and a brave man,' Agricola said from behind them, his voice hoarse. 'Regardless of his choice of religion. Honour, courage and helping his comrades were the most important things to him, as they are to all of us in the legion.'

'Do we just leave him hanging like that?' Ceridwen asked.

Fergus looked around the temple as though for inspiration then shrugged. 'We don't have much choice. But let's not throw his sacrifice away. Ferchu is bound to come nosying around soon so we need to get moving if we're to have any chance of escape. Grab those witches' cloaks and let's get out of here.'

46

Fergus unbound his hair, letting it fall around his shoulders like a native. He and Ceridwen helped Agricola wrap one of the priestesses' long black cloaks around him to conceal his Roman uniform as far as possible. Ceridwen wrapped the other around herself.

With Agricola hobbling between them, Ceridwen and Fergus made their way across the temple to the door. Cautiously, they opened it and peeked out. Fergus, realised he had lost all track of time as he saw with surprise that it was the dead of night and the sky full dark; however, there were no guards immediately outside.

Exiting the building and keeping to the shadows, the three of them paused to take stock. Despite the late hour and the chilly darkness, there was plenty of activity in the hill fort. Big fires, torches and braziers burned all over the area to provide light. They could see that the main gate was a hive of activity. It and the ramparts round it thronged with warriors, all facing outward and ready for war. The ballistae on their carts were positioned there as well and every now and then there was the crack of one firing down the hill at enemies who strayed too close.

Some distance away from the main gate, however, the

ramparts nearest to the temple looked deserted. This made sense as the queen only had enough warriors to defend one part of the fort's circumference at a time, and the attackers evidently did not have enough warriors to attack in more than one spot at a time.

'Let's get up onto the embankment over there,' Fergus said, pointing. 'We'll be able to see what is going on better from up there and maybe see a way out of this place.'

With all the attention of the queen's warriors focused on the main entrance to the fort, there was no one to challenge them as they crept to the edge of the rampart nearest to them. A set of steps was cut into the earth embankment and with some difficulty they manhandled Agricola up to the top. Once there they had a magnificent view of the chaos below. After the slaughter that had ended Comux's first assault it seemed that the fighting for the hill fort had descended to stalemate.

Looking around, Fergus could see that the rampart on which they stood offered no means of escape. The outer wall descended in a sheer drop, about the height of four or five men standing on each other's shoulders, until it met the natural rock of the hillside, which then fell away in a steep incline. This was why the rampart was deserted at this point. No attacking force could gain access here and any attempt to jump would be suicide.

Casting his gaze further afield, Fergus could see that the queen's grandiose villa still blazed at the bottom of the hill. The roof had gone and the walls looked to be on the verge of collapse. Other fires had been lit by the besieging forces so that they could see what they were doing and keep an eye on what the defenders were up to. Comux's forces were gathered around the base of the road leading up to the hill fort, just out of range of the ballistae. The slaughtered corpses of men and horses lay scattered all the way up the hill to the entrance gate of the fort, the remnants of the failed assault. It seemed that Comux still had hundreds of men though. By Fergus's reckoning they outnumbered the defenders by about three to one, even after the hammering they had taken earlier.

Warriors, their arms and armour glittering in the firelight, howled in the night like wolves. Someone had found that the cellars and larders of the villa had been stocked in anticipation of the queen moving in and now most of Comux's men were merry with drink and feasting. Despite the ballistae, it was obvious that they were still full of confidence.

As he watched, Fergus spotted Comux himself, recognisable by the great crested bronze helmet he wore. His chain mail glittered. He held a long bladed stabbing spear in his fist as he rode along the lines of his men on the back of a splendidly painted, light and agile war chariot. He was waving, encouraging and invoking cheers from the assembled warriors.

'Cocky lot, aren't they?' Agricola said.

'Why not?' Fergus said. 'They know it's just a matter of time until they take the fort. They outnumber the defenders. Sooner or later the ballistae will run out of ammunition and then victory awaits.'

'What's that noise?' Ceridwen said, her head to one side as she strained to hear.

They all listened. Fergus heard it first. Drifting through the darkness, above the clammer of the drunken warriors below the main gate and the crackling blaze of the burning villa, a rhythmic drumming could be heard, the unmistakable sound of hooves on soft earth.

'Horses,' Fergus said. 'Lots of them.'

Almost immediately came the blare of Roman buccinae and cornua out of the darkness.

'It's Pomponius!' Agricola said, his face brightening. 'Looks like we are just in time for the show.'

'We're not out of the woods yet,' Fergus said. 'He wants us dead, remember?'

'According to the queen, yes,' Agricola said. 'But can we trust her word on anything?'

'I wouldn't put it past that bastard,' Fergus said.

'Careful, trooper: that is a senior officer in the Roman army you are talking about,' Agricola said, trying his best to sound reproachful though his tone betrayed his own suspicions.

Fergus did not reply. This was not the time to explain everything that had happened between him and the praefect. He glanced sideways at Ceridwen who he saw was watching the unfolding scene outside the fort with intense interest. Whatever the outcome, her prospects were bleak. With an unsettling lurch of his stomach, he realised that he actually cared.

Shouts of surprise and alarm came from Comux's troops as the sudden attack from their rear slammed into them. Into the firelight galloped ranks of Roman cavalrymen, letting fly a volley of javelins as they arrived. The Gaulish cavalrymen roared war cries as they charged in, and the clash of weapons rose as *spathae* were drawn and battle commenced.

Up on the ramparts a cheer rose from the defenders at the sight of their enemies being attacked. The cavalry hacked and slashed, cutting deep into the ranks of the southern Dobunni before they had a chance to group themselves into a co-ordinated defence.

'Help me get closer,' Agricola said. 'I want a good view of what is going on.'

Fergus nodded. Most of the defenders were concentrated around the main gate with only a few guards at the cardinal points along the walls to watch in case of a surprise attack from a different direction. This meant they could move along the top of the ramparts and get very close to the main gate without being challenged.

With Agricola leaning heavily on Fergus's shoulder and Ceridwen carrying the spears, they stumbled cautiously along the top of the embankment, stopping when they were as close as they dared go to the warriors who defended the rampart above the gate, hovering in the darkness just beyond the light cast by the fires below.

'It's not the whole regiment,' Fergus said quietly as he looked down from their new vantage point. 'Judging by the number of cavalry fighting below I'd say about five turmae. That's maybe a hundred and sixty troopers. Fewer men than Comux has. What's Pomponius thinking? Surely he is not just relying on surprise?'

'He hasn't come alone,' Agricola said, pointing to a new body of soldiers arriving out of the darkness. Forming up in ranks with their big, square shields locked together, pila at the ready, reflected firelight gleaming on their polished bronze helmets, these men were clearly Roman legionaries.

'Looks like a cohort of the XX Legion,' Fergus said as

he caught sight of their standards. 'Valens's comrades have come too late to save him.'

'That's good news for us, though,' Agricola said. 'If we can find some way to reach their officer, Pomponius won't dare try anything in front of him. If he really does intend to kill us he won't want witnesses.'

At the base of the hill Comux's forces had managed to regroup and form themselves into a tightly packed line, spears bristling at the front to ward off the horsemen. The surprise attack had caused a lot of casualties, but the southern Dobunni were still a coherent fighting force.

Cornua sounded a signal and the Roman cavalry disengaged, turning to ride back towards the legionaries. A desultory cheer rose from Comux's warriors at the sight of their enemy retreating. Five noblemen in their war chariots trundled forwards in pursuit and the rest of the Dobunni warriors began to advance behind them.

'Works every time,' Fergus said, a grim smile on his face. He noted the fascination with which Ceridwen was watching proceedings and a slight pang of unease entered his chest as he realised the druid was watching a master class in Roman cavalry battle tactics.

At another cornu blast the cavalry reined their horses to a stop and wheeled around once more. They charged back towards the advancing Dobunni and as one released a volley of javelins. The missiles rained down on the approaching British warriors, many of whom were running full tilt. They had no time to raise shields to defend themselves. Hard spear points smashed into men's chests, legs, necks, even heads, sending a whole line of warriors tumbling to the ground.

Having inflicted another wave of casualties, the cavalry turned around once again, divided into two groups and flowed back around either side of the line of legionaries who now stood behind them.

The British warriors raised another bloodthirsty battle cry at the sight of the foot soldiers. Now they had before them at last an enemy they could both get to grips with and fight on an equal footing. They surged forward with renewed fury, the chariot-mounted nobles speeding before them.

At another cornu signal, the rigid line of legionaries divided in the middle and wheeled inwards, forming a sort of funnel of troops and also revealing what was positioned behind them.

A groan of dismay came from the Dobunni that was audible even at the height of the rampart top. Agricola gave a short, grim laugh at the sight of eight more Roman ballistae that had been positioned behind the legionaries. Similar to the four in the queen's possession, these were also the new, experimental cart-mounted weapons. They were set almost horizontal, levelled straight at the charging Dobunni.

The ballistae loosed their deadly volley as one. Their targets had been carefully chosen and the five chariots that led the charge were annihilated. One simply disintegrated as a ballista stone smashed through it, spilling charioteer, warrior and horses to the ground. A bolt from another ballista killed the right-hand horse of Comux's chariot, powered through the creature's body then decapitated the charioteer. Out of control, the vehicle plunged forwards, flipping its rear end in the air and sending Comux spinning out of it on a trajectory that took him in an arc through the air to land with a bone-smashing impact in the dirt.

A fourth chariot had its left wheel shot off and veered sideways out of control. Its horses pounded over Comux's body before the trailing platform of the chariot turned what was left of him to little more than a bloody smear across the ground. A fifth, well-aimed ballista bolt shot another nobleman off the back of his chariot. It exited his body in a spray of blood and travelled on to take down two more charging warriors behind. The other three ballistae loosed stones that ploughed deep, bloody furrows through the ranks of the oncoming Dobunni warriors.

'It looks like the queen will need a new consort,' Fergus said.

'I don't find that funny,' Ceridwen said with a reproachful glance. 'Comux was a fool, but I take no pleasure in watching my countrymen die at the hands of Roman soldiers.'

'I'd stop watching this, then, if I were you,' Fergus said. 'Because you're about to see a lot more of that.'

The ballistae, quickly reloaded, loosed another withering volley at the oncoming Dobunni, taking a further, devastatingly bloody toll. The stones smashed eight furrows through the warriors, killing everyone from the men in the front ranks right through to the less enthusiastic warriors trailing at the back. Incredibly, even after shattering and passing through so many human bodies, a couple of the stones still had enough velocity to carry on, bouncing in the soft ground until one finally embedded itself in the turf while the other simply rolled to a stop.

The remaining warriors were too close to allow time to reload the ballistae. The legionaries closed ranks again in front of the artillery weapons. They had done their work. Little more than half of the men who had begun the charge remained upright and still advancing.

To Agricola and Fergus, what happened next was entirely predictable. It was standard Roman military tactics. The legionaries threw the first of their two pila. The heavy wooden javelins sailed through the air into the advancing Dobunni warriors, piercing mail and exposed flesh to inflict further casualties. Those who were able to raise their shields in time found that these became unwieldy once the iron head of the pilum had embedded itself. The legionary's javelin was designed with a long, weak neck and a heavy wooden shaft so that it would bend on impact, weighing down the opponent's shield and rendering it useless. Most of the warriors had little choice but to drop their shields, leaving them defenceless as in quick succession the legionaries launched their second and last pilum to similar effect.

'This is not battle. It's just murder,' Ceridwen said.

'It's the Roman way of warfare,' Fergus said.

There was an audible metallic hiss as simultaneously each legionary drew his sword, the short, broad-bladed gladius designed for close combat. The Dobunni now faced closed ranks of legionaries standing side by side, their big, curved, square shields locked together in what looked like an impenetrable wall.

It was the final straw. The British warriors, reduced by so many in so little time, no longer had the stomach to continue an assault that was mere suicide. Of those who remained, the charge faltered and stopped. Their own close order fell apart, panic and self-preservation took over and the warriors turned and fled. Caught now between a hammer and an anvil, the only way they could go was backwards towards the hill fort.

With a blare of cornua the legionaries began to advance. They stepped as one towards the fleeing warriors, gladius at the ready, shields still locked side by side. Behind them, the carts carrying the ballistae began to rumble forwards also.

Seeing their enemies sudden reversal of fortune, the defenders in the hill fort finally felt emboldened enough to leave the defences and sally out against their besieging enemies. Roaring their war cry they rushed out of the gates and down the entrance road in a hectic, frantic charge.

The two rival Dobunni factions met near the bottom of the road that led up to the main gate. Desperate, chaotic fighting ensued. Men fought men hand to hand in a wild, undisciplined melee. Warriors cut down other warriors in a frantic killing frenzy. Swords hacked, shields countered, spears stabbed and men died in welters of crimson blood that sprayed from opened wounds or gushed and spurted from severed limbs and heads.

The advancing legionaries stopped just a little distance from the fighting, forming a wall of iron to stop anyone fleeing. The cavalry turmae galloped back past the legionaries on either side, cutting off retreat in either flank. What remained of Comux's forces were now trapped in a killing zone with no escape.

'So the Romans stand back and let their barbarian lapdogs do the killing,' Ceridwen said. 'Are they afraid to get blood on those nice uniforms?'

'Clever tactics,' Agricola said. 'Why risk our own men?'

Very soon it was all over. Those few remaining southern

Dobunni who could still stand raised their weapons and called out surrender. There were about forty of them and they stood, ringed by their enemies, panting and looking around to see what would happen next.

Out of the gate and down the hill rode Queen Finnabair, her black hair blowing in the wind and her long cloak trailing behind her. At the sight of her, several of the defeated warriors fell to one knee, bowing their heads in supplication. One of them, a tall, red-haired nobleman, raised his face and said something but he was too far away to be made out.

'He's probably asking to surrender,' Fergus said.

Finnabair looked down at him from her horse, her face a mask of contempt and disdain. She spat at him and shouted something. Again Fergus, Ceridwen and Agricola could not hear what it was but its meaning was clear.

Whooping, Finnabair's warriors rushed in and slew the remaining southern men, running them through with their long Celtic swords, slitting their throats or simply beheading them as they knelt.

The last anguished screams of the dying faded, leaving only the moaning and cursing of the mortally wounded and a quiet that was all the more significant for the deafening clash of arms that had preceded it. Fergus looked up towards the horizon and saw that the first grey streaks of dawn were creeping up the eastern sky.

'It's over,' Agricola said.

'What now?' Ceridwen said.

'Hush, the pair of you, what's the queen saying?' Fergus

said, straining to hear and squirming flat along the rampart to get nearer.

Finnabair raised her voice and shouted something towards the Roman lines.

Fergus spotted Pomponius straight away. The cavalry praefect's silvered crested helmet gleamed in the light of the various fires and his crimson cloak streamed out behind him. His body armour glistened with polish and neither it nor the pristine white body of his horse were sullied by any splashes of blood, likewise his ivory-hilted sword, still firmly in its sheath. Typically, he rode forward from well behind the lines of the Roman legionaries. Fergus spat over the wall as he saw Sedullus riding just behind the praefect, following him like a lapdog as always. At the same time he noticed that behind the ranks of legionaries from the XX Legion, the carts on which the ballistae were mounted where still moving forward.

'We need to get down there,' Fergus said, spotting a nearby flight of stairs that would take him down from the rampart to the gate. 'Something is going on and I can't hear a damned thing.'

'Don't be stupid,' Ceridwen said, laying a hand on his forearm. 'You'll be killed.'

'What do you care?' Fergus said, making a face. For a moment they locked eyes, then he looked away. 'Give me your cloak and wait here. I'll be back when I find out what Pomponius and Finnabair are up to.'

47

The news that the battle was over spread like wildfire through the hill fort. Women, children and the elderly who had been cowering inside the relative safety of their houses emerged and rushed to the gate, desperate to find out if their menfolk had survived the fighting.

Fergus wrapped the long black cloak around him and pulled up the hood. Spear in hand, he hurried down the steps to join the stream of people who now thronged the gate. Anonymous in the crowd, he was able to push his way forwards until he was actually in the open entrance. Finding himself beside one of the ballistae carts he glanced upwards then immediately looked down again as he saw that the weapon was manned by Ferchu. The bodyguard had a strange expression on his face, a mixture of triumph and disappointment that the battle was over and he could not kill anyone else. Fergus kept his head down and moved away from the ballista into the middle of the open gateway.

From there he was able to look down the hill where the queen sat on her horse before the ranks of Romans.

Pomponius had not ridden out to meet the queen, but instead sat on his mount level with the front rank of legionaries. He was speaking with the queen and Fergus was gratified that he could now hear what they said.

'I trust you have what I want?' Pomponius said.

'Of course. The sacred spear is inside my temple.' The queen smiled. 'And your troublesome Agricola has been dealt with too, as has his Hibernian lackey.'

Pomponius curbed his prancing horse and sat motionless for a moment, gazing down his nose at her, his face a mask of solemn authority. 'My lady, are you telling me that you have murdered a Roman tribune?'

The queen frowned, clearly taken aback and confused. 'What are you talking about?' she said.

'It's like I told you all,' Pomponius announced loudly to the Roman troops, 'this treacherous barbarian queen, this woman, has killed the Roman envoy party sent to make a peace pact with her.'

He gestured at the ballistae. 'See: they also have the artillery weapons captured from our forces the day before yesterday,' he said.

Fergus breathed deeply through his nose, feeling his anger rise at the praefect's bare-faced duplicity. The queen's confused reaction was enough to show him that what she had said before about her plot with Pomponius was true and now he was double-crossing her as well. Not that he cared a damn about Finnabair, but his commanding officer was despicable.

Things were about to take a turn for the worse. It was time to go. Fergus turned and began pushing his way back through the crowd, keeping his head down and fighting the urge to break into a run. A few annoyed people pushed him back as he passed but most had their attention fixed on what was happening below. He made it back to the stairway up to the rampart without incident.

Hastily mounting the steps, Fergus went along the rampart to rejoin Agricola and Ceridwen.

'Pomponius is up to something,' he said, quickly relaying what had been said.

'The lying shit,' Agricola said. 'It was him who wanted us dead.' Wincing at the pain from his wounded leg, he pulled himself up onto the top of the rampart and sat on it.

'I'm going to say something,' he said. 'I'm going to shout down to our men and let them know we are alive.'

Fergus laid a restraining hand on his shoulder, looking anxiously along the rampart.

'Get back down, you fool! Those Dobunni warriors further along will see you,' he said.

Agricola glared at him in rage.

'How dare you speak to a Roman tribune like—' Agricola began to splutter.

'Look.' Fergus tapped him, pointing at the legionary crews manhandling the artillery. 'They've reloaded.'

As he spoke the ballistae fired with a series of loud cracks. Agricola blinked in surprise. The queen flinched in her saddle, her horse rearing up, but the missiles passed high above her head. They had other targets. In groups of two they fired on the ballistae of the queen's forces that were positioned to defend the main gate. With loud crashes the boulders smashed the weapons to ragged splinters of wood and metal. Fergus saw one boulder destroy the cart platform one of the ballistae stood on. A second hit Ferchu, who was manning it. The stone slammed straight through his pelvis, releasing a mist of blood and taking off his right leg completely. Ferchu toppled into the wreckage of his destroyed ballista, blood spurting like a fountain from the horrible wound.

The queen wheeled her horse around and galloped back up the hill to the gate. Pomponius signalled and the Roman cornua sounded. With a roar the Gaulish cavalry swept forwards, rushing up the hill after her.

All hell broke loose at the gate as the crowd who thronged it turned in panic and tried to escape back inside the hill fort. Children and the elderly fell in the crush and those who went down were trampled under the feet of those trying to get away from the onslaught.

Fergus saw the ballista swivel to point upwards towards the ramparts.

'Get down!' he shouted, grabbing Agricola's shoulder and hauling him down off the rampart top, ignoring the tribune's shout of pain. Fergus looked round again and saw to his dismay that the warriors further down the rampart had clearly heard their noise. Four of them had detached from the others and were approaching to investigate.

The ballistae loosed and their stone balls hammered into the tops of the ramparts around the gate. A section of the wall nearby Fergus and his companions disintegrated in a welter of stone shards that obliterated two of the approaching warriors outright and sent the other two tumbling off the ramparts into the darkness below.

With a measured, rhythmical step the legionaries of the XX advanced behind the cavalry in the stolid, ominous silence that was the signature of Roman soldiers going into battle, the only sound they made being the clumping of their hobnailed sandals and the clanking of their shields as the edges clacked together.

In contrast, the interior of the hill fort was filled with a cacophony as men shouted, women cried out and children screamed in terror. People ran this way and that, trying to flee or find cover. The chaos was increased as some fell, tripping over bodies lying on the ground. Several stray ballista stones landed in the midst of the crowd, adding to the casualties.

Fergus, Ceridwen and Agricola cowered on the ground behind the wall as ballista stones crashed into the ramparts, working methodically along their top to sweep the defenders away to their deaths or send them diving for cover. Either way it stopped them from raining slingstones down on the Romans marching their way to the gate. As the queen galloped into the fort, her warriors made a desperate attempt to close the gates, but the remains of the destroyed ballistae and carts prevented them from closing more than halfway. The warriors attempted to clear the wreckage, but the Romans were already halfway up the slope.

'They'll be inside in no time. We need to get out of here,' Fergus said, as they cowered behind the rampart wall. He could feel the percussive impacts of ballistae stones hitting the outside of the rampart and hear the zip of their bolts as they soared over the top of the wall mere inches from their heads.

'We can't get over the wall,' Ceridwen said. 'The queen's forces are at the gate. Where do we go?'

'I just need to talk to the troopers and the legionaries,' Agricola said. 'Tell them who I am. Show them my uniform.'

Fergus shook his head. 'You won't get a chance. We're on the wrong end of a Roman assault. You of all people should know what that means. The leash is off and no mercy or quarter is to be given. The orders will be to kill everything that moves and keep killing until you are ordered to stop. If you stand up in front of those men they'll cut you down before you get a chance to speak. We need to find somewhere out of the way to hide until the assault is over. Then you can introduce yourself.'

'We can't get out of this hill fort but what about the Roman fort?' Ceridwen said. 'Couldn't we hide in there?'

'The queen turned the captured artillery on it,' Agricola said. 'It's half ruined.'

'The walls are still standing though. We could hide in Valens' quarters,' said Fergus, who saw the sense in Ceridwen's plan straight away. 'If we can get inside we can take cover until the main attack is over. At least they will be more careful around a Roman fortification. We can show ourselves when the signal comes to stop the battle.'

They all exchanged glances and nodded to confirm they were in agreement.

'Leave me,' Agricola said. 'You can go faster on your own without having to carry me as well.'

'It's very noble and Roman of you to suggest it but I don't think so,' Fergus said. 'Me and her both look like locals. When the legionaries break in I'd rather be standing beside a man in a tribune's uniform.'

As if to prompt them, another large chunk of the rampart wall a few paces away exploded under the impact of a ballista stone, leaving a gaping, ragged hole in the defences.

'Let's go,' Fergus said. 'The Dobunni have too much else to deal with right now to worry about us.'

Ceridwen and Fergus positioned themselves either side of Agricola and he wrapped his arms around their shoulders. Crouching to avoid the ballistae shot howling over the wall, they hobbled down the steps from the rampart and back into the hill fort interior. They were close to the temple and near it the huge royal house, but the little Roman fort was quite a distance away through the maze of roundhouses and animal enclosures.

The interior of the hill fort was in complete chaos. Panicking women and children ran about in different directions in panic. Some warriors, deciding that the battle was already lost, had abandoned the defence of the gate to run and find their families, hoping to somehow escape the coming slaughter. A herd of pigs had broken out from their enclosure and were charging around wildly among the throng.

Ceridwen, Fergus and Agricola picked their way through the anarchy. As Fergus had predicted, they were largely ignored by people who had greater things to worry about. As they neared the royal house, there was a sudden flare of light and heat from overhead. A large plume of flame erupted from the roof. The three of them instinctively flinched and ducked. Looking up they saw another small, flaming object flying through the weak grey gloom of the dawn sky from over the rampart. It came down beside the horse corral and exploded in a mushroom of fire.

In sheer terror, some of the remaining horses in the corral leapt clean over the fence while the others kicked and bucked at the fence or each other in a panicked attempt to flee.

'Fire is raining from the sky...' Ceridwen gasped in shock, her fingers of one hand going to her mouth, her eyes wide with disbelief.

'It's Greek fire,' Agricola said.

Ceridwen stared at him uncomprehending.

'It's a liquid war weapon,' he said. 'It burns with a fire that cannot be put out – unlike our magic spear. They fill jars with it, set fire to them and lob them at the enemy.' He turned to Fergus and said, 'They must have an *onager* catapult out there too. Pomponius really has brought the works, the bastard. I can't believe Suetonius can have sanctioned this. We need to take cover if we don't want to be incinerated.'

Several more blazing missiles landed, exploding, setting buildings ablaze and incinerating people and animals. Behind them there was a crash and Fergus turned to see that the first of the Gaulish cavalry had broken into the fort. The foremost riders leapt their horses over the wreckage of the queen's ballistae and through the gap in the half-closed gates.

The reckless bravery of the first two in was rewarded with a swift death at the hands of the defenders, but within moments more horsemen drove their way through the gap and the tide turned. Stabbing with lances couched under their arms they slaughtered the defenders around the gate. Realising the position was lost, the remaining Dobunni warriors fled into the interior of the fort. Several cavalry troopers dismounted and swung the gates wide open.

The rest of the cavalry troop poured into the fort. At their rear rode Pomponius. Beside him rode Sedullus and behind them marched the legionaries of the XX Legion, a wide wall of rectangular shields that quickly filled the gateway, blocking the only means of escape from the hill fort.

'Well at least that'll put a stop to the Greek fire,' Fergus said. 'They won't risk one landing on their own men.'

Havoc ensued. The warriors knew the battle was lost but there was nowhere to flee. Horsemen rode this way and that, killing men, women and the screaming children who ran in every direction in their panic and desperation to get away. The thatched roof of the royal house was fully ablaze. Ceridwen winced at the sight of a toddler trampled to bloody ribbons under the hooves of a cavalry horse as the trooper mounted on it decapitated its screaming mother.

'The Roman fort is too far away,' Fergus said above the din as he assessed the distance they still had to travel. 'We're not going to make it. Perhaps we should try seeing if your uniform will stop them after all.'

Agricola nodded and they turned back in the direction of the gate. About fifty paces away were a turma of cavalry, riding in close formation unlike the rest of their comrades, who were riding randomly seeking targets. Fergus recognised the leader of the turma immediately: it was Sedullus. The rest of the men were not from Turma XV or X, however, and he did not recognise any of them, nor would they recognise him. In the middle of them, protected from attack on all sides, rode Pomponius.

Another rider approached from the left. It was the queen

on her white horse. She trotted up to Pomponius's troop and began shouting to him. Her words could not be heard amid the screaming, war cries, crash of weapons and frightened bleating of terrified animals, but her hands were raised and the look of supplication on her face made it obvious she was trying to surrender.

Pomponius made a curt gesture and Sedullus spurred his horse forward. He brought his heavy lance up. Before the queen could turn her horse the blade drove into her chest, half lifting her out of the saddle. The point erupted from her back and she let out a scream that was half anguish, half fury. Sedullus yanked his spear out of her and she toppled off her horse into the dirt, her blood and her life gushing out from the wound where she had been spitted.

Agricola lifted his arms off the shoulders of Fergus and Ceridwen and, waving and shouting 'salve' to get their attention, he began to stagger towards the Roman cavalrymen.

'Wait! I don't think that's a good idea...' Fergus said, laying a restraining hand on the tribune's shoulder.

At the same moment Pomponius turned and caught sight of them. At first a look of dismay crossed his face but it was quickly replaced by an expression of anger and they could see him barking orders. Sedullus shouted to men on his left and right. With obvious intent, their lances couched under their arms, the troopers started forward towards the trio.

'Jupiter! They're going to kill us!' Agricola said, his voice laden with astonishment.

Fergus looked around to see if there was anywhere they

could run and hide; anywhere at all that might provide some sort of defensive position.

Then something caught his eye beside the temple.

'Could you drive that thing?' he said to Ceridwen.

Her eyes widened when she saw what he pointed at.

48

A little way off, near the temple, sat Anfad's scythe chariot. The two horses yoked to it – one grey and one coal black – were trained for war. They waited patiently amid the chaos and noise around them for their master who would now never come.

Ceridwen shook her head. 'It's a special skill that takes years of training,' she said.

'Aye,' Fergus said. 'I know the fundamentals though. Try and get the tribune to the fort. I'll distract Pomponius and his troopers with that thing.'

'Don't be a fool,' Agricola said. 'It's suicide.'

'Suicide isn't what I have in mind,' Fergus said. 'Murder, maybe.'

He ran to the chariot, climbed onto the central driving platform and unwound the reins from where they had been tethered. Placing his feet in a wide stance on the driving platform, he twisted a rein around each of his wrists and with a lash of the reins and a yell at the horses he braced himself as they whinnied and took off. The chariot moved forwards, gathering speed as the big scythe blades rotated faster and faster with an accompanying whooping sound.

Fergus aimed the war chariot straight at the oncoming troopers. As it accelerated the whooshing of the blades became a steady humming beat. Once again, Fergus lashed the reins across the backs of the two horses, urging them on to greater speed. Suspended above the main axles by animal sinew and catgut wires, the highly sprung steering platform bounced and bucked, but absorbed most of the jolting that would have been expected from the wheels rolling over the rough ground.

Gritting his teeth to avoid biting his tongue, Fergus's heart leapt into his mouth with every lurch that threatened to send him toppling off the platform to the right or left where the revolving blades would chop him to bloody pieces.

Sedullus, with three troopers on either side of him arrayed in arrowhead formation, galloped towards the chariot across the patch of open ground before the royal house. Fergus saw the look of surprise and consternation on their faces as they saw him coming and a strange feeling of wild glee came over him. He aimed straight for Sedullus, delighted at how light and manoeuvrable the chariot was. It was not a surprise: in Hibernia he had seen the greatest warriors ride into battle in chariots whose charioteers could make their vehicles leap over fallen trees, cross gaps, traverse crazy inclines and generally follow anywhere their horses went. Fergus just wished he had the knowledge and experience to drive in the same way.

The distance between him and the onrushing cavalry closed in seconds. In the face of his unflinching charge, the formation split. Sedullus went to the right, taking half the troopers with him while the other three went to the left, leaving a gap for Fergus to pass through. Instead he yanked the right-hand rein and leaned in the same direction to turn the chariot. The vehicle responded instantly and veered to the right. The deadly blades grazed past the flanks of Sedullus's horse, but scythed deep into the front shoulders of the horse ridden by the trooper behind. The impact made the chariot buck and rear to one side, but the revolving wheels impelled the blades to continue turning and a horrific wound was opened along the horse's side. As the blades rent open the animal's belly they also severed the leg of the trooper riding it, just above the knee. Suddenly unbalanced and unable to grip the saddle he toppled screaming off his mount. Hot, steaming loops of guts spilt from the torn side of the horse as it collapsed sideways to the ground.

Fergus mercilessly goaded the horses to pull the chariot on its right-hand trajectory. The second trooper jumped his horse in an attempt to escape the deadly blades. Only its forelegs made it, however, and both its back legs were severed above the hocks. As the horse screamed and fell, spilling its rider behind it, the impact caused the chariot to skew sideways and to the left. This, however, merely impelled the blades on the opposite side into the flanks of a horse passing by on that side, causing it to rear up and throw the trooper off its back. Howling, the man fell backwards right onto the revolving blades. As he landed his forearms and lower legs were chopped off. His torso bounced up once then fell again to be shredded by the scythes.

Fergus felt hot blood splashing across his left-hand side. He briefly considered he was killing comrades, but his battle rage took over and banished such thoughts from his mind. It was kill or be killed. There was no time for discussion about it.

A new threat presented itself as Fergus realised he was on a collision course with a roundhouse, but the well-trained horses had no intention of ploughing into it. Not waiting for their driver to turn them, they veered left. The sharp turn took Fergus by surprise. He leaned hard into it to avoid being pitched off. The left wheel lifted slightly off the ground and he felt a brief moment of panic, fearing the vehicle might tip over, then the wheel came back down again and the chariot completed its turn, just avoiding the roundhouse. With barely time to think, Fergus dragged the left-hand rein to keep the chariot turning, this time at a slightly less dangerous pace, so that he completed a semicircle to end up facing back in the direction he had come from.

Only then did he get a proper look at the bloody remnants of the men and horses he had killed. Glancing around for Ceridwen and Agricola, he was relieved to see that they had apparently taken advantage of the distraction to take cover somewhere as they were nowhere to be seen.

A deep feeling of regret stabbed him in the gut when he saw the fallen horses. It was not right to kill such magnificent animals. The men he felt less worried about.

The big royal house was now blazing furiously and sending thick roils of smoke into the grey dawn sky. Several other houses were ablaze too and the smoke from them drifted around the hill fort, adding to the chaos and panic that was all around.

The remaining troopers had also turned to face Fergus again. Sedullus was bawling orders and pointing his spatha at the chariot. With a roar Fergus goaded the horses forward, noting with fierce delight the look of trepidation on the troopers' faces as they saw the war machine, which had destroyed half their number in as many seconds, coming at them again. They were well trained though. Their discipline held firm and Fergus saw they had sheathed their heavy lances and now held throwing javelins. He quickly checked around him and noted that there was not a lot of cover on the chariot if they launched them at him.

Side by side, the troopers came on in one line, javelins ready. Fergus had no choice but to drive straight for them. The distance between them closed in moments. One trooper launched his spear early. It was well aimed but Fergus had time to duck and felt the wind of it passing only inches above his head. The others maintained discipline, waiting until the last possible moment.

'Loose,' Sedullus screamed when mere yards separated them.

The other two troopers and Sedullus all threw their javelins at once then veered their horses away to escape the whirring blades. Fergus had to drop the reins and throw himself flat on the driving platform. There was a thud as a spear landed just behind his back. A second spear hit the spokes of the right wheel and smashed to splinters. Sedullus, though, had not aimed for him. The black horse in the traces screamed in pain as the javelin dug into its flanks.

Fergus was unharmed but had dropped the reins and the chariot now careered out of control. He clung on grimly, all too aware of what would happen were he to slip off the platform. With the reins trailing uselessly along the ground and no one to control the horses, one of which was maddened by pain, they plunged onward, skirting around the side of a thatched roundhouse and heading further into the interior of the hill fort. Frightened people and animals desperately ran to get out of the way of the war machine with its wicked revolving blades.

Sedullus and his troopers turned their horses and came after him again, now with spathas drawn. All Fergus could do was continue to hold on to the careering chariot and pray it did not crash or tip over. If he jumped off and managed to avoid the blades, either the fall would kill him or Sedullus would ride him down in moments.

The horses burst out of the maze of roundhouses and animal pens onto the wide open space of the parade ground at the front of the little Roman fort. The troopers, riding at full gallop, were catching up and would certainly do so once onto the open ground. Fergus had to do something to regain control of the horses. Looking down he could see the reins trailing beneath the chariot, but knew he had no hope of recovering them; the lead trooper was just behind him now.

Screaming a war cry, the Roman cavalryman leaned as far forwards in the saddle as he could, spatha raised, preparing to bring it down.

Fergus, one hand gripping the side rail, ripped out the javelin that was still stuck into the driving platform. He flipped it round and launched it straight at the rider, now mere yards away. The spear hit the trooper in the face, the point going through his open mouth and smashing out through the back of his skull, knocking off his helmet and sending him flying off the back of his horse. But there were still more troopers and Sedullus pounding behind him and Fergus knew that unless he regained control of the horses he was done for.

In his youth, he had seen heroes of his tribe perform the feat of the chariot pole. He had never done it himself, but he reasoned that it was now his only option. The trick involved balancing on the shaft between the horses. The nimblest and bravest would run along it and back again from the chariot platform, but it was extremely dangerous and at the speed he was currently travelling, potentially suicidal.

Gingerly he clambered over the front of the driving platform and placed his feet on the pole. Below him, the ground rushed past in a blur while on either side were the heaving flanks and flying hooves of the horses, the one with a spear still in its side beginning to slow, causing the chariot to slew unevenly in favour of the stronger horse. The slightest slip would mean falling beneath those pulverising hooves and if that did not kill him, then the wheels of the chariot would finish the job. Briefly he tried to balance on the bucking and bouncing chariot pole, but found that it was impossible.

For the first time he realised why the heroes ran up the chariot pole rather than walk. It was not to demonstrate their ability but because forward momentum was the only way to stay on. Arms wide on either side of him, he bent forward and ran, planting one foot before the other squarely on the pole.

In four steps he was between the horses. His fifth step slipped and he lurched sideways to his right. Instead of falling off the pole he fell against the grey horse. Grabbing a handful of its mane Fergus swung himself up onto the animal's back, clenched his thighs and hung on grimly. Now at least he could perhaps regain some form of control.

Glancing over his shoulder, Fergus saw that Sedullus and the last two troopers had caught up with him. They divided, Sedullus going to the right and the two troopers going left, skirting the dangerous whirling blades to draw level with the horses pulling the chariot. Mounted on the right-hand horse, Fergus looked round and saw Sedullus, sword drawn, preparing to close in to cut him down.

With no weapon, his only hope was to try to skew the chariot so the blades would force Sedullus to move away again out of striking distance. He grabbed the mane of the grey horse and wrenched its head to the left, digging in hard with his right knee as he did so.

The horse began to turn, but at the same time the black horse gave a hoarse grunt, finally overcome by its wound. Its haunches suddenly weakened and dropped, it stumbled to the right, crashing into its partner and squashing Fergus's left leg between them. The grey was knocked sideways, lost its footing and stumbled, releasing the pressure on Fergus's leg just as both animals began falling to the right.

He had to somehow throw himself as far away as possible from the horses or go down with them and be crushed. Fergus launched himself upwards. Screaming in terror, the horses went over, twisting the chariot pole and tipping the vehicle over with it. There was a loud crack of splintering wood as the chariot flipped over. The giant rotating sickle blades on the right-hand side tilted and struck the hard ground with full force. The first one to hit snapped off and went flying through the air, spinning as it went. The next two did the same in quick succession.

Sedullus was immediately behind the chariot. Before he could react, the first blade scythed into the front left shoulder of his mount. The second severed its left hind leg and the shrieking horse fell sideways, spilling Sedullus from the saddle. He hit the ground hard, rolled over onto his back and let out a scream as he saw the chariot, still in motion, flipping towards him. The spinning blades still attached to the left-hand end of the axle came right over and landed on him, shredding Sedullus's body into a bloody mincemeat that was unrecognisable as human.

Fergus landed on his right-hand side, hitting the ground with an impact that drove the breath from his lungs. He bounced and rolled several times before ending up sprawled face down in the dirt. Behind him he heard Sedullus scream and the smashing and rending as the chariot shattered.

For a few moments he lay stunned, his head reeling. He was unsure if his eyes were open or closed. All he could perceive were coloured, spinning stars. He seemed to hear a compelling voice at the back of his mind telling him to sit up. Shaking his head, he dragged himself to his knees, but had to stop as his vision swam and he felt as though he were about to throw up or pass out – or both. His right arm hung down and felt strangely numb.

As his head cleared again he looked up and saw the last two of Sedullus's troopers reining their horses to a halt and wheeling them around to come at him again. They approached, spathas drawn and ready to cut him down. Fergus staggered to his feet. They would be on him in moments. He had no weapon, his right arm seemed not to be working properly and he had no hope of outrunning the troopers' horses.

It looked like he had finally run out of options.

49

Fergus looked hastily around. He was almost in the centre of the wide, flat parade ground. About twenty paces away lay the mangled corpses of the Tungrians who had been massacred earlier trying to break out of the Roman fort. Their weapons and armour lay discarded on the ground, but he would not be able to reach them in time. Even if he did, his right arm was numb and did not seem to be working. It was either broken or his shoulder dislocated. Behind him was the smashed wreckage of the war chariot. The injured horses, still alive and trapped in the traces, struggled to rise, whinnying in pain and kicking out wildly.

There was nowhere to hide or take cover.

He braced himself, ready to spring in either direction to avoid the troopers' swords but aware they were coming at him from both right and left, leaving him little option. There was nothing he could do but wait for death and curse the discipline and training of his Roman comrades.

Loud blasts erupted from nearby Roman buccinae and cornua. Fergus was dimly aware of other instruments around the hill fort repeating the series of notes that relayed the orders: stop fighting and hold positions.

The confused looks on faces of the approaching troopers

showed they too were puzzled by what was going on. However, it was equally clear that their blood was up and they intended to finish the current job before working it out.

'Stop!'

The command was barked from a little way off in Latin and with a strong tone of authority. Both troopers slowed and Fergus, swinging round, saw a Roman officer wearing the red cloak and crimson front-to-back crest of a tribune. He was striding towards him across the parade ground.

Fergus recognised Agricola limping along beside the new tribune, supported by a legionary on either side. Looking more closely he saw the officers were accompanied by about four contubernia, which numbered around thirty-six men, all armed legionaries from the XX Legion.

Fergus lifted an eyebrow and exchanged glances with Agricola, who grinned back at him.

'Troopers, leave that man alone,' the tribune shouted. 'At once. That's an order.'

This time the troopers reined their mounts to a halt, a mere horse-length from Fergus.

'Sir, this man is a traitor working with the British,' one of the troopers said. 'We are acting on the direct orders of Cavalry Praefect Titus Pomponius.'

'And I am a tribune of the XX Legion,' the Roman officer shouted back. 'My orders supersede any of an auxiliary commander.'

'Sir, this man killed a decurion,' the trooper tried one more time, reluctant to disobey a direct order of his commander.

'Do as I tell you or I will have you flogged,' the tribune screamed at the trooper. His face was puce with fury. He shot a derisory look at the Gaulish cavalrymen before turning to Agricola with a savage grin.

'Fucking Celts,' he said. 'You can't trust any of them.'

'What's going on here?'

The sound of another voice, angrily raised and accompanied by approaching hoofbeats, made everyone turn to see who it was.

Across the body-strewn parade ground rode Titus Pomponius Proculianus, his face red and glistening with sweat beneath his gleaming, silver-coated helmet.

'I gave express orders that that man be put to death,' Pomponius said. 'Where is Decurion Sedullus?'

'He's over there,' Fergus said, gesturing to the red and white mess of butchered meat that lay among the wreckage of the chariot.

Pomponius managed to look both puzzled and annoyed.

'Who has disobeyed my orders? This man is a traitor.' He pointed at Fergus. 'I identified him myself.'

'It's you who is a traitor, Pomponius,' the tribune said. 'Luckily I was able to identify the tribunus laticlavius of the XIV Legion, Gnaeus Agricola here, and he has told me all about your ridiculous scheme, which is nothing less than treason.'

'Your plan worked then,' Fergus said to Agricola as he drew near.

'Luckily Quintus here happened to be with the detachment from the XX,' Agricola said, cocking his head towards the other tribune. 'He recognised me straight away when I showed myself to him.'

Fergus nodded. Now his battle fury was subsiding and he could think straighter, what Agricola said made sense.

There were not more than twelve military tribunes in the whole of Britannia. It was natural that they would know each other.

'He is a friend. We went to school together,' Agricola added, confirming just how fortuitous it was that Quintus happened to be here.

'You'll be crucified for this,' Tribune Quintus said to Pomponius. 'You've led me and my men a merry dance. We've started a war against an allied nation, all because of your lies.'

Pomponius stiffened in the saddle. 'I am a Roman citizen. I cannot be crucified. I was simply fulfilling the will of the general,' he said.

'Well, we'll see what he says about that, won't we?' Quintus said. 'Men, this man is relieved of command and now subject to military discipline. Someone take his sword and his armour.'

'Mind you,' the tribune said out of the corner of his mouth as he turned away, 'he probably did us a favour in a way. We would have had to take this place someday.'

Pomponius let out a roar that betrayed his frustration and rage. For the first time since the battle began, the praefect ripped his ivory-hilted sword from its sheath. He spurred his horse forward, aiming directly at Fergus.

With the removal of immediate danger, the adrenaline flow had subsided within Fergus to be replaced by a wave of exhaustion. Aside from which he was still concussed so did not react. He simply stared as Pomponius closed in on him.

Agricola shouted a warning and Quintus turned back to see what was happening. 'Masivo!' He barked another curt order and pointed at Pomponius. 'Stop that man.'

Almost immediately Fergus heard the sharp crack of a ballista. Something shot through the air, moving so fast as to be almost imperceptible. Instinctively he flinched down, turning his head to see where it had come from. A short distance away he saw that several of the ballistae carts had been pulled right inside the fort and he recognised the architectus – Masivo – who, having taken careful aim and loosed a bolt, was now bent over one of his machines loading another.

The first iron-tipped missile, shot with devastating accuracy, hit Pomponius's horse just to the left of the centre of its chest, right between the pumping forelegs. It passed through its body, lacerating all the vital organs on the way and exploding from its flanks in a cloud of pink haze. The horse gave a grunt and simply dropped to the ground.

Pomponius's fat body sprawled over the animal's head and landed in the dirt, sliding forward, his sword arm leading the way. It seemed that only his dignity was injured, however, for he began to rise to his feet straight away, his venomous gaze still set on Fergus and his rage making him deaf to the tribune's urgent commands.

Fergus, his right arm still numb and limp, staggered sideways, catching sight of a couple of weapons beside the corpse of a dead Tungrian auxiliary lying nearby.

Now on his feet, Pomponius stumbled forward, raising his spatha and wheezing out a roar of anger as he came. Fergus glanced down at the gladius still gripped in the Tungrian's dead grasp. The gladius was much shorter than the long cavalry spatha clutched in Pomponius's hand. In close-quarters fighting where there was no room to swing a spatha, this was an advantage, but that was not the case here. They had the whole parade ground to themselves. Fergus could also only use his left arm. Pomponius, despite his portly build, had a distinct advantage with his working arm and longer sword.

'Fuck it,' Fergus concluded. No one said it needed to be a fair fight. Leaving the gladius, he picked up the unused pilum from beside the Tungrian's corpse and spun around with it in his left hand to see that Pomponius was nearly on him.

With no time to think, Fergus launched the heavy spear underarm. It had barely left his grasp when the tip of the blade entered Pomponius's gut, going in under his shining cuirass. Fergus stepped in, catching hold of the shaft and thrusting upwards to tear through the praefect's vital organs.

Pomponius squealed as he realised what had happened then screeched in agony as the metal head of the pilum tore through his innards. Fergus released the spear and the heavy wooden base of the shaft dropped to the ground and, as it was designed to do, bent the metal top. Its weight pulled Pomponius forwards, threatening to wrench the tip out of his body cavity, spilling his entrails along the way.

Pomponius dropped to his knees, gasping like a fish hooked and trailed onto dry land. Fergus returned to the dead Tungrian and this time retrieved the gladius. He stalked back to Pomponius and looked down at him, then glanced in the direction of Agricola.

The tribune simply nodded. Pomponius looked as though he were about to say something, but Fergus swung the gladius backhanded and the blade sheared deep into the cavalry praefect's neck, cutting right through to the backbone.

A torrent of blood gushed from Pomponius's severed neck all over the front of his polished bronze cuirass. The dying man's mouth worked soundlessly as he raised both hands uselessly to his throat. Fergus swung again, a more measured stroke. This time the neck bone separated and Pomponius's head toppled end over end from his neck to land on the ground between his knees. His sightless eyes gazed up at the sky as his lifeless body fell backwards, one last spurt of crimson blood jetting from his neck before his heart finally stopped.

For a few moments there was quiet.

'That saved us a trial, anyway,' Tribune Quintus said.

Fergus dropped the gladius and walked over to where Agricola stood, still supported by the two legionaries.

'It looks like your right shoulder is dislocated,' he said. 'It's hanging much lower than your left.'

'Tell me something I don't know,' Fergus said sourly.

'My *medicus* can fix that,' Quintus said with a grin. 'Best damn medic in the army. Valerian!'

'We can at least now go and get what we came for,' Fergus said to Agricola. 'We should go back to that temple and get the spear.'

He had been going to ask about Ceridwen, but then thought he should not mention her in front of the other tribune.

'Yes indeed,' Agricola said, nodding. His face suddenly brightened. 'Perhaps there's still a chance we can salvage something from this whole debacle and actually get what General Paulinus sent us here for.'

A short, dark man in full legionary armour, but carrying a leather satchel over one shoulder, came forward. He examined Fergus's upper arms, running practised fingers around the back of his dropped shoulder blade. With the typically serious expression of a medic on his narrow features, he nodded.

'It's dislocated all right. Look over there for a moment, will you,' Valerian said, indicating with his right forefinger the bright red ball of the sun that had risen above the ramparts of the hill fort.

Fergus did as he was told, realising at the last moment, as the physician grasped his right arm in both hands and wrenched it outward with a sickening sucking sound, that the man had merely been distracting him. There was a loud pop as his dislocated shoulder slid back into place. A wave of pain and shock overcame Fergus. His vision swam and he passed out.

50

Agricola and Fergus stared down at the floor where they had last seen the sacred spear.

They stood inside the Dobunni temple. The embossed bronze cauldron still sat before the three altars, the blood in it rank and half-congealed. Flies buzzed across its surface and the strong coppery odour from it mingled with the stench of burnt flesh. The corpse of Longinus still twisted above the pit.

The sacred spear was gone.

Agricola shook his head in disbelief. He looked lost.

'We shouldn't have left it behind,' he said.

Fergus frowned, spotting something on the centre altar. He walked closer and picked up the smooth, round ball of coloured glass, turning it over in his hand and examining the neat round hole that went through the middle of it. He grunted, his mouth cracking into an ironic laugh.

'What is there to laugh about?' Agricola said. 'Who in Hades' name took it? The queen, Comux, that cursed big druid and Pomponius are all dead. Perhaps those damn priestesses...'

'It was Ceridwen,' Fergus said.

'How do you know?' Agricola said.

'The priestesses are dead. We passed the corpses of those witches outside on the way here. They must have come round, run out of here and straight into the legionaries,' Fergus said. He held up the glass object. 'This is the druid snakestone I gave Ceridwen. She has left it here to let me know that it was her who took the spear. When was the last time you saw her?'

'When Sedullus charged at you we took cover in a nearby house,' Agricola said with a shrug. 'Shortly after you all flew off towards the parade ground I spotted Tribune Quintus coming in the main gate with the cohort of the XX and those mobile ballistae. I hopped out to meet him but told her to stay behind. I'm in a Roman uniform but they'd have killed her. To tell you the truth I forgot all about her. The bitch must have crept back in here and taken the spear while everyone else was busy.'

'If she worked out a way to get out of the fort she just had to carry it away,' Fergus said. He shook his head, still smiling, privately admiring the resourcefulness of the woman.

'How did she get out? Our soldiers are all over the gates,' Agricola said.

'These forts often have secret tunnels out of them,' Fergus said. 'They're usually small crawl spaces that go down from under the floor of one of the main buildings to emerge somewhere way beyond the ramparts. They are there for the royalty and nobility to escape if the fort falls. I'm sure quite a few others got away with her.'

'You knew about this?' Agricola eyed him with disbelief and a sudden wariness.

'I'm guessing,' Fergus said. 'Most hill forts have an escape tunnel. I'd be very surprised if this one doesn't, that's all. I've really no idea how she got away.'

Agricola sighed and they both turned and walked back out of the temple into the light of the new day. Smoke from the burning buildings drifted across the hill fort. The royal house was completely aflame, black smoke and red fire roiling up from its destroyed roof into the sky. All around the bodies of the dead – butchered warriors, animals, women and the small corpses of children – lay scattered where they had been killed or were piled in heaps where they had made a stand. Discarded and broken weapons littered the ground. Pigs, goats and the odd stray horse ran wildly around in terrified panic.

There was blood everywhere, either pooling around the piles of corpses or splashed and splattered across walls of buildings and the arms and armour of legionaries and cavalry troopers. They could smell its thick, coppery tang in the air, mingled with the greasy stench of roasting flesh. Groups of defeated Dobunni who had been spared when Quintus had ordered the attack to cease, stood huddled together here and there, surrounded by wary legionaries. The warriors tried to look defiant and hold on to some semblance of dignity, while their womenfolk were pale with terror and grief and the children howled with fear. What lay ahead for them was uncertain. Perhaps death and if not that then probably slavery. The only thing to be sure of was that their world and the royal seat of their kingdom from time immemorial had just been destroyed before their eyes.

'Rome has come to the Kingdom of Dobunnia,' Agricola said.

'And Dobunnia is now Rome,' Fergus said, looking at the

white, traumatised faces of a couple of young Dobunni girls who stood nearby and wondering what seeds of resentment and resistance had just been sown. How many potential recruits had just been created for Ceridwen's planned rebellion against Rome?

'I'll have the whole fort searched,' Agricola said, his face pale and a look of clear concern on his face. 'If she is still here – if the spear is still here – I want her found. We simply cannot go back to the general without it.'

'But it isn't the right spear,' Fergus said. 'Not the one Suetonius meant, anyway; the one the Christians hold sacred, remember? It was Lugh's spear. The Lúin of Celtchar. What we saw was some druid magic staged for our benefit. As you said, it was a trick that made the spear burn. The queen was just passing it off as the Christian spear. She had a "magic" weapon and she knew the emperor would want a Christian relic more than a druid one. And it worked. It was the bait that lured the general into sending us down here to negotiate sending Roman aid to help her gain supremacy over Comux.'

Agricola looked lost. 'But we cannot return to Suetonius without the spear,' he said. 'We simply cannot. Our punishment will be severe. It will be the end of my career…'

The tribune trailed off realising that the disgrace, demotion and embarrassment he would have to suffer would be considerably less harsh than the possible beatings or worse that would be meted out to a soldier from the ranks like Fergus.

Fergus stopped walking. He was looking down at the scattered debris of battle that littered the ground around them. The smile returned to his face and he looked up at Agricola.

'Longinus said an interesting thing at the feast last night,' he said. 'When I asked him about the spear he said their God Jesus was crucified by the Romans. It was an ordinary legionary who stuck the spear into him when he was on the cross. So it made no sense that the Christian spear would be a shining magical item like the one the queen had. Their spear would simply be a standard-issue Roman weapon.'

He bent down and picked up a fallen Roman cavalry javelin that lay amid the wreckage that was scattered all around. For a few moments he and Agricola locked gazes and nothing was said.

'Are you suggesting I deceive the general?' Agricola finally said.

Fergus shrugged and held out the javelin. 'All I'm saying is one Roman spear is like any other,' he said.

There was another moment of hesitation, then Fergus winked.

Agricola smiled, nodded and took the javelin. 'We must never speak of this again,' he said, trying to assume an air of superiority commensurate with his rank.

Fergus nodded. 'Why would we?' he said.

Agricola cleared his throat. 'It occurs to me, trooper, that with the death of Sedullus, the XIV Turma of the Ala Gallorum will need a new decurion,' he said. 'And this war has only just begun. Would you be interested in the position? I'm assuming you are still on our side, of course.'

Fergus looked at the carnage and destruction around him, then up to where the smoke from the burning buildings drifted out over the ramparts. Where did his allegiance really lie? A short time ago it had all seemed so clear to him: Rome offered a civilised light in the barbarous darkness where druids kept the people enthralled with superstitious magic and tyrannical gods like Crom reigned supreme. Becoming a citizen of Rome seemed a noble goal. Now, looking at the devastation around him, Ceridwen's words came back to him from the night she was a prisoner in the legionary camp. Rome crushes all in its path, enslaves the people, steals their wealth, burns their homes and then when there is nothing left but a desert, calls it 'peace'. In Erin, Fergus was of noble birth, but would he ever be more than a second-class citizen in Rome?

He thought of Ceridwen again. She was somewhere outside the fort, now with the spear of Lugh, continuing her own war to unify the tribes of Britannia against the Romans.

For the time being, perhaps the best thing to do was to carry on the path he had chosen and see where life, and Crom, took him.

Bringing his gaze back to Agricola, he nodded.

'Yes, I am still on your side,' he said.

For now anyway, he thought to himself.

About the Author

TIM HODKINSON grew up in Northern Ireland where the rugged coast and call of the Atlantic ocean led to a lifelong fascination with Vikings and a degree in Medieval English and Old Norse Literature. Tim's more recent writing heroes include Ben Kane, Giles Kristian, Bernard Cornwell, George R.R. Martin and Lee Child. After several years in the USA, Tim has returned to Northern Ireland, where he lives with his wife and children.

Follow Tim on @TimHodkinson and www.timhodkinson. blogspot.com